L. M

D1584431

# SANDBARS
## THE POWERFUL NOVEL OF A WOMAN COMING TO TERMS WITH HER OWN LIFE.

## SIGNET Canadian Bestsellers

# SANDBARS

## A Novel

## Oonah McFee

ℚ

**A SIGNET BOOK**
**NEW AMERICAN LIBRARY**

TIMES MIRROR

Published by
Macmillan-NAL Publishing Limited
Scarborough, Ontario

This is an authorized reprint of a hardcover edition published by
The Macmillan Company of Canada.

First Signet Printing, August, 1978

2 3 4 5 6 7 8 9

SIGNET TRADEMARK REG. U.S. PAT. OFF. AND FOREIGN COUNTRIES
REGISTERED TRADEMARK — MARCA REGISTRADA
HECHO EN MONTREAL, CANADA

PRINTED IN CANADA

COVER PRINTED IN U.S.A.

*for*
Pierre Delattre

# ACKNOWLEDGEMENTS

The completion of this book was made possible through grants from the Canada Council and the Ontario Arts Council.

## AUTHOR'S NOTE

I should like to acknowledge with gratitude and affection the time and thought so generously given by Dennis Lee, who, from the book's first draft to its last, was critic, friend, and mentor.

That this volume was even begun is due to Harry Hall, who is remembered here for the trust he placed in me.

O.M.

What seas what shores what grey rocks
   and what islands
What water lapping the bow
And scent of pine and the woodthrush
   singing through the fog
What images return
O my daughter.

**T. S. ELIOT**
Marina 1930

# SANDBARS

# I

———◆———

For the first few minutes I wasn't getting anything tonight. It kept fading away; that's the trouble with the shortwave band, on a transistor anyway. But I held out. One of those autumn nights when, arriving home from a party, something about the night, the stillness perhaps, suggests you pour yourself a drink and see what the transistor might pull out of the atmosphere, even if it is garbled.

What's taking place at the other end of the world—is the sun just rising? the moon coming up over a hillside? You get hooked, watching the needle move along the dial. Suddenly there's a squawk, what's this? another squeal, then more dead air, and now a surge of balalaikas from nowhere, vanishing; you double back. Where have the balalaikas gone? A crash of sound. Could be anything.

But! A lucky stroke of tuning! A ripply voice has said the Grieg "A Minor for Piano and Orchestra" is to follow. A transcription, the announcer tells his listeners: "This program comes to you from the transcription service of Radio (he pronounces it Radd-io) Nederland."

Radio Nederland!

The first time I heard those words it was summertime and I was out on the verandah watching the cows come down the hill, looking up from the pail of raspberries I had just gathered and was picking through in search of ants. I couldn't sob. I just sat. Mute. Seeing, and realizing, in those short moments, what was happening down at the river. As I see it now and turn my mind away from it.

————

At the time, while I was pawing through raspberries on the cottage verandah, my father was inside fiddling with his ham radio station in a corner of the living room. I listened to him dit-da-ing away as the fruit stains dried on my pinafore, and I thought, Today is a *best* day. I love it when it's summer. A thunderstorm had already begun, loud with lightning strikes. My mother was frightened, and once or twice I went in from the verandah to tell her it was still far from our hill. She said I could stay outside a little longer.

I was perhaps ten then, maybe eleven, a time when the arrangements of life were all in good order, and I would be watching, or listening. Or doing. My needs began and ended wherever I happened to be, days that saw me tumbling into bed at night, a sleepy nod to myself as my eyelids closed, unfearful, the mind drifting off, the sounds of curtains ruffling . . . wonderful . . . the hot wind . . . what's in store tomorrow?

That summer my parents were indulging in a wry and tender tug-of-war. The feud was over my father having eased his ham operator's station into a choice location: the living room of the cottage. My mother pretended to be livid. And my father pretended to take the broom to her, but always ended up patting her on the bottom. Then back he'd trot to his transmitter: for two months a territory under constant siege. But the fact was the cottage had no basement. And it hadn't occurred to my father beforehand where he was going to put his wireless. He just dismantled the parts and lugged them up on the train.

"Of course!" I can hear him telling himself. He was thinking of the space on either side of the fireplace. Pleased with his logic, he began carting his precious apparatus into the living room. Since he was left-handed, the first of five cartons was set down left of the fireplace. I sat on the couch to watch: the soldering iron, the coils, the little crystal domes. I liked to be around whenever my father got down to business. Then too, I wanted to be there when the first beeps came over VE9GW, from a sky that was above a hill and not a city. That seemed a different matter, somehow. Out of the heights of a wilderness, you never expected to pick up sounds, except maybe crows and hawks.

At the first screech of code my mother came running in from pruning the lilac tree, her shears poised in mid-air as she drew up short, arrested by the *fait accompli*.

"Why that one?" she shot out, her eyes measuring the cubic space now taken up. "Why the one closest to the kitchen, for heaven's sake?" She stood in front of the wireless-panel picking twigs out of the shears, internal murmurs slowing her down, settling the wash of the surface she had cut across. She was wondering what might look nice in the room, what camouflage she'd make. "I'll have to run something up on the machine," she said, "something pretty that'll keep the dust out." My father was wreathed in smiles. "I expect I'll have to cut a pattern first," she added, taking in the details of coils and tubes. What appeared a few days later should itself have been camouflaged: a roses-and-rhododendron chintz cover with flounces, like a pillow sham with growths. At such close range to the fireplace it seemed attached, like an unmentionable symptom.

"Perfect," my father said, arriving home from work one evening, his eyes seizing upon the chintz before he was half in the door.

Though he'd put up the two aerial masts the previous autumn, this was the first summer my father had tried out his transmitter at the cottage. From the moment he finally decided to build himself a station (three or four winters earlier), it had to be in the class of a coastal wireless station. Not many years before, after all, he had been the resident wireless operator at a Government ship-to-shore guiding station on the Nova Scotia coast—a posting he coveted for its bleak isolation amid round-the-clock distress signals. Subsequently transferred to Ottawa, which meant sitting all day at a desk, my father missed the unique conversations—catching rides on a journey with strangers, as he put it. He would have his own station.

It took him two years to acquire the components, and from the time he first assembled the conglomerate he'd been storing in the cellar fruit cupboard, my mother never went near this marvel of wires, condensers and eternal CQs. It was not woman's business. But at the cottage, with the thing right under her nose, man's business eventually got the better of her. I remember the first day she poked about the panel, whistling guiltily as she turned first this knob, then that, pretending to dust between the maze of wires and shining coils, a mask of crystal and metal snouts which in my mind seemed to be defying her sudden interest. Then I noticed the whole works was getting dusted sometimes twice a day. On would go the cover again, and off down to the river she'd go (or into her bedroom with the door closed), an operator's manual hidden between the pages of *Good Housekeeping* or *Woman's Home Companion*. And once she got the hang of things, had boned up on what little Morse she'd had time to learn, she'd whip

off the chintz and go to it. But only when she was by herself.
I mean without my father around. The fact she'd fashioned a
flouncy covering by no means meant she accepted the thing
in the living room. She held firm against any interest for fear
it might encourage my father to set up in the living room in
town.

Her tack was prompt. Carried out with finesse. Whenever
she went about straightening the room, or was merely passing
by on her way to a bedroom, she would arch her neck back
for a highly effective glance down her nose, as if she had
been affronted by the remains of something, a carcass. On the
other hand when it was her turn to sit at the panel her neck
all but scorched itself at the tubes. Evenings, while she was
sitting around waiting for the train to bring my father from
his office, or else when he was off playing tennis or fishing on
the river out front, she'd settle herself down with the intensity
of a pro determined to give her all, headphones arranged precisely under her dark curls and those brown eyes of hers
dancing half out of her head, stirring up, over distant continents, God knows how many poor souls; improvised dits
and das thrown in that could have meant anything! A kind of
pig-Latin Morse only she could have fathomed.

Encouraged by her expertise in these first early disserta-
tions, which never lasted more than fifteen or twenty minutes
around supper time (when my father's appearance was immi-
nent, but the only free time she ever seemed to have), my
mother re-organized the routine of her day. Why, she'd just
barely get started when she'd have to shut down in the
middle of something she was enjoying hearing about, or, as
was more often the case, abruptly leave dangling whatever
yarn she'd launched into. She began hurrying through the
breakfast dishes, the bedmaking, scatter mats rolled up as
one, shaken out on the hill with a snap that sent sand and
caked mud flying round her head like pieces of flint. On to
the next routine, the one my brother George and I waited impatiently for and which my mother saw we never did without: outings that opened up vistas, countless moments of light
and subtle dark and wondering in the strange yet familiar setting that was, to us, the best place in the world. It might be
nothing more than a short trip somewhere in the rowboat,
perhaps to the tiny island of pines and rock-shelves, or else,
in another direction, seeking out, discovering some new corner of the hills and forest that surrounded us like a giant
arena.

George and I would go to bed hopeful but not quite certain of the next day's outing, for my mother planned these excursions according to what the sky looked like at sunset the evening before, which, she vowed, told her more than any weather forecast: if the sun went down behind a cloud, bad; night dew on the grass, good. On some days, when the sky was nothing but blue and the air was fragrant and shrill with the happiness of birds, we'd start out early in the morning, tramping through fields of grain, over the hills to climb one of the mountains (not mountains as such, but having been raised in the Highlands my mother regarded any wooded elevation as another Ben Nevis); and as we picnicked she sewed, or read, leaving us to find our own interests, to sense by touch and smell the creation around us: a shoot of fern, a spread of moss and lichen, and the birch-bark Indians had once made canoes from.

And now all this wandering hither and thither, crawling under barbed wire fences, pausing waist-high in a wheat field —what was that rippling through the grain, a skunk? the hum and whirr of insect and animal life, fresh hoof-marks, a deer? All this, which even yet held awe for her, was not being lived for itself alone but as something fresh, a new spectacle she could present to her friends in the wireless world, summoning her regulars, drumming up new ones. Oh, she had lots to talk about; with my father in the city all day, sometimes it got lonely up there. It wasn't as though she had George and me; not that way. We *were* the day, the today. And props belong to the stage, they aren't part of the audience. And so she rhapsodized by the hour, amused but at the same time cursing the groundhogs nibbling her new carrot-tops, clacking away about the voile curtains she was making, the new Eaton's catalogue that nobody she ever talked to had heard of. All this made for good mind-copy, a flowing banter for sailors at sea, or some octogenarian still in command of his ham-operator's faculties. Lonely people depend on the outside world. It's more interesting than what relatives have to say; it is something they can react to, a sense of immediacy.

"When are you going to let me try, Mamma?" I asked one day, my hand chafing at a stone jutting from the fireplace. She had taken the earphones off and was blowing on them, polishing the rims with her apron, like a pair of glasses.

"You already have," she replied, shifting position, crossing one knee over the other as she prepared to resume the CQs no one had as yet answered.

"But you shut the panel off first," I said accusingly. "How could anyone hear me?"

"They weren't intended to," she laughed, untangling a cord that had caught on her silver snake-bracelet.

"Does that mean . . . ?"

"It means exactly what it says. I can't have you bothering people."

"I know a code," I burst in, edging onto her chair. "I've got secret ways of doing Morse. You don't have to have dots and dashes for every single letter, do you? When I practise with a spoon on the side of the boat I can hear the words, it's the way you *make* the sound!"

"Then you must teach me sometime," she said, putting on the earphones again. I went outside, I'd better find that bent spoon, I'd need to practise some more.

Despite her deep preoccupation at the transmitting panel, my mother was smart enough to see that my father never caught her at it; she still had to go on playing livid. There was her precious living room in town to be considered; for whatever need she had of VE9GW, she too could sit by the furnace.

As for her secret hours of dit-da-ing, she did not feel it was necessary to say to George and me "not a word", as she did about other things—my father's birthday presents, or the visit of the man from the credit office. There was always a special feeling when things were really private. If she didn't sit down to answer our querulous eyes, then George and I knew enough not to let on, even if we were right in the middle, bursting to blat out the news to anybody.

But one factor my mother had not bargained for: the ultimate piping up of one of her contacts, who just happened to find my father at the other end of VE9GW one summer night.

"Hey, Cec. That wife of yours knows her way round the frequency band. Tunes in on a fellow's wavelengths too, makes a chap feel like a man. Is she pretty? Does she have good legs?" My father of course had been writing it down and my mother, having detected something in his facial expression, the way his pen moved, leaned over his shoulder reading as he wrote.

My father's pen stopped.

"Am I pretty?" That was all my mother said, standing

there, defenceless, grinning, a red-faced radiance, pulling a curl round and round her ear as she examined her ankles and calves.

Then it was out to the verandah, my father leading her, and a vivid recounting of two months' names and conversations: the fire-ranger's account of an out-of-control forest fire north of Rimouski, the population of North Dakota, a flagpole sitter who fainted, fell, was revived, climbed back up again with a dislocated shoulder, her supply of news spewing without letup. On to the next one, Jacques somebody, a French-Canadian trapper in Northern Ontario who was making a pine cradle for his first-born, how she told the trapper it would be nice if he had a son and spelled his name *Jock*. The sound of her voice, animated yet dreamlike, living in the reaches of North Dakota, Rimouski, in the to-and-fro rocking of a new pine cradle. Like rain falling, the kind that lulls you with a sort of excitement. My father lived, inhabited every word. As my mother went on from her limitless source, they were sitting on the porch couch, my father nodding, smiling, slapping his knee, joking, a little misty in the eyes, his hand gently running up and down her thigh. It was as though the two of them had turned into one person, you couldn't tell who was one or the other. It was wonderful . . . and yet it was dimming. I would miss my father taking the broom to her.

---

After all her snortings, after my mother's brilliant and utter disdain for the wireless-station holding down its space in the cottage living room (her sustained antipathy, the marvelous, unflawed totality of it, I cannot even yet comprehend), that was the way things at the transmitting panel slid into place. And it was about this time, perhaps a week or two had passed, that the wonder of "Radd-io Nederland" floated into the earphones slung around my father's neck. That night I was to realize the first sorrow I could do nothing about.

I think of Gladys. Sweet absurd name. I try to see her but frightened swallows swarm across my vision. A protective shield? No. The swallows are not an illusion.

There is another picture too, which, like a suture, dissolves in the tissue of my memory cells, a wound that leaves me, at this moment, dumb, without words. But I have reached a point, almost, where telling about it will come more easily, eased by the kaleidoscope of events my eyes do not wince at:

the hours preceding the terror; precisely, the day before. Until now, so unexpectedly detached.

I remember it was a Sunday in July, and I remember it significantly because it was the day after acquaintances of my parents, people they had met only once at a party, had chosen, in fleeing the city heat, to light upon us. How had they located us on the isolated, little-known side of a half-deserted river? Address book in tow at a party, their list of passive acquiescents, they could scarcely have missed out on my parents since everyone present had either been to, or was aware of, our Cannery Row summer place. No directions asked for. Into the black book: name, place, number of beds. They were good at finding their way, they said.

One of them, I can't remember which, got diarrhea, so they pulled out around midnight that same night, leaving us to once again make our own din: my mother, my father, my little brother George, and me. The discovery of their absence next morning is one reason I remember that day: it was what we were feeling at the time. Everything simplified. The smells of summer, the running and jumping, the back and forth love-play of my parents. When you've had to go around trying to answer dumb city questions, you feel you're all the time biting your tongue trying to hold your breath in; when you finally let it out you're on a trapeze. I remember when I got up that morning and found them gone, the first thing I did was go out on the hill and turn somersaults. Next I wanted to go around hugging everything, Scotch thistles and all, and for good measure, the bumblebees there ahead of me with the same idea. The fact I didn't have to keep sitting at the table after I was finished, even that did me just fine. All through breakfast my father kept saying, "Thank God for some people's diarrhea," muttering it again as he dragged pails of river water up the hill, ending his trips with a loud *diarrhea* as he turned the pails into the rain barrel.

On the day of this sudden emancipation, there was nothing exceptional, nothing we hadn't done other summer days, I suppose. But as I said, the way we were feeling heightened our relation to things we'd known for so long; it was as though we were rediscovering—a blade of grass, or a swallow, the lichen rock in the next field, and the cows who followed us when they got tired. It made you want to run your hands over each and every one. To say you were back again.

After breakfast I decided to sit on the verandah steps and let my buttermilk pancakes settle. There was lots to see.

Across the river, over in the French-Canadian village, it was a special day too. A day of masses in the little Roman Catholic church, the only one for miles.

I sat on the top verandah step counting the slow-moving cars, families from Wakefield, Lac Philippe, Alcove, and north; from south as well, Cascades, from outlying farms back of a service road known as the Loop. Old jalopies mostly, some brand new, sedans, roadsters, a few buggies, all clogging the river road, slowly turning up the narrow one, past the village and on as the churchbell rang: 9:00 a.m. —10:00—11:00. I watched the dust from the road moving over the car hoods, each an indeterminate shape in the wind, as though drawn in its own separate devotion towards the pealing bell in the white spire. After the morning's final bell, when the mass was over at 11:30, I thought of how it would ring again in the early evening; at seven o'clock, exalting the Saint, and the faithful who came to kneel. Already I longed to hear its peal, for in the evening the sound carried across the water, primitive, dreamlike, a hushed peacefulness renewing the tapestry of the hillside.

But when it sounded that night I was not looking its way, not seeing the glistening white board church in the field, or the cars winding their way to its roadside setting. I was looking instead at a small space beside the river which now lay trodden and silent, a patch of earth broken with a violence that haunts me today. It was only hours later, when I was falling asleep, that my mind lay beneath the churchbell's ringing, willing the sound back, to overtake me, and I wondered at what exact moment in that terror I had half-heard its peals.

———

The village had had its Saint's Day festivities. And we had had ours, less saintly, nevertheless no less loving of the eternal: the river, the mountains, a sudden opening of blue in the sky.

It was when evening came that everything changed— though not at first, because it began with jubilation, at the wireless panel. Some time, likely in the late afternoon when my mother wasn't looking, my father had gone out to his aerial and hooked it back onto the mast. (All day thunderstorms had been threatening and, to please Mamma, the aerial had been unhooked and grounded with a boulder. She was certain lightning would head straight for that wire and blow us to bits. My father never tired of his back and forth trips: drop the aerial, hook it up, drop it again. It added a little spice to the feud over VE9GW, proof of its presence if nothing else. And when my mother's façade was uncovered, the kid in my father had to go on with what was left of the game. He'd wait for a roll of thunder to die off in the distance, and out the back door he'd go. Without batting an eye, up went the aerial, as though swinging in the wind with the gentle glee of his mind. Except that on this day the thunderstorms seemed to be more threatening, and there weren't quite so many expeditions to the mast.) The cause for jubilation was that, static and all, my father had turned fluke airwaves into a burst of Morse that had him hopping about as if he'd been stung by bees; it was the first time he had picked up Holland. At least as far as I knew. At the age of ten you keep track of your father's hopping about, but not his wireless log.

The next thing I heard was his quick staccato, whacking out his replies so fast I couldn't understand a word of it. No facial expression to go by, nor that habit he had of decoding out loud to himself. The rapid-fire sending, the urgent pleasure of it, was all I could take in. This time he was using two fingers, which he never needed, always that left forefinger with the thumb a brace underneath. I didn't think he even knew I was standing there. I decided to go outside again; I had to finish cleaning out the leaves and ants from the raspberries. Then I heard him shout, "Quick. Come and listen," plopping down the earphones as he summoned my mother, who had hidden herself at the first clap of thunder an hour before, had rolled herself into an eiderdown quilt and was sitting on the floor of the front bedroom cupboard.

"Quick, Mimi," my father says again. "Come and hear what I've got on the line." His footsteps halt at the cupboard door where he tries to talk my mother into surfacing. *"Der fliegende Holländer,"* he adds, doing a jig, and in a whir of his own flies back to his headphones. But my mother is having none of it. She calls (through the comforter, which means she shouts because she can't hear herself), "Has the rain started yet?" A few feet away, outside the screen door, I sit on the verandah with my brother George, one year younger. Gingersnaps tide us over till supper as we watch the sky in this storm just breaking, watch the way sudden workings of wind make dark patches on the river, the way the weary cows carry themselves in their trudge to drink at the shoreline, where the water is still blue. In a minute, in a futile moment—or is it seconds?—I will drop my gingersnaps and scramble to my feet to try to run inside and cry out what has happened down at the river. While a man in Holland is sending signals across the infinite. Unaware what elements carry them over the Gatineau hillside.

It was all that sudden, the thing that happened, something you didn't think could be real life, like a dream you were having. I couldn't move. I just sat dazed. What explanation was there? The trees and water were real, so was the reflection of our rowboat tethered near by, and the mound of brown spruce cones we'd gathered. How significant they all became, their realness, as though they were there as revelation, and my mind gathered them in to protect my mixed-up disbelieving: presences of split-second duration. The spruce trees. Did I hear a car going along the road across the river? or was it only the wind? Another sound, the sound of pain, coming up from the riverbank below. The outline of an animal prancing, a cow, turning against a branch and falling. Were they being skittish again? But another cow was thrashing around in the grass and slipped suddenly, soundlessly, over the bank of the river. It was then I knew for sure that something was wrong, and in the part of my head that cringes with fear, instinct muzzled me. I got to my feet, I got that far, but something prevented me from tearing indoors to tell; I must have been afraid for my father, not wanting him running down there after them. Which he did anyway, he had picked it up through his earphones, the commotion . . . the cows, all of them screaming like that.

All that distance ago. Yet now, the sweep of Grieg's "A Minor", music which really has nothing to do with the story but seems tied-in somehow and is passing through the room like a person; that, and the repeated identification of Radd-io Nederland's transcription service between times, relays much beyond the pleasant soundtrack it is. While it does bring recollections of my father's Flying Dutchman, it's the rest that leaves me, still, dragging that soundless sob through time, place, places, beyond all days. How could I know then that tears, certain tears, unlike time and change moving on, could stay wrapped up inside you, like something trussed you feel wanting to get out?

———

I see myself sitting on the verandah on that July evening, with nothing adventurous or magical, except maybe the magic of being. Coming down the hill there is a parade, a special breed, a faint cowbell where breath and flesh and steamy hides seem to be looking at me. All six tons of them, free as the hypnotic wind back on the hill, a wind and a day my mind will never hear the end of. I taste it the way something bitter and unpleasant ages on your tongue. I have decided to turn off the Grieg "A Minor"; to admit, in silence, and to put to sleep at last, what I am reminded of.

How strong the scent of wild raspberries in the gully! A red dye runs through my mind, touches a nerve centre. I am there. I am there in the gully beyond the cottage, where a bluebird drops a feather, a soft pale feather, still warm. In the sumach he sits above George and me as we count the heads of the cattle standing under the elm. All twelve accounted for. Up and down the bark they take turns scratching their necks, sideways the ears, the stumps of their sawed-off horns, lazily, joyously. They know that tree. They trust it. Cowbells jangle the song of a pasture, the fields of July when the grass is still green and the clover buzzing with bees. With our lard-pails, wax paper in the bottom, George and I return to our berry-picking and the canes of raspberry bushes swing back into place, leaving their empty hulls to stare at us with moist little eyes. The bluebird takes stock of the crop left to him. Not for many more minutes will the smell of wild raspberries fill the gully. A storm is coming. You can see it gathering in thunderheads to the north, in the blackening river below the hill. The bluebird has left the sumach. And the cattle begin to move.

Stifling heat presses through the air as they cross the hayfield and then close ranks, herding one behind the other down their trodden path to drink at the riverbank. Their river and ours, George's and mine. Scarcely is the herd half-way down when the first bolt of lightning rips a jagged scar upon the earth. The storm is still far away, I know, but we run, George and I, bare legs ripped by thorns in the climb from deep in the gully. Our pickings, in pails filled to brimming, spill before us like shiny wooden beads as we hurry on downhill to the safety of home.

George says, "We beat the cows all hollow." And I tell him they weren't racing. "All the same," he says, "we should of slowed down, we should of waited for them." He likes to talk to his favourite, Myrtle—a boy's cow, coal-black with a white face and a horn that's starting to grow again. Myrtle has a pick on the rooster, chases him round and round the hen-house until it dawns on him to run for cover inside, which sets the hens going, the ones that are laying. He flaps at them, jumping up and down on his claws. He has to get even with someone. Gladys is the cow I call mine, she's dark red and smooth all over. But it's not because of that she's my fa-vourite. It's this act she puts on, like a performer, my mother says. She kicks over the bucket of milk, waits till it's full too.

Right now she's the last in line, coming down the hill as though the heat got her, gave her the heaves, as Mr. Carman calls it. He's the farmer, who holds his temper when Gladys spills the milk pail. He thinks it's funny the way I stand there laughing. I pretend I have to go to the bathroom; I do that for fear he'll clout her one. I wish now we'd stayed to walk down the hill with them. Gladys has a bigger belly then the others and it's bothering her, that sag of weight swaying in the terrible heat.

Heat and no sign of rain; only double forks of lightning, yellow tongs that come together as though trying to kindle the hillside. Onto the cottage verandah we land with a thump that sounds like the thunder itself. Our raspberries may have dwindled to half the supply but our heads are filled with the shifting pleasures of brother and sister. While we catch our breath we pretend to pant hard, to show we are that done in. Inside: my father about to hear from his Nederlander; my mother solidly, inveterately cocooned. Still panting, we run to the kitchen for gingersnaps, out again. And there we sit, George and I, watching the cattle lumber past as they make for the river, calling out the names we have given all twelve.

I could give you every name, but it would take too long. I'd be wanting to tell you something about each and every one. Maybe I should mention Yvonne, named for the wife of a man across the river in the village. She was the only cow Mr. Charbonne had, and when his wife died he had to sell her to pay for the funeral. And after Yvonne came over here to the farm she followed Mrs. Carman everywhere she went, into the vegetable garden even, standing stock still in the furrows watching her hoe; and without so much as sniffing a turnip, or treading on the lettuce. That's why George and I didn't pick her for a favourite. She had made her own choice. Then there's Winnie, who can't make proper moo-sounds ever since the hired hand lost the head off the axe chopping wood and it caught her full on the throat. And Irene, who's always getting sores. But melancholia, a hole in the neck, or running sores, they journeyed through our lives as if all along they had been waiting for us, had come to life out of our picture books. And not all sillied up with flowers behind their ears, or big crooked hooves. Often, when it was close to milking time, we'd run up the hill and into the barn where they stood waiting, each in her own stall. We'd walk along the row of cud-chewing heads whose eyes faced straight ahead as the wooden halters were moved into place; we'd hear buckets and milking stools being banged around, then the first squirts of milk hitting the tin pails as George and I wandered between the pairs of brown eyes that seemed to be half-closed, their lips still chewing as we stood with our arms around their necks, laying our faces against the warm pelt while they eased a stance. More than a routine; much more. The cows were our best friends.

Nothing impedes this downhill trek of theirs, a long way down without so much as a stop en route. This time it's taking them longer. The heat, maybe, and still full of all that milk. As they lurch ahead, a cool ballooning wind sustains them. We like the way they hold their heads outstretched facing into it, which we imitate. "Here's Myrtle," George says fondly, sticks his head forward and with his hand rolled into a fist makes the shape of a stunted horn on the right side of his head.

Electrical currents recharge themselves. From the verandah we can see that deer flies have followed the cows, riding out the swish of air fanned into being by a flagging energy left in their tails. In all this time, not so much as a spit's worth of rain. Instead, mutiny in the heavens, coming closer now, bolts of lightning exploding out of the north as well as the south, meeting head-on and rocking the air with salvos, like detonated battleships. The whole cottage shakes and I hear my mother's voice, muffled, the whinny bordering on hysteria, addressing no one in particular: "Where is the rain? It's always better when it *rains!*"

A soaring wind ships across the river and the cattle trail the last few yards to its edge. Plodding gracefully now. Where the ground is flatter. They seem not to notice the sky's vibrations. Not until the flash that splits the oak tree before them.

They seize up, stall at the smashing sweep as the great tree gathers in the power lines, snaps the pole bearing the transformer, and heaves down into the water. The cows back away from the torn-up root and stand there puzzled, refusing to budge, eyeing the sprawl of branches, and the choppy river that slaps through the foliage. An alien sound to their ears, in a place they go to as readily as to their stalls in the barn. One makes a move, another follows. They jam together and stare, thirstily, at the fissured trunk blocking their way. They gape and gape, crane their necks and swing their tails like a cat disturbed, and then furtively lower their heads and moo; a soft bewildered lowing at the barrier denying them water.

Was it animal instinct that urged them on, drawing them along the river's bank? that drew them nearer, inexorably to where the high voltage wires lay hidden, in grass soaked by the tree's splash? The fear of God was in those power-lines—that we knew, on account of being forbidden to climb trees down there; bare wires that could electrocute us, we kept hearing, drummed into us daily from the moment we first set foot on the hill.

I see them now, the cows, and feel myself cry an empty sound, with pain that breaks through me charting its voyage over fibres time has not yet toughened. It is nine o'clock here, in the soft twilight of September, 1974, where rain is about to cross the Toronto sky. It was going on for seven then, but the light of a summer night, as if still clinging to an edge of the horizon, lost its hold; there was nothing to stop what was coming behind, there was more than rain in the sky.

I see the cattle edge closer, advancing on the fallen tree by way of its tip where the branches are thinner. They band to-gether in threes, in fours, joined by their impossible, stubborn curiosity. Bessie, the lead cow, suspicious, a tobacco-brown statue at the head of her herd, thinking, sizing things up, de-cides now to make a move, the benefit of backsides and nos-trils that prod her ribs standing by. With her bell so soft a tingle she puts her nose low over the ground; a tentative nudge and she stumbles on contact.

On contact. Living cells that, at birth, picked themselves up, stood on all fours and bleated, a consequence of nature that chewed, and roamed, and lingered in shade. What is there left now? a quiver, a mechanical arch of her chest as she lets out a cry and topples sideways into the water, taut. Is she dead? Bessie! Bessie! It is happening. It is not happening! I fumble for George's hand and open my eyes again. I am afraid; everything going round in circles down there. Bits of mud and twigs spin through the air. Why must they all herd so? I tell myself they are trying to reach Bessie; their haunches stagger about in the tangle of wires, passing shocks one to the next and the next. Which makes them stampede into each other. Down goes Irene. The wet wires . . . hidden, under broken branches. A black wire twines itself around Irene's hind leg; I shake with her screams as she rolls down the slippery bank, hoofs up, dazed, rigid. A splash into the water. And George, trembling too, puts his hand over his eyes. I slip my arm around his waist and pull him closer while I try to find Myrtle and Gladys. I want to say something to him but my mouth . . . my voice doesn't happen in this unreal world, the spread of hoofs and hides that are betrayed, that in a matter of seconds die as we sit, beyond understanding, beyond our taking in.

Bessie. She was the one with spirit, made of fine instincts and quick with her wits. And now in the turn of a whirlpool I see her white underbelly, clean and fresh, untransformed by the voltage that streaked through her. And right behind, Yvonne, like a puppy staying close beside its mother; it is the eddying current that puts her there. Yvonne, who had two years at the farm, and a calf for each season. In the hayfield three miles back, right now, they frolic through the greening stubble, her healthy heifers with the same odd patches of white and coppery-red, a distant obedience to her likeness as she drifts away.

I see Yvonne with more hurt because of her beautiful will to love. I picture the sight of her that June morning, led by a rope out of the Charbonnes' yard, trudging down the village road, over gravel, through the sifting dust of the sawmill, the smell of the marsh, past all the sounds she knew, then standing alone on the scow, looking straight ahead as she was rowed to her new home. Rolling hills and pastures, the wide open land she wasn't used to. With joy I feel new life springing up in her, dropping her nose in my hand, melancholy slowly dissolving, left behind in the lettuce patch, in her end stall in the barn, the starched swish of the blue-coloured apron Mrs. Carman always wore; Yvonne . . . pretending to chew at the cleanly washed apron blowing on the clothesline. I am filled with the vision of her brown-eyed serenity, the touch of a vein in her warm neck, the story of her need to belong. Which she carries through to the end now as she follows Bessie, drifting, controlled by the small waves, the current, as if the river were making sure of, was granting her one essential: her journey alongside. And the thing at the river is happening all over again. I can't get Yvonne out of my mind, stumbling, her cry a muted bellow, then that small sound is gone as she slides headfirst down the embankment. Her lips are parted, as though she were kissing the grass. The grey river receiving her washes a wavelet over the fuzz of her tawny-red crown and I find I must think of it now as a silvery flow, the pat she would have needed.

I wonder how I saw it then? No. I don't wonder, because I know; the wailing and shrieking, the pain of animals we loved, knowing they were being *burned alive*. That's what I saw. One following the other, two at a time, one more, one more. So fast.

Myrtle. I saw Myrtle, spinning by herself in her own patch of ground off to one side. Why did she have to go down like that? I never told George, not then, not ever. She fell over a stump and dangled there, until the sheer weight of her front quarters pulled her over, her pink stomach turning purple till the splash covered her black hide, her white forehead. Why Myrtle?

The water settles and Myrtle is turning in the eddies, between logs. I say to myself it didn't take place, I didn't see it. I try to pick out Gladys, to see if she's backed away from the shore.

Screams of burnt flesh. I want to run away where I can hide with my ears covered; I can't move. I open my mouth to call for my father, then the screen door bangs and he is vaulting over the verandah railing, jettisoning his old tennis shoes because they haven't any laces in them. Headlong he plunges barefoot, slipping on the uneven ground and barking his shins on stumps he doesn't clear. There's only Little Jean left, who is the smallest and the most timid. My father tries to head her off. But he's too late. She turns her head the other way, to where she must, in that one direction to which she is bound. It is not for her to leave the herd. Her ears go forward as she lows a plaintive, forlorn call, and bounds ahead—into contact. . . . But you can't hear Little Jean. The others are still screaming.

How the chipmunks agitate, alerting. Swallows dip in and out of their sandbanks, like a flypast. Their quick bird-songs cry in terror, tongues of nature crying. My father paces back and forth, pulling his hands through his hair and across his eyes, the way he does when he comes up from diving. He is not ready to come back to the cottage. Instead, he looks out at the cattle, floating like swollen debris in their journey out through the eddying current. And the storm pours its rain at

last. Grey bandages of rain driven by the wind. Holes in the
verandah roof allow the rain to drip upon my brother and
me; swift, heavy drops, uncontrolled. It is lonely here on the
verandah for there is that sound, the one that has stopped. It
plays on, through the rain and the high wind, a sound that
won't cease because it is still in our vision. We hear the cattle
moan. We always will.

My mother has come out of the cupboard and above me,
at the bedroom window, she pushes her forehead against the
white cotton mosquito netting. The eiderdown quilt covers all
but her face; like an Arab hovering there, a wordless Arab.
She suspects something is up at the river but the silence
puzzles her, the silence of wind, and swallows who fly low
over the water and do not call now. George tells her he
thinks Myrtle is dead. Electrocuted, he says, with a terrible
emphasis, making it sound like an achievement.

"Nonsense," my mother says, which is what she always
says when she wants something not to be so. She rubs her
hand quickly over the windowsill as if checking for dust,
looking then at her fingertips. "Where's Daddy gone?" she
says. I am the one she's looking at because George has his
head down. But I don't want to hear myself say the words. I
can't.

"He went to the privy," I tell her. And that's not a lie. He
must have had to go *some* time today.

"What? In this storm? Couldn't he have held it?" It is the
quilt she is asking as she draws it tighter to her ears and goes
back to sit on the floor of her hideaway.

———————

When he returned my father didn't mention the cows, so
George and I didn't. We had long before learned from that
certain quiet in him (when he'd become pale-looking and
drawn without losing any of his colour) that when there was
trouble he saved us for the last. It took longer. It wasn't only
our comprehension that was important to him. He wanted to
let us see how everyone, even he, could take things badly
sometimes. So we wouldn't feel it so much, I guess, seeing
him. I decided that when the time came I would try not to
keep asking show-off questions or speak out of turn.

Meeting our eyes as he came up the steps, assessing how
deeply, how darkly our minds had received the events, my father bent over us to pick up our raspberry pails. He knew, he
understood; that shock, for the time being, was sparing us

from the worst; that the real enemy was the anguish to come. With his fingers around the wire handles he held first one pail and then the other to his nostrils, inhaling as he observed us through plops of rain that spilled, intermittently, from where a shingle had been torn loose by a gale.

My father's wordless presence, the wonder of it, balancing our pails, leaning over us, tension trapped in his breath, the life in him trying to tell us . . . There was nothing we could have done.

Like an immense seawave the rush of his concern closed around me. Order of a sort beginning somewhere: splashes of rain falling over my father's shoulders, his bare feet raw with scratches and sharp cuts, and our raspberries, their wet smell lingering fiercely. Had my father sensed the shiver that rose up in us just then? On impulse, in a motion that cut through our reflection, he let his arms sag down as though the pails were laden, and before setting them on the window ledge asked us what we felt they were worth, would we sell them to him for Mamma's supper?

All at once we didn't want him giving us anything. In unison we hung our heads and said, "No. That's all right." He started to say something, I can't remember what, and put his hands on our heads, bunching the hair at the crown as he fingered the tufts, speaking to us that way. How could we take from someone who had given the rest of himself, going into the thick as he had? It was our turn to give. He was the one with wet in his eyes. He pulled change from his pocket and left it on the table beside us, going then back down the steps to retrieve his sneakers; one had landed right side up in the juniper, and the other was down the path a way. He turned them over to let the water run out and carried them inside and hung them on horseshoes nailed to the wall above his wireless. I saw him copy down the call letters of his new Dutch friend before shutting down, smoothing the chintz cover with words going on in his mind.

It looked as though he might come outside again, but no, he was on his way to Mamma's cupboard. "You better come inside now," he said through the screen door, "your mother will be worrying." And I thought, That's why he has to go to her first. She's the one who's frightened and nervous. And being afraid is worse than being sad. He turned away but in a matter of seconds came back to tell us we could play with the good deck of cards.

The pack was in a leather case on the mantel. I could hear

him pushing the vase of chicory aside to get at the cards, the
vase scraping along the stone again as he moved it back. I
knew that sound. It was home, it was many things. And what
really mattered was to acknowledge what my father was trying to do, letting him see our attention was taken up. Already
George and I had gotten to our feet. Torrential rain blew
sideways into the open verandah and trickled down the awn-
ing of the stacked chairs, speeding past us in rivulets where
the verandah floor sloped. We climbed onto the bench and
stood at the stained-glass window, an oblong transom that
opened from inside, was now hooked to the ceiling above the
living room table. Because of the wind the light shade was
swaying wildly, the huge parchment shade banging against
the kerosene lantern my father had just lighted, casting circles
of white up and down the walls and around the floor. As my
father broke open the seal a spin of light passed over his
head and I remember feeling, briefly, the anguish he was
concealing; something I sensed but couldn't explain. There
was no droop to his shoulders, no set of his lips; he was
standing erect, seeing to our pack of cards, his shirt and tennis ducks so wet they stuck to his frame and squilched as he
made his way to the table.

At that moment I wanted to go inside and stand beside
him, loving him so deep in my heart it hurt. I think I was becoming aware of what we meant to him. I caught, and held in
my mind, that instant's awakening, the way he glanced at the
window just then, catching sight of the two of us; the ache in
him . . . for the cows, and for us, who can't tell him, cannot
give him the words we have yet to learn. What solace would
he have found as his eyes met ours? George's face barely
above the window ledge, mine scarcely higher.

He knew we were waiting for the high point: his way of
spreading the cards across the table, always as though offering them to someone to pick a card. Up would come a longi-
tude of mountains with snow, like an exotic shiny fan. That
was the way my father laid down every pack of cards, with a
flourish; he could never just plunk them. This time a lesser
reflex, habit by itself, guided the cards. The fan shape came
out crooked and there was no long range of mountains span-
ning the tabletop. He made a quick stab at poking them into
place. But I saw that his hand was trembling.

We said yes, we'd come inside and play Fish and tracked
our wet feet over the living room linoleum, staying only long
enough to pick up the cards; went out again by the kitchen

door, and with the thunder silencing our footsteps, returned to where we had been. The lightning wouldn't come twice in a row, not when it had so many other places it could go. George and I did not speak of that place down at the river. We were sitting there simply because we wanted to be near. We were their kin. This is what we were feeling: that by not leaving the porch we kept faith. How could we leave them all alone, like that?

Springs creak in the cot as my father stretches out, and when I raise myself to look through the netting I see my mother's arm come out of the cupboard, pulling his right foot down until it reaches the floor; she has to make sure he's grounded. Out of his wet clothes now and into the sweatshirt he saves for tennis.

"No," I hear him say. "I was down at the river. I heard a tree come down and I wanted to see before it gets dark if the wires had fallen." My father will tell her about the cows now, in his way, so it won't seem so bad when she's in this panic. I don't want to listen to them. I don't want to hear a word of it. It is so lonesome out here on the verandah. Do parents know how you can love a cow? Rain splashes over the coins my father had left, as George and I sit without taking our eyes from that one place by the river, with the light of summer gone out of the hill.

It wasn't the tangle of wires or the broken tree that seemed to fasten us. It was the trampled grass where the cows had gone round and round. The last thing they had left us that was still part of them. Their cries seemed almost to be calling to us, out of what was left by their feet. That was the worst part, I recall, seeing the open, flattened space. Was it that that made us look there, not southward where their bodies were still specks on the river but right there where the real sadness was? Or was it something deeper, unknown, beyond what we were now feeling? an indefinable physical force as well? Were we dwelling on the bizarre, the madness?

---

It is night-time of *that* night. The last storm must be way past Ottawa by now and my mother has started the supper dishes, by candlelight because the power-lines can't be fixed until tomorrow. Bedtime, and my father sits on the side of my camp cot, tracing hopscotch-squares with his fingernail on the seersucker bedspread. In the candlelight, which we have too, I can see from the way his eyebrows shoot up and down that he doesn't want to talk much. But it is here where we always do our serious talking, at bedtime when it's quiet and settled down. George is perched at the foot of the bed, holding the drawstrings of his new, too-large pyjamas, and I have my knees on the pillow, leaning back against the wall. The rain, hard on the cedar shingles, makes something to listen to while we're sitting like this; rain that's on our side now, a friend. It is no longer armed. My father does not say, 'There's no use this' or 'There's no use that.'

"There are two kinds of pastures," he begins.

"Are they in Heaven yet?" George says without looking up, pretends to be more interested in looping a drawstring around his thumb, but I know it's to give him something to do, like my father's hopscotches.

"There's no such place as Heaven," I say. And my father looks at me hard, startled too, with eyes that say, 'Can't your mother and I ever talk without you listening, when you should be fast asleep?' I slide down and draw the covers up under my chin, and snicker into the pillow, nervously. My father's look of a moment ago does not turn out to be the reproach he meant it to be. Any outlet, however reprehensible, is welcomed. George has his drawstring to fiddle with, and Daddy his hopscotches. I snicker. I am the one who thinks everything's funny when it's the opposite. My father leans over me, bobbing my head up and down on the pillow, his teasing squelch.

It is my turn now not to want to talk. I have not forgotten the river.

"She thinks the cows are caught in the boom down at Cascades," George says, emphasizing the "she" as he looks at me with hurtful eyes, as if it were my fault he has doubts of his own.

"They're no such thing," I tell him, sitting up again, "they're too heavy. They'd sink 'way before that." My father's brow furrows, a wince in his forehead.

"Your mother doesn't seem to share your feelings," he says with a note of censure, "and neither does George." George does not say anything, but I know from the way he meets my eyes he is taken aback by the suggestion he and I are divided in thought. His mind speaks in his face as he looks at me, as though saying 'That's all right, Daddy didn't mean it that way.' My father does not miss this exchange, and clasps first George's hand, then mine.

"Tell me something," he continues, "wouldn't you say that

Heaven could be many places, and many things? It could be here . . ." He pauses, draws us closer.

"Is it in this room?" George wants to know, puzzled, "right now? The way God is when we're saying our prayers?"

"I don't think Heaven's a place at all," I say. "Besides, Daddy means Sumach Point, George, not just the cottage."

"Yes, indeed I do," my father agrees. "But also, where else? What other places?"

"Not the river," George whispers, his eyes on the floor.

"Oh I'd say it's there too," my father replies, his voice low, passing a hand down the back of his head, does so again, slowly, as if trying to understand things himself. "Heaven can be very near," he adds, "or it can be very far. Doesn't matter where, just so long as it's there. Don't you think that's what counts?"

"The cows got killed. That's what counts," I argue, not meaning to.

"But what also counts is believing they might still be with you, somewhere else," he replies. "Why don't we agree that the part of them you remember, whatever it was that told them to lick your hand, or follow you out of the barn, that part still lives on and is somewhere in the universe? You don't have to call it by any name, just a place of their own, where they don't have to work for their keep, a pasture that's safe, nothing for them to stumble into."

"Like the night-pasture," I suggest, seized by the suggestion of their existence.

"Exactly," Daddy says, "now you're catching on. Think of them there now, never being parted, never having to stand up in the barn all winter. Wouldn't you agree the cows are much better off?"

But this is not my way of seeing things. We are expected to make a straight exchange, to swap pastures we cannot imagine for the ones out there on the hill where Myrtle and Gladys belong. It was all right as it was.

My father lets go our hands and clasps his hands around one knee. There is a less-strained look about him, his eyes drifting here and there, at a chair in the corner with a basket of ironing waiting to be done. After a moment he pulls his white sweatshirt down below his waistband, where it has curled to the underside of the fleece. It is smooth-looking now. He slips his hand under his backside and sits swinging his legs over the edge of the bed, as though we had just made plans, we could relax and think about them. My mother's dishes clatter in the kitchen. She hasn't said a word through the beaverboard that separates the rooms. She has been saving it, just in case. "Don't forget the important part, Cecil," she calls, and I hear her carrying the basin of dishwater out the back door where she throws it into the grass behind the cottage. My father lights one of his Turret cigarettes, the first I've seen him with all day.

"Now that the cows are gone," he says, "we should compare how they went." I know he is feeling his way, that he *wants* to explain, and yet he doesn't. "If they'd been taken into town . . ." He doesn't finish but rubs his head as if he were seeing them being loaded onto the scow.

"Where they get killed by a man with a board," I say. My father rubs his head some more and agrees. "Yes. They get killed. And their backs aren't turned either, so they sense right off what's coming. What's more, there's nothing around them that's familiar, no one they know. So, either there's the plant in town, or the less terrifying way of—a while ago, which was more painful for you than it was for them. Some day you will understand." There was not a finality to the sound of those last words; it felt more like a page being turned in a book. At the end of a chapter.

My father blows out the candle by my bed, and even though the night's still hot and humid, he gathers in the bedclothes and pulls them up to my chin and it gives me a feeling of being safe and snug. Almost. He takes George's hand to gesture him off the bed now that it's time.

"There'll be tears in your heart when you go to sleep," my father says, with his arm around George and his head looking down at me in the dark. "But try to think of the cows as having won out."

---

I thought all the pieces of glass I felt in my stomach would stop hurting after that. But nothing made any difference at all. Because there's sleep in your eyes it doesn't mean you can turn over to the wall. You start counting cows. Which is exactly what I did. It was all set up in my head, like a one-reeler I was being forced to sit through, over and over. I tried reminding myself of what my father had said, to think of the cows as having won out. But when you're that young the heart is not so generous. I picked my doll Wampa up from my pillow and held her as I sat up in bed, leaning into the netting at the open window, with the wet smell of the mountains and the pine cones lying around the barn, the fields empty and silent except for the slow beat of rain and the frogs croaking down in the pond; all the arrangements of things I loved. How long I sat and stared out at the black night, listening to the rain and the frogs, waiting for the night to be over, the night to go and the dream that would come to stay: that everything would right itself and be the same again. And when I lay back on the pillow I told myself, Next summer another herd will stand under the elm, seeking its shade. I thought of the wild raspberries that would grow in the gully, of the bluebird that would come to sit above us in the sumach, watching the cattle as George and I would; the heifers born last year, this spring, now back in the third field: the calves of Bessie and Yvonne and Little Jean, and . . . We would give them new names. Yes. There'd be fourteen new names to think up; a one-syllable name, two-syllables, three. I heard them in my head. They had a nice ring. . . . I went to sleep then.

I went to sleep because of a sound that had stayed with me, a sound circling the valley, burying itself in my flesh while the cows were borne southward by the eddying current, past the pines and the birches and the river's great width ten miles down. Sitting there on the verandah, with the rain dripping on my head, with George's first quiet sobbing for Myrtle, around the corner so no one would see him, and my father inside talking to his Mimi, holding her hand, I think, as he gave her his guarded version, the pain in him a more painful thing than my mother's pale comprehension, through all of this I could hear the seven o'clock churchbell over in the village. Faraway. Close by. Entering my mind obliquely perhaps, somewhere behind my own soundless despair. It pealed through the rain and the lost time, hammering out sounds that for an instant restored a sweetness I could not explain; perhaps in the resonance a sober, merry blessing folding its arms around the violence, and perhaps just the promise of continuity: that soon another summer will come, and on hot afternoons we will sit down beside the cattle. That it could be so, again. That's my need.

# II

———◆———

There's a place, an old house, where I live by myself now, and sometimes it's as though nothing had happened at all.

I ask myself, What do I make of it? Autumns and summers slip into place, and the great swoops of night and traffic and longing that see them through have become the background to a mystery I can't seem to let rest, the question of why I am here at all. Except to live.

Am I no longer seeing the world under bright lights? The earth is so busy and dreamless. There once was a time when a blade of grass served a purpose, cool and slippery between the lips, no more than that. It was what you found, what you came upon, whether a single blade of grass, or the sudden smile of a child with a nickel to spend, a child who turned out to be yourself, who ran then to swing under the hypnotic sway of pine branches on a sultry day. In the flesh, a jangling that was soft; a sense of streams rushing past, and clouds, looking at them and wondering where they might be going. I miss that feeling.

Half of me belongs still to another city, and the summertime Gatineau Valley of my generation. The other part, the woman, belongs here in this city that's been mine for twenty-five years. I am divided into these two parts, not trying to make them match, like a pair of shoes, but to bring them together as one, which they aren't. I've been taken over by original claim.

I am like a churchbell that rang for an age over a single meadow, until moved to a steeple that rises out of a hundred others, whose peal is no longer singular with the fresh innocence of pastorale but a chime of neat and tidy habitude. An essential caught up in the pace of realisms.

Sometimes I go back to the places where I lived with my parents and brother. And spend time poking around, things

26

won't have changed all that much. A winter, or a summer, or on the day of a sudden impulse, I jump in the car, on the train, perhaps take a bus. Excitement inside me as I step out, identifying myself to the air: the city, the village, the river, and fresh tracks in the snow through a bush, footprints same size as mine. You get the feeling the wind should be the same because you've come back, that known sound of a train whistle, the neigh of a horse in a field, the footsteps you sense behind you on a sidewalk. Things of beauty and measure, humming, caught in a faraway drift of churchbells greeting the night. A thousand details, with no relics. For something else is taking place, begins its own mystery every day in all the details of being born, and loved. Seeking and losing or finding and losing. Or perhaps just waiting. Is that what I'm doing—waiting?

And then I return, back to the sounds of this other city, the lights of Toronto that tell me I'm home. Back to my rented house. The lower half of a rambling old dwelling, with high windows and ceilings and well-worn floors that sigh with the history of time. A house where my cat and dog play with the silk lampshades I fashion and sell to interior decorators. A house where friends come to relax, or blow their tops, or put the lid back on mine. A place with a back garden, a fireplace, and all gucked-up with treasures from flea markets. Where people party with me, young, middle-aged like myself, some older than I; friends who paint, or work for the government, sell lingerie or surgical instruments, teach music, make love, on occasion get drunk; in groups or in twos, threes, fours, asking ourselves questions: what do we love, what are we afraid of, who threw up at *The Exorcist*, who's turned on by Noel Coward, or Von Daniken, or acupuncture; passive whimperings (and shouts) of "What's happening to the world?" Isn't it the same question we used to hear our parents asking themselves?

The street itself is a peculiar assortment. Easy-going hippies content with their love-nests, the constant new arrivals in a flurry of guitars and Burmese cats; children armed with toy guns and interesting words, the poetry of those clutching a handful of jellybeans or pussy willows their parents have bought them at the corner; perhaps a single, a twenty-year-old or a pensioner, instinctively concealing his private desperation. For variety there's the Rolls-Royce to add an established, conservative air, the King of the Castle hard by the laundromat. A city street I have come to love, noisy, peaceful, indifferent as time ticks away at the future. The order of daily processes, scattered sounds and movements involving people I don't even know but whose ways I associate with. For I see them as I see myself, confident, unsure, the soft yet tough will of the spirit caught up by whims of fate, even so, not giving up; like moths in search of a flame. We are the voices and shadows on patios, the faces in attic rooms, the bodies who huddle on a sofa in the bay window of a town house. Inconspicuous in Ramsden Park where we skate nights; the park where we sit with an ice cream cone when it's too hot for sleeping. The whole of the city around us, with crowds and trees and movement and the sounds of momentum idly caught in the subway's open cut. Cultures and passions comprising the conditions of human lives. So many conditions. So many partings.

I must listen to myself, both voices: the I that was and the I that am. It has come to that. On my ceiling, outside my window, in the pulse of my being, something immediate and fearful and radiant trips a trigger in my brain. And in my throat there rises the same cry: I am here where I've always been. Forever the same cry.

Identity is not what I am seeking, I know who I am; no more, no less, I'm an offspring of time, my flesh a chunk of the universe. My true identity exists in the soles of my feet, where they have taken me, what they have shown me, the steps we have climbed, those we have fallen down.

I am looking for something, I think. Out there. Where beauty and things of consequence seem buried somewhere.

But what *is* this something? Is it a person, a place, an astral body, or just a feeling? Or is it an embodiment of all four? For a long time I have waited, a standstill journey I seem to be on, a crowded direction which moves through history, memorabilia, joy, anguish. All the silent arrangements of time standing between me and this sound journeying within, a cry that keeps calling my name and yet I cannot get through.

If I'm being summoned to answer, then a time of sitting still is what I need. Going back to examine a river and wordless fields—what do I ever find? that I was young there, and the fields have forgotten? They have not freed me. I wander the hills at dusk, and stroll through the disconnected sounds of late night in the village; but it is not enough to go back. Not that way. You bring only your eyes, and, keeping silent, bow to sound. One's voice, mine . . . I tried. I opened my mouth, Did I, had I just seen a certain man, a certain woman, and that youth, and her, that little girl? Yes. Yes! And a sign in my head, bringing it all to an end: it's over. It is over. And in reply, my throat . . . and then I left. I left the stars over the river, the blurred pines, fireflies; it was very late. I was bailing the boat, there was no one around, I had wanted to call out.

But to what? to whom? The shooting stars?

That's why I must do my journeying deeper within, settle down and let my being live more fully the life it knew.

What'll I see, I wonder? No skimming past, can't pick and choose. Or pretend not to notice. Will I sit, stand, wander, will I speak out loud, and glance away? Notes of music . . . a sticky table—what if I don't remember?—I'm thumbing a ride, there's a letter in my handbag. I cover my face with my hands. No. No picking and choosing. Should I begin in the middle? and after that . . .

There's time, the space of time is very small. It is autumn now, smoky haze hours . . . what if I can't remember? oh, but I will. There was the Grieg "A Minor", I was in the armchair here, and I heard my voice again, and again, I saw the cows . . . it wasn't just fancy. I could *feel* that mark—the scratch on Myrtle's horn. If that night I could come alive, and be as I was, touching a drip of rain on the sill, pressed against the window netting in the ragged flannelette nightie I wore, with its blue embroidered collar wrong side—was I wearing it inside out?—then why can't I again? Yes. I won't close my fists. I will remember. I will talk into Indian summer's rusty light. On an October lawn I will sweep the leaves, and, under the fierce blue I'll bank flames at the edge of the sidewalk; twists of smoke coiling, up and away, airborne; chatter of passersby, what will they be saying? I won't hear them. For I'll be six or I'll be twenty, I'll be Hannah with chocolate cake on my face, or a freaky wave hanging down from my hair, and a bracelet I'll toss high at a peg on the wall. There'll be the Minto Follies . . . and crooners: "All of Me" . . . lah-la-la, dum-dee-da-dah-da-da. It is the last day of September, tomorrow a new month begins. And the moon at night a glacial glimmer; frost in the air, already a wintry chill once darkness falls. Perfection I think.

Perfect haze. Perfect frost. And the language of silence— before the rainy nights come. I can almost hear the racking wind. I lay my head back and wait for the wind to stir. The window, even in winter. Yes. I must listen to myself. And listening is the price I must pay.

# III

I am in a region of summer hills and clouds set to music. And of time, for my mother is young. We are by ourselves, sitting in a field where daisies droop, seem disorderly. It was of course the heat. Yes. I remember the encumbrance of my mother's dress, her skin so covered up with all those curious tucks and ruching. Furlongs of blue gingham she put into its making. But it was the fashion then. Like my pinafore.

Am I six? No—seven. My mother has just said, "Not now, pieface," and, after a minute's reflection, examining my toes, I clasp my hands behind my head and ask, "When, then?"

"In a while."

As usual, I wanted to know if we could go for another swim. It's inconceivable that with a whole river under our noses we have to sit wasting precious time, have to stay put on this hard bare rock staring at it.

Nothing much is happening apart from the distant jabber of birds, aroused by a hawk, and my mother turning the pages of her new *Needlecraft* open on her lap. I pick up a broken cedar branch and swish flies away, collecting my wits: studying a heap of cow dung, and a whir of locusts, fancying I should catch one to add to my collection. Would it eat my caterpillar, though? That slow fat one, what would I feed it, raspberries or ants? chocolates? I pounce. Missed!

"Here, what are you doing?" Mamma says.

"Nothing." I retrieve the branch and sit down again, fingers coiling fresh cedar-leaf warmed by the sunlight, now drawing the tip of the branch across my nose as I gaze at the river, moving indolently, deliciously, thirty feet away.

"Know what?" I ask. "I'm hungry. So if I fall asleep will you wake me?"

"Be still," my mother replies.

"Are we poor?"

"I said be still. And stop sucking that cedar. Do you want to poison yourself?" I lay the branch down, arrange it across the cowflap, like a tablecloth.

"Mamma?"

"What now?"

"Am I bothering you?"

"Yes, of course you are. And I don't know what I'd do without you either. Anything else?" She bends my head into her lap, blows into my ear, releases me. Placidly she leans back on her elbows and the magazine slips sideways on her lap. She picks it up again, rolls herself over onto one elbow, begins flipping through pages. I decide I won't talk any more for a little while, or even move as much as my big toe— unless she wants me to give her a hand, tie her hair back maybe, find the ribbon for her in the sewing basket, that'd take a minute, and some doing, it's always so snarled. She'll look at me and say, "Calm yourself," or else laugh, pretend to be outraged and ask, "Any objection?" as I hold up the tangle of knots, feeling she should see for herself. "Excuse me," she'll laugh, and I'll ask her why she keeps porcupine quills in there, and that small piece of my hair from when I was being born.

---

"I don't have black hair," I'd said the previous week. "That's one of *your* curls," this emphatic denial having been uttered in the cottage living room.

"Really? You don't say!" she had replied, rubbing her nose. "And what would I want with a piece of my own hair as a keepsake? I assure you it's your hair, not mine, and it came straight from the back of your . . ."

I was very fair, light-skinned. So why keep insisting that this ringlet, sleek as a blackbird's wing, was mine?

"I know," I broke in, sitting down beside her on the stuffed chair, "it's one of the curls you had left over. Remember? when you snipped some of yours to glue on my golliwog? You brought this from Canso!" I could hear my father in the kitchen, hacking at a piece of ice with an icepick, singing and whistling "The Golliwogs' Cakewalk".

"Nothing of the sort," my mother said. "That's the way

you came into the world, a black shock of hair thick as a
Scotch thistle. Couldn't believe my eyes, but there it was, a
wad of it behind your left ear. I might have known you'd arrive on the scene with something to say for yourself, before
you'd even opened your mouth." She paused, looking down
at the needle case now lying open on my lap. "My, what a
funny sight," she mused. "You yawned in my face and then
turned your head away. I thought I was seeing things. I
remember wanting you to have hair like your father, and not
all the colours of the rainbow. Well, I certainly lost no time
snipping it off at the roots."

I was not, I then discovered, found under a cabbage leaf,
nor anywhere else on the ground; my parents had been
forced to look farther afield. Cabbages, they said, and for
that matter the best-tended garden patch in the world, could
not grow where they lived at the time. Not even ferns. My
father had returned to the room and was sitting in the other
padded chair opposite us. I glanced over at him.

"Radishes?" I asked. I wanted to believe I'd been swaddled
and watched over by rabbits, waiting their chance to hand me
over.

"No, nothing, I'm afraid," he replied. "I guess it was just
too cold."

"Icebergs," my mother murmured, looking pleased, smiling
with memory as she sipped the drink she and my father were
having while waiting for visitors to arrive from the city.

"Icebergs?" I repeated, dismayed. In my mind, looming before my eyes in a flash—massive blue-white icebergs, majestic, frightening; we were in the dory boat, my father gunning
the engine as we raced through high seas for an opening in
the reefs, the one passage that would allow us to make it into
shore. I had tried not to remember that; it was long ago,
when I was five, and the world and I were now seven, there
was nothing here to shrink from, the sandbars and logs were
things to have fun on. "You found me on an iceberg?" I said,
my voice tissue-thin, feeling the prickle of goosebumps shivering my skin, the gurgle in my mother's throat as she downed
another sip of her drink doing nothing to help matters.

"Of course not," my father said gently, "your mother was
just thinking of a certain morning in the middle of summer.
She had seen a couple of ice floes, they'd come down from
the Grand Banks and it struck her as funny. She'd been out
coaxing along the poor little fringe she hoped would turn into
carrots . . . and this blast of cold air, straight from the

Eskimos. Seems to me that was the day your mother finally gave in. She stood looking down at her carrots and she said, 'They'd need the kitchen fire after that.' " They smiled at one another, similar or separate images glimpsed, thought about for a few seconds. I waited. Curious now. No vegetable patch to be scooped up from. So where? I trembled with excitement: what nooks and crannies had they searched? there was no grass that I could remember, the bushes were scrawny, and the sands kept shifting it seemed to me. As for the winds, I'd have been blown away.

"Well?" I whispered after a minute. I moved down onto the floor and sat cross-legged, they'd see I was still there, waiting for an answer. Did they find me under a rock? I inquired, sucking my fingers.

"Hmmm," my mother interjected before I had any further suggestions, laying down her glass and then bending over to retie the ribbon in my hair. "One evening after supper, around sunset, wasn't it, Cecil?" she asked, blithely, innocently, of my father, and went on, "By some strange coincidence, there was this low pink cloud that broke apart, it was sitting on the edge of the sea, and . . ."

"Your mother and I were down digging for cross-eyed clams," my father said "and we wondered what was that coming down? Should we go out and see? So we set the pail in a rock-pool and waded out to meet you, because you were . . ." He slipped his hands into his pockets; it was my mother's turn.

"When we reached the cloud you were lying on your side, sound asleep."

"Was I drifting on the water?" I asked, fancying that I'd somehow been contained within the cloud, and, like a toy inside a cardboard Easter egg that slips out as the two halves break open, I'd sailed through mid-air, out of the cloud and down. "Was I floating?"

"Oh no," they replied in unison, surprised, my mother's disavowal carrying through on what she had initiated. "Your cloud wouldn't give you up until we held out our arms and lifted you off."

"What did you say to me?" I asked, getting to my feet, my eyes wandering in the direction of the screen door.

"We said, 'So there you are,' " my father replied.

"Did you say, 'I never dreamed she'd have buck teeth' then too, Mamma?" I called over my shoulder, and ran outside. I'd remembered something: Oswald, my pet toad, by now there'd be a good catch in the spider's web, and if I left it any longer, another toad might get there and make a meal of it.

But in the course of the few days that had since passed, instead of being completely forgotten, the question of how I came to be had been slipping in and out of my consciousness. Fantasy was gone; the pink cloud and I were no longer a pretend-story, for I was now trying to see in my head, experience that bare and perfect moment, an instinct clamouring inside: if only I could gather it in, like something furry I could lay my head against.

Who can forget the first rush of awareness, where you were and what you were doing when you discovered that you hadn't, after all, been clambering around rocks from the beginning of time? Mine was there, sitting on the rock with my mother, holding in my hands once again this token of hair, furnished, only short days before, with history, my mother's words, '. . . the way you came into the world' repeating themselves in my brain, while the river shimmered, sparkling and moving away as if at high tide, the sky salmon-coloured at one end. All at once I found myself communing: what lay in that distance overhead where I had come from? I felt ready to burst, and I did not know why. In silence I sat fingering the twine of hair. A funny feeling—as though I'd suddenly come upon an integral part of myself, vital almost, like an arm or a leg I'd found; not knowing I had it before, I guess. I heard my mother say, "What a strange place to have a birthmark." She reached across and began parting the hair above my ear. I scrunched my shoulders over her fingers. What interest did I have in a strawberry mole I couldn't possibly see? I was now trying to steer my head in another direction, I had to be on the lookout for pink clouds, what they would look like when they broke apart. I always would.

----

"What are looking at?" my mother wants to know.

"I told you."

"When?"

"You weren't listening."

"No? Since when?"

"Before." She is reading, or rather, turning pages. Has she lost her place? or is it one of those times she's pretending to read? I deposit the needle case back where I found it, covering it over in the bottom of her workbasket—wool, folded makings of an apron, and a carrot that's supposed to be a pincushion, pushed aside to make room. What's she saving these dried pumpkin seeds for? to make some more beads?

Looking up once more. What will the sky tell me? what now? A changing light, and so a change of focus; the mind is lost, sails upside down in the brittle wings of a dragonfly; attention detaches itself, flits about, and goes back to where it was—swishing flies, eyes wandering, what's near, what's far.

We used to sit nearer the water than this. But now that I've got it through my head the river's dangerous, "treacherous" my mother says, the minute we start out in the morning it's this flat rock she heads for. First she fusses about the little mounds of anthills, "new colonies" she announces with a sigh, vexed as usual, muttering that she thought she'd done them in yesterday as she gets down on her knees and spears them all over again. And while ants scurry and retreat to cracks in the rock, she distributes around us the day's bundle of treasures: the things she brings for herself to play with. She unrolls her sewing and spreads the pieces out on the rock, coloured strips that blow all over the place, along with pages of old letters, and recipes. What else? I see she's brought pink wool, to knit Granny *another* pair of bedsocks? and some apples she'll start peeling for a pie; and a piece of tartan, who's the tam for this time?

At first I kept running back and forth to the river, I had things to check on, mudpouts and minnows—I was afraid the pools I made for them would dry up, or leak. Still, there's more going on here now, it's in her head, notions that have to do with herself. She's the only person I know who makes things up in her head. Even with her eyes closed she knows what's going on down at the river. "What a picture," she'll say, looking at her fingernails, or lying back on the rock with her hand over her eyes.

"Where?" I'll ask and screw up my nose. Another thing that pleases me is when she takes out her Yardley's Toilet Water and puts some on me too. It's like having some of her secrets, right in my skin. Sometimes she asks me what I'm thinking about and then watches me. I look about and don't know what to say, feeling it a privilege to be company, even if I don't understand.

---

Her name was Mimi, which is what I called her too when I was small and was trying to pronounce her name, Marie—the name my father instinctively called her by soon after they met. He did not think her given name, Mary, suited her one bit, he wanted something that went with . . . what? what else besides dark curly hair? And in attempting to mimic my father, perhaps "Mimi" was the first word I ever said. I remember calling her that again when I was a bigger child; it slipped out certain times, the feel of it, an emotion really now that she was teaching me new things. I was learning about the whole of the world. Before I grew up. The ways of the world came after.

The field I mentioned—my mother was right when she called it our field. A part of me is put away there. A hilly farm field that was no longer in use, except as a wandering ground for livestock. Without staying long, sheep and cattle meandered from place to place and gawked around as though they had memories. The signs were still there: stone foundations of the old farmstead, an apple orchard gone wild. And here and there giant daisies the cows took a swipe at en route to the river. But mostly it was a terrain of sunken rock and parched weed-grass, with the ragged sound of bulrushes in the swamp stretching against the wind. At one end of the field, not far from the cottage, the remains of a sprawling sandpit, overgrown in spots where grass had scratched and seeded itself, withered brown clumps that stood out like hair transplants rimming the bottom. When they tore down the old homestead by the river, and moved the farm back over the hill, the rest of the hillside just died, soon missing the warm scent of animals, the thump of life it had known. Lost ground, so faultlessly pure in its desolation; pure and therefore more lovely. Was it this perfection that made it different?

I had no words to give then, I could only express myself in excitement. To me the field was a kind of light, in the summer years it was always here I ran to, running dreamlike, an expectancy too vague to define, pounding along the hill, everything the same as the day before until I saw it again, with my mother to say, 'Tell me, what do you see, what do you hear?' The first time she said it took me by surprise. I thought I had missed something, a dead animal maybe, that always brought me running. I guess that's how you begin, pounding along beside your mother, like a calf.

---

Sometimes it's like this, this distance that looms up, pinioning me to that one area of time, forcing me to stay near, not to leave for a while. The other evening, for instance, I was scooping out a pumpkin, and when I got down near the bottom I found myself with the pulp shoved aside, one hand on the chopping board and the other abstractly tracing indentations up and down the shell. And I could hear crows, in the soundless kitchen they cawed as if over my shoulder, then the sound faded away. A sound of pleasure to be sure, the fields, the sandpit, a spent pine at the landing; but why this sudden cry of birds I couldn't see? My mind pushed farther, deeper. There were no responses . . . I lost track of the glimpses, they were too brief. But the sensation, as though I had been turned around—was wandering. Why am I forever being pulled to that pasture?

I see my mother in that blue gingham shirtwaist, made from one of the endless patterns she would cut from brown wrapping paper and then iron out flat. Its long skirt, sweet with the toil of her embroidered rosebuds, lies between us fresh as the day itself. Cloudless sky, butterflies the colour of lemon and ginger all over the place, the river still as a pond. She is reading, I am thinking. Soundless words float on the air of surmise as I hear myself being discussed again, as though I were the pick of a litter eight weeks old. The evening before: "She has her mother's eyes." I have no name. I am always she-who-has-her-mother's-eyes, no face of her own. Still, it's enough to make me curious and I try to see once and for all why eyes must consistently be singled out when they all seem the same to me. I roll over on my stomach and rest my chin in my hands, pretending to look at ladies in nighties on the cover of her magazine; there's a way of going about it, mostly not breathing loudly, so she won't think I'm nagging her or hinting for something.

No. My mother's eyes are not a bit like mine. Hers have a restive look about them, insistent yet soft and mysterious almost, being so deep a brown, a pair of eyes that declare another world stirring within. A world I cannot possibly know. Her perfume has an edge to it, though, all that's required to assure me of things I do not know: her perfume, her joy in bare feet, the wild abandon when she suddenly lets fall the scoops of curls on top of her head; instead of a hairbrush, hands drawn through tangles that brush my cheeks, something silky which seems to hypnotize me; eyes closed, opening again, sitting perfectly still as I feel with both hands the texture and then let go. At close range, past my nose, ebony loops tumbling in the wind, full of the smell of Pears soap.

And now, in a drift of silence I see beyond the tilt of her eyes. Her face is like a clear voice, instant and sudden, with that expression turned inward. Into it I read what I wanted, gave myself simple answers. I am wondering when it was, or how it was, we were eternal for a time.

# IV

"Mamma, show us how you danced. Show us how you and Daddy danced at Canso." Words that are not a whimper, nor uttered on impulse; they are a loud need directed straight at my mother, who is in my line of vision. Her face is turned to me but her eyes are closed, as if she was asleep, or dead. She could at least answer, or open her eyes and just look. She draws away, no—circles away, like someone wandering around in their sleep. One hand is loose around my father's shoulder, the other arm sticks up in the air, bent at the elbow; their fingers are locked. What kind of dancing do they call that? What was wrong with the way they danced at Canso?

They're having a good time. An interlude I pay attention to, for I haven't yet discovered the rock, or sat by the bulrushes as my mother sewed. Late afternoon. A September light that's pale, no diamonds in the air, no sparkle. And the wind so quiet. This awful cottage. Where is the blue green white grey, the sea? And the pine with my swing? What can it mean? That we're never going back? Have we left Canso forever?

I am no longer happy; newly six, I'm anxious, apprehensive. We've moved somewhere, and everything's the opposite to what it was, which puzzles me. It's like being sick in bed with a temperature: you're there and you don't know why you should be.

Yes. What did it all mean to me then, those first few nights? Trying to match scents and sounds, another tiny bed,

my forehead on its pillow, contemplative, shoes on the floor
ready to step into in the morning, as the eyes open and close
in drifts of sleep. Lashes closed. Asleep; as yet having no idea
we had said goodbye to the green fury of the sea, the veiled
mists.

The key to the house in Canso, still in my father's hand.
That's what I see now, a silver skeleton key. Why did he
have it with him on the train? Sitting solemnly, my tongue
licking at steam on the window as I took in explanations all
the way to Ottawa. I search their faces, and turn back to the
window. My father, exalted, the key turning in his hand; yet
his brows drawn in, vulnerable to my mother's rebellion. Repeating again—is he talking to me this time? "Wait till you
see where we're going! A brand new place to live." And my
mother, weeping, "We're going the wrong way, I want to go
back." All the way there on the train. In the hotel too, before
they found the cottage, she cried. "I'll never get used to it,"
she said. "I'll never feel at home here." And my father, telling her he would find a cottage to rent somehow, we could
stay there until the house in Ottawa was ready to move into,
she'd have the feeling of being out in the country again.

"I thought *this* was our house," I said, "isn't this hotel . . . ?"
They didn't hear me then either. We were in the dining
room and my father was too busy leaning across the table
asking my mother not to cry, he had to go where the Government sent him, and something about a river and mountains
not far from town, he'd do his best to find us a shack by the
water. And Mamma, blowing her nose and weeping louder,
"Water! Water is not the sea!"

"Now, Mimi . . . in no time at all . . ."

"Can we leave the table?" George asked. "We want to go
and slide down the banisters again."

"*May* we leave the table," Daddy corrected. That meant
we could go.

"May we?" we chorused as we ran out the glass doors.

"What's a shack?" George said. "Does it have stairs?"

---

'Wait till you see where we're going.' Well, I have. For
three days I've seen, and it's not like it used to be at all. It's
never going to be again. Not ever. This awful cottage. When
I get up in the morning I have to ask myself, Where am I?
Nothing means anything.

It does to them though. Or are they pretending? Do they

lie awake nights too? The roar of the sea, that always put me to sleep. The wind putting waves onto the shore. Here there's only a river. In the daytime I used to be able to *see* the wind, it was blue, even in the rain.

"Show us, Mamma?" The music goes its own way, slow music, a new record I've told them is silly. They got it just before we left, that and another one. Daddy brought them back with him the day he went to Mulgrave to see about our train tickets. And neither one of them sounds the same as the old ones. It's a good thing there wasn't time, or they'd have been dancing like this down there too! But now that there is, ever since we've gotten here they've never stopped. I wonder why they don't like the old records any more? What about that one . . . what's it called? My father's back is turned but I know it's no use there either; his eyes are shut too.

It's this new way of dancing, not a word or a sound out of either of them. It was easier before when their records didn't have words about moonlight. It was smell then, those times. They jumped around all over the place, or foxtrotted, laughing all the time. They even fell down on the floor they were laughing so hard. They said they had to get their breath back. Mamma wet her pants once, I saw her holding herself.

I pick up my crayon and chew the wax as they circle past the table where George and I have been given something to do. We're supposed to be colouring elephants, circus elephants with chairs on their backs, and tigers in bare skins. Mamma says I've been peevish all day, that's why these big crayon books were brought out, the expensive ones with pictures to copy, they're for when we have tonsillitis. I've been told to sit here and be content, well-behaved like my brother. It takes him longer to colour, that's the only reason he's quiet.

"Mamma," I say again and climb down from the chair. "Show me?" To give them room I move backwards, I can't go any further, I'm at the wall. If I'm patient and wait . . . I run my hand over the mahogany gramophone and the wart on my finger catches on the lid where there's a chip out of it, and scratches down one side.

---

I remember the day it got that chip, the afternoon it arrived, and my father's lack of concern when he saw the scratches. "Couldn't be helped," he said opening and closing the small door underneath, squatting down to open it again.

"See!" he cried eagerly, turning around and motioning us nearer. But how could we, without landing on top of him? And the sense of immediacy demanding we crowd in closer, the light from the kitchen window ablaze on the mahogany veneer. "It's even got shelves," my father announced. "And there's not a hinge or a nail loose anywhere."

"I think it's swell," Mamma replied. "Who gives a hoot about a chip out of the lid? It's a wonder it got here at all, the angle the man had it set at bringing it over. He must've just dumped it against the nearest seat in the dory and let it go at that. One big wave and the whole works could have toppled into the sea. Who was that gink anyway? Was he from Canso, Cecil?"

Canso. The nearest town to our bungalow far out on the coast, the easternmost tip, where my father was in charge of the Government wireless station during the twenties. The town itself familiar only in name; as I remember, miles and miles from our home, and the only route out by way of the sea. A bleak reach of shoreline, a neck of land beyond whose farthest point seagoing ships and schooners seem forever at the mercy of storms and gales.

Cliffs, the wild sea, sun and fog and moonlight breaking in through clouds. Our parents, and each other, were all we had. The world to ourselves—except for the two men who took shifts in the station with my father, and who lived in the bunkhouse alongside the station's mast.

And so the Brunswick Victrola, its impending arrival, had held us captive with curiosity: Mamma and Daddy with all their talk at the table—the dancing they'd be able to do, and they'd have a chance at last to listen to John McCormack, and hear "The Swan of Tuonela". They could even take the Victrola down on the beach and play it there if they wanted to. George and I didn't know what it meant but it felt good, all the while waiting for this wonder to arrive, each morning the two of us getting up early and running into the living room to see if it had come while we were asleep.

"Got word from Canso, Mimi," my father finally said, "the Victrola is on its way." He turned back to us, grinning broadly. "Here's what it looks like," he said suddenly, and grabbing a pencil from behind his ear, drew a picture on the back of the kitchen calendar. Except for the legs, it looked the same as the woodstove in the living room.

"What do you do with it?" I asked. I had never seen my father so excited. He had dropped the pencil and was leaping around, at the same time throwing his cardigan up in the air and catching it.

"Can I have it?" George wanted to know, conscious of the spindly oversized handle my father had attempted to draw, something to wind up, like his giraffe.

"Sure," my father replied, "of course you can. But this is not a thing you keep for yourself, George. It's something for all of us. Your mother and me too." He grinned again, and tossed his sweater onto a chair. "Good Lord," he said at the sight of George and me, puzzled, noticeably intent, realizing just then we knew nothing of what this was all about. "*Music,*" he exclaimed, "that's what you're going to hear . . . that's what it does, plays music, like this."

The peace of the kitchen, briefly lulled, erupted again as off he went into a succession of sounds, and more jigs, a splendid and joyous sight but an odd one, more of a spectacle, his fingers pretending to play the piano (we didn't know what a piano was then either), while Mamma accompanied him singing, having difficulty following his tunes. The sight of them! Not to mention the noise. "That's what you'll hear coming out of the gramophone," my father said, slowing down, puffing, gasping almost.

And so the gramophone came to us like magic, out of the sea George and I thought, maybe the man in the dory boat found it some place. For days the two of us had sat waiting in a cove below the cliffs, watching for the maroon-coloured dory to come through the high waves. We had done this before: the new hammock, the roll of linoleum, George's kiddie-cart. And now it was the Victrola, itself not too important—it was the sensation of the boat coming in, that's what we were really waiting for. Slippery getting the gramophone up over the rocks. But we helped some, George and I had hold of the legs. The man in the dory asked me how old I was and I told him five. "Then you shouldn't be sucking your thumb," he said.

I felt safe when we lived there, doing things in the place I was born in. I could be trusted to stand back from the cliffs, and find my way in the fog, and best of all, I could sit and watch the schooners get shipwrecked. Those things felt right. But here at the cottage, nothing does. I don't know what to expect. Mamma says she'll show me after the valises are unpacked. I wasn't talking about that, being shown things. That doesn't tell me why my father's gone all day, we were used to having him around when he worked, now he goes to an office somewhere, and when I tell Mamma it's not the same, I can't run and ask him something, she gets annoyed and says, "I don't want to hear another word about it."

---

Wan September light, no sparkle. Out in the kitchen, haphazard piles of valises and crates that tell me of a journey, of a place that's far away, they smell of the sea. I trace my fingers down the side of the scratched Victrola as over the floor our parents glide. *Glide*! In their bare feet. Dancing in bare feet. They could get slivers, the floor's not linoleum like the one at home. I wonder why they never danced without shoes until we came here? It's this change in everything! At Canso, when they danced the other way, their feet went fast, and Mamma's legs made funny kicks and her beads flew round and round. And since they brought all the old ones, why don't they change the record? Put on one of those for once? I'll make a big sigh, that's what I'll do . . . no, they wouldn't hear me. I should try a strange noise, something they're not used to. I could put my fingers in my ears and blow like I'm filling a balloon. There. I blow so hard it hurts my glands, the place they get swollen in, near where the tonsillitis goes.

Mamma and Daddy aren't paying the slightest bit of attention, won't even look at me. I stamp my foot. It's *always* like this now, when my father puts on "Moonlight and Roses". What's more, I always know when it's coming. First they sit on the couch and squeeze hands, they don't say anything. There's sound though: they mutter. Mamma is so pretty when they sit like that, it's because they have secrets with each other. The way they stare you'd think there was a game going on in their heads they had to concentrate on. I don't know what it means. It makes me feel dumb. I stand in front of them and never once do they ask me to sit down with them; they don't even tell me to run along and play. That's when I feel dumb; either they want me there or they don't. It's important to know. I'm one of their children. It's not as though I'm interrupting, not if I just stand. Maybe that's why they get up to dance—maybe I *am* bothering them.

"Moonlight and Roses". Slowly they turn, moving away, slip, slip, sli-i-i-ip, back again. I want to tug my mother's arm, and my father's elbow when he turns; if I stood on my toes I could reach that far, *then* they'd hear me. I don't though.

Back I go to the table and pick up a crayon, this time a purple one.

"My elephant's going to have a purple coat on his back," I tell George, and rip the paper covering where the crayon's blunted.

"So's mine," he says, and for a change slips his fingers into his own crayon box. A purple one; it's never been used. He saves his, when he can get away with it he uses mine. As he begins his fingers slant the crayon, light mauve, gently he colours the head and trunk, deepens it to purple.

"Copycat," I tell him and put my hand over my elephant so he can't see what colour I've decided to do the fringe.

"It's orange," George says. I couldn't hide the crayon, it's longer than my fingers.

In the far corner of the living room my father is busy winding the gramophone, now he turns the record over. "Beautiful Ohio". I pay no attention, I go on colouring the fringe orange and red. I don't care if they play "Beautiful Ohio" and "Moonlight and Roses" all night. I don't give a hoot. What's more, I don't even hear their bare feet any more. Sli-ip, slip, sl-i-i-i-p. It's only the crayons making that noise sli-i-i-p, slip.

No. It's the soles of their feet, coming nearer. Stopping. I won't look up. But down on the floor, clear as day, I see their toes, dusty-looking. They've got dirty feet. I feel their bodies swaying lightly, standing beside my chair. I glance across at George, who's still shading-in purple, doesn't know anything's different. I take a sideways peek at their toes again. My mother has moved her foot on top of my father's. It looks silly. Why do they stand and do that?

"Thought we hadn't heard you, didn't you?" my father says, and when I look up at him he lays his hand on my head, "You mustn't always be thinking you're number one, you know."

"Run on into the bedroom," my mother says, "and you'll find my beads in the bottom bureau-drawer."

"No they're not," I tell her, and drop my crayon. "They're in your sewing basket." I hurry to get them, bump my funny-bone on the door frame.

"And while you're at it, bring your mother's headband," my father calls out. "Might as well do it right," he adds. "Think you can find it, lass?"

"In the bottom drawer!" I shout from the bedroom, "where the beads *used* to be," emphasized, to let him know I keep track of where they put treasures. I have to know where important things are.

I crawl underneath the bed to get their shoes, they'll need their shoes, the best ones. I push the pee-pot out of the way, the shoes are in behind. First I blow the dust off, my head hits the coil springs as I pick fluff out of my father's laces. Now I get to my mother's black satin pumps. I spit on the buckles and crawl out again quickly; I have to shine them on the pillowcase before the spit dries. Her mascara! To look right she should have her mascara on. It's in her secret drawer. There. I gather everything up in my arms, except for the beads; I put them around my neck. Mamma comes to meet me, I was dropping shoes.

At the gramophone, my father waits, a record in each hand, the jackets still on, one is green-coloured cardboard, faded, and the other thin brown paper, torn at both corners. He's watching my mother, their eyes meet. Her headband in in place, her long yellow beads sparkle beneath the overhead paper lampshade. I stand beside my father at the gramophone, I don't move, the only thing I do is breathe.

"Which'll it be?" he says. "The Charleston? Or the Black Bottom?"

"The what?"

"Right hand or left?" he laughs and holds out both hands. I choose the left, it's the one nearest. He pulls the record out of the green cardboard one and tosses the empty jacket onto the couch.

Away they go like sixty! I don't even have to watch. With my eyes shut I know exactly what they look like, just by the feel of it.

I go back and sit at the table. I don't crayon, I just sit, and sit, in the September light, it sparkles. And the wind is blue. Yes.

My father winds up the gramophone again. "Ready, Mimi?" he says. It's a slow one. This new kind of music is soft, I notice, it has a faraway sound, like the ocean. Yes, it's like the sea. My father is singing, holding my mother close as they move across the floor.

"Who-oo-oooo? stole my heart away?" my father croons, and my mother answers.

"Who-oo-oooo? makes me dream all day?"

"That's a nice piece, I never heard that one before," I say to George, who goes on with his crayoning, doesn't even look up. I take off my shoes so I can tap my toes, my bare feet thump. "No," I say, "I never heard that one before, not to speak of anyway."

Patterns of movement and sound as I tap my feet on that September afternoon. The wild, familiar disorder of feet, arms, legs, beads; my mother's green georgette dress, her talcum and shiny mascara, my father's striped blazer, the rakish way he tips his straw boater over one eye as he gathers Mamma in his arms. They waltz away, "Beautiful Ohio" again. Their heads come together, my father frees one hand and removes his boater, and I see it sail through the air like a pieplate, ending right side up on the couch.

"Will you marry me, Mimi?"

"Go on!" A vase rocks on a table they bump into, they don't even notice.

"Will you?"

"That depends."

Everything back in order, our own again, waiting for tomorrow, ready to spring out of bed: "Time to get up, kids."

---

The shack! whose surroundings in a strange and opposite way were so like the wilderness we had left behind, giving us our bearings again. How quickly it happened.

Out on the verandah George and I play, we raise our voices to the winds of September, to the summer-burnt fields and the coursing river, to the savage snap of sheets and towels on the clothesline.

"That one?" George asks, holding out a piece of sod.

"No, silly, it's too big," I tell him, "it has to fit or the roof will cave in." We are making a house for the toad that comes onto the verandah every night, to catch flies in the spiderwebs at the kitchen door. Our hands pat and shape mud, sticks, and curls of birchbark that do for windows.

We thought of Canso, and the sea, but it was gone; this was our world now. Time had become suspended once more.

Some weeks later, toward the end of October, as George and I sat on the floor putting dry pine cones on the fire shortly before bedtime, our parents dragged out the suitcases again, explaining we must leave for a while, the house in Ottawa was ready, and this wasn't a place you could stay in during winter. We saw nothing wrong with that and yawned contentedly—having already sensed this was not the same as leaving Canso. Why, half our clothes were being left behind, and they hadn't packed all our toys either. Then too, we'd seen Mamma fold her favourite pink Japanese kimono and put it away in her bureau.

"I won't bother to bring these," Daddy had said of his hip rubber boots. I sat down again at the fire. I had wanted to make sure my doll was still where it should be, on my pillow, and not stuffed into a drawer along with the kimono.

"And we don't need *both* piles of gramophone records, do we Cecil?" Mamma said, mixing them all up, "we'll have enough with what's lying on the couch." She holds one up so my father can see the label. "Shall we bring this one?" she asks, and I notice her eyes are misty. "Moonlight and Roses"? Did I ask if they were bringing that one? did I remind them?

"How long is winter?" I say, turning around from the fire.

"As long as your nose," Daddy says.

"And as short as your memory," Mamma adds, laughing. "Where's that bag of clothes pegs you were going to bring from the kitchen?"

Late afternoon—next day? The Gatineau train was running late. Stopped at the bottom of a hill. People standing up in the aisles, others crane over one another at the window. "A dead horse on the tracks," the trainman tells us, "heavier'n a rig, so she is, have to wait fer to get help to lift . . ." He examines his grey cotton gloves; that's how I know he's the trainman.

"No, you can't get out to see the horse," my father says, anticipating me, "the train might start up and we'd be left behind."

"Can you not think of something more appropriate?" my mother cuts in. "What on earth would you want to go and peer at a dead horse for?"

"I hope it isn't hurt," I say. Mamma winces, bends over me and whispers, "Just sit quiet, there's a girl." My feet dangle idly, unconcerned.

"I hope they don't hurt the horse when they lift it," I say after a while.

And now, having left the train at Union Station, instead of skipping through the shine of the tunnel to the hotel as we did arriving from Canso—we're in a taxi, twilight darkening the orange sky, and streetlights suddenly, mysteriously, blink on—George and I had never seen streets before! At the hotel, when we looked out before, all we saw was the Parliament Buildings, the Rideau Canal and the tops of trees skirting the Ottawa River. We'd hear a car-horn tooting, "Ah-oo-gah", and Mamma'd say to my father, "Would that be a Ford?"

and he'd reply, "Sounded like one." George and I thought maybe a Ford was some kind of boat. And so we had never seen cars either. Or a streetcar. Or priests! Priests swinging along Rideau Street, a monk in a brown habit and sandals, and his head shaved. Craning our necks, faces glued to the back window of the taxi. Why are these men wearing skirts? and beads?

"They're called Quebec Highlanders," Daddy said, pleased with himself.

"Good Lord," Mamma exclaims, "where in the world did you ever hear that?"

What do I remember of that first night and the small two-storey house, smelling of paint and wet plaster, the curtainless windows and bare shiny new floors? Was there furniture?

That night my father stood for a long time at the bottom of my bed, blinking as he smoothed the flannelette cover. "It's sure a great place up there," he said. "For all of us, Mamma too." I suppose what he was trying to say was that Mamma's mind was at last off Canso, her tears were behind her. I guess he had to tell somebody. He pulled up the blind and opened my window a little. I saw the white moon shining, seeming at that moment as if it were sitting on top of the branches, on the edge of the roof. "Same old moon, looking at you," my father said. It was the first time I ever thought of the moon being in so many places, all the places I had been.

In the next room, I can hear my father talking to George. "Sure we're going back. But not tomorrow morning, son . . . of course I promise."

We were so young then.

The cry in my throat rises again. What *was* it about that place? I can't seem to get at the feeling, not yet. I see a red sweater. And someone's hand reaching for a flower. Colours and sound, pieces of sound, float by. I cannot stop them. Train whistles . . . a lone swallow . . . yellow dandelions. And watching the mist burn off the river; a girl and a boy who see their reflections in puddles on the verandah, or in the sandbar's bay. One and the other inching up through the rain and sunlight, through the strange unknown hour of some shared experience. Is that real? I've lost my place. Nobody's there . . . we've gone from the cottage . . . there was a funeral. And another. No. No! there wouldn't have been, not for . . . that was earlier, earlier. Things blur—it's too soon. I must bring it back. I *must*.

I see every rusty nail, each spike. Yes. Outside on the

verandah, bathing suits hanging from spikes. Broken shingles, lying half-hidden on the shelf above. I see the path going downhill to the river, moonlight on that path, and rain, now I hear the rain coming closer, torrents pouring through a funnel of torn tarpaper on the roof.

Moonlight lining the path. But that was later. What of the days, what of all the searching seconds before that time? I see the stones, the rocks . . . my hands close, as if closing around rocks. Yes. There was an old tree I wanted to climb, it was beside this big rock, and every day, well, nearly every day . . .

# V

" 'The Lost Chord' sounds terrible on the piano," my mother says to the back of my father's head. She's standing behind the piano bench; from her implacable stance, I get the feeling she's miffed, almost hostile. "It's supposed to be played on the organ," she adds pointedly. My father pays no attention, goes right on playing, intent, sinking lower and lower over the keyboard as if he were about to disappear into the keys, not to mention the pedals. On either side of him George and I sit with our legs dangling, toes almost reaching the floor, an elbow propped at our end of the keyboard, seriously, comfortably, following the music. Piano or no, "The Lost Chord" sounds all right to me; besides, the way he works the pedals my father makes it seem like an organ. "Why don't you play something more cheerful?" my mother goes on. "Do you *have* to play that?"

"The kids want to sing it tonight," my father explains. "They have a plan up their sleeves." For the first time he takes his eyes off the keyboard. "Eh George?" he adds, bringing him in on the conversation. George is polite, and shy, more inclined to wait until he is spoken to; he is more comfortable that way.

"So far we've only learnt the words," George offers, turning to my mother, and explains we still have to learn how the tune goes.

"We're practising," I tell her. "After supper tonight we're going to sing it for Mr. and Mrs. Nolan. It's her favourite piece."

"That woman doesn't know one piece from another," my mother counters, sniffing. Then she reconsiders. "It's like her to pick a dirge. Why don't you sing her something else for Heaven's sake? Goodness knows you've got enough to choose from."

"*No*," George says, quietly defiant, and swings his legs, one foot over the other back and forth, that's his way of speaking up. "She gives us shinplasters to put in our bank," he says brightly, the brown eyes avid, shining like varnish, hardly subtle.

"For singing? Since when?" my mother demands to know. "Shinplasters are for buying your warts back and nothing else," she declares, peering at me: did I not know this grownup's game was reserved for one thing and one thing alone? the same as putting your tooth under the pillow for the fairy? "What gave you the idea the woman's going to be forking out money to hear you sing?"

"Because we don't have any warts left," I announce. "That's why we're . . ." I'm embarrassed, I don't want to admit to such things: "*You* know, Mamma . . . you know. Mrs. Nolan always opens her purse, soon as she sees us. And we need to thank her *some* way," I whisper impatiently, and pick up the tune where George and Daddy are going back over a phrase.

"What a racket," my mother says, and I feel the brush of her dress against my arm. I know the music and words in the next line . . . it's my favourite. I turn around and sing into my mother's face:

It may be that Heaven's bright angel . . .

"You've got it all wrong," she says flatly, "it's *death's* bright angel, not Heaven's. You're as bad as Mrs. Nolan, you don't know one piece from another." She nudges my father to lift his behind off the bench, she wants to get at the sheet music. "Here," she says, pulling out a tattered sheet, which she places on the music rest. I read the block letters out loud: FINLANDIA. Daddy doesn't need music for that, he knows it by heart I tell her. I do it on purpose—she won't come right out and ask him to play it because she's mad at him; she doesn't like Mrs. Nolan. And I know why. Her hair's dyed! And the rouge she puts on makes her look like a clown, my mother says. But there's a lot more to it than that! I watch Mamma every time Mrs. Nolan teases my father; she tells him he's too handsome for words, no woman should have him all to herself.

"What's the matter with that drip of a husband of hers?" my mother will say after the Nolans have gone. "A spineless nincompoop," she'll add. Every time. I hear them talking after I've gone to bed. It's as though I wake up on purpose, to make sure they come upstairs happy, there's a way I can tell. I guess I'm not really asleep until I know for sure. "Now, now," my father will begin.

My mother pushes me forward and sits herself down on a corner of the piano bench. Her back is to us, she has to have somewhere to put her legs. Facing into the kitchen she mutters "Finlandia," like someone having the last word. *Finlandia* sits before my father, open at the page. But "The Lost Chord", far from being lost, warms the Sunday afternoon while my father and George and I ready ourselves for our shinplasters:

> But I struck one chord of music
>
> Like the sound of a great amen.

My father is in his element. A flash of white shirtsleeves; feet busy at the pedals. And George getting ready for the next line. He opens his mouth on a beat, murmurs, feeling his way:

> Will speak in that chord again.

And now his voice rises,

> It may be that Heavunnn's bright ainjulll . . .

I join him:

> It may be that only in Heaven
>
> I will hear . . .

My mother thinks it over, her eyes on my father now as he bends over the keys. She yields. Joining in, but with a compromise. That's as far as she'll go. Against our notes, the words we are learning, she comes in on another line, one that's supposed to come later. Is she making fun of herself?

Does she want to have a good time too? She sings to the air in front of her:

> I knew not what I was playing
>
> Nor what I was dreaming then.

And George and I, taking care not to make any mistakes, with the piano to lead us, sing louder, which puts my mother off key.

"Here, Mimi," my father says, leaving off where we were. He begins right in the middle of the end. "This is where you were," he says gently without looking up, and to George and me, "Come on, kids, join in with your mother" (she has stopped singing), "let's see if you two are able to pick it up from here. If you can come in at the end of a piece, hit it right, that means you've got the tune." His hands move slowly, chords hum, for the first time he sings,

> Nor what I was dreaming then.

My mother sits, her back to us still, singing on key now,

> And I struck one chord of music,
>
> Like the sound of a great amen,

her voice not musically devastating, in fact dreadful; even so, eager, almost a quiet wondering, her hands folded in her lap, lovely.

The marvel of it: the communion they shared, a kind of light in the way they were being themselves. The way it should always have been.

# VI

Late afternoon and the river is washing past, empty of logs for a change. But the tang is still there; the water-level has dropped, and it's hot and still, softening the air with spruce-gum and pine and waterlogged driftwood. Close to shore, where it's shallow enough to wade just now, the current goes backwards, water smooth as an eyelid moving upriver, circling the sandbar and reversing back downstream. Farther out the sweep of the current is another mood, the speed reduced in some places, as if having to reckon with the restless eddies, nail-holes in the water.

The river, the sepia sandbar, the moving grass. And the lichen rock down in the pasture. Where grass-songs carry, from note to note, the tune of the earth. Rocks and mud and dead insects and crinkly sheep turds to play with; a spear-toothed skeleton bone to rap time on a derelict hay-rake. And my mother, lying on her belly, bitting a hangnail, thinking, abandoning her cuticle for a taste of the ragtime tune she's entertaining herself with, off-key, as though she's making it up.

A little distance from her, I make myself comfortable on a boulder where I can see everything, my breath drawing in the deep smell of rotted stumps and mud and slime. Below me, on a long flat rock, not two but three bathing suits spread out to dry.

And that signalled instant flash glancing a blow off my insides was the mind snaking back, fixing itself upon an exact moment earlier, when it was still morning and my mother's attention, showing signs of flagging in the sweltering heat, was divided—before my brother, in response to the distant whinny of a black horse, had exclaimed, "There's Daisy!" and bolted for the path up the sandpit.

We are down at the shore, feet cushioned in the goo of the mudflat, treading water that's clear and green and chilling the tips of our knees. And now my brother's face is turned to the wind, sunburned, quizzical, absorbed by something he sees across the river. His mouth is open and his head is to one side, eyes squinting into the sun. My mother is trying to brush his hair: damp black curls on a head that looks diseased, patches of skin showing worse than ever where he got at it again with the scissors. Voices murmur: his, hers. A moment that holds until the detail bends out of focus, as in a dream.

Landscape now, blue sky and the jagged line of open hillside. My brother's back is seen at a small distance, he is running, short pants and checked cambric shirt scampering up the hill. He crawls under the barbed wire fence and turns around to wave, then swings into stride again, the top of his head bobbing through the wheat field, disappearing from view. I am fond of him, we have some pretty good times.

The same age as me, he claims; according to him we're both
seven this summer—except he's a year younger. That's why I
look out for him, it's my job. Not ten minutes ago we were in
swimming, and the moment Mamma said the two of us
looked waterlogged out he came, collected his shirt and pants,
went looking for his shoes, then like a shot took off for the
farm. He likes going into the barn. That's his territory, his
and Jimmie Carman's; this is mine.

Now my mother is talking to herself, hunched over, fiddling with something. "Fool of a thing," she says, and I feel
her voice bite into the sultry quiet, irritably, impatient, the
same as when she trips over something. Maybe she needs me,
I tell myself, and swing my legs down off the boulder. With
my hands on my knees I squat alongside her. "Keep still a
minute," she exclaims, and I wonder why since I'm not doing
anything. She's fussed about the dress she's making me, the
one that's given her all the trouble this week: pink dimity,
blue forget-me-nots with yellow eyes, and rose-coloured
smocking below the white lace collar. The dress I see is finished, and hangs from the shoulders on a dead sapling, a
mess of brown-leaved twigs sticking out of the neckhole, like
a granny-face with a wig, and, drawn through the sleeves,
withered branches, skinny arms in short puffed sleeves held
out to the breezes, fingers missing on one hand.

"It looks like a scarecrow," I whisper, so as not to stir. She
didn't say anything about keeping my mouth still.

"What are you whispering for?"

"I don't know."

"Then hand me one of your crayons," she says and tips
herself forward on her knees, tells me she thinks the dress is
uneven at the bottom. "The fool thing's longer at the back,"
she sighs. I offer her the crayon, I keep shoving it against the
back of her hand but she doesn't even notice; she's too busy
yanking at the hemline. Another impatient tug, and the
sapling bends forward and almost snaps. The dress swooshes
back again, jiggles like a one-legged windup toy. It shudders,
comes to a stop all lopsided, the right side trailing on the
ground.

It looked all right as it was, I tell her; she should have left
it alone. Down on her elbows now, pulling up tufts of moss
and sniffing them as she watches me take hold of the sleeve
and fit the branch through the armhole, her bare foot nudging my bottom as I rearrange the wig-leaves the way they
were on top, like curls. There's dirt clinging to the lace collar.

Now how did that get there? I flick away bits of lichen and dried cowflap, plus two ants. Swivelling around on my knee I turn to look at my mother, pleased.

"Think you're smart, don't you?" she laughs, mad at herself. She reaches out and pulls me down beside her, and with the wax crayon draws a moonface on my knee. A green moonface with ears. I bend the other knee, so they'll match. "Not on your life," she says, and begins the circle higher up, above the scab.

I look up from my moonfaces. Before we leave, will Mamma rip the hem back some? Should I get the pins ready?

No. She has taught me patience. If she can sit beside the fool thing, then I can too. Doing nothing—that's a way of keeping busy. You read your mind. I study hers instead. Engrossed, her thoughts sail past me. She could be anywhere. With a forefinger I trace a moonface in the moss, first one, then a second.

"I guess George and Jimmie are jumping in the haymow by this time," I murmur without looking up. No reply. Not a sound. I say it again, staring in front of me. Coloured strips of material blow around the rock and I leave them. Let them blow; I don't have to talk either. The pieces scatter, they flutter and leap from twig to rock to thistle, like syllables, like words, my own. My withheld words. Have George and Jimmie taken the dog and gone with Mr. Carman to bring in the cows? My mother, surrendered to thought, glances at the tattered odds and ends, her eyes follow as they scatter idly, this way, that, all over again; like my chatter a minute ago. Still, there are other ways of talking. I seize my pack of crayons and tilt it sideways, thumb and fingers working diligently, deciding between them which colour would be best. Obstinate now. I need three colours—where's the green?

My mother hasn't moved, a kind of sprawl, and I can tell her mind is back on the dress. She studies it as if she were about to tell its fortune. I peel the paper on the crayon, sharpen it with my teeth first, then chew the wax and swallow it. I decide my drawing's going to be more like a tattoo, and on the side of her ankle I draw a large flag. What'll I put for an emblem? I reckon I'll do a special flower, she likes pink roses. One petal. Two. Three. Petals opening out. When's she going to admire her surprise? Will she think it's an interesting thing to do?

And speaking of that . . . "George says there's more to do in the barn," I say. "I guess that's why he's always in such a hurry to leave." Didn't she hear me this time either? *If you please, Mamma!* What's she doing that she doesn't answer? You'd think she'd be glad I'm not always running off to the farm too. Too bad I didn't. Down on my knees, silently turning over a poppy-red crayon. She doesn't understand. "I could have gone too, you know," I begin again. Should have saved myself the effort. For suddenly I realize the train's been blowing; it's a freight, shrilling across the water, taking forever. I know very well she heard me, though. Why does she have to keep twisting her wedding ring? And moving her leg away. Crossing one over the other. You see! I can't *make* her answer. And I have to tell her something, I don't know what it is. Head down, red crayon following a bend of her anklebone, round and up the shin. I add another rose, and then a bud, they should have buds coming along for when they die. And some showers to water them. I pause . . . I never drew rain before. My hand, moving above the buds, speaks, that is to say it draws—draws splashes, which turn out to be fat, and pointed, like teardrops, like the one that spills down onto the crayon box. There's no such thing as silence.

---

I cried that night too, I remember—even though my mother had in the end (after how long? minutes? seconds?) brought herself back. Without making a formal pronouncement, she conveyed her approval of the nosegay on her ankle. "Half a mo," she exclaimed, jumping to her feet, and scurried down towards the shore, where she retrieved two sizeable discards of material snagged on a sunken stump (a pair of voluminous sleeves she'd cut out wrong), turquoise and mustard-yellow polished cotton with black, purple and peach harlequin squares, knotting the two ends together as she returned to the rock, folding it lengthwise (what was she doing? making a sling?) before sitting down. With a thumb holding one end against her instep, she flapped the length of cotton over and wound it round and round her ankle and instep, like a bandage or a mummy-cloth. So she could show Daddy he had an artist in the family, a large brass safety pin in the corner of her mouth, sucking back saliva: at suppertime we'd borrow the boat from the farm and row across to meet him at the station. "Why not?" she laughed, winding intently, awkwardly, unevenly, glazed cotton slipping from her grasp, paying no attention to the bulges overlapping, until the entire flag, buds, roses, every last leaf, was covered over. "As for those swanks," she added, her eyes skimming the distant tops of a half dozen roofs deep in the woods beyond the stationhouse, "those fops in their manor houses over there" (*what was a fop?*), "they can go to blazes"—seemingly unaware of the ground to be covered beforehand, after she'd tied up the boat, the fifteen-minute walk ahead of us. What about the people we'd pass? padding along the highway, the spectre of this grotesque-looking plumage, scarcely two minutes old and already loosened and hanging down over the heel of her shoe; and strangers, *perfect strangers*! doing double-takes, truckers adjusting their rearview mirrors. . . . "There," she said, fastening the brass pin, the winding over with, sitting there patting a leg that looked as if it had mumps, "that'll keep the bloom on the rose."

Did I stir then? rouse myself and get up off my knees, pleased at what I'd heard? snickering, telling her I thought the rags around her ankle looked *awful*, she couldn't go over to the station like that? Or, before the train blew, had a certain moment come and gone? the essential of that one perfect twist of air beyond recapture, crayons thrown into the long grass, pushing my mother aside now, it was too late. I don't know. What can I remember of that child's heart? of the ten seconds or the hundred seconds, a rib of the universe beginning its struggle—with itself—stubborn, full of pride, dependent, independent, defiant, not capable of understanding this shock of emotion: these first deep tears, no mashed finger or split-open head to its advantage, no known cause, wind ruffling a tuft of my hair, bare arms pinned to my sides, drawing in tightly, tighter, against the line of my body, while my mother draws her hands apart, ceases twisting her wedding ring, and is off down to the shore to fetch her harlequin squares.

Sun tilting high in the sky, metallic river ribbed by its light. And the wild, dumb, arrogant, mocking harlequin squares slicing across my vision, my mother's swaddled foot in the air, one knee over the other, bobbing her leg up and down. I can't stop the feeling, that ground, that white slab of rock! the illumination . . . Yes! I remember! My drawing . . . it was a message to her. It was as though all my days and nights till then had been lived for that one moment, its communication; the spill of a minute's pondering: 'George never wants to stay here, he says there's more to do in the barn.' Words that were not merely a passing observation, no longer just plain *words*, tuneless, silent on the inside, like the teacher

at school, or a minister saying the Lord's Prayer. What I was
trying to tell my mother had come from my socks. Without
having to say so directly, I'd found a way of telling her I
liked being there with her best. This awareness had never
happened before. It felt like a power inside me, a new language.

It's thrilling! seeing myself then, dabbing away at a new-
found level of consciousness, touching beyond instincts I was
familiar with. And it's funny too! The passion of the inner
self, emerging, sounding its voice. While a train came up the
valley and blew away my words.

# VII

My mother and I. As close together as we would ever be.
That's why I must stay there, discover her again and again,
alone! When she and I were alone in that pasture.

Against the sky and moving clouds her face impassive,
wisps of hair blowing across her brow and cheeks and at intervals pulled back into place; sunlit temples and hands and
the turned-up toes of bare feet as a piece of conversation.
Sewing doubled across her lap. Thimble back in place. And
she takes the first of many darts with the needle. Stitches
divining the very air about us. In all it told me a kind of
story, and what I presumed I accepted; it was real, like a
silent movie. I'd see her smile to herself, lips parting as if
coaxing out words. Thoughts cordoned off in silence, a
stillness shaped by land breezes, the cattails moving, like the
swamp-reeds and small cedars. It was her eyes that held the
ring of sound, seeming for all the world as if they were answering someone, which had me imagining the field and river
were somehow connected, that they had played with her
thoughts, bewitched her. Presently, a yawn, shifting to a less
bony ridge of rock as she scratched her behind, and dreamily,
or bemused, with whatever messages she might have received,

.or given back, she would adjust a hairpin, rummage through her workbasket—intently picking through the tangle as if she were at a bargain-counter—and end up tying a piece of ribbon on the end of a forefinger. Sometimes she'd wiggle it and suddenly burst out laughing.

When she did that I'd say, "Is this where you like to live best, better than in the city?" At first I was saying it every day, but to myself. Watching her, the serenity, life taking place, the earth confiding its creation. Dimensions taking on flesh. And us seated above the whole of life on a table of rock veined with quartz sharp as white bone, the Gatineau River's blue freedom riding below the sounds of logs in the sucking eddies as it followed its path southward. In its rounds of blooming and dying, bleached lichen hugged our rock like a knitted cap and as we ran our hands back and forth, its silver wicks crumbled and whispered in the hot sun. At what point did I realize it wasn't a question I was asking my mother? rather, I was seeking to confirm that I too was being drawn beyond the visible around me. And when did she decide I was now ready, nearly so, to receive what I could not see? Hearing my voice again I was of small age, I think. The smell of licorice, I remember jellybeans in a small brown-paper bag, they were melting in the hot sun. I had picked out what was left of the black ones and was licking the stain on my fingers, facing into my hand, or behind it, a need to be out of sight as I made my enquiry.

"Is this your favourite place, at the cottage?" This time determined, a tone firm as the set of a pair of eyes.

"Why? Why do you keep asking?"

"I just thought you're always doing funny things here." Out from behind the hand now. Squinting up at her face. "You're different from in the city. You act peculiar." She laughed again, a small sound that flowed on the air, as the river flowed, idly, a tune, all song and no words.

"So I do funny things, do I?" She looked at me, waiting, her brow elevated; I was supposed to go on, she wanted to hear more. Pretending again, as if she didn't know what I was getting at, and I thought, That's how they find out what you're thinking. I kept silent, my hands working away at nothing.

"And what, pray, exactly what are these . . . the thingummybobs I do?" She prodded my stomach with the bow-knot finger.

"In the cottage you dance in bare feet with a cushion," I

exclaimed, "and outside you're all the time talking to the air
. . . and you go running over to the sandpit to spin pieplates
off the top. Mammas aren't supposed to do that, are they?"

"Silly, isn't it?" She smiled to herself and pulled a cedar
branch down, it shaded her face, the sun was in her eyes.

"You even climb trees," I said. I was thinking of the dou-
ble-trunked cedar at the riverbank below the cottage, it was
crooked and leaned out over the water. Now that I had told
her, had actually come out with it, all of a sudden I was
seeing her licks of abandon as part of my own ways, an extension, one of the other; I felt excited, I liked hearing about
it from myself.

"Why shouldn't I?" she said. "It's fun. I enjoy it." She
toyed with the end of the branch absently, brushing the fringe
back and forth across her face. "Yes, this is where I like to
live best. It's the only place to be, the mountains off in the
distance . . . and every morning the hills and river to wake
up to." She gazed around. "There's a special kind of language
in them, did you know that?" she said turning back to me.
"They've each a tongue of their own. It tells you so in your
storybooks—'the language of the forest'. Some day you'll
hear for yourself."

"Is that when you talk to the air? Is it because you hear
voices?" Her eyes widened, she let go of the branch. It
swooshed with a snap.

"So that's what you meant! Well, yes, though there
wouldn't have been any voices, not the kind you're thinking
of. Sometimes, when you catch sight of something lovely, a
cloud that suddenly turns pink . . . or you hear a sound you
never heard before, say it's the trunk of a dead tree you
come upon and all of a sudden a small animal starts rooting
around inside, the noise reminds you of something, at first
you don't know what, so you stand perfectly still and listen
and think; maybe a squirrel or a skunk just woke up and he's
hungry, such a racket, in a hurry too, like somebody going to
work. You can make up anything you like. Seeing things for
yourself, that's how you grow inside your head." She slipped
her hand into the jellybeans, the bottom of the bag, red ones,
she liked cinammon. "And Mammas are no different," she
added emphatically. "They still have to keep growing too." A
pause, and a glance down at her bare feet. "I'm not that old
yet, you know," she added.

"I know," I said, dimly embarrassed that I wasn't certain
what she meant.

"What do you know?"

"That Mammas have to do thingummybobs too."

"To remind them . . ." she sighed, then: "funnymagigs!" and repeated, "funny-ma-gigs," prodding my middle syllable by syllable as if I was three years old. I guess sometimes she wished I was. She liked to pick things up and hug them, some part of her communicating, spilling over, shyly, hands instead of lips to do the talking. I absorbed the proddings as part of my due. Over the performance of "funnymagigs", on the last syllable, our heads collided, and the next thing I knew she was singing:

> When the red red robin
>
> Comes bob-bob-bobbing along,

her little wooden dressmaking ruler now gaily tap-tapping against the lid of her sewing basket. "Who knows?" she broke in suddenly, eyeing me speculatively, the ruler held against the fluted edge of the lid, like an organ pedal holding down her words, a softness hanging in the air as she paused, speculation gone out of her now, her tone more a conviction, yet whispered, as if beseeching. "You might turn out to have your father's ear, then you'll find yourself listening for more than dead tree-trunks."

But that I scarcely heard, for I was sitting with my legs out straight, puzzled, suspicious, not quite certain what the whole thing was about. The river didn't seem any different. I listened, the sounds I heard sounded the same to me. But were they? "Shhh!" I whispered suddenly, in case she spoke, my mouth ajar, letting the brass button I held slip from my hand. What *was* different? That light off the river, if I took another look—*was* there something invisible coming through?

Did I only imagine that first swift communion, the unseen too mystical to hold to reveal itself? It was there, and yet it wasn't. I pulled my knees up, concentrating, my eyes and brain a single process searching the points of infinity, inviting to come to me all the things I did not know.

Moments that passed, were renewed, nested in the coloured air, the shapes of sounds. And in my mind I too would talk to the river and pastureland; the perfect mimic, gazing around, above, away off down the shoreline, for good measure scratching my backside, the Persian thimble on my thumb and my mudcaked toes poking at frog-spit beaded on the grass. We would do this forever I thought.

There is a particular afternoon on the hillside. I remember.
That terrible storm. When the creeping dark sky drew a cavern around us.

I hadn't sensed the stillness, the motionless cedars as the
rushing wind started to hold back. I was close to catching on
to "Drigo's Serenade", humming it all but in tune, concentrating with my eyes closed. And midway through a bar, my
mother stopped, told me we were leaving. "It's turned black
at the north," she said. "In fact it's bad over the river too.
Sneaked up on us." I felt her urgency and took a look for
myself. Black thunderheads, on top of us almost. "Damn
storm," she muttered and pulled in the spread of her dressmaking. A jumble, buttons, sewing basket, scissors, pins, her
compact: they all slid down the chute of material. I heard
them collide in its pit, my gingham dress a sack, with the
workbasket upside down in the bottom, thimble pinging
against the spools as we tore across the sandpit. "Just look at
that sky," Mamma whispered, as if afraid she'd be overheard
and singled out by the first bolt. "A humdinger." And it was.
The earlier clarity was murky as underwater, the air heavy
with silence, cocoon air. In the half-light my mother's bare
feet thumped ahead of me; the ground sounded hollow.

But I wasn't afraid. I didn't know what it meant to have
fear of thunder, or the bull, or for that matter anything at all.
I only felt threatened when my parents quarrelled.

"Sing 'Drigo's Serenade'," I called to my mother's back.
But she was anxious, didn't hear me. "Tomorrow," I told myself, "tomorrow when the storm's gone," raising my voice to
make of it a promise.

"What are you muttering about?" my mother panted. "Get
a move on. This is no time to be chattering. Whatever you
have to say, save it for the cottage for goodness' sake." She
thrashed along, the reed-grass and thistles flattening into a
swath behind her.

"What's for supper?" I demanded. I always had to have the
last word. She turned around, distracted, fuming.

"How would you like a thick ear?" Stung, I ran past her,
through the gate, up the hill, leaving her struggling to fasten
the gate with her hands full. The screen door banged behind
me with a sharp crack, a fitting "so there!" as I waited inside,
lower lip pushed out, well into my pout. Then I heard the
whop of the sewing basket; I knew that thump. On the last

lap, the path uphill, it had sprung loose from the gingham sack and tumbled upside down on the hill, contents spewing like dry vomit into the worn-down grass. The sight of my mother as she chased after spools, squatting down to gather up every last pin, shamed me, my eyes smarted. I wanted to run and tell her I'd pick everything up, that she could go on inside, I wasn't scared of the storm. But I didn't. I thought she might push me away, dismiss me like something that was in her way, which always seemed worse than being slapped. I decided to wait and hold open the screen door; that would tell her I was sorry. Sudden rain accelerated her scramble, a last handful of sand and grass and embroidery thread. Clutching the workbasket under her arm, the refilled chute of material swinging and hitting her legs, she took the verandah steps two at a time.

"Which are you scareder of, a storm or the bull?" I asked, with the wind almost taking the door out of my hands.

"They're both a menace," she replied. "And you don't help things one little bit." The wind blew big raindrops onto the roof, sounds of censure, drumming at me. I spoiled the whole day, I thought miserably, you always think of it afterward; why do I always have to act bold? She went directly into the bedroom and I followed; standing beside her I searched her face as she reached for a towel above the washstand and began wiping off her workbasket. The damp smell of Indian-grass rose between us, seeming sharp and bitter-smelling in the precarious silence.

"You didn't get so very wet," I said, and then remembering we'd left our sneakers behind, dove under the bed for her good tennis shoes, to ground her. . . . Now she was peering into the mirror, drying her face with her head turned side-ways and her back to me, so I laid the shoes alongside her feet, first nudging her toes with the rubber so she'd know. At the head of the bed, rain pounded against the windowpane, a hard sound, tense like I was. A cloudburst, the sky able to rid itself of desperation. As she bent down to tie the laces I stood leaning against her legs, holding back tears as I pushed my shoulders against her thigh, and I thought: Trying to make up for things is the worst part, you can't tell if things are really back to the same. Presently we sat down on the brass bed, sank into it, the bed was old, the springs half shot, creaking painfully under our weight as we swayed and bounced up and down with a gentle motion, a soft rhythm against the driving rain splattering the windows. Nothing else

was happening and so looking straight ahead I recited into
the air:

Spring has came,

The snow has went,

It was not did

By acci-dent.

It was something to do, I thought, keeping us occupied. But
Mamma didn't say anything. I guess she'd heard my verse before.

"I didn't mean to be cheeky. I don't ever mean to be," I
said in a low voice, not wanting to refer to the thing at all.
Ordinarily, she was supposed to be marching me off to my
room, that's where I was always sent, except now she was
scared of the storm about to break and didn't want to be
alone. So I put my arm around her and sat very still, suggesting I understood. Taken aback, she turned suddenly and
pulled me in closer; she thought I was the one afraid! "We're
safe in this room," she whispered, as though in a conspiracy,
"this time the storm's coming from the south."

---

*The storm's coming from the south!* That's what my father
would always say to reassure her. For it was she herself who
had staunchly declared that a storm from the north was a
bad sign, but there was nothing to worry about if it was coming from the south. Needless to say most of them did—or so
she was led to believe. A rumble in the distance, north, south,
the back of beyond, and my father would do a reconnais-
sance, drop whatever he was doing and proceed to the living-
room window that faced downriver. "Looks like it's over
Ottawa," he'd call out. "Yep, the storm's coming from the
south, Mimi." Content now; but impatient with each ensuing
rumble, expressing herself with a series of "achs" and the occasional bravado of "Go to Hell", eyes roving across the beaverboard ceiling, as though penetrating the heavens.

"A lot of fartin' around is all it ever amounts to," she'd
say, harping away. "That's the worst of these bleeding storms
from the south, they go on all day." Nevertheless, still taking
cover in their bedroom, the only room in the cottage with
blinds on the windows; pulling them down, the bedroom door
bolted. That, and the cave of a bulky eiderdown-comforter

drawn up around the pillows, it seemed, would ward off the lightning strike ultimately destined for our hill. "It's those blasted fiends from the north," she'd mutter as sheet lightning flared through cracks in the blinds.

And George and I, sitting on the camp cot in his room, preferring this vantage point because his bedroom was off theirs, would look up from his Meccano set and tease her, eyeing the curve of her swaddled body on the bed as we played our mouth organs and chanted:

> Loony as a bedbug
>
> Choking in the sheet.
>
> Bit your mother's pimple,
>
> Thought it was her seat.

"Don't mock your mother," Daddy said overhearing us one day that same summer, appearing from nowhere at the door, his face wet with rain and his hair blown into wild disorder, doing up the buttons of a dry, freshly laundered shirt (had he been out grounding the aerial again?).

"Awww, we made it up," George said, visibly concerned, raising himself on one knee as he glanced through the doorway. Was Mamma offended? "We were only fooling." Sitting down again: "That's only our rhyme for when she gets under the covers, to make her laugh," he said. "We have to *help* her, when there's *lightning*."

"All the same," I put in, "I think it would be a darn good thing. . . ." I hesitated, climbed onto the pillow at the head of the bed and braced my back against the wall, a seat of authority from which I might deliver my gospel according to Saint Molly, Mrs. Nolan.

"What would be a darn good thing?" my father asked, grinning.

"Well, in a storm . . . we shouldn't pay *any attention* to Mamma."

"Oh?" he said. "We shouldn't?"

"No, we shouldn't. Let her take her mind off it herself. That's what Mrs. Nolan says. *You spoil her.*" Twigs, twigs and nails rolling across the tarpaper on the roof.

"Yes, that's true," he replied, holding the underside of his wrist up to the light at the window while he buttoned the cuff of his shirtsleeve, taking his time, deep in thought, the silky rustle of Egyptian cotton releasing a muted sound, something

not unlike, not far from the tongue of his mind, a voice as
near, as alien, as dreaming and melodic, as grave. "That's
true. But you see, she's all we've got."

---

*The spring has came, the snow has went.* Creaking up and
down on the bedsprings, singing in my head. And my mother
and I, our shoulders silhouetted in the half-dark of the room,
and the rain dripping inside on the windowsill where the
frame was warped. As we sat out the fizzle and crackle of
lightning, I passed my hand back and forth over the bedspread, thinking not about the cows in the pasture but the
bull, his habit of standing off by himself when the rain was
coming down hard, and the rain-soaked cows herding together, as though sheltering one another. What did it mean
that he acted like an outsider, gravely absorbing the driving
rain, sullen and alone in the middle of the field?

There was no denying it: that summer we had to be wary
of this new bull, though he wasn't new in terms of his arrival
at the farm. He'd been born in the barn up there on the hill,
and from the first day I laid eyes on him, all legs and a big
furry head, I looked upon him as mine and named him Ambrosia. As gentle and distinguished as any calf born. But then
for some ungodly reason he grew into a wild devil of a thing.
Not pleasing to look at either. The gleaming henna hide pro-
claiming Ambrosia's birth had turned a hideous blood-brown,
and the white crown that once was his exquisite head had become yellowed and splotched with the mud and manure of
his wars. Added to these distressing features he had a torn
nostril (no longer sound enough for a ring, since he had
wrenched free from every chain) that seemed to be forever
running pus, blood, leftover saliva from the wrathful sweep
of one great slab of tongue. Here was one bull even the farmer made certain was given a wide berth. Except when the
woeful creature, for one reason or another, had to be cor-
nered. Then it took two hired hands, Mr. Carman, and his
snapping cowdog to bring him in. I remember how Ambrosia's eyes blazed as he stood in the small pen outside the
barn, caged, scarcely moving, his hide damp and steaming,
goaded by pitchforks jabbed at his face, up his behind. Gone
forever was my manger friend.

Locking Ambrosia up was senseless. If he was in a mood
he'd smash his head through the barn window, turn around
and kick the stall down and then charge headlong outside,

butting whatever machinery he found lying around the farm-yard. Which meant relegating him to cool off in some deso-late pasture miles back of the woods. Pitchforks in hand, they'd load him onto the stone-boat and tie him down. And off he was carted over the rutted roads of grainfields and backwoods, let loose in the middle of nowhere, where for so long a time I was afraid they would leave him to die. If noth-ing else, Ambrosia had character and it hurt his feelings. Sometimes, when the wind was right, I could hear him bel-lowing, high-pitched, a terrible sound to listen to when night was coming on.

"His Majesty is touchy when he comes back," Mamma would say. Every time. His Majesty! I knew that, I mean his being touchy and all, but I didn't want to rub it in on him. On his first day back you could see him standing at the top of the hill, as if he'd had to come and make sure the river was still there. And if he had a notion to, he'd start down the hill on his own and before we knew it there he was, crossing the sandpit not fifty yards away. Either way, with or without the cows, that was about as close as we dared allow. Most times he dawdled, purposely doubling back through the sand-pit to scratch his neck on a boulder, hiding behind it, peering round one side, other times perversely pretending to chew at the leaves of a shrub, bloodshot eyes turned on us. Some days my mother gambled he'd turn back, maybe go the other way round through the far gully. Either route was fine, as long as we made certain we had our fifty yards between . . . another five minutes, and I could have patted him, that's what I'd be thinking, and one day I said so.

"Do you want to end up in the river?" my mother fumed. "One toss of that head and that's exactly where you'd be, my lady."

"Well, there was a time I could have!" I retorted. I didn't want her to lose track of things.

"Be quiet."

"Why?" She looked down at me but didn't answer. A lesson, a reminder. Not to be exasperating. As we laced up our sneakers I'd sigh all over the place, kicking at the picnic hamper because I was mad at myself for running from him.

Where did we run? To the cottage a hundred yards away. Actually, the fence between was what we headed for, which was scarcely half the distance to the cottage, seeming decep-tively near until a sudden departure was necessary. His Majesty sneaking up on us. Stumping ahead like some lumbering four-footed giant, snorting so hugely the grass divided, like hair parting. Reaching the fence, my mother and I would fling our bodies over the rickety stile, leaving him doggedly swaying along, head down, intent, as though he too were going somewhere. We were his excuse to end up at the stile, his favoured stamping ground midway between the top of the hill and the riverbank.

With a petulant lumpishness he'd sag that grotesque weight into the poor fence, pawing the stricken ground, the pussnout buried in the dirt and his haunches screeching the wire. And while staples dropped off and the fenceposts retched in a peculiar, at-odds slant, dry earth rose magnificently over the heaving back, like brown hoops swirling and disintegrating in the carrying wind. By the time he got going, once he'd rediscovered his potential for fury, the scene never varied. I'd sit on the verandah steps, wanting to get my hands on those furry ears, disconsolate with the sense of loss, the memory of that once gentle head, the yearning it always seemed to bring, and yet so quickly seized with the glee children cannot contain but must project into the goddess-laboratory of destruction. Demolition uprooting the hillside: turf, sand, stones, raining down on his back while he roared as though possessed by the devil himself. Red-eyed, a look around; finding nothing but the neutral hill, the indifferent fenceposts, Ambrosia would get bored and give up, satisfied that his territorial rights had been established, that his virility left no doubt.

Ambrosia. Silly dumb name for a bull, yet a majestic name to bestow. His profile. The giant aristocratic head, bloodshot eyes turned to the cooling wind. Suddenly I see him going through the motions. Under gigantic clouds and bewildered swallows lining the powerline-wires along the hill, he flings his final great bellow skyward. Stringing out villainous high Cs, a half-dozen echoes touch bases, reverberating through the rockfaced mountains a quarter of a mile away, belated falsettos penetrating the distant chasms further beyond. He looks up, rigid, taut, ears thrust forward searching his own alien sounds. Certain he is about to take off and charge across the hill, I have tears. I make no sound, but my face is running wet. And my mother, sitting across from me on the old garden swing, not so enchanted as I, tells him to be quiet. "Put a sock in it, Ambrosia," she says. A demand he pays no attention to until he is ready. Stones still flying through the air, grey pebbles, silver coins that twist and spin high against the winds of sunlight. My mother sees my tears, starts the swing moving. "Don't be concerning yourself," she says. "He thinks the echo's a cow from another herd."

"But he wants to fight it, I can tell by his back. Look at him, trying to make himself look huger and stronger."

"Get on with you. It just seems that way. He wouldn't fight a cow, *that's* not what he wants."

"Then why does he look so mean and dangerous, and not friendly?"

"It's part of him, to keep control of things." She is trying to keep it simple, her expression is asking questions of the air. She dries off my face with her fingers and then clasps her hands together in her lap. "It's his territory," she goes on. "And even though he thinks it's a cow, his instincts tell him to show who's king around here, in case it's another bull somewhere." She wiggles her toes on the step of the swing. "That's the way nature acquaints itself," she adds, fingering her hair, "the wind carries their messages, and then they stand up to be noticed." She twines a curl around her ear and I feel in her gesture a soft caress; it seems to be part of something we're talking about, the way she's thinking about it. Yes. She is imitating; maybe it's the same for people. Slow-motion almost, she rubs one foot over the other as the swing idles, and I hear her say again, "That's the way nature acquaints itself."

Which made that powerful head against the sky a thing of sentient beauty as Ambrosia awaited the returning call. Then would begin the thump thump of his descent downhill, a dust-caked cumbrous sight as slowly he'd plod along to rejoin his herd at the river, grumbling to himself while he stumped and lurched, the same day-in-day-out path through the low-level sumachs. Meek as a calf now, an air of benignity accompanied his journey along the riverbank as he drew near to his harem, standing up to their bellies in the slow-moving water. His wrath spent and his atrocious ugliness sticking out all over, he looked so forlorn, turning this way and that, bumping into the cows who for some reason must band close together while they drink. How I envied them his faithful return. But nothing will divert their lowered heads. A tail swishes at flies, then another; ears flap them away up front. A fitting silence of dense concentration under the scorching sun. This is the time of day they like. The long trudge through the back-barn fields ends at the river. Contentment lies in their lidded eyes as they skim their lips over the cold Gatineau water.

I see their wrinkled reflections, flesh so warm and sheened in the sunlight, and it turns within me and gallops, for my sense of possession, my need of it, belonged for a time to that fabric of tawny hides steeping in the jade-coloured water above the sandbars.

---

The picture becomes impossibly exquisite. Voices prolong its exposure. Whispering lichen. And logs smashing the shore. A dialogue in this scatter of cattle and "Drigo's Serenade". This intact nearness. One miraculous Olympus not yet eclipsed by rival priorities: by vanity, pirouetting, my mirror appraising me, moonstruck, sensuous, did I have oomph?

I see my mother leaning back on the rock, barefoot, ginghamed, ringlets caught up loosely and dangling, girlish arms pulling a cedar branch over the crescent of sunburn high on her brow where her hair had earlier protected it. She is close at hand, humming her "Count of Luxembourg Waltz": "La, la, Can It Be Love?" And then all is still. There is no "la, la". Or is it that I am no longer listening, or hearing it?

Yes. That fact was so. My teens were pushing me away, out of my mother's life. And I had to tell her so, find some way of letting her see me, that I was different now. Did I tell her, just then? I cannot remember exactly, nor even the time of year . . . oh but I can, *oh*! It just seemed to happen, the "say-goodbye" that was meant to be deep and close, but instead came out dismembering; a meat cleaver in the stomach. I was fourteen. And there had been that boy in the baseball sweater. I could smell his athlete's sweat, could feel that hard chest. Flat, like mine once was, I was thinking. The insistence of my own mystery, unwinding too fast. I thought and thought. I couldn't just say "I have breasts now, almost." Had she noticed? No, she would have said something. Suddenly I was angry she hadn't, so I blurted out: "Why do you have to sit on that same old rock doing nothing but sewing and humming? That's not fun. It's pins and needles in a workbasket, that's all it is."

My mother was kind. She didn't reply but kept biting at the thread and rolling it beyond need between her thumb and finger as though it were the last moistened knot we would ever share. I didn't think it so final. All the same, something about the way she began arranging spools in her workbasket, moving them about and putting them back in the same place, told me she had of course known. Those expressive hands. Though she did stop jockeying the spools, her thoughts were hopping all over the place: *so soon?* And I thought right back, not giving an inch, *I'm not a kid any more*.

And that was true. Not that I was after something better. I sought the same thing, only different, the difference being in the way a girl needs to grow. With passageway. In a sense, to be locked out with nothing more than her own breath. I started arranging the spools myself, thinking about it. I was happy, and unhappy. Against such going round in circles my mother's focus came back, as casually as if she'd just turned a page, or rounded a corner. I knew by the way she hunched her knees up, hugging her arms around them. I thought maybe she took consolation from the water-under-the-bridge sense of it, reading in its river-image what she wanted to know: that I would be back and that I wouldn't have dropped anything. But even so, I couldn't be satisfied with the river-image she took consolation from. It was all right for her, but I didn't want to sweep things under the rug with a "There, that's settled." I needed something in addition. Like sitting down and talking. She was still clasping her knees, so I clasped mine. Somehow it felt like the time on the garden swing when she told me about Ambrosia. The same fullness of moment. It was good to hold it again. This time I was conscious of a sudden and fierce intensity, that something wonderful would one day be happening to me. It came as a kind of light. And yet, quandary, and a sense of restlessness, however obscurely, kept intruding; I edged closer to my mother. Her bracelet had slipped along her arm and I moved it back to her wrist.

"Daddy gave me that before you were born," she said. Glad of this simple answer to nothing, I thought. But was I judging? Was this an opening? She wasn't looking at me but at the bracelet.

"Hear me, see me, for Pete's sake!" my mind retorted. We still aren't saying anything so I ease the bracelet off my mother's hand and try it on, hold my arm out to show her. I let my wrist fall limp and delicate. Like in the movies.

"I want to be grown up," I say. "I don't like being just a girl. Not any more."

"You shouldn't be wishing your most precious years away like that," she replied, still not looking at me. Now that's a strange thing to say, when she can do anything she likes, and knows everything there is to know. Has she forgotten what it's like? this imagining and yearning? And not being certain what for either. I push further.

"I want to be grown up," I say again. "Like you. Not just pretending."

"You don't know what you're saying, child. It's then your troubles begin."

"You don't have any troubles, so why should I?" Now she is looking at me, fingering the bracelet. She *knows* this sea I am in.

"I used to feel you were a long time growing up. Don't know why, really. But I did."

"When? This year? This summer?"

"Half a dozen times this summer. I'd see you climbing down out of a tree and I'd wonder what in Heaven's name you were doing up there, and I'd think, Ach, sure she's still only a child; she should be encouraged with these gymnastics; what nonsense that I would worry about the hem of her dress being up above her knees."

"That's because you *made* them that way in the first place!"

"What? In what first place?"

"All you did was buy patterns for a ten-year-old and cut them out bigger. And those kiddish sashes, and puffed sleeves, like they put on dolls. No one else my age wore them. Wears them. Look at my winter coat!"

"And what's wrong with your winter coat? A lovely coat."

"It looked better the way it came, with bone buttons, not those pom-poms you . . ."

"I don't know," she broke in, looking childlike herself, the tips of her fingers easing back and forth across her kneecap, like a child with a secret to tell. "I guess it's because I wasn't in any hurry to see you growing up, not for a while anyway."

"And now you're going to tell me I've got the rest of my life ahead of me; go on, tell me, 'there's time enough for that'."

"Oh no I'm not. Not by a long shot."

I glanced at her quickly and sat up straight. What was this? I would wait, say nothing and wait. If I'd said, "What's that supposed to mean?" she'd have answered right off, "Never you mind." We were sitting by the window on the couch in the cottage living room, her eyes drifting over her flower beds, the woman now, for that instant anyway, the quiet grace of a woman's passion, head tilted slightly, fingering her hair as she gazed across the slope of the hill and on, over the long grass beyond the fence, above the sandpit the lone elm tall and still, seeming then to have been such a long time in the world, ageless, like the sky. "The rest of your life ahead of you . . ." she said after a moment, "yes, you sure have. And I don't think you even know what it means.

"No. You may have thought I'd say There's time enough for that. But there isn't, lassie, not when you've found the one you want."

"You're barmy, Mamma. A minute ago you just got through saying your troubles only begin . . ."

"I know, I know. So be prepared for plenty of them, some that'll make you laugh and some that'll make you cry, and some to spare. Why, you've already begun—don't you think I know that? the doubts, the longings? But you'll figure them out. Be patient. They'll come to you in their own good time. I can't tell you, or explain. You have to come across them, experience things in your own way. You're a woman now, and I needn't . . . You've seen enough of your father and me. Why should I try to tell you what's beyond the gestures?

"When I was a girl, well, you wanted to still have something . . . yes, it was the discovery." Hesitating, pulling a wave back, ". . . but only when I was ready." She sounded as though she were talking to herself. "Granny was right," she added, and then stopped.

I thought she might go back to her spools again, and finish, spoil what she had to say by being a mother again, reminding me I wasn't even fifteen yet. But no. Her eyes were smiling. And trusting. They also had a sharp look in them that said "keep your wits". She knows I don't need things spelled out, I thought; only her blessing.

It was then I felt a grave kind of joy, a strange sexual flow through the whole of my body, and the breath in me rose full as a sailing wind, enough for the other self squeezing my heart. That night I sat at her dressing-table mirror. I got out her lipstick, puckered my lips together the way she did to make the line deep and curving—Pure Flame Tangee set off against the tan of my skin. Next I combed my hair around my face—with kiss-curls and bangs I put spit on. And I asked myself, Why did she always say I would not be like her, that I was like my father?

In September, when my birthday came, I had lipstick of my own. In a brass case with coloured stones. But the other present meant far more to me, for now I wouldn't have to go around in cotton bloomers all the time. I sat with the box on my lap, tissue paper rustling, and my father said, winking at my mother, "Can't for the life of me think what's in it. Do you know, Mimi?" Not one but three pairs of pink rayon panties. With a rosette on the waistband. "For parties," my mother said. But I wore them to school every day. Under my bloomers.

---

I think of the river-image, its dimensions. For passageway has led me through darker tunnels, and en route has stuck barnacles on the gingham. But there is some obscure carry-over: like a spark that seems to keep burning, flicking both shadow and light on the walls of my insides. Of circumstance I am an heir, a kin now rich, now poor. I do not walk easily away whenever debacles overtake me. I stand and howl. And whatever the patinas, the bandages, all have a permanent sheen, for they are vintage.

Descendants of time: an Indian-straw sewing basket, here—here on my night-table. Realities moving softly. I stand and look at it, wondering at its long survival. Somewhere inside I hear the voice of tiny red stitches choosing partners as my mother sings the "Count of Luxembourg Waltz", and I feel myself skimming over the sand to a lichened rock. Nothing is changed, I think. I lift the lid. I pick up the Persian thimble I once put teethmarks in when my hands held my mother's pins. In my head I hear the sound of a river washing past and a cowbell coming down over the hill.

"It's not fun any more," it says.

# VIII

I am in another reach of time, a meridian of white peonies and purple candles. The house in Ottawa. And it is evening. June? Odd that we'd be in the city. But no matter. My eyes have singled out an interval. I'm in summer clothes, what are we . . . ? The bronzed chords of Chopin fall across the dust in the sunparlour. That is all the sound there is, this funeral march. It is enough. My hands bind themselves in my lap as I listen and duplicate history, something stately, maybe the funeral of a King, a pageant I imagine as unbannered and broken off, smudged with cold rain. I feel the warmth of the mahogany piano bench, my father's aliveness as he pulls me close when left-hand passages allow. He has perhaps chosen to play this "Dead March" for its feeling of reality. Sometimes its happening tells him more of what life is. He can do this only at home, thinking out loud with that piano of his. His glimpses are all beyond me. But I pretend I catch them. Am I nine years old? Ten?

We have just returned from a wedding. (My mother dropped cannel coal on her foot this morning, and I went in her place.) A mistake. Decidedly out of place in my stillborn, taffeta cut-down. And the more so in that the bride was the daughter of my father's wartime commander, and I'd never laid eyes on a one of them. I was proudly displayed among the lot, an underfoot barbarian. Turned loose in a sea of Puritan icebergs aground at the punch bowl. Given a sticky orange instead of punch. Hastily. I only wanted to try it.

My perception of the bride introduced me grandly. Her plate-shaped headdress resembled my Sunday School bookmark so closely I saw her as a Madonna with Child. Though her arms were busy with bridal things during the ceremony, I was somehow convinced that a diapered cherub nestled in her kangaroo-pouch of tulle and Brussels lace. Silently convinced, until the service was over. Trailing my father down the reception line, with nothing to say to anyone, I thought of the altar I had just seen, and the Madonna.

I would ask the bride.

"Where is your baby?" I inquire, probing the tulle. Corsets stiffen, at eye level my ears feel the stays stretching.

"Her first wedding," my father offers, turning to the comic, jowly kingdom standing in judgment. His observation hangs deliciously in the ought-to-be-cane-whipped sublimity of their faces as he takes me to meet other, more splendid children. . . .

———

Bong goes another chord, and another, two more, heavy and round and solemn, dum . . . dum . . . dum-dum. I ask myself, Why does my father begin with that "Dead March"?

Is it what I did? No. It has nothing to do with me, or weddings, or my mother's sore foot. It's just that he can finally let down, feed his mind through his fingertips, paint sounds now that he has nobody but me, who doesn't understand them but sits beside him all the same, feet dangling the black patent shoes that have spilled punch on the toes.

Black patent shoes. Stubby buffed-down shoes. Polished with spit on the toes where it shows most. And deep, deep in the dark, memory dives into a cupboard that's crammed with clothes and suitcases and Christmas decorations, and boxed wonders put by for measles and mumps. Down on the floor, scattering things not mine, a brush of musty perfume and shaving lotion as my mind drags out the shoebox. Same old shine. Stages of my life bent into the soles. Where did I tramp in that far time? And what did I leave behind? I'm just passing through again I say, defensively. I take my young hand and go through. There is a feeling of descent, a white brilliance, strobe-like. Corridors swim as in a dream, corridors with music behind the walls. I belong here, I tell myself. The songs have been waiting. They need my voice.

Have I got it right? I expected some change. But—is the house empty now? Is it summer, and we're at the cottage? Yes. I see fields backing into the mountain, fields of ripened grain like tawny pelts weaving themselves into the blue wind. And a sunset my mother says has broomtails. Broomtails? Rain follows, a muttering sound on the broken roof shingles. And a gale whistling through the knothole above my bed, which has a lumpy mattress. Soon it will be autumn.

And now the house in Ottawa, a January night? Pitch black in my bedroom. Night-sounds under the feel of my blanket. I hear the red wooden streetcar creeping uphill through the bush, and closer, under my window, the dog's bark at the back door. Vaguely I catch sound of my father opening the door to let him in, my mother at the icebox tearing off bits of cold roast. Faintly, on the kitchen linoleum the dog waltzes around on his hind legs. A "clop" from the big black-freckled mouth. Then silence.

A child's whole continent. Winter, summer, the passage of time looking back at me: January in the late afternoon, a May night. Where I am standing gusts of night winds call my name: the child, the woman, I answer to both. The winds are a single voice of course, my father's. It is one day. It is another. Right now he is playing the piano again, improvising. *Forte, fortissimo.* Preludes that run through the house, conducted, strangely, by the arm of a pine bough swaying in the twilight wind. He flips the lid of the piano down and leads me to the kitchen, pulls my winter playsuit from the chair over the register and checks to see if it's dry. Out into a snowstorm we go bundled and mittened, trailing a toboggan behind us. We walk down the middle of the road where the plough has been, half-closed eyes, glistening faces scrubbed by the wind force. On the empty street snow falls into a diamond silence. It is no dream. It is the snow that is opaque.

And it's coming down heavier here. We are on the brow of a hill and my father is cleaning off the toboggan. The hill is long and steep and every time down the spray catches us full on. "Gee it has a great feel," he says, "taking off into all that clean snow. Let me see what it's like going headfirst." He lies down on his stomach with his chin resting on the toboggan hood; the fierce wind scoops snow-swirls high over his head.

A routine, as firm and faithful as winter itself. Every snowstorm, after supper or before, we get the toboggan out; the same hill, past vacant lots, over a fence, through the bush. My voice shrills across open space, as fresh wax sends the toboggan headlong. But the hour claims us. Twilight, or nightfall. Through three-foot drifts and the soundless open land we pull the toboggan home. Snow fills in our tracks, leaves no traces. My father in a windbreaker, or his overcoat. Always a hat. The wonder of it is that he never seems older but set in that one perfect bend of time, somehow, untouched by summers giving me my own design.

---

There is a piece of music, Fauré's "Elégie", that brings back happy glimpses of my father, the time I could never look away, when I saw in his eyes a stillness that gave my world its first anxieties. For his reveries were totally beyond my comprehension. And I would move about the house playing catch with a ping-pong ball against the dining-room wall, or else seize the dog for a game of rough-house down on the floor. Noise going on all around him but my father is deep in the dream of his mind; whatever happens will not register. If the doorbell went, or someone asked him a question, it was as if he had to come to first, as though he'd forgotten he was even around . . . a juncture my mother never failed to pounce on.

She would ladle out little servings of censure, always something different to start off with: head-in-the-clouds-Charlie, or bats in the belfry, and the one I always thought had a very nice ring to it, like a song: cuckoo in the treetop. "Your father's daydreaming again," she'd say and start singing "I Dreamt I Dwelt in Marble Halls", with a nod directed at his upside-down book or a sudden shrug of his shoulders, reacting to a conversation with himself. Then to no one in particular Mamma would sigh, "The Irish with their dramas. They're all alike!" And I would go out of my way to remind her she didn't call it dramas when we had people in, so why did she have to say it now? "That will be enough out of you young lady," she'd retort, and tell me if I didn't watch myself I'd grow up to be a dreamer too.

Once I asked her if that was a bad habit; I saved this discussion until I was helping her dry the dishes, when she never missed a word I said. "Should I train myself to talk a lot?"

"Tell everything? Heavens no," she cries, calamitously, as though amazed at herself. "You keep your thoughts a while, ponder them some. Otherwise there's nothing left to surprise me with."

"Well then, what's so terrible about daydreaming?"

"Nothing. Nothing in all the wide world. It's tender and deep. What you want of someone." How contradictory, how fickle she is. And then I think, maybe there's something to be said about Mamma wanting to be deep like that too. For she tells everything, all the time. I have a notion she's only pretending to be irked; and what's more, she doesn't want my father to know it. He might change. Well. It's like trying to do my lessons, only harder.

Mostly my father's "dramas" were just a certain note of quiet, except when a letter came from Grandmother Watson in Ireland, and then it really was a drama taking place in his mind, a troubled drama. But he made up for it with his gentle, afterthought kind of whimsy. That and his affectionate nature. Troubles he kept inside; anger I never saw in him. If there was any, it never showed. Instead of letting fly like Mamma, he'd go down to the basement and switch on his ham radio, monitoring CQs squawking from earphones draped around his neck, while he fixed a neighbour's radio (the place was littered with them, mantel sets trotted up to the front door after supper and dropped into his unprotesting hands with a thought-you-might-tinker-around-with-this, my mother trailing him down the cellar stairs asking why he didn't pay for the parts as well, to complete the service). Other times he sat on the parlour sofa looking out the window, cloistered in that private-midnight reverie. Which meant my mother gave up and found herself something to do, like making a banana cream pie, maybe washing her hair.

---

Without knowing exactly why, I soon came to feel the sadness in my father when he was quiet like that. It was there in his eyes. I'd walk by him with my ping-pong ball in case he wanted to play, scanning his face when he thought I wasn't watching. And I'd tell myself, that's the reason Mamma bakes a pie and makes her hair pretty. But then I'd think, What if Mamma feels lonesome too because he is? I remember I would remain indoors, busy myself at the dining-room table with my colouring book, or make a new peep-show, imagining my presence would speak for itself.

Memories of my father: a language that breaks away and leaves me, now, with pieces of sound that belong, where? At the moment nothing seems fixed in place with all its parts. The view from the toboggan hill, for instance. I can't remember if there were trees. Or if we saw rabbits and winter birds on our way home through the bush. Did our clothing pick up burrs? Together we pull the toboggan behind us through the silent snow, the silent winding trails, the empty land that draws dusk onto its breast. I do not chatter. We take long looks at things like trees and burrs. Influenced by this quality of muteness, walking side by side, something is transmitted, a catch of inner light that quickens. I know that whatever my father is thinking will pass itself on to me. I am not so aware of external things when I am with him. I am deeper into his mind and he in mine.

Was it always that way? Or was it that one thing I said one night that brought us close? "Mamma is your sweetheart," I said, a conception I had that gave me a sense of well-being. My father was straddling a stool in a soda fountain at the time, about to take me to my first ice show where he picked up extra money nights, shining spotlights from a cubbyhole in the roof of the Auditorium. He had chosen the opening night to bring me along, getting me in free because I could squeeze in beside him in that black little space high in the rafters. A rinkful of ostrich plumes, Frick and Frack, and Sonja Henie. The lights certainly kept him busy, all elbows as he pursued the skimming flash of a solo now rounding a bend at the far end of the arena. But he had more fun than the audience. He put so much of himself into it, the timing of those red and blue lights, sometimes two at a time, criss-crossing the flying-by jumps and spins. Did a few jumps of his own on the side if a passage in the music moved him.

He stood throughout the entire performance; backed up against a cement wall, or crouched at an angle beside me. Wow. I'd be following a single skater, a swirl of chiffon white as a blowing feather, sequins glittered through a spray of snow at a sudden stop, and then the electrifying, roof-shattering surge of the concert band soaring, up full, dipping, swooping, and my father ready and waiting, his floodlights aimed at one end of the semi-dark arena, and whooosh! the white chiffon, Sonja Henie, in one silver stroke, the iridescent sequins deepening from pink to red, gliding the length of the ice.

"Gee," I said just as his hands shot up in the air and suddenly began clapping with the deafening applause, "tomorrow night it's George's turn to come. I wish it was mine." He didn't hear me, couldn't, the background noise, and the band repeating the final reprise (was it "Iberian Night"?), and him thumping my back now instead of his hands. Relieved that my rush of words had gone unheard, I looked up at him fondly, remembering Christmas morning not four weeks before, guiltily, when George, trailing a tangle of ribbon and red tissue paper, leapt across the room to show me his new Brownie camera, and I, dropping the white fur mitts I'd been hugging, swung around exclaiming: "And I didn't get one!"

"Do tell," my father said looking me in the eye. "Girls aren't interested in cameras, now are they?"

A hard way to learn a lesson. I remember my father was still in his pyjamas and dressing gown, lying on his side, stretched out full length on the floor beside the Christmas tree, one foot crossed over the other, up on one elbow and with his chin resting in his hand. I ran over to him, my heart as sick and dark as it had ever been, as it is at this moment, picturing . . . experiencing again the burden of my eagerness, close to tears as I scurried back for my fur mitts, stricken by my negation of what was lying about me, gifts that, in spite of the Depression, my parents had planned and scrimped for, had done without themselves, I was thinking, in order to surprise me.

And as if that wasn't enough, Mamma added her contribution to the gift-opening ceremony, her expression of gratitude a real dandy.

Seated in an armchair by the fireplace, the folds of her li-

lac kimono and nightie turning crimson in the blaze of firelight, legs crossed as she prepared to open my father's gift,
one slipper showing beneath the hem, a velveteen mule hanging loosely, about to slip off. I remember glimpsing the lid of
a small Birks box falling from her lap as she held a tiny
gold-coloured hand mirror, a delicately scrolled Florentine
accessory for her dressing table, with petit-point on the back
casing and pin-dots of pink and aqua enamelled on both sides
of the handle, and I heard her say: "What good is a little
squirt of a thing like this? You can only see one eye at a
time."

---

When the appluase in the Auditorium had died down, and
my father was poised, his fingers squarely on the hood of
each spotlight, the rink dark and hushed as the Follies skaters
darted about at centre ice in search of their places for the final bow, I said, "How long will it be till next year? Do I
have to wait that long to see the Follies again?" I had
climbed up on a wooden crate, and was perched with one
arm extended wide, to suggest all the extra space there was,
hinting, though not venturing, that maybe I could come too
when he brought Mamma on Saturday night. And the second
I brought my arm down I saw him bump his head; he was
trying to swivel one of the lights around without making me
feel I was in the way.

Afterwards, on the way home, the first thing he said was,
"So Mamma is my sweetheart. Yes. I suppose she is." He
looked down at me, curiously thoughtful, then in a minute
his face lit up as if my observation had taken care of some
attendant doubt, had told him I was aware of what was most
important in his life. Almost midnight, my eyes full of sleep,
we sat on the streetcar in the subzero night, disclosure precious in its seal. No longer did I feel separate, or alone with
myself. That night when I said my prayers I included myself.
If I should die before I wake I left out. Please make sure I
come down in the mornings, I asked, I have to be around in
case things get clouded over. It was clear to me grownups
needed things explained too. They can't always see everything
for themselves.

Perhaps the night of the Follies I saw in his eyes a recognition of self, my own self with his, how the heart is only at
peace when loving is present. Fear of its non-existence was
all I could share, or give.

But music affected him more than anything else, and the piano was his slice of the absolute, his bagatelle mountain. I was still quite young when I began to realize that the sweet sounds coming out of the piano were a part of himself, a voice deep in his gut. Once home from the office, leaving behind the continual beeping of radio signals from connecting offices and a desk scattered with government business, which so often took him to foreign places, he'd barely be in the door when I'd hear the first meanderings of treble. Straightaway I'd race to the piano bench; *I* couldn't wait either. The dog would lie down beside us, the length of him pressed against the side of the piano with his head sideways on his paws and his body absorbing the vibrations.

The first harmonies roll softly and tentatively as I watch my father settling in, the life of him become music in his head. Around him an aura of calm, or, once in a while, a conflict inside growing urgent with release. In a white shirt, with metal-link armbands, tarnished silver that gave signs of wear and were always getting caught in the wide sleeves, his body never stopped moving as though living out the sounds coming from the old upright. Inhaling spirals of smoke, a cigarette rolled from Turret tobacco moving from side to side in his mouth, his eyes half-closed, fingers travelling up and down the keyboard as he reflected. A shy man in his daydreams, pouring out his love and sometimes his woes.

In a manner of speaking I knew all the music my father played. That is, it was familiar, and when it wasn't I'd pinch his sleeve: "What's that called?" In the beginning I thought he never heard but soon I caught on; so deep into the mood, his eyes most of the time shut, he'd keep on playing, with a secret fascination as though he were walking on water, until a sweep of shirtsleeve told me he was pleased as he listened, right to the last dying-away pedal. Then sideways at me a waggish smile, pleased with his sharp three-note staccato, a mimic "what's-that-called?" The armbands pushed back up again and off he'd be, going over the whole thing reflectively, or whimsically, depending. Telling me what it was about, who wrote it. And in a way I'd be certain to remember too. Hitting chords as he made up words to "The Hall of the Mountain King", and through his eyes I envisioned all the mountain kings of Norway, the mourning for Ase. On edge for fear I might lose track I sat twisting my fingers, staring straight ahead into the gold-lettered HEINTZMAN centred in the mahogany shine. Creatures and streams and great forests and caves just beginning to fall into place. And the next instant, tomfoolery. His own "Surprise Symphony": "Here," he'd say, "time for the blight of the fumble bee." And he'd see to it that the bee had someplace to go: "Bald Mountain" going on in his left hand the the bee in the treble, a high-pitched drone worrying the life out of the bass. And then back again, something quiet as a lullaby, suggesting immortality, such as a statue or a flowered balcony. Mixing things up, as though his mind couldn't sit still and be content with its one set of blocks. That's what he'd do. It was always like that.

Except when company came. And then his playing was different, the sound was never the same. People had a habit of dragging in sheet music (which his ear promptly rearranged), and for hours at a time he'd oblige. But the familiar patterns, the flow of the line had a silence in it somewhere. I thought it had something to do with their asking where he learned his music; no matter what he played, sooner or later it got around to that. Who'd taught him, how old was he when he started, was there someone musical in his family? I remember one night a man asking him was it true he had accompanied John McCormack. Well, yes he had. And he shrugged, embarrassed it should have come up. But the truth of the matter was it took him back. And he didn't want to go.

He never went over things. For him it was all past. That much I knew: there was an empty space I sensed in his life, one I didn't care to ever have knowledge of. Now that he had us, nothing could hurt him again. That's what I told myself: things stayed in his mind too long, that's why he looked out the window. Whatever the thoughts, the maze, the montage, he had to wear them down that way.

I don't remember exactly how long this logic secured my world. But later, when I was older and could no longer ignore my concern so handily, how often I longed to say something to him, anything; instead of always putting things aside, letting them fester in the bog of my own silences, I might have lifted that hushed thing that was buried so deeply. . . . But what could I have said anyway? "Did someone you once loved die?"

I see myself sitting on the bed looking out the window. I was upstairs in my bedroom trying to think of words I could say. And my mother, pausing in the doorway: "There you go again, concerning yourself with things beyond your ken." Everything so normal to her. Nothing interwoven, nothing out of focus. If you can't put words to things, if you can't talk about them, then they can't mean very much. If something's happened: "Don't lose sleep . . . why bother your head . . . it's over, have done with it." She's shaking out cushions: "You win, you lose." And stirring a pot on the stove: "It's only temporary." Sometimes I want to scream at her. But why, when she doesn't understand? Hanging up her coat in the closet: "Make do, lassie." Mamma!

For a long time I kept telling myself, Some day, some day very soon, when I can bring myself to let in his darkness, now becoming mine, I would go after first-hand knowledge, find someone who could tell me about that door in the past my father had closed. Friends—there was bound to be one he'd have talked to. Then, without mentioning a word, without his ever knowing of my intrusion, I could try to make things up to him. When I went to bed at night, no longer did I lie awake over my poor showing in Latin and geometry; a miracle in that department was easier to come by—not that I counted on it though. And I didn't care. For no matter what, my struggle was now concerned with what I might say or do, how I might go about taking the place of this unknown something when I hadn't been able to before.

The day never came: I knew myself too well. In my sleep, playing a role I had no business in, I seemed to be all over the place, chattering a blue streak, in and out of doors, at the table, even showing up at his office after school. And always my insides in a quiver as I saw myself attempting to draw my father out, enquiring eagerly about things of no consequence. As a result, the very first time I was faced with an actual moment, when my father had suddenly turned off a radio he was fixing in the basement and wandered upstairs into the living room, I thought it would be easy to wander in there too, why not just make a move and suggest that I'd been sitting all day, how about a game of tennis? or did he feel like taking a walk with me, we could go down through the bush to MacKay Lake, see if the trilliums were out yet.

I sat where I was in the sunparlour and kept on reading, like all the other times, afraid to try for fear I'd find myself standing alongside staring out the window too, in the loud hush my mind thinking the same thoughts as he. Why, he'd have guessed right away, and realized . . . How could I take a chance on causing one more sadness for him, when he saw mine? discovering that what he thought he'd been keeping to himself had communicated itself to me. It is now, at this very moment, that I feel the pain. In both of us.

On the day my father was buried I asked his friend Mr. Mahoney to tell me about John McCormack, and Tipperary. Translate for me. I could ask anything I wanted now—once I could find the words. They'd been close friends for so long, I was thinking, born in the same town even. My mind hearing its own dialogue, the long-put-off silence, my own, springing up in me as Mr. Mahoney removed his coat. He'd been *there*, who else would know?

An unplanned conversation. But then I hadn't expected to see him.

That morning, at the funeral parlour, I was standing by myself, face to face with a day I had never known before: the casket and flowers I owned as if mine and would soon follow through moving traffic, along side streets, past school playgrounds and people burning autumn leaves who would look up, waiting for us to pass, their attention then turning back to heap and bury successions of rakings. It was almost time for the service—an hour to go? What time was it? How much longer?

People holding forth, voices speaking back of me. Not that they were interrupting—I wasn't talking to anyone. No, I didn't, did I? I was too busy wishing they'd all go away. I hadn't invited them, and I had so little time left. The burial. I wanted to talk to my father. It felt . . . the way he was dead, I mean from the way he looked, the way I saw him, he seemed—what? And so I spoke, I was saying things to him. I thought he might still be able to hear me. Is that what others, is that what everyone does the first time? I wanted to tell my father I needed him, he would understand. Before this I was too confused, but now, in a little while they're going to take him away, I won't be able to stand here. How do other people manage to endure, not show? That man over there, the one with the *Reader's Digest* . . . has he ever been through this? Did he once get a phone call when it was too late?

My voice, did I begin with words, out loud? single words, double, my head is bent low, "Canso . . . fireflies . . . the river . . . your turn." What am I saying? I stand and wait.

My fingers move across my father's tie, a special tie, it was part of him. Yes. I was waiting.

For what? a feeling to come? would it touch the air? I'd recognize whatever happened. My father's face, pensive. How could he not know? Protected by the influence of wondering, imagining—until I heard my voice: "I am here," I said. And then I couldn't talk any more. I didn't want just the sound of my voice alone. I didn't talk to my father again, not then anyway.

In the time that was left, finding myself in utter silence, coldly indifferent to anyone who set foot in the room as I stood guard, looking down . . . on eyelids, my other self returned, fingers twisting at my father's lapel, as though imploring. It cannot be true, give me back my father.

I jumped at the touch of someone's hand laid upon mine. Mr. Mahoney.

I hadn't seen the man since I was in my teens; a dentist, he'd moved his practice to Vancouver, I suppose nearly twenty years had gone by. And the sight of him, never dreaming he'd be there . . . that he'd come all that way.

He asked me if there was anything he could do, almost his first words as he stood with an arm around my shoulder; words I didn't fully take in until I realized who it was saying them. "Do?" I said. That's when I turned around and guided him in another direction, pushing people out of the way so we could find a place to talk. They weren't doing me any favour by being there. . . . Was that necessary? Did I show it? I tried not to, but they couldn't understand. How could I pretend to sit down and listen? Words failed them, they kept saying, "The accident . . . but then of course, that's life." Of course! And what would they know of failed words in this, my room, my space, mine! and Mr. Mahoney's.

I suggested the other end of the room, I wanted to get away from the flowers, they were wilting. Mr. Mahoney asked two people sitting on a sofa would they mind? I had seen them there before, they had come each day and brought their lunch.

The sofa was angled into a corner where once in a while a faint breeze stirred through the windows. Wedged between empty porcelain vases, a mantel clock in a glass case showed twenty past eleven; more than an hour and a half left before the service. Perhaps more though, I seem to remember the clock being fast.

I was blunt. "Why did my father always clam up like that?"

Without realizing until now, this very instant, could that have been what was pounding at me before Mr. Mahoney arrived? Was I trying to tell my father I'd known all along, had understood, and that he'd never been alone? Canso was the first thing I'd said. And, fireflies, I mentioned fireflies for a very good reason. I couldn't help it . . . I'd remembered the night I'd found him sitting by himself inside the cottage, and I knew it was one of those times, he was far away somewhere, so I went outside and caught him two fireflies in a jar. He said we shouldn't keep them closed up like that, why didn't we go out on the hill and watch them in the dark? we'd be able to see them better.

Fireflies. But then—what did I have in mind when I said "Your turn?" The toboggan? Likely. The wind and the winter quiet of Sundays when it was going on for dark. That was a good time, it was swell, the best of all. The toboggan hill *and* the walk we took afterwards down through the bush; blizzards swirling around his brown hat, the blue snow shadows, my wet mitts, the smell of wet damp wool. By ourselves. Unobserved. Creaking branches topping the silence. And him telling me I was good company; that was what he said one night when it got dark early and we lost our way in the bush. The snow was so deep I had to follow his tracks. I stepped in the holes his boots made, and got behind. "How are you doing?" he said. I wonder. I'm still trying to step into those hollows—they're what I have to fall back on.

Mr. Mahoney. Beside me on the sofa. His lovely face, for instance. A few lines on the brow, at the corners of his eyes as well, but the auburn hair, the freckles, still the same, his small frame no heavier. The hazel eyes are patient, solemn, meditative, and twinkle mistily at something he remembers.

"It wasn't like my father to be abrupt, not with anyone, and for him to clam up that way . . ." With his eyes on the floor, Mr. Mahoney listened attentively, taking in what I had to say as if it were new to him. "I used to dread those moments," I went on, "people blundering on . . . they met someone from Ireland the other day, couldn't find the place on their map, would he show them? And postcards . . . what place was this? was he ever there? . . . wasn't he from County Tipperary? Meaning well, I suppose. But opening up a wound. If he were at the piano, I'd feel him wanting to shove his hands in his pockets, as if he'd have given anything to get up and leave the room."

"And the yellow piano light shining full on his features," Mr. Mahoney said, nodding soberly. "No one would ever have known what he was thinking; that same composed tilt of his head, attentive, congenial. Never letting anything show in his face."

"No, he never did, did he? That's what made it seem worse, the way he kept playing. The music, so empty suddenly—it changed into neat and and perfect notes: the piano giving a concert. Sometimes I'd get the feeling I was the only other person in the room with him, regardless of who might be there, nothing they said was heard by either of us. The sounds inside him were louder."

"Yes," Mr. Mahoney conceded, "there was a vulnerability beyond his power to conceal. Still, there was many a time he'd catch my eye and wink. It broke the tension."

I glanced about the room, the far end now a confusion, middle-aged men mostly, shaking hands. "What's new?" "Exactly . . ." "No, not since the war . . ." "Come now . . . Anthony Eden . . . Suez . . ." And still more coming in the door, like a contingent. I was glad of the business suits—I couldn't see the flowers any more.

"You knew my father all his life," I said turning back. "Did it have something to do with his mother?" I reminded him that my father had never bothered to answer his mother's letters, nor even read them. "Whenever a letter came," I said, "he left it lying on the hall table as if it were a circular he might find time to look through. Then after a few days he'd toss it into the fireplace, or the garbage. In all the time his mother was alive I never heard him mention her. It did cross my mind she might have had . . ."

"His mother," Mr. Mahoney begins, and leans his head back, contemplating through half-closed eyes. Is he going to dodge the issue? I try to read him; does he find my determination odd? are my fingernails leaving a mark on his wrist?

"Your grandmother couldn't have been very proud of herself, the way she treated her son."

"Then it *was* her after all," I said hesitantly. Mr. Mahoney looked up and glanced about briefly, as though searching for a familiar face.

"Your own mother, I've been meaning to ask—is she not well?" But I wanted to change the subject; this was no time to be discussing my mother's odd spells, the possibility that

her memory was going. "I was here for a few minutes last
evening," he added, "on my way from the airport. I didn't
see her around."

"No, she's not well. I mean she's home and everything, but
the shock . . . she knows something's happened but she can't
seem to take anything in. The night it happened, when I got
to the house the neighbours told me she'd heard the news on
the radio. And you know how local stations play these things
up. The army captain who lives next door heard it too, he
said they didn't just refer to the skid marks—the man who
went through that stop street—but they gave all the details,
how my father's car had struck the light standard, the angle
and the marks and everything. When he went to see if my
mother knew, he saw her through the living room window
. . . she was sitting on the floor rocking back and forth, like
a child being cradled by its mother after it's had a bad fall.
Except she was alone."

"That's terrible. The poor woman!"

"Since that time, from the moment I arrived all she's done
is wander around her room. Her conversation's making no
sense whatever." I shifted uneasily. I had left my mother sitting with her hat on and a letter in her hand. She was waiting
for me to drive her uptown to see my father at his office,
there was something she wanted to ask him. The letter was
ten years old.

"I'm sorry."

I remained silent.

"Well now," Mr. Mahoney sighed as he crossed his legs
and plunged both hands deep in his pockets. Perusing the
floor again, his thoughts more at ease down there.

Flies buzzed against the window screen and fell on the sunlit sill as though in a stupor. In the parking lot a car door
slammed, and then another. Mr. Mahoney raised his head and
smiled affectionately, his head turned sideways to face me.
He was waiting for me to say something.

"Was it when he was very young, when he was still a
boy?" I resumed casually, absently, as though it were taken
for granted. Making a stab, I had to begin somewhere. "During his childhood?" I press further. Mr. Mahoney does not
want to be overheard; his hands, in prayer fashion, tap his
lips.

"Both during and after, but especially when he was small
and needed her most. No attempt at being a mother, or anything else."

"Was she that unfeeling?"

"Totally. To be perfectly honest, a wretched woman. Something of a tyrant, who thought herself above her station in life . . . her, a shopkeeper's wife in a country town! To hear her tell it, she was simply not interested in extending herself to the likes of them. And as for children! She never forgave your grandfather for wanting a son, and regarded your father as a proper nuisance." I turned away, the thought had made me shiver. I always have to feel, visualize, I can't just hear about something, and pass on.

Mr. Mahoney shook his head and was silent for a moment, reflecting. "And so it went on," he said, pausing again as he took hold of one of the drawstrings at the window, "the years . . . loss of his boyhood, his youth. A terrible thing growing up alone, the way your Dad did."

"Alone? What about his father?—In other words, he made no difference."

"A lovely man he was; even so, no match for his wife. I daresay you knew your father spent all his school life in boarding schools, but did you also know he rarely saw the inside of his home from one year's end to the next?"

"No, I didn't know any of it." My voice lowered, I was counting years. Flies thrummed against the screen, like a tabulator.

"The bakery thrived, but as for the home above," Mr. Mahoney sighed, cutting short his words to thrust aside the cord of the Venetian blinds. "If ever there was a matriarchal household, that one was a prime example. When I think of the times I tired to sit down—and was politely shown the door. I called in from time to time to visit your grandfather in the shop, to bring him news of his son. 'Who's that?' your grandmother would call from the top of the stairs. I must say he handled it well. He wasn't embarrassed, he showed a slight irritation perhaps, but his manner remained amiable, the mark of the man's dignity. He'd reach for his coat and say, 'Mind if I come along?' Her indifference didn't surprise me, I don't know—maybe the way she closed the door behind us, formally, as if we were strangers, told me her mind could go back to whatever had been interrupted upstairs." I imagined the stairs, dark and narrow, and carpeted, I thought. I also caught a glimpse of my grandmother from behind—was she small? tiny? I saw her eyes . . . I was going to ask Mr. Mahoney . . . His voice broke in, "We'd go for a stroll across the fields where it was quiet, and he'd ask what books we vere reading in school, a soccer game, had there been one, hat had we been up to lately with our friends, things like hat. He'd listen quietly, imagining, his lips in a smile and at he end he'd say, 'I love my son.'

"Yes, I'm afraid that as far as your grandmother was conerned, one man in the house was more than enough; your ather could find his own way."

There were a number of people standing close by in small roups, almost on top of us, faces averted but obviously inent, sniffing nervously as they picked imaginary lint from heir shoulders. "Not an ounce of love in those cold veins," Mr. Mahoney declared, his voice resounding like the final vords in a soundtrack at a moviehouse. "Something sinister bout the woman." It was then, noticing the audience, Mr. Mahoney seemed suddenly taken aback by his words and ooked apologetic, his face shrinking back into his scalp, as if e had just pronounced a terrible judgment on someone andicapped. "God rest her soul," he added, a flush rising up rom his neck.

What I needed to know: a boy's reach for his child's coninent, stepped on and forgotten. That's all it was. But for me nough. Silence overtook me once more as I pictured my faher climbing the steps on his first day of school, small for his ge I imagined, and reserved. Up the steps alone. With the rand new suitcase to last seventeen years. From primer to aledictory, a boarder.

It was now noon, still an hour to go before the funeral ervice. The ceremony. Already the organ had started, I could hear it in the chapel, the right kind of music—to cut you in half. It's part of the ritual. I went directly outside and valked along the Driveway, wondering who had arranged the ervice in the first place, a man in my father's office? somene from the department? I certainly didn't.

It was there, I was thinking—here on this Federal Drive, his is the real ceremony, leaves stirring, the bare earth alive, abbering birds, suddenly speaking in private phrases. Where lse, I thought? what more fitting service? I stood still for everal seconds. Suspension. September. And the blue wind hat always comes back.

Over the grass, past flowerbeds, my feet measuring the lind distance ahead, like a sleepwalker, following the asphalt footpath, grey and white behind the noises of the city.

Around me was a cloak of willow branches as I stood beside the Rideau Canal. In its brown reflection I could see

the roof of the Auditorium, the old arena where I ha
watched my father's spotlights shining down on Sonja Heni
and although it was now mid-September, I was sitting on tl
streetcar with the windows frosted over and my father scra
ing a peep-hole to let the night in, and me dropping off
sleep with my mind set among the wonders to come.

I leaned over the railing, the water softly lapping the c
ment abutment and the shallow bed clear under the autumn
sky. Yellowed poplar leaves dropped on the surface, saile
sideways smooth-skinned and beautiful in the catch of su
behind. My eyes followed the sailing leaves, pretending the
were in a regatta, an attempt to idle my thoughts. It was dif
cult trying to keep down the rancour I felt as I thought of tl
house in Cashel, Tipperary. "One man in the house was mo
than enough"; the words kept springing back at me.

I knew what Mr. Mahoney had meant, and yet I didn'
not fully. Only the background, that's all I knew . . . tl
cold eyes of his mother, his dear father. The part of his li
he had closed forever, what did I really and truly know
what had he felt those times? I couldn't hear his boy's voic
calling, I couldn't visualize and say, So there he is. The co
sciousness of it scraped in my head. I knew I had to redeer
that closed space. For myself.

It was immediately after the burial service, right there i
the cemetery; I walked over to where Mr. Mahoney ha
moved apart and was standing with his hands behind h
back, more or less a stranger now. I cut through shoulde
blades, a homburg was doffed, a hand held out, Mr. M.
honey's presence being all that mattered. Catch phrases sti
festooning the air: translations of His will . . . untimely d
mise. For three days I had listened! and still, the senseless g
ing-on about the car crash. Like wares lined up at the mark
counter, I thought as I turned away. Which did not come a
a shock at all, this turning upon a kindness at once repelle
to me. As it was at the funeral parlour, I could not then se
beauty, the caring in the rustle of gestures, those waxen face
about to arrange themselves around mine. There was som
thing I had to get on with.

Mr. Mahoney's hand reached out. "I need you," I said, an
realized he had been waiting there for me. His eyes were re
Now it was over. And there were only the two of us, or so
felt. "Tell me about my father," I said, ". . . the summe
holidays in Cork with his relations, for instance. You starte
to mention that this morning."

"You'll only be the sadder . . ." he said.

"No," I interrupted. "It's what I still don't know: what I can't describe to myself—not being able to feel I am at last saying to him, 'So that's what you saw and did! how old would you have been then?' That's what makes me sadder. All my life now, wherever I go, I'll never be free of that voice calling to me. 'How are you doing there?' And I will want to answer . . . I will turn around. . . ."

Mr. Mahoney raises his brows; I see nothing unusual, won't my father's presence always be there? ". . . seeing myself as if I hadn't changed at all," I continue, "the child tagging after him, following him somewhere: 'See! Do you see how I'm doing? I *am* you, I am that time. It isn't lost any more.' This is what I'll want to cry out. A while ago that's exactly what I was feeling, it came over me unconsciously.

"I went for a walk this morning after we talked, I wanted to go over things in my mind, I wanted to make them come alive, your school, fields that carried certain sounds. I ached to picture them and I couldn't." I seized his forearm. "Can you appreciate that?" I said, "that I have to see it for myself? otherwise a corner of me will always seem missing." How could I get it across when I could scarcely make words for myself? "What my father was, I am," I said, as if to myself. Autumn sunlight, a single leaf falling; workmen on the ridge of a hill putting rocks into a wheelbarrow. A woman passes, nods, and Mr. Mahoney raises his hat. And then I hear him say: "What you're really asking is whether you carry the same loneliness as your father."

I suppose that was when I sat down on the grass, the maple was something to lean against. Mr. Mahoney sat down too. I don't know—was it my imagination, or did death have a hold on me? my mind dense, immune from shock, groping for a sign, or signs? I couldn't say, No, this is the *end,* that's all there is. At the time I couldn't. There in the quiet, I was convinced all my thoughts were heard, as if being carried in that soft wind. I couldn't get over the wind; the air wasn't empty any more. Which meant I didn't have to sit there trying to believe in something.

Mr. Mahoney had propped one foot over the other and was leaning into the tree-trunk. His pipe was out, Edgeworth tobacco and his thoughts sinking under the thumb packing the bowl. His face inscrutable—summing up? used to me now? or what? my twisting fingers and the soundless cry in me exposing the child, afraid, lost? I don't know. "You

know," he said, "one of the joys of life is bringing up a child.
You listen for them when they're little. Watching over, and
watching for. All you can hope is that they don't grow up to
hate you. I wonder if a parent, when he goes to his grave,
ever knows which one he takes with him?" A match flares
suddenly against the sole of his shoe, an Eddy match, one of
the long ones that will last while he ignites that brown
shredded mass. And I smell with incredible waves of vision
an exact place, an exact time—Sunday evenings, and the
house on Elmdale. In his face, a face shot by the indifferent
light of flame in the wind, I see tracings of worry and laughter; sixty years of bric-a-brac and consequence, and a scar on
his temple I don't seem to recall.

"Tell me about my father," I say. "His music, he wanted
to be a concert pianist, at least that's what I heard my mother
telling someone. Though I never heard my father say so."

"That puts me in mind of a concert he'd played in Cashel
one evening. He'd have been . . . oh, about sixteen, I suppose. After the concert he invited some of the lads to his
home, he wanted to keep on playing. There must have been
seven or eight of us, all dressed up in our best clothes, full of
chatter; it was quite an occasion being asked back to someone's home that late of an evening, and wasn't this grand? Instead of returning to the cold, pewter-smelling air of a
dormitory, here we were warming our hands by a fire.
Many's the time I've thought of that night. Carpets on the
floor, and newspapers lying around, framed photographs
about, the smell of things, you know? Then of course there
was the piano, and your Dad playing away at one end of the
room.

"I tell you, none of us wanted to leave. I'd heard him play
many times, but that night . . . You see the relations he
spent his summers with, an elderly aunt and uncle in Dublin,
both of them musical, had taken him to concerts there, and
to London once, so that—hearing famous artists perform,
and with his ear, what came out sometimes on the keyboard
was the sound he'd carried away with him, not the notes but
the sound of it. And that's what we were hearing. Say, a
descriptive thing by Mendelssohn—was it the 'Spinning Song'
he tried that night?—or a nocturne, or something by Debussy, impressionistic, 'La Mer' for instance. He was experimenting, taking the melodic line but finding his own
harmonies. What music! so expressive! and the movement of
his head, the abandon. Can't explain exactly. And all of us

sitting quietly, without a move really. And that dim room, shot through with the light of cranberry glass. A person doesn't forget. It seemed as if the night itself—well, you could have been saying, What lad is this with such music in his head? Do you know what I mean? . . . Yes, I see you do. What your Dad was feeling, what he had to give . . . Mother of God, it was beautiful." Mr. Mahoney stopped then, and looked down, caressing the grass alongside his trouser leg, a man cut off from the present, as if invaded, compelled by the improbable sound of chords long beyond reach, now resounding inwardly.

"I can hear it," I said, leaning forward and bracing my elbows on my knees. "I can hear Mendelssohn and that hollow echo, the sense of water dripping when he'd . . . that's how it always struck me, not just his hands but his whole body shaping the sounds, hunched over the keyboard, 'peering into Fingal's Cave' he once said."

"And does it bother you? Is this as far—?"

"Of course not. Why would you think that? I'm . . . really, it's fine."

"All right then. Still, by all that's holy, there's one thing I've a mind to leave out—the outcome. Don't seem to recall whether it took place after, or if our months were still full. I just remember the plates of little cakes getting lower and lower. Anyway, your father had carried on with his playing, not looking up at all, in fact totally unaware of his audience. Then he stopped, rubbing the palms of his hands together. And suddenly he swivelled around on his stool and announced he'd decided to turn his studies to music. He'd been thinking about it for some time, he said, and what did we think of the idea?

"In a shot your grandmother had jumped to her feet, crossed through our midst like an angel of terror, and closed the piano lid. She locked it with your father still sitting there. No one in the room moved.

" 'No son of mine will be an itinerant musician,' she declared, and left the room. . . . What she was saying was she disapproved of the stage."

"And approved the lot of a civil engineer," I added.

"Your grandfather had been that proud as he sat there, beaming at his son. I remember he went over to him and put his hand on his shoulder, told him maybe he could do both, he thought he'd make a fine pianist. Why, he'd had the same thing in mind for him all along. 'How would you like to

study in Dublin?' he asked. 'When you're through at Kilkenny, you could go there.'

"The poor man never knew his son's lessons had been ter-
minated then and there—your father would never have burdened him. From that night on, your Dad did his practising
at the home of a family who lived near the school. They'd
heard him in a concert there, they had a piano, they said, and
they'd be honoured to have him come and play."

The tides I needed were washing into place.

"I knew about the family in Kilkenny," I said. "I mean I
can place them because my father wrote a song for them,
'The Windows of Kilkenny'. I remember my mother one day
asking why he didn't turn it into a foxtrot. Which he did. For
her." Something he invented before I was born, I was now
thinking. I could hear the fluidity of those rolling chords, the
minor key. It had always reminded me of a river, not slow
and peaceful at all but a river with currents and bends.

"You know," Mr. Mahoney went on, "no one knew the
song existed till the end of the term that year. We were in the
middle of writing a final exam; I looked up and there was
your Dad filling up his two pages with the score. I couldn't
believe my eyes. When I think of those precise little notes,
and the carefully printed words below—like sheet music."

"Was that like him? I mean he had a lot of whimsy in him
and everything, but . . ."

"I think he was trying to tell the new master there were
other things to learn besides fractions and being good at
games. I remember the lyrics had a lot to do with children.
Likely your father was looking back on his earlier days then,
and the young ones, the new lot arriving for Fall term."

"What did they say?"

"Say? . . . oh, about the sheet music! Wastebasket. But
not before the pages were held up in front of the class. Without anything being said."

"Did he get another try?"

"Goodness knows, I can't quite remember." He searches
the sky, shakes his head, ". . . it escapes me. They'd have
passed him anyway, he was always good at school."

"The Windows of Kilkenny". I glanced over at the grave.
Petals. Petals in the wind . . . vague sounds . . . yes—the
people—I should return. I've never been in a cemetery before, the sunlight . . . why does it strike sound, a shrill
brassy sound?

"Tell me something that's crazy, Mr. Mahoney." I watched him through his pipe smoke, drifting past me in blue layers.

"Ah well," he said, glancing around at the tombstones as if they were creatures about to reprove, "a bit of the devil in your Dad, you know. Take the time in Dublin, 1913 I believe it was. Now that must have given him a show of his own back-talk." Mr. Mahoney edged nearer and inclined his head as though his words were intended for our knees. "Climbed a lamp post on O'Connell Street with a Rebel flag, he did, tied the thing to a bolt under the globe, then gave it a wee flick so it'd catch the wind. And him a Protestant! I would say the impulse was out of a dare, though, your father had enough strife of his own without inclining himself to others."

From the look of him, pleased and pink as a cherub, I wondered if Mr. Mahoney had been the one who gave the dare. Drawing harder on his pipe, a funnel of smoke shot triumphantly out of his mouth and curved away in the wind. "Of course things were different in those days," he pointed out. "Not like the troubles that followed, what with the Easter Rebellion and all," he added reassuringly, purposefully, I thought.

"So it *was* you who gave the dare."

There were leaves blowing around us, little piles of scarlet and gold that settled like bright badges at our feet. I remember too the intermittent gusts tackling Mr. Mahoney's thick hair while he regaled me once more with the feat of O'Connell Street, recounting in even greater detail how the two of them had watched from a pub as the banner was taken down. Shaking his head as memory trickled light into that September afternoon. For me, his soft brogue bringing back to life that cold space beyond, the earth-hollow where December snows soon would fall—blizzards, and winking stars . . . and fireflies? I thought of a lot of things like that. In my mind I could hear the sound of a Gatineau train whistle, and the putt-putt of a dory heading into the waves at Canso; sound by sound my senses articulated the rhythmic stoke of the furnace coming up through my bedroom register. All the night sounds you pay attention to as you gather in the lonely-sweet concord of their company.

"Right there on O'Connell Street," I heard Mr. Mahoney say again, his voice in a higher pitch, pleased that the conversation had gained new distinction. But I was now out of talk—the smell of fresh-dug earth had drifted past, overpowering the roses and carnations fluttering lifelessly in the sun.

We stood up, our minds returned to globes far from
O'Connell Street: the white moonfaces of mourners I scarcely
knew. Six of them left now. Tirelessly waiting. They tiptoe
around in aimless circles. Disembodied whispers. Faces looking longingly at their parked cars, calculating the distance to
the cemetery gates. Two taxis waiting. The meters running.
Why don't I make some effort? My behaviour . . . all this
time paying heed to no one except Mr. Mahoney. "I'll go
with you," he had offered when we stood up, "it's no place
for you to be standing. I'll walk over with you and explain."

But no. Not yet. Those sounds I heard a minute ago, running through me, something, out of focus, but fixed. My
mind reaches, my eyes peer, and see myself. I'm being put to
bed without supper. What are they talking about? what do
they mean, "She's not fit to be in the same room"? What
have I done? I see my eyes are burning. But no tears, my
face is shining! At the top of the stairs, a bedroom . . . the
stairway is long and narrow and dark. My Grandmother
Watson's house? The focus, no distortion, no, I'm visiting my
grandmother in Cashel! Now what? My mother is with us,
she's there but my father isn't, I don't see him at all. Strange
surroundings. . . .

Formalities could wait, I decided suddenly, and steered
Mr. Mahoney off course and down a grassy slope. "There's
something I want to tell you," I whispered close to his face.
Still cherishing his O'Connell Street memories, Mr. Mahoney
was moist in his eyes. But mine had come alive, to honour
malice.

Was he listening, paying attention? I pulled at his sleeve
and asked him again.

"Do you remember when my mother took us to Ireland?"
He said, yes, he did indeed. I would have been four or five.

"Well, I guess I had something to say to her after all. We
were in the front parlour, I think it was there; anyway, she
was on the other side of the room, sitting by the window with
her eyes fixed on me. I can't remember exactly what I was
doing at that moment but I suddenly got up and kicked her
in the shins, once on each leg. Mamma said, 'Whatever did
you do that for?' And I told her I didn't know. I just felt like
it. I just felt like it!"

And that was perfectly true. Later that same night, before
I went to sleep, I got out my crayon book and drew my
grandmother's legs. With bruises up to the knees. Then I
started telling myself that tomorrow I would go to her and

say I was sorry. But in the morning, when she looked at me, expecting it, I never let on I noticed. I didn't want to lose hold of the mystery of why I did it, a secret I seemed to treasure.

I wonder, did Mamma ever tell Daddy? I hope so, I hope she used some red and blue ink, to show him exactly. Maybe my grandmother did, in one of the letters he never opened.

---

The door closed softly on my father's Irish history, a significant softness when, along with his suitcase—sheet music and the hope of his mind cramming it full—he swung into that one final spring day: a sun in the sky or a drizzle to see him off, his freedom one step ahead. Surely a grin on his face. With his degree in his pocket and a kitten he'd found in a pail at the railway depot, my father left Dublin forever and set sail as a wireless operator on the first boat that would hire him. Among the passengers was John McCormack. And with him at the Captain's table sat the newly-signed-on crew member who, later that evening, was to accompany Ireland's great tenor at an impromptu concert in the First-Class Saloon. "Kathleen Mavourneen", "Macushla", "I Hear You Calling Me". Once more, for old times' sake. And the sounds falling upon the ears of passengers and crew, on the ears of someone perhaps sitting in a corner off by themselves. Nights at sea, mid-Atlantic, a steamship plying the dark swells, her lights blazing and all around the wash of the infinite.

But he needed his roots; it was there he had learned to speak, had seen his first flower, and stood on a stone bridge, momentarily brushed by the braid of his mother's hair as she stooped to pick him up—the coil that stood for something then. And always would I guess. He lived, he died. And banked by those still-intact roots, I understand better now. Not at the cemetery, when I sat on the grass with Mr. Mahoney, not then at all. So just when? now? this minute? last year?

I think now of an evening in September. We are at the piano, my father and I, weary and on edge from sleepless nights of paralysing city heat. For over an hour the house shook to its last brick. I sat on my corner of the bench, plugging my fingers into my ears at the dissonances between keyboard and elements. But then! A lightning bolt ripped through the sky hitting the transformer across the street. My fingers came flying out of my ears and my elbows crashed

down at the bass. I whinnied at the sparks shooting from the
piano light a sit sputtered off in a gangrenous smoke. My father was quick with his wits. Darkness and all he plunged into
the "Indian Love Lyrics". And, accompanying himself, wailed
like a bagpipe. His scuffing of the keyboard combined with
his wailing drowned out even the thunderbolts.

A break in the music, and I hear two spoons tapping.
"Sweet Georgia Brown," my mother calls out from the
kitchen. Between them, they do keep things going! My father
perhaps hasn't heard, does not honour my mother's request,
for he has bounded off the bench and into a half-demented
and circuitous softshoe. And keeping up the silly bagpipe
whine. My mother appears in the kitchen doorway clutching
an old Campbell's Soup tin she uses for her homemade
candles. "Sweet Georgia Brown," she sing-songs, vocally
stamping her foot, and proceeds to disgorge a few bars on
her own. Two rhythms going there. Comic relief. Catching
hold of me and my terror. I sit on the rug hugging my knees,
crying and laughing (though mostly weeping), at the vaudeville, the cacophony, and at the dog that has retrieved my
hair ribbon and lies with it between his huge green teeth. My
hysteria, become voiceless, buries itself in the burr-matted
fur. It does not seem so bad, after all.

Afterward, when the piano light blinked on again and the
night was quiet outside, my father let down, a barometric
drop that made him seem suddenly removed, in a space of
his own. His eyes appeared to be looking right through the
room and beyond, as though he were rolling up the honky-
tonk into a now-passed memory. Something, I don't know
what, brought him back. He picked up a slipper that had
gone flying into a corner during his dance and as he fitted it
back on he looked into the kitchen and winked at my mother.
I felt eased. But even though he starts back to the piano and
hitches up his trousers over the bends of his knees, even
though he pats a spot for me as much as to say "Well now—
storm's over, on with the programme," I know there will be no
more alehouse pibroch. Not tonight. Something I sensed as
strongly as if he'd written it out.

And I was right. His fingers pressed down firmly into the
keys and he held them there long through the pedal, as
though he had found himself at an organ high in the transept
of some great cathedral. It was "The Children's Prayer". And
it came out lonely and lost. I watched him, bent low, as if
taken over by the mission of children, as if it were his own

blood crying softly. Was it my tears? He hadn't seen me cry before, not like that. I want to tell him it was exaggerated. Except that would be a lie. And he knows more of what I think and feel than I do myself.

The piano bench holds our silent dialogue, makes unnecessary the telling of broken or mended certainties. I am glad I did not mention the uncomfortable version of "The Children's Prayer", for whatever symbol or shadow my dismal panic made relevant, my father's mind is rid of it. I feel new glimpses racing back to him. He has made the switch to "Musetta's Waltz Song". What now has come into that mind, that tuneful ear? What's *La Bohème* got to do with children in a forest? It has me wondering again, the way he mixes up his music. Those traces of tallow wax smoke from my mother's candle have gone deeper than his nose, I tell myself. Bringing back the sometime-somewhere-*Bohèmes* scored through the sum of him. He has furrowed his brow (something he does more from habit than anything else, I've noticed; a sudden self-revelation he voices between his eyebrows). He pauses to roll another cigarette and doesn't say anything. I have a feeling he will play it right through this time. I can tell by the way he's hitching up his trousers, the down-to-business of it.

As though in a prelude of its own making, the room has taken on a sober quiet, and it is symmetrically dim—there's only the piano light, with a squat, brass shade that compels the bulb to stare at the keyboard. One more waiting eye, listening for my father to begin. And try as I may, I cannot prevent myself from shifting closer as he slips into the tender and dark *Bohème* I know. Even if he is immersed in that same back-and-forth trance. With his eyes closed. I close mine too and hear the music through its images, sorting out destinies through their faces and hands, and the candlelight in the garret, believing that soft and immense flaming, the foretelling. But I become vulnerable to the foretold as it recedes into a terrible beautiful sadness. The pedal tone holds. What's left in its dying-away sound becomes illusory, exotic, as I make of it what I want. I leave a door open. I do not imagine death.

A curious mixture, "The Children's Prayer" and Puccini's flamboyant intensity. What other silenced songs is my father counterpointing in his mind? I sense somewhere in him a harking back: to "cut boughs". That's what I've heard my mother say. Cut boughs! Perhaps across the tallow wax scent, made retentive by the mist-thin rain still falling, some remembered fragment joins edges. A footfall. A particular possession. A loss grown diminished.

A light dances in his eyes and my senses feel its chords. He is telling me something, I think. But I do not comprehend. What can it mean to me when I have not heard a gate clang shut on all the lost time? The wounds I bear are no deeper yet than the scabs on my knees. This light in his eyes. It's a voice I feel. But that is not the same as knowing. Still, I am his child beside him on the bench, his leaf of darkness and joy. I am his edge of dreams, his white-socked, listening flesh pressed close, trying to talk his language in a tongue he longs to remember, as I do now, while the branches outside my window scrape, as if to come in from the storm.

# IX

As if to come in from the storm. Even the trees. Elms a hundred years old cracking in the cold, expressing themselves. In another moment a gust will lift the bare boughs and hang them elsewhere, away from my window; they'll claw the darkness instead.

The night is alive with choruses of the pitching wind, late November gales that have me wide-awake, going in the direction of things I cared about. From the window seat I shout at the top of my voice, in the sleeping night I cry out to the beautiful wind. And the huge elms shrug; trees understand these things, I tell myself. They are our incarnate selves, they also have pores.

Often when the wind blows like this, in a fury, ruthless almost, and the sky without moon or stars, a dead dimension black as a grave, then the night stares back at me like an insistent voice, as though it too had things to say. Overhanging streetlamps in the rear laneway swing crazily, dramatic spins of light that climb the backs of houses and down again over the flat-roofed garages, circling once more high into the arch of trees. Up and down the lane, the metal shades tilt; intermittent rushes of light redesign the earth, seeming at times to weave temples and columns, tracts of land luminous with mists that shroud human forms. And beyond this present world, yet seeming very close, I imagine an ancient land that's earthly and permanent and set in the quiet of evening. It makes my flesh leap; an emotion, with the power of an anthem. Unreal and once in a while unsettling. But it registers. I jump up, seized with an urge to climb to a topmost limb; and accustomed once to this straddling of branches, in my mind I am up top again, hands tight around the thickest joint, riding fierce as the wind, my voice shrill, streaming, a current answering the other side of the world.

Standing in silence I hear myself uttering my name, my own, and I sing out: I yell, "It's me! Wait for me."

Sometimes it's like this when the wind is wild; deep down I'm trying to convince myself—I want to believe in what I call out.

I dream of my exchanges being answered, or heard. It's better than nothing.

# X

Nothing? Whatever made me say that? when I think that even blankness is made up of something, an energy force maybe, standing in its own significance like a vacant lot.

In this room, a fixed kind of silence, set off against shifting howls of wind and a garage door that's come unhinged—and the centre of my being breathes easily. Acceptance, perhaps, the senses having wandered, pulled through an afternoon of emptier gusts: the slower, more serene wind of the cemetery.

I was thirty-five the year my father died, and late that night, reaching Ottawa, I went upstairs to my old room and sat alone in the dark, thinking of him not as he was in my

adult years, nor even while I was a youngster, when he had
sat on the bed too, listening to my prayers. I was thinking of
a time before that, trying to imagine, to bring into focus a
young man's face, the motion of his slender frame scurrying
around the bungalow at Canso, imagining too what his words
to Mimi might have been. In my mind I saw him stopping to
sit beside her, her weary half-smile as he smoothed her damp
hair; then, later, leaping about the bedroom as he welcomed
his firstborn. What would they have said, afterward, when the
ordeal was over and it was quiet again, and the stars already
pale in the dawn? I couldn't seem to think of anything else
that night. But then, what else would have come so swiftly to
mind? It was my birthday.

There's no retreat; I know that. The other self grows
louder, is in control; at least tonight it is. I push my hair
back, and fiddle with the chintz pad on the window-seat.
How strange to be sitting here, one body, two voices bound
up each with the other, still unscrambling this name, that
place, what followed. Who can translate all these locked-in
presences, and why must they linger so in the mind? springing up to face you like something out of a time zone, naked,
intact, as if lit by flares. That's what it feels like. No wonder
I want to yell.

Three minutes ago is the past, I am thinking; everything
taking place becomes memory. Will these trees ever look as
lovely again? or as ruthless? branches pointed downward, up,
the creak, snap, lashing; battling the winds higher, and
higher, lyrical riffs for the mind to catch, implying victory?
Memory is snow, and that train ride, and rainsoaked blueberries; memory is a trombone, and a hotel parking-lot over in
Hull. Memory is stairways and doorknobs, a certain doorway
I walked through, another, still others, adding up to cities,
towns, villages.

My hand grips, squeezes, not the old Teddy Bear I saw in
my mind just now, nor even the softball . . . but this glass of
rye and ginger ale. Backside leaning against the kitchen
counter; shoeless, half-conscious, muttering rapidly, a pang of
this, and the relief of a shriek bursting my lungs. But good
God! how long have I been poking around the kitchen?

Back to the window-seat, the chintz. What is covered up in
all that sky? That's what I keep wondering. Which mysteries
are real? People die, but after a while there's no sense of
death having distance—they seem to know something and
you want to talk to them, as if you'd made a promise. Or is it

only my need? They played music, and burned leaves, and watched eclipses, and answered the loons, and bought you a red dress and three gold and silver bangles for your first dance. And now you can't get rid of the sounds, the smells; the colours; something inside you rises up, spills over, in me it does.

———

I was remembering a school in Edinburgh, and snow falling on the Braid Hills at Christmas in that same city, and then a steward aboard the steamer *Letitia* who gave me a broken string of moonstones. Images of the winter I was eleven, that rushed through my mind in a fragmented way, some disintegrating like ice splinters, others holding moments that came clear. I saw myself with a face screwed up, unpleasant, George's quality of harmony putting me to shame. I was reminded of being somewhere I didn't want to be: away from home, from wherever my father was.

He hadn't come with us. Why not? It must have seemed like a long time then. Everything so far away.

Now that we were settled in, in that draughty flat in Scotland, I got the feeling we would be staying with Granny White forever. If we'd just come for a visit, which is what George and I had been told in the fall, then how come it was winter now? It seemed there would be no end, no end at all. And all the while a vague, indeterminate sense of loss, the days passing, as if life had suddenly sprung a hole and everything was spilling out, away from us.

Glancing across the table at my mother: does she think this is a nice place to live? George and I sitting glum-faced, solemn-voiced, chewing the sleeves of our sweaters, minds picking up pieces of conversation and then slipping away, escaping as we sampled the other sleeve. Five of us around the table. Talk, talk, talk. Our Aunt Isa and Uncle Tom, Mamma's elder sister and younger brother who lived with Granny too, flushed and obsessed with their Scottish complexions, insisting we'd soon be real Scots, *Hielanders,* polite and well-behaved like other children, and before we knew it we'd have roses in our cheeks, the same as other bonnie lads and lassies, "Who eat their porridge every day," one or the other was quick to remind us, between mouthfuls they slurped up like soup.

"The children had roses in their cheeks when they arrived," Granny called out from her bed one day.

"We didn't have chilblains, though," George ventured, and held up a set of puffy red toes, rolling up his pyjama leg so we'd have a better view, for some reason examining the shiny skin proud as could be, as though it were a trophy.

"Feet belong on the floor," Aunt Isa put in softly.

"Oh they do, do they?" Mamma's voice, hissing like beads of cold water sputtering on a woodstove. "And who says so?" Then turning her head, the fire cooled down, "You're at the table, George."

"I've got chilblains on *both* feet," I announced.

"Trust you," Mamma sighed, waving a spoon in the air. A gob of treacle pudding dropped on the lid of the brown sugar bowl. "You always did have to have two of everything."

"And you know where she gets that from, Mary," Uncle Tom said. "Her mother."

"Maybe," she replied.

"Maybe!? Maybe, you say!" Uncle Tom bent low over the table and gathered us all in with huge brown eyes. Good night. Are they going to start *that* again? That's enough for me. I knew what was coming: what else? during these Sabbath suppers: having been into the bottle and the "wee doch-an-dorris" 's and "It's a braw brecht moonlecht necht th' necht". That accent! I used to sit and listen to them, Aunt Isa, a beaming, bright-eyed and happy woman, and Uncle Tom, newly engaged, being teased by my mother, chairs drawn up before the small Victorian fireplace, faces aglow in the late afternoon, the front room pungent with the gas of coal fumes and savouries and wallpaper smelling of boiled meat. "Having a wee tot," they'd say. "Keeping the Sabbath."

"Will ye no' have a wee drop?" Uncle Tom would call down the hall to Granny, who would reply from her bed, "What dear?" At the sideboard, the tinkle of a glass touching the rim of the bottle of Scotch whiskey, Uncle Tom filling up his glass. "Again?" I would ask. "But you had one. You had yours!"

"Ah," he'd reply, "but you see I like mine neat." And I would sit down again, satisfied, having somehow come to the conclusion that if you didn't add water, you were being more sparing, that's why he had come to the end of his first, that fast. Except my mother did too, right after, I noticed. And Aunt Isa with hers. The room would grow dark, firelight playing with fringe on the velour armchairs, across brass urns, the fire-tongs, and I'd hear their voices low, alive, "tak a cup o'kindness" . . . "yer a' recht", and another wee "tot".

If the drinks went to their heads I wasn't aware: all I could think of was, Why are they *happy* talking that terrible way? *It's a braw brecht moonlecht necht!* Why do they have to carry on so? like folklore. We were supposed to laugh, George and I. But I didn't think it was so comical.

That's how it was that night at the table, Uncle Tom fishing for something in his pockets, his face (with a pipe clenched between his teeth) urging us to listen, while he dealt with the important subject of where one of my characteristics had come from.

"Maybe!?" he said again to my mother, the tongue getting ready to roll. "Thurr-rrr's nae doot aboot it, Mare-rry."

"I hate it when you talk that way, Uncle Tom," I said quietly. "And her name is not Mary, it's Mimi."

"She's Mare-rrry t' me lass," he replied, giving me a close look as he reached for a clothespin, clamping one of my curls to the hem of my dress.

"Would you like to see my other foot?" George asked, his head bringing up part of the tablecloth as he straightened, taking it all in his stride: whatever grownups said, or what he believed them to have said, of no consequence.

"Yurr-rrr othur-rrr foooot?" Mamma laughed. "Ae George, but it is no' enough t've seen t'othurrr one?"

"I want to go home," I said, reaching across the table and pulling at my mother's arm. "It's crazy here."

Without first asking permission, I left the table and wandered into my grandmother's room. I sat beside her on the bed, my head down. I felt ashamed, and was close to blubbering. The smell of the sick tray, wretched with slicks of boiled milk, and bottles of medicine and an enamel vessel heaped with discarded wads of cotton batting, yellowed and sodden with camphorated oil—I did not want to be in that room either.

"Is it not bonnie spending a wee whiley with your Granny?" she said. "Is it not home to you?" Her voice so soft and caressing as she untangled the clothespin from my hair.

"It's okay," I said, not looking up.

"You've not been giving it much of a chance, now have you? Why, scarcely three weeks have passed . . ."

"No, I guess not, Gr-r-r-ahnny," I said, my tongue taking a run for her benefit as well as my own. I wanted to make myself laugh, having learned that tears often turned into laughter.

"Just think!" she exclaimed. "All the things you'll have to

tell your father when you go back." She leaned forward from the pillows. "Why not write him a wee note this very minute?"

"I already did. Do you know my father?"

"Of course I do, wee lass."

"Then he wasn't just *saying* that?"

"Saying what, dear?"

"About you . . . when he was seeing us off at the boat, and . . . did you know he came all the way to Montreal with us on the train? Well, we were out on the deck, it was after the funnel blew . . . the funnel was still blowing and he hugged me and said: 'You'll love your Granny. Will you tell her I said that?' I was crying. I wanted him to come too, and I thought he was just saying that to make me feel better." She took my right hand in both of hers, her fingers seeming so tiny as they stroked, the sweetness of her for some reason flowing past me. I was suddenly embarrassed. "Is he going to come and get us?" I asked.

"We'll see he has lots of letters," she said, ignoring the question. "We'll keep the postie busy." The back of her hand not veined but pure white, and fragile, transparent almost, and I drew away. I didn't know her very well, I didn't know her at all. I sensed wanting to feel close to her, but only to talk, we could be close with thoughts. I didn't want her to touch me—she would have expected me to love her back, put my arms around her neck, but that was something I wanted to save for my father and mother.

---

Weeks passed. November, early December. George and I were enrolled at school now. Gone all day, each day a fusion one with the other, fading from the night of one into the late afternoon of another. Upon reaching home, no longer did we run breathless up the four flights of stairs to the flat. Anything to dawdle, we thought, to lose ourselves. I'd stand perfectly still on the stone stairs, leaning over the spiral banister and looking down into the stairwell, as if seeking within that clammy darkness the answer to how long we would have to stay.

I remember a late afternoon, shortly before the Christmas holidays, George and I were sitting on one of the landings midway up the stairs. Our shoes—brogues—were caked with dried mud, and wordlessly we scraped away, George using a twig from a holly bush he'd found on the sidewalk, and me the less wieldy point of a cloth-covered textbook. "What muck," we muttered. "Not clean dirt like it is at home."

Seeing myself now, ourselves, huddled together, preoccupied, pushing the little mounds of Braid Hills earth into a dark corner beside the wall—it was a pretty good time; we were more on our own. Maybe that's what felt wrong. We were used to being a family; breakfast, the Sunday funnies and the hubbub of who's-got-what-section? twilight . . . we were our own island, nobody was somewhere else.

And here we were, transported from the trafficless plain of a neighbourhood to the whirl and confusion of jewellery shops, bakeshops, booksellers, theatre marquees and sidewalk artists, the bums and the fashionable of Tollcross in the heart of a big city. Gone for hours at a stretch without anyone seeming the least worried, or even surprised. As I think of it, would there not have been a few hawkeyed shrieks? the shops on Lothian Road we darted in and out of, for instance, and riding the two-decker buses until asked for our fares, the policemen we stopped to talk to? Secrets? as we moved through the multitudes, unknown, criss-crossing the intersections to see what was afoot, peeking up and down laneways, like urchin conspirators. Would there not have been moments, conscious or otherwise, of Can I stay here forever? Or did the sights please only our eyes, glances of curiosity with no emotion, our minds closed to these streets, to the smoke sailing above twilight chimney pots, experiencing them merely as particulars associated with being on our own? Maybe that was what was wrong.

The senses. Spoiled, and yet that is not quite true; we were far from pampered, that was important, and we accepted our punishments as coming to us. We had been spoiled in another way. And so were unaware our resistance to change was only the first, the shock that pointed the way, telling us nothing is permanent. Right then, was the early, taken-for-granted promise of life being taken away? How could we have known, clumping around in those enormous foolish brogues, that we were learning to stand on our own feet, that sooner or later people have to live for, within themselves? they have to forget about the Sunday funnies, a pet kitten, conversations in our own accent: they're gone. The self is there in their place, has become the sum, and, good or bad, is the one thing you cannot change.

Is it better, I wonder, if in the beginning you're not made soft by the warm padding . . . is that the best way? no fun, no rubber boots and a rowboat to remember, or a hero to look back on, no one who cares much, the spirit toughened up good and early, growing hard, no places and voices and winds to hold it captive?

I know my own answer.

Anyway. Now that our clumpy brogues were cleaned off, the soles good as new—not because of Granny's floors, she wouldn't have minded what George and I tracked in; it was on account of school, the headmistress had made us sit a whole day in stocking-feet, our dirty shoes outside in the hall—we lingered on the landing under the skylight, as though we were sitting in a waiting-room, the straps and buckles of our schoolbags less sharp under numbing behinds, feet knocking together, like pistol shots ringing through a catacomb. The two of us were laughing, but I was also angry, mad at the whole of Scotland. We were talking about letters to our father, and the pantomime we'd seen the day before.

---

The pantomime at the King's Theatre had already started when we sat down, and the comedian, a lumbering giant of a man who hadn't bothered to shave, was in the process of making what he said was his prize cake recipe. Clouds of flour and shredded coconut flew about his shoulders, as well as egg yolks, and handfuls of fat, slug-like raisins. Looking closer, I confided to George they must be either June bugs or sheep dirt. As he measured and added the ingredients, the comedian announced in a loud voice what each one was, sucking his fingers noisily, nodding at his pint-sized assistant, a timid clown with sunken eyes who in turn held up over-sized boxes and jars, the contents identified by jagged block lettering, like children's printing. Nutmeg, gumdrops, sage (*sage?*).

"And now," said the comedian craftily, "we need some thyme." Slyly stroking his stubble, he grabbed the tin box from the clown's hands. Then, after holding it at length above the mixing bowl, he turned the contents upside down and dumped in an alarm clock. We jumped, ohhh . . . had someone played a trick on him? the clock's alarm going off, ear-splitting shrieks ricocheting off the walls, hysterical people falling half out of their seats. And George and I looking around and wondering what everybody was laughing at. Thyme? We had never seen that word before, and the lady in front turned around and asked Mamma would she mind saving her explanation for the intermission. "I was talking to the children," Mamma told her. "Do you not have anything better to listen to?"

That's what I was laughing about on the landing with George. Not at the thyme joke, which Mamma had explained later (letting us taste a sample at Granny's kitchen cupboard), but at the back of the woman's head: a foul, fish-smelling dome rigid on the long neck, the wild frizzy hair, the hat, not moving, like a target dead ahead. To keep from laughing I had tried not to look—but that head! I couldn't stop, it was funnier than the show.

"You made it up," George said suddenly, vexed, his voice carrying lightly down the stairwell, the skylight too dim to reveal his expression, "those weren't June bugs. In my letter to Daddy I'm going to put they were raisins." He shifted his schoolbag, slid his cap over one of the steel buckles and eased himself back.

"Me too," I said.

"Are you going to tell him about the lady in front?"

"Sure. I'm going to tell him everything." I picked at a crevice in the wall, flaking the dried paint. "I always do. Don't you?"

The building was cold and damp and the windowless hallways had grown suddenly dark, the glass fanlight above us blotchy with wet filth, perhaps it was snowing, melting as it fell. It was close to Christmas, and I thought of the pink map in the Atlas. In my mind I saw snow falling on white ground, and clumps breaking away from the crook of a branch onto the blue shadow of a snowdrift. What would my father be doing now, I wondered?

Someone's doorbell rang in a flat below, a jangling sound, more like that of a fire-alarm box. That was the only sound we heard, magnified in the vast space surrounding us. After a while I said to George, "I think us being here's got something to do with Mamma . . ." breaking off in the middle when my jaw cracked.

"Gee, is that a tooth?" George asked gently. I shook my head, and pulled the side of my mouth open for inspection.

"I saw stars though. Boy, did I ever!" We were eating—crunching—flavourless boiled candies, a bag of "sweets" one of the teachers had given us, unexpectedly.

"It's on account of Mamma we're here," I began again, unnerved by the explosion of the last crunch constricting the top of my head. "I just know it is. Something to do with her not wanting to leave Granny." Opening the bag wider, on his lap, George searched through the mix of satiny pastels and multi-coloured stripes, settled for a green striped oval and held it flat against his coat as if it were a button.

"Something, I guess, the way Mamma is always putting her arms around her," he said wistfully, working the candy through a buttonhole. "Something, I guess," he said again, the tone lighter, resigned, the tone of an adult shrugging, "Who knows?" The green stripe into the mouth. Resting his chin in his hands. Frowning. The taste?

No. He was thinking of something to say. "I like Granny though. I feel sorry for her . . . she has nothing to do. Is Granny very old?" I did not answer; every day at this hour we asked the same questions, at last letting these exchanges go by, and sat with elbows propped, as though unseen in the fading light.

What it was we did not know. We did not understand these things. We just kept saying, "I hate it here, don't you?" or at least I did. And George would reply, "Sort of," and look away, uncertain, but not displaying the gloom I was, the hopelessness as I passed my hand back and forth over the worn stone.

A door in the hallway opposite opened, a woman's face peered out. "Oh, I didn't know it was you two," she said, and closed the door. Flicking the last of the dried mud from our clothing, we got up and climbed the remaining stairs.

Dislocation . . . the extent of it! This was not the same as when we left Canso, no similarity whatsoever. Things went on happening then, the same as before: clotheslines, the wooden doorstep, the dining-room table, it meant tooth-brushes in a glass and napkin rings the Indians had made. And something else: a place where I had never had to say to myself, I am afraid.

Was this, then, my first encounter with fear, the sense of it rising up in me? At school in Ottawa I used to say, Who wants to be going around scared all the time? I'm not. Brave me! I wasn't scared of the dark, nor of a bogeyman, nor for that matter of anything else children are supposed to be frightened of, like a drunk man or a runaway horse, and certainly not of the mysterious, face-blackened ragpicker from Hull, who I'd heard dragged children into his junk wagon and made off with them. As for the neighbourhood bully—I thought nothing of walking up to him and landing a good punch. No. My sense of wellbeing was not disrupted by things I could get at, or reason with, like the dark. How different now, this fear, like a sharp weight, a metal cone turning inside me upon the first realization, vague and elusive as it was, that I might one day wake to discover my home was gone, I didn't have my father any more. Why, you heard about orphans all the time, I kept thinking.

Did this burden of love start there, in Scotland? Was I trying to protect myself from it even then?

And! I see something else. As I walked in the winter dusk, past a railroad station, down an embankment, the Firth of Forth, under the bridge and on, eleven years old, and the self turning its head . . . there was something. Or, as I stood on the grounds of a square, tapping to the prance of horses in a military parade, what of the gleam, the martial airs I could hear? As I tapped, as I slept, was I not being awakened to love in a more mystical form—the pull of my own land?

By now (was it almost Christmas time? I remember there was holly hanging on the wall, and talk of St. Nicholas), I knew that Granny was very sick. I'd heard Mamma tell the man in the butcher shop that's why she came home: ". . . very sick," she was saying. "And I wanted to see her once more because she's dying." I didn't know there was any connection between "dying" and "dead". I took "dying" to mean the same as having to stay in bed all the time; there was nothing else I could think of. At the time, I had just scooped a handful of sawdust from the floor into my pocket and now had my head under the green curtain in the shop window, I wanted to touch the dead rabbit hanging up, and I thought: That's what all grandmothers do, I guess. First they get sick in bed, and after a while they just go away some place.

I loved my grandmother, as a child loves all gentle things, like a pet bunny, or someone warm and soft that's nice to sit and talk to—until the novelty wears off. Already I had stopped asking was there anything I could get her, I didn't bother bringing her a glass of water when she had a wheezing spell either. For I had begun to resent her, she was the cause of our being there. Everything was all her fault. And so one day I decided to ask her how long she was going to be dying.

Pink and shining, her blue eyes too bright, she was sitting up against a bundle of pillows, which is the way she went to sleep too. She held out her hand and said, "Bless you, child. Not long, dear. And what did you and George do today? Did you go up to the Castle?" Same old question. Except that's where we went after school most times, it was near where we lived; schoolbags strapped to our backs, the Castle a retreat now, the dungeons a kind of home away from home, pretending as we descended below that we were escaped prisoners searching for a secret passage. And Granny, waiting for us to come home, always the frail arms outstretched.

She liked us to tell her about the ramparts, and the cannons. In our own words, she'd say, an excuse to hear, once more, by word or enactment, what was going on in the esplanade where the kilties walked up and down—as if what had been there for centuries had, with this latest visit, changed overnight; the mixture as before but with new ingredients, wanting to hear everything, pleased with the gleaming blue eyes: "And what did the pipers say to you this time? Did you do the Highland Fling for them?" In those moments, me on one side of the bed and George on the other, excited, both talking at once, two sets of eyes confirming, telling her what she wanted to know, that we were having fun, and maybe, just then, at least for a little while, we did not miss home. Though what I remember most now is not the Castle at all, but the cripples. World War I over twelve years before, and yet here it was, its presence all around us: amputees; empty trouser legs, folded-up sleeves; faces of the shell-shocked; faces of those who'd been gassed, or blinded. Jesus. I'd see them on the streets, in railway coaches, and in tearooms, shuffling and groping about platforms at Waverley Station. Pensioners—in their twenties. What was really going through my mind then, I wonder, as I stared at a burned-out hole for a face? I used to worry about them: how do they eat without any hands—or a mouth? will they be well again one day? and see again? finding nothing in what Granny or anyone else had to offer by way of explanation. After a while, I didn't mention it any more. For I had ceased to be shocked, no longer compelled to turn around. My age had mercifully imposed a time-limit on my concern for the scars, the injustices sustained by others. The reality was: they belonged to one world, and I to another, 3,000 miles away.

In the front hall, standing under the gaslight fixture on the wall, what do my brother and I talk about as we buckle our schoolbags? conscious of a tap running in the kitchen, Mamma doing the breakfast dishes; the door of Granny's room ajar and Aunt Isa braiding her hair; Uncle Tom in the bathroom with his foot on the tub, polishing his shoes before leaving for work. And with the exception of Granny, all bossing one another, their voices carrying from room to room:

"Pigheaded!" . . . "Go soak your head." . . . "Tom, I'll bust you one in the kisser!" Sooner or later one or the other appearing in a doorway, attention suddenly diverted: "Haven't you two left for school yet!?" No, we've been too busy listening. *When are they going to mean what they say?* with hard feelings, then we'd *have* to go, they'd want us to be on the next boat. "Is this all you're going to fight with Uncle Tom, Mamma?" I asked. "Can't you say worser things?"

"Fight? About what? On your way, or you'll be late for school." Navy blue velour hat and a James Gillespie School beanie down the flight of stairs, early-morning fog sweeping the narrow streets, swallowing us as if within another greyness.

What else but for George and me to run away? That's what we did. Early one afternoon, it was—had school been let out at noon that day? or was it one of the noon-hours we had sat on a hillside bench overlooking the cricket green behind the school, and said, "No matter what, we're never going back *there*! having to stand up and sing daft songs, shouting 'Men of Harlech' and 'D'ye ken John Peel?' with a bunch of sissies in kilts."

We had put the mail back in Granny's letter-box at the main entrance, no letter from our father. And there we stood, feet planted wide apart on the concrete floor, hands behind our backs, butts bumping monotonously against the plaster wall, faces rubbing back and forth against the inside of our coat collars: "What are we going to do? . . . I know!"

Counting our pennies (would there still be enough for an orange and some sugar-cakes?) then wham! out the big metal door, turning right, the shop on the corner; cream-buns and a sugar-cake in a paper bag, a slice of ham and some figs mooched from the butcher in another, as we headed out— across the street to the Cameo movie-house.

Already, weeks before, we'd treated ourselves to a snooze in one of its curtained boxes, availed ourselves of the toilet as well. We had just walked in, one Sunday afternoon when the cleaners were there; the doors were standing open and we wanted to see where the smell was coming from, formaldehyde, and other strange smells. "Why don't they ever bring us here to the pictures," George had asked as we sidled past a man with rags and a set of brooms, "when the movie's right where we live?" We had lingered, walking up and down the empty rows, would they mind if we sat down? A small theatre, with wine-coloured plush seats, roomy and low down

so you could sit watching with your legs tucked under if you
wanted, and, except for the funny smell, *exactly* like the Re-
gent in Ottawa, we said, where we'd been taken to see Charlie Chaplin in *The Gold Rush*. "Comfy, eh?" I said, putting
my head back on the seat.

"Cosy. Cosier than the dungeons even," George whispered
into the silence.

We could live there, we decided now, nothing wrong with
the Cameo . . . "Will we have to sneak in behind big
people?" . . . dodging a tram, "Should we show our money
to the ticket-lady and explain . . . ?" hopping over an excava-
tion where workmen were burning tar in the middle of the
sidewalk. Slowing down now, face to face with the cavern beyond: in all that dark no one would ever be able to find us,
we weren't afraid, we had each other.

In the last row, in a corner against the wall, we sat, slept,
woke up again, through God knows how many showings of a
silent movie: a pretty lady in a long satin gown who cried a
lot; smudges of grief and desire in her eyes, a limp, broken-
hearted handkerchief being knotted and unknotted, what rare
moments of tragic splendour as they lay on a quilted chaise-
longue, and walked up and down this one room, an *artistic*
room, more like a garden—or a palace! so many things, balconies, mirrors, trellises, a grand piano, lemon trees, statues
and marble benches, boxes of chocolates lying about, and a
treacherous-looking cockatoo poised on a circular stand
above the chaise-longue. There was a pleasant, smiling man
with sleek black hair and a thin mustache, dressed in a tux-
edo and white spats, who kept coming in and kneeling down
beside her, he'd give her a rose and she'd slap it away. What
does it mean? we asked one another, the way she clasped her
hands together, and then wringing them, why? when the man
was being so kind to her; the conflict was wonderful! his mas-
tery when she stopped crying. "Good!" I shouted out loud.
But then she got up and began climbing the winding staircase
and stopped half-way, crying again. It was very confusing. In
the pitch darkness down front, we could see the pianist's
arms, out of the pit white shirtsleeves thrashing against the
beam from the projection room as he pounded even more
drama (Beethoven's "Appassionata"? Vivaldi?) into white letters running across the screen, words that kept changing so
fast we couldn't remember what they said, we had to spell
them to ourselves, first, before we could read them.

Sound asleep on the floor when Uncle Tom found us—past midnight.

"If it weren't for Granny, I'd give the pair of you a thick ear," he said, marching us out, one in each hand, the metal cleats of his thick-soled golf shoes exploding in rapid succession across the stone floor, like shots from a firing squad, all but trampling us in his haste, the fringed outer tongues snapping threateningly as we burst forth under the marquee lights.

"What time . . . is this another day?" Goerge asked, Rip Van Winkle at last managing to get the breath out of him. "What day is it?"

"What *day* is it?" Uncle Tom thundered. "Tomorrow! That's what day it is."

"Would you like to hear about the movie?" George pursued, wide-eyed, full of ginger.

"What!?"

"I guess not," I said faintly, frowning, wondering to myself, Gee, does Uncle Tom have Mamma's quick temper *too*?

"It would be more to the point if you heard what *I* have to say," he snapped.

"You're not our father, you know," I said, stopping as he paused to turn up his coat collar. A lamp standard, the lone streetlight, deflecting through a drizzle; and Uncle Tom, dark-haired and brown-eyed like our mother, a tall rangy man, dapper and well turned out in rust-green tweeds under a belted trench coat, the thick hair slicked back, head tilted downward, regarding us.

"Ae, lass, I'm not your father, and it's times like this I think I haven't missed much. It's only once you're gone . . . Some Sunday afternoon, a day that's no' so far off, I'll be keeping the Sabbath and thinking to myself . . ."

"Well?"

"Ae, I'll be a man stretching his legs afore the fire and I'll be saying to myself, Now then, what is it I'm missing?"

"Is it all right now, Uncle Tom?" George put in, back in favour, striking while the iron was hot. "Would you like to hear about the movie? It was a *love* story!"

"Spare me that, laddie. Your Uncle Tom's had enough scenario for one night, your poor wee mother off up in the Braid Hills, prowling around with a lantern. . . ." Knocking ashes out of his pipe.

"A lantern!?" The pipe into the mouth.

"And your Aunt Isa, bless her. But Lord God of Creation! beleaguering every policeman, anything in a uniform, the In-

firmary . . ." The empty pipe being shifted, clenched between two back molars. "As for you, young Lochinvar! Save
your tale of the cinema until tomorrow, George. You can tell
Granny all about it then."

"I know the real reason he doesn't want to listen," I
laughed, pointing fie! to my uncle as we mounted the curb,
and, letting go of his hand, sprinted ahead and pulled open
the iron door: "Uncle Tom canna wait to get upstairs th'
noo! T'sit doun wi' his wee tot!"

"Did you not hear what I said about a thick ear?" he shot
back. "Hold your tongue! or I'll give you a thick lip as well."

"Oh-ho-ho, 'Little Brown Jug'," I mocked, egging him on,
singing as I ran up the stairs:

> Oh-a-do-si-do,
> You and me,
> Little brown jug
> Don't I love thee?

"You!" he cried. "You're your mother all over again."

"Oh no I'm not! do-si-do, I'm my father all over again."
And my voice reverberating, echoing down and around the
stairwell, coming back at me, do-si-do, a thousand decibels,
ringing, ringing, sounding through my brother's footsteps, my
uncle's, up and down the walls, the stone slabs, the spaces
. . . fading, dying away, indecipherable to all, to everything
but the seconds and the song I was singing to myself while I
leaned over the railing at the top of the stairs in Scotland.

---

Had my mother known all along? that we would not be
there when Granny died? Was it . . . did she decide to return
because of us? or my father? Did she too yearn for the river?

Coming back on the steamer, I stood on the lower deck
beside the cabin steward, throwing the moonstones he had
given me into the ocean, one by one.

"Can I?" I'd asked. "Would that be a terrible thing to do?
Do you mind? I want to see if they'll turn into pearls!" I
shouted excitedly, having a strange idea—I remember I was
convinced that before long I would be hearing of a find in
the middle of the Atlantic. It would be in all the newspapers,
I fancied, they'd think they were real, and I wouldn't let on,
it would be my secret.

"Mind? No, I don't mind," he said, tossing one in for
himself, "but first make a wish each time you throw. Wishes

are more likely to come true than pearls. But who knows? maybe they'll both happen."

A shiny moonstone sails into the May wind. I lose sight of it as it curves behind the spray of a seawave.

"What did you wish that time?" the steward cries through the wind, his hair tossing wildly as he buttons up his jacket.

"No fair's telling," I laugh as I throw another, and another. I'm going home, home to the river, the fields. I don't need the wishes, after all. Or the pearls.

# XI

"Is that a broad hint?" My mother's voice, words that touch the air gently, languidly, intimate as a mating cry, and I remain silent, standing with a bar of green soap in my hands—how can I break in on this moment, when the grin of the world covers my face? My father is prodding her bum, she's in the downstairs hall bending over a suitcase and my father wants to squeeze past, he's carrying a duffel-bag full of pots and pans. But where's he going to put it? there's no room left in the kitchen, you can't move in there . . . he'll have to take it down to the cellar, he says. They're packing, tomorrow we're moving up to the cottage. Late May; all the windows are open, curtains billow, and make a faint sound. I imagine them as trilling, almost. It must be a warm afternoon, my mother's in a thin dress, a pale-peach chiffon, torn under the armholes, a party dress once; did she pull it out of the rag-bag to work in? I see she's perspiring. Then I should be barelegged, in ankle socks, but I'm not, I've got long wool stockings on, and those awful suspenders that don't keep them up properly; they're all wrinkled, and look as if I'm wearing gaiters or leggings.

"Can I go outside for a minute?" I ask. "I forgot to say goodbye to the milkman."

"What for?" my mother demands, wheeling around. "He's a galoot."

"He is not!" George exclaims, shocked, his head looming above the arm of the easy chair. He's kneeling on the floor beside little piles of nickels and dimes and coppers he's emptied out of his telephone-bank; he doesn't know which ones he'll bring to the cottage. "He's a nice man," back on his haunches now, insistent; "he says next winter he'll take us for rides on his sleigh. He's going to let us get on!"

"Yes, and that's not all," I say, adding to the tally, "he doesn't mind one bit when we feed the horse oats outa the bag."

"He's still a galoot," Mamma says, sniffing, her apology. She knows he's a nice man but he's dumb, she says, his brains are all in his feet.

"Who's a galoot?" my father enquires coming up the cellar stairs, his voice merry. He loves packing, he's as excited as the rest of us.

"What's-his-name," Mamma says without looking up, she wants to get on with what she's doing.

"Who?"

"That bird the Producers' Dairy has delivering the milk now."

"Is he?"

"Is he! Haven't you seen his handwriting?" My father sets down the bottle of beer he's brought from the cellar, and musses her hair with both hands.

"What's the use?" Mamma sighs, and sits on the floor beside the suitcase, laughing as she pats her hair back into place. "You're all a bunch of galoots!" she adds. "How do you think we'll ever be ready to leave at this rate?" They take turns drinking out of the bottle, the quart of Black Horse Ale passes back and forth between them.

"We'll be up half the night," Mamma says after a minute.

"Oh . . . there's not that much," my father replies, and holds the bottle up, assessing.

"I wasn't referring to my kidneys," she points out. "Just look around you. Take a good look. Then go on upstairs and see what's piled on the bed." My father takes a fast swig, promptly gets to his feet and heads for the piano in the dining room; he has decided to play standing up, more weight, and note by note. "The Anvil Chorus" shakes the whole house. Next they will dance, first they'll shove the suitcases and cartons aside to make room, and then they'll undo the rope around the gramophone, unpack a record. My father grins, my mother blushes and kicks off her shoes. Music. I think it's "You're the Cream in My Coffee", yes, that's it . . . past half-filled boxes they whirl, tripping over the rug. Curtains billow, and trill: You're the salt in my soup . . . they glide nearer, and George hunches over his coins, shelters them with his arm so they won't get stepped on. He pays no attention when they dance like that, but I do, I have to make sure they're holding each other the right way, close in. Sometimes they don't, and . . . but this time they are. I pick up my hoop and wander outside to look for the milkman, maybe I'll find him in the next block. I want to tell him I'll be seeing him again in the fall.

Sun on the sidewalk, dappled circles, and patches of tar covered over with sand. With my hoop I begin to run, no, I'm skipping, You're the cream in my coffee, I keep time with my feet, and sing:

> You will always be
> My necessity
> I'd be lost without you.

George catches up, he bounds ahead, coins jingle in the metal bank he has his fist around. He turns, and runs back, tells me I should hurry up or the milkman will be gone. "It's early," I shrug, "he's bound to be around some place."

The milkman, perspiring too, asks no questions. He listens, amused, as if what he is hearing is very important. And it is, *very* important, now that George and I are home again; it's a barrage, to make up for what we've missed! His backside leans against the side of the wagon, long legs crossed one over the other as he licks the paper of the cigarette he has rolled. Everything about him is big, not just his feet: a loose-limbed, lanky body, huge teeth in a basset-hound's face, the droopy eyes, pouched, like his mouth, like the sag of his arms. Head not moving, the watery brown eyes roll in my direction, impassive, almost dazed-looking, but with a sweetness that stares at you. And through the smell of horse flesh, and smellier urine, I chew on the reins, I like the taste, somehow seeming part of the moment as I wonder what he is thinking. Maybe he was just having a rest . . . a smoke. And then I think, maybe everyone tells him the same things—except I don't know anyone who goes to a cottage. Mamma says no one, only ourselves, would be caught dead—in our place, anyway, she laughs. I can tell she's proud of it!

"Sounds like the two of yiz have a pretty good time up there," the milkman says, and places a hand on each of our heads, like paws.

"You can come and visit us if you like," from George.

"That's wonderful!" he replies. "I'll remember that." The paws slip the reins from my mouth and transfer them to the hook on the front of the wagon. He waits, grinning, wet-eyed, while I pick up my hoop.

Still turning round to wave goodbye, the wagon all but out of sight in the block beyond, George and I wander home. Mission accomplished.

On the way, George starts to say something, changes his mind; his eyes linger on the sidewalk as he stops, his hand working at the rim of my hoop.

"What's up, George? Don't you want to go home? We're almost there, and we should . . ." Now, being asked, he begins walking again, slowly. "Do you ever get afraid?" he says.

"What? Of what?"

"Oh, things."

"Like what?"

"I don't know."

"Then why'd you ask?"

"I dunno." He didn't say scared, he said afraid, there's a difference. He walks beside me now, takes hold of my hand to pull me forward, his mind returned to catching up, by way of a shortcut at the end of the block, on the packing we're supposed to be helping with.

What was he trying to ask me, or tell me? He never spoke about being afraid again. Never. Whatever it was that day, I guess he decided to keep it to himself. Maybe, just maybe, it came out later, in something we found ourselves talking about, some joint vulnerability, sensed more than voiced, finding a common spirit.

Long after, when I was older, I would remember that afternoon, the two heads moving along, caught by the wonder of a sidewalk journey, "Lookit!" . . . "Did you hear something?" . . . "That's a live piece of worm." . . .

My hoop, bright red, paint worn away where it's chipped. And George's foot pressing down on the bottom rim to hold it upright, puzzled that I must waste these minutes refastening my suspenders. "But I had to!" I said.

I am trying to see him now, the short pants, one sock up, the other down. Would he have had that brown sweater on? the one he wouldn't part with? so full of holes Mamma couldn't mend it any more, the darns wouldn't hold. And his telephone-bank—how much did he have in that little black box? What wind and patterned sky did we see?—is that what this sound is now, traveling through me?—what neighbours' front porches and breathing leaves did we glance at as we hurried to find the milkman?

Did I answer George when he said, "I bores be the one to tell him where we're going tomorrow."

---

In our minds, and for many a summer it seemed, there was for the Ottawa Valley but one train—the one that went up the Gatineau. As for the stops en route, and those the coaches went on to, to these we remained indifferent, possibly unaware; we only knew where we got off.

For the cottage was that one track on which our lives moved. On Christmas mornings my mother could be heard to exclaim of any and every gift that it was just the thing for Sumach Point. A feather boa, mukluks, satin pumps, an Indian sari—it wouldn't have mattered. "Perfect!" she'd say. "The very thing for the cottage." In an embarrassed voice my father would agree, and tell her that's what he had in mind when he bought them, half-believing it himself.

With no sense of killing time, they seemed able to weave a spell around the grey dragging winter; days passing, indifferent to snowploughs and ten-foot icicles, comfortable at the thought of being housebound when snowdrifts were up to your hips, reasoning their kids out of frostbite and frozen ears, and by March, their brows knitting as they wondered had the ice been put in the ice-house yet . . . would the cottage roof have collapsed under the avalanche of the record snowfall? Then in the same breath, "Don't you think it's time we wrote away for the new seed catalogue?" And out would come the previous year's book; they thought maybe it would do.

I was the impatient one wishing winter away. For my senses seemed to retrench, as though trying to sleep through it all, yet with a silent unvoiced temper in me. Like the subzero day I put my tongue on the school fencepost, knowing full well what would happen. But still pigheaded. The whole of my tongue, back as far as the tonsils, stuck on the frozen steel, and in a furious rage I ripped it away. But then I guess you have to begin somewhere, shedding that first layer of soft skin; there are more to come, and the tongue is as good a place to start as any.

Mamma said it served me right, that I was being taught a lesson for moping about. But I did not agree. It was winter proving itself. And if I was, as she had said, a sorry-looking sight, it was only because I couldn't stop dreaming of summer, the wind blowing life into the fields of grain, and nights when you could see every star in the universe by just standing on the hill. I would look at the patches of blackened snow still clinging in the slow-moving spring, measuring them day by day in my mind's eye as I waited for the brown bruised grass to come green again, yearning to walk barefoot through patches of June, with pine needles cracking like eggshells in the silent woods, the miracle of July so distant, that shimmer of thistle and sleek grass, the *feel* of it trampling down the new-mown hay as it was forked into the barnloft. That's why I daydreamed in school; the teacher said I was wool-gathering and complained to Mamma, who said, in a nice way, "She's like her father that way."

But I had discovered, had come to the conclusion, that summertime was in no way related to the city. I was about twelve then.

How could it, I thought, when the summer I knew lasted half a year? I'd get up one morning in May, and not be back in the same bed again until November almost. (With nothing more than a malfunctioning fireplace and kitchen woodstove, how did we survive the cold? patches of snow in May, shrinking back into the earth under the verandah; October nights, a glacier moon. . . .) Long after the last Gatineau cottager had boarded up for the winter we would still be there, spinning out the remaining weeks commuting to school by train, homework done in the glow of a kerosene lamp. And so, returning sometimes after the first flurries of snow had sprinkled the hill, I could never disassociate the face and voice of the city, then anyway, from the season that had now begun, the months ahead not just a time of waiting but a way of life removed, a feeling that seemed to say, So this is what the city's like.

Winter belonged only to the frozen vision of sparrows trying to keep warm in the silvery sun, a time of bright cold streetlights transforming the bare trees into skeletal death stares. At night, a kind of crisp hard silence where there was no sound to go by, like the look of a far-off boat rocking. Everything about seemed so unloved, the vanishing shadows of afternoon, blinds being pulled down against the night. I was probably very young, but I remember my childish impatience at having to scratch holes in the frosted windowpanes so you could see out when morning came.

Nothing ever seemed to touch our anonymous beings. George and I would make angels in a fall of snow, yet the patterns made by our bodies were as remote as the rumple of overcoats shuffling along the snow-rutted streets.

But summer! An alliance all around us. In the pitch dark we could sit on the hill with the night lights of fireflies blinking as though regulated by our breathing. We *touched* wet raspberries.

You can never forget that. You can't even pretend to.

―――――――――――

What an age! I remember that as soon as the year's new calendar arrived from Jolicoeur's Épicier-Boucher—a huge, year-at-a-glance, kitchen wall-hanging, complete with its reproduction of some medieval epicurean orgy, fleshy and buoyant, tankards held aloft by fat dimpled hands, the equally fat cherubic faces of frilly-shirted squires, their faces seeming both ancient and childlike above the roasted pigs on the table and the live ones rooting through the sprawled legs beneath—the moment we learned the new calendar was up on the wall, George and I would race to circle the 24th of May, climbing up on the chair beside the stove with a bright red crayon, that holiest of days circled round and round and round, the day of our move waxed into being, George's hand, mine to follow, both having to take part in this ritual, a feeling: proof. In the warm kitchen, in the warmth of urgent feverish hands, the wax soft, glistening. And the scarlet eye beamed, as though winking.

While I frittered away the days—except those of the piano hours. And the toboggan hill.

Then! In the week preceding the 24th of May Holiday, when everyone else in the neighbourhood was laying in firecrackers, my parents would be filling the old steamer trunk with summer clothing and stuffing fruitbaskets full of tinned foods, and immediate things liked rolled oats and toothpaste, and, now that the gramophone was left behind in the cottage for the winter, a new batch of records; the oddest mixture: Rachmaninoff's "C Sharp Minor Prelude" and Victor Herbert's "Natoma". And of course, dance tunes; they were dancing tangos now.

Where did they put everything? I mean what did they pack things in without getting them all mixed up? Like the day George and I went to find the milkman; the first time we had seemed aware, were conscious of the chaos going on around us, delighted at being underfoot, *participating*, potato masher in with the tennis shoes and pee pot. Maybe they said, 'What does it matter?'

And what a collection of marvellous, shiny junk assembled beforehand, suddenly appearing as if from nowhere. In the dining room the top of the poor old piano became in that final week a depot for last-minute purchases (bought after payday, the fifteenth), a clutch of playing cards, mosquito netting, books, sewing patterns and yard goods, dominoes, nail polish, fishing tackle, nails, rope and lengths of chain, a new saw, a bigger hammer; great piles of disarray that toppled—invariably in the middle of the night, which set the dog barking. And then silence again. Going back to sleep with dreams in my head: things get better all the time . . . is that what my parents are thinking too? Did the bottle of iodine fall off the piano and break? . . . and the peanut brittle, is the dog eating our peanut brittle? . . .

Looking at it now, the preparation involved in this move, the whole thing seems unreal. All the clatter and shuffle of a travelling circus; what was to go, what was to stay? Mamma's voice deep in an upstairs closet: "Are you taking *two* grey flannel suits again this year?" And Daddy from somewhere in the basement: "What?" Twitching with eagerness, George and I would run up and down the stairs squealing our jumble of messages, translating everything to suit ourselves. After a while, all roads leading to the living room. A suitcase turned upside down and emptied out, one of our parents admitting *that's* the wrong one! they meant to put all the shoes and rubber boots in instead, the thing repacked. "Where's the bleeding bridge-lamp?" from my mother. "Didn't you send it ahead by C.P. Express?" from my father. "Of course. I'd forgotten. But the light bulbs . . . where in blazes are they?" A hugging embrace, or a yawn, the piano starting up at once: "Sleepy Time Gal". And my mother's favourite expression slicing through the opening bars: "Who says so?", turning to us, who sit observing from the chesterfield, "The cheek of your father! when he's the one who yawned first!"

On the day of departure, trussed rolls of bedding would be placed in the downstairs hall, along with the rest of the clutter waiting for the taxi that would take us to the train. The

last one out, my father would lock the front door, and
George and I would say goodbye to the house on Elmdale
Avenue. We would look out the back window of the taxi and
see our street running away from us, an emotion that was difficult to explain. I'd see our house at the end of the block, the
trees and lilac hedge soft-hued, disappearing from view, at
once seizing me with an inner silence, wishing we could drive
around the block, one more glance. I didn't know what did
that.

———

By this time, a lot of hard work had gone into improving,
if not restoring, our seven-acre estate of grasshoppers and
groundhog-holes. For the cottage, erected ten years earlier on
the uninhabited side of the river smack in the middle of a
steep and treeless hayfield, had remained empty, unoccupied,
some of the floorboards missing, door-handles lying about
where they'd fallen off the doors, fungus the size of pumpkins
under the windowsills—until the "bums" came, the Canso
prospectors. Us. Had other people taken one look and fled?
appalled as they skidded back down the hill on the previous
night's fresh deposits, praying for deliverance and a safe return (by the leaky rowboat thrown in with the rent, fifty-dol-
lars-a-season), eyeing the far shore from which they'd come,
vowing never to leave its banks again?

———

I like to go back there sometimes, in the autumn when
there's no one around, doors padlocked, windows boarded up,
the only other family to occupy the place still holding on to
it. ". . . Children grown into their late teens now," they tell
me in the village. In the tiny post office I ask, *"S'il vous
plaît,* can I borrow *un bateau?"* and they nod: today I can
take the green one, or the red one, whatever is anchored below Gagnon's landing at the end of the highway fence, warn-
ing me the boat leaks, or the oarlock is broken, then handing
me a pail in case the boat is full of water.

I row across and sit on the verandah steps, sunlight exploding diamonds on the water, movement of trees, a bird lighting
on a slack Hydro line at the riverbank. And I think, All this!
I was living in luxury: it's not what you give a child, it's what
goes with the giving.

———

Wild raspberries. Moving in a dark wind. A shoe . . . a hat . . . gypsy moths, white-on-silver floating past in the half dark. A quartet of cows harmonizing in the barn, a moment of silence. And eastward, over the dew-sodden hill, the Northern Lights, like a green shield trailing across the night sky. Standing by the woodpile in my pink flannelette nightie, clutching what's left of my moonstones, head tipped back, staring; "What's the *aurora borealis*, Mamma? Who *makes* it?"

"I *said* it's time you were back in bed. Are you deaf or something?"

"Is it the Indians doing that, Mamma? Out in the Northern Ocean?"

"In the *what*?"

"Look! the green lights flashed higher! Is it the Indians turning mirrors against icebergs?"

"Something like that," she says, a cigarette between her lips dropping ashes down her front as she wraps her cardigan around me. "You'll catch your death. Don't tell me you were out on the hill with nothing on your feet!"

"What's all the chatter?" my father says through the window netting. He comes outside and sits on the woodpile. "Mimi?" he asks, reaching for a puff of her cigarette. "What makes you say it's the Indians? Isn't it the Eskimos?" The air is warm with the smell of the woodpile, freshly sawn pieces, the slimy bark-ends flaked with compost, oozing pine- and spruce-gum in the sleeping night.

And now it's another night. After supper. Must be late fall; it's dark; my father is toting buckets of river water up the hill—our supply for next day; one more trip and the rain barrel will be filled. From which George and I with smaller pails will then replenish the buckets lying empty in the kitchen. Is this one of the nights we forget this most important of our chores? and in the early morning, before breakfast, must look for a stick to crack the ice that has seized the pails? We're supposed to see to that, the least we can do.

The recollection of one such morning I relish for its sheer astonishment, the resonance of its visual command. George and I, feeling sheepish about neglecting our chore, had shivered out the kitchen door to be confronted by a huge, anxious-looking bullfrog embalmed dead centre in the ice-sheet crusting the pail. His head, like a fossilized gourd, was poised above what had been the water line; we squatted over him, peering at the balloon-skin of his eyes opening and clos-

ing as he waited for us to free him. Too old to jump, we
thought, dozing there in his bucket-pond, the warty head
propped on the icy headrest. But with the first splintering of
ice, his leap shot him clear over the verandah railing. Daddy
was standing at the screen door. "Allemande left to the corners all!" he twanged after the frog.

---

The cottage had no plumbing, and in the years that we
were without electricity, the chill was taken off the water by
keeping two battered preserving kettles steaming at the ready
on the kitchen stove. And in a galvanized tub, scarcely big
enough for a knee-to-chin fit, George and I had our sort-of
bath. That too a nightly routine, but a seasonal one depending on how frigid the Gatineau River was—late June the ear-
liest you dared put more than your big toe in.

"Wash as far as possible," Mamma would say, and then
add: "and 'possible' gets washed Saturday night." Giggling to
herself as she retreated. She liked that one.

I remember the shock it always was the first night there,
sitting in the middle of the kitchen floor, angled into the tub
and the water spilling over the side, the cake of Lifebuoy
squirting out of my hands and skittering across the bare floor,
retrieved under a table or chair, full of sand and whatever
else it had picked up; nevertheless a pleasant sensation drying
myself as I gazed around, flypaper coils from the previous
summer dangling from the ceiling, the walls decorated with
mended tubs, enamel washbasins, mops, lanterns, cobwebbed
wheat-sheaves, a butterfly net, the bucksaw, empty spikes,
and spikes holding rusty chains, canvas gloves, ice-tongs, a
tennis racquet without any strings, washboard, the vegetable
garden's scarecrow on a stake propped against the window,
and scattered about the top shelf of the curtained cupboards,
mousetraps, candles, paper napkins and rolls of unopened
toilet paper chewed at the edges. Meanwhile, our parents
scurrying hither and thither, back and forth from room to
room as they get on with the unpacking, trying to figure out
why they can't find the mate to a shoe, the fork belonging to
the carving set. "Say, are you sure you packed the stopper for
the hot-water bottle?" A torso straightening: "Must be there
somewhere. Look inside the enema bag." "No, doesn't seem
to be, maybe the dog—oh, here it is, in the sugar bowl."

And George and I, bathed, hungry again, following them
about, a chunk of hastily cut bread slathered with Lyle's

Golden Corn Syrup in each hand, waiting for the next
suitcase to be opened up. More attentive now. For suddenly
it's not the same thing all over again, the child remembering
other times, aware of the activity he's participating in, but
not of its core. Now, watching, absorbing this flurry of motion—the sudden knee-bends into a trunk, the exchanges,
tosses of books and words and peanut brittle and fishing
tackle, scissors flying through the air: "Here, use these to cut
that knot," and the reply, "That was an offside pass!"—our
parents are seen in other lights. We can't tell exactly . . . it's
a feeling, all mixed up in the brain and flesh, our mother not
just the mother who took us to sit on a rock by the river,
standing over us as we put on a sock, seeing to it that our
shoes are properly tied; our father not merely Daddy whom
we welcome home from an office, who pours himself and our
mother a drink, and helps her set the table, who puts on a
record and dances with her while the vegetables are boiling,
or sits playing a game with us on the floor. For somewhere,
and magically, between one year's winter and the snow-
roofed night of another, on a day waking up to summer
breezes or the sound of the bread-wagon's sleigh bells, all at
once you knew that everything your parents were doing,
word, deed, thought, was indivisible, the smallest fragment of
their world a part of yourself; not just two familiar voices set
apart, two beings separate from our two when night came,
and in the day even. There were four voices, vested, belonging together since the beginning of time? the slow-dawning
realization that they always had.

And so we stand, George and I, silently licking goo,
dribbles of Lyle's Corn Syrup running down a wrist, scissors
flashing back and forth. That's what I'm seeing now, and
*feeling*! the cold steel, sticky hands picking them up, and firelight, a shower of sparks shooting up the chimney as a
charred log caves in in the middle; wind whistling through a
hole in the attic . . . there it is again! no matter. That box,
this carton, empty, are they saving these? padding around:
what *else* did they bring this summer? is there something that
slipped by us, packed when we were out playing? For instance, where's the new kitchen-table oilcloth, the pride and
joy of our mother's kitchen?

Its whereabouts no mystery. She knew exactly which packing case: no danger of it being in with the carton that had
the bottle of ink, or glue, or turpentine, or Lysol. And, like
the booze, a kind of celebration she would save for a later

moment that night, the kitchen oilcloth not to be unpacked until messing with supper was over, dishes, pots, canisters, tinned goods all put away. And then! what a ceremony as she dove into a packing case; carefully, lovingly, the shiny tablecloth taken out, her dark eyes aglow, sighing softly, a hand caressing the slippery folds; patterned in roses, of course. (Mamma had this thing for pink roses: her dishes, curtains, dresses, sets of jazz garters, bathing cap; a satin rosette sewn onto the dog-collar when the spirit moved her.) Year after year the oilcloth's floral design honey-combed with tiny buds, the daintiest of blooms, like something on a baby's nightgown—though by midsummer the roses would look blighted, from the furious scrubbings with Old Dutch (ants swarming day and night, "leaving their pee stains," she'd wail).

But! did she really *mind* having to throw the thing out in the fall? All through the winter, tripping back and forth uptown, as though viewing at an art gallery, sizing up bolts of oilcloth at Freiman's . . . what might Zeller's have? back down to Woolworth's, over to the market. Coming home empty-handed—she'd have to compare notes in her head. Back uptown another day. And again. Once more. . . . How could she even remember the difference?

And finally, on a late afternoon in spring, landing home with her treasure. Standing in the front hall, still in her coat as she untied the brown-paper wrap, unfurling the roll for George's and my benefit, and then: "Don't let me once catch you with a knife . . ." Gazing at it as she draped the length over her arm. "Didn't cost much," she'd say, or, "Paid a pretty penny for this one, but don't tell your father." The grand unveiling repeated when my father returned from work; cord, wrapping paper removed as before, sitting with it on her lap. And then later that evening, stored away in the bureau drawer along with her summer dainties, lingerie, lavender sachets, pink bathing cap.

"Your mother's 'Limoges roses'," my father would say, referring to this article of faith. She liked that, it gave her kitchen class.

And encouraged her all the more: to stand on the night of the 24th of May, before the kitchen table, a childlike innocence in her, almost hesitating to release it from her arms, holding the oilcloth tenderly, as though it were an infant's christening robe.

And always George and I would stand watching her pat down the flowering rose, and tell her how pretty it was.

"Prettier even than last year's," we'd say. And she would whirl around and tell us, "Then mind you take better care of it and not be leaving the jam pot out! You're big enough now, goodness knows," regarding us with chronic scepticism, our lowered heads nodding agreement at the phrase that shamed us now that we were a year older. What was it we were always doing we were now too big for? It went on and on. For years.

# XII

Like that day on the train.

If anything was a case of plain bad luck, that was. Nothing whatever to do with my age—eleven. Soon I would be twelve, I was reminded, with a heavy sigh.

The 24th of May and there we were, decked out in our fanciest as the train bore us northward for one more summer, the four of us squashed between hampers, suitcases, duffel-bags, and the wicker dog kennel at an angle, down on the floor and sticking part way into the aisle.

My mother and George rode with their backs to the engine, my father and I facing them. I had the window seat.

So many things to look at, I was thinking—not so much that they were new, or different, nothing was changed; the difference was in the way I felt about them. A year was a long time.

The window was open, and I had my head out as far as it would go—not just to see; the wind on my face a lovely thing as the train rushed along—the river seeming a deeper blue, wider than I had remembered. Small whitecaps flicked over, deepening the blue to violet out where the water was choppy. In close to the shoreline, where the current was almost nil, gusts scribbled lines across the blueness, like writing.

I was wearing my new straw hat, a Panama with red gros-grain ribbons, and two yellow cherries and leaves on the band. In the seam at the back, a piece of jagged straw had been caught in the lining, driving me nuts the way it kept making the back of my head itch. Finally I put my fingers underneath and scratched, still intent as I craned out of the window, drawing rushes of the wind into my open mouth. I guess my knuckles must have tipped the hat forward, for off it went, hurtling down over a bed of rocks and onto the shore.

I saw it lying there, right side up by the water. Almost a grownup's hat. That's what I was thinking that morning as I put it on, in front of the mirror, like Mamma.

My father leaned out the window and said, "You should have been more careful, a big girl like you." And my mother, full of an appalled sigh: "It serves you right. You'll just have to go back to an elastic band. Money doesn't grow on trees, you know." Which made it all the worse. Not because I should have known better, but because the hat was the first possession I had ever treasured. I mean I had a special feeling about it; you always love your doll best, or a tiny bracelet someone once gave you, but that's different—something you *own*. My hat was something I *appreciated*, its meaning: the gesture, the acknowledgement I was now out of pigtails. And the hurt was with myself for losing it.

I thought about my hat all that summer. I still do.

There I sat with my burden of guilt. Mamma took up her embroidery hoop, as though nothing had happened, I thought. Daddy had gone back to his *Wireless Manual*—though he couldn't have been concentrating all that hard for he looked up and said, twice, "Never mind . . . it's all right." George, with concerns of his own, busy flicking cinders off his white sailorsuit. Saving the big ones.

Dejected, my pride cut to the quick as tears smarted, I glanced across the aisle at the woman in the blue-flowered voile; somehow the ripple of the sheer blue and white material seeming soft and free, like a caress when drafts of wind gusted through. She had come late into our coach, her arms, indeed her stomach as well, laden with brown-paper bundles knotted with ends of string, the kind you keep in a tin can. A reek of farm dung, mixed with liniment, came out of her every pore, the pungency so immediately staggering I could not understand why I hadn't noticed the smell before. She caught my eye: "What'd you have to go and lose your hat for?" Pleased and grinning with her intrusion. And I thought, What's so funny? I made a face at her and turned away.

Mamma looked up from her sewing and said, "Well. You're a sorry-looking ticket."

"I know," I said, my eyes drifting beyond her, above, a cobweb, pale brown, metallic in the burst of sun.

Coming to collect fares, a mournful-looking conductor clanged open the door, and my mind was transferred to the sudden flurry of activity: the lift of voices, feet and legs uncrossed, hands rummaging through pockets and handbags, a boater taken down off the rack and the ticket removed from the greasy hatband.

Not until the conductor arrived at our seats did I look across at the woman again. And I thought, She must know him pretty well; gee, I guess she does.

All the time he examined my father's six-months commuter-ticket, which took forever as he puzzled why it had been clipped to Mamma's one-way, the woman leaned across the aisle and nudged his arm, holding her forearm against his and pressing down hard, laughing with a hideous strident excitement—seconds? a minute? I couldn't take my eyes away from her face, moist and glassy-eyed with the uninhibited relish of this private, unprivate matter. Clearly she had forgotten all about me and my hat, and I decided I'd take advantage of the lull in her fix on me.

My once-over would have to have tact, I thought, not be vulgar. Slyly I sneaked glances around the conductor's back; I even put my hand up to my eyes, pretending they were covered, somehow imagining she'd think they were. At first I could see only the lower part of her body, and I remember being surprised, in fact fascinated, by how short her legs were. Like stumps in lisle stockings, full of darns in the knees. Because her big behind took up so much room, her feet didn't quite make it to the floor, and the more strident she became the more her legs bounced about, the heels banging against the wooden supports under the seat. Small feet, they were. In black shoes with brown laces.

With a flourish befitting its worth, the conductor took out his gold Waltham and checked the time against the landscape racing by. Making the most of this pause, the woman raised a puffy red hand and hooked her thumb and forefinger into the empty watchpocket, and pinched hold of the lining—either that or his skin. After a quick glance around, the conductor shoved her hand away as he slid the watch back in behind, and rested his arms on the luggage rack above. Of course I couldn't hear a word he was saying, but it didn't matter . . . he may have pushed her hand away, but now he was being attentive. Her feet bobbing again, face pink as a cherry blossom.

Crestfallen is what I felt when the conductor moved on to his next passengers, the woman's legs still as fenceposts as she sat looking wistfully after him, fingering the knottings on one of the bundles.

But not for long! I don't think the conductor could have been more than four seats away when she called down the aisle, shrilling his name as if he were two coaches away—was his name Percy? How could you tell, what with her raucous hee-heeing and the succession of sharp slaps upon those bolster-thighs? The poor man never let on he heard. He had his ticket-taking to keep him busy, turning them over again and again, upside down too? he wasn't the amiable, chatty kind, and he had to do *something*! "Percy? All right for you, Percy! Come on!"

My parents looked up, went back to what they were doing.

The woman. Her face searching the aisle as she waits for the conductor to turn around. Can't he even *wave* to her? The tall head; towering above low voices. I fidget, afraid he doesn't like her in return. She deserves his liking, I think, right there and then. For everyone to see. All that love in her—I didn't want it going wasted.

And so I kept my eyes on him, I just knew he'd turn around, he had to! Which he did; did he ever, he winked, *and* was that something! a long-drawn-out closing of a granuled lid. Only then did I sense this moment as being familiar; even if no words were exchanged, wasn't this like my parents' own peculiar way of dropping off into whispers? Here was that identical truncated adult-code—pushed to a frenzy by the woman's florid giggles, the hands and feet working, spurred, I noticed by Percy's awkward nods in my direction. But she liked that, yes, she did. The sharing. "Eh, dearie?" she wheezed, catching my eye.

This time I did not look away; as the train lurched on, the whistle blowing, people talking, I found myself staring, no longer seeing a pink sweaty face but an image, luminous, still. There is nothing piercing about green eyes, but at that moment hers had touched my tap root; I felt my senses quickened by the living and breathing world, as growing things reach for nourishment, vital air. Her whole expression

spoke nothing but the teachings of something indefinable and
fine. Love. Eyes giving as much light as they received. A
stranger; who had squeezed me into her being.

No longer did I feel modest about peering like that. I
wanted to remember her. An emotion came over me, I recall
a sense of wanting to go over to touch that brown hair; such
a curious-looking frizz, like a Fuller brush mop with its
streak of grey, obviously hacked at, an isolated flash of silver
that had grown in again standing upright, like a royal crest
above her temple. What was she thinking as she sat alone,
grinning to herself? In much the way a sunrise does, or a sudden cloud, or the slow song of a waterfall, her face seemed to
grip my senses, a face whose only lines were the tracings left
by decades of smile, the person behind that smile a kind of
wonder the sunlight played upon whenever the train shot out
of the woods.

Now that the conductor had disappeared into the next
coach, and with all that vigour refusing to be contained, she
battened every eye—overalls to grey flannels—not in the least
hesitant as she focussed on someone seated, or a man walking
back from the water-cooler, a new passenger getting on. And
the eyes of the women? They found a sudden interest elsewhere. Anywhere. The way Mamma was doing. And she, the
woman, the mystery of her talcum and animal instinct insistent, inhabiting its own world, her chunky body leaning forward, oblivious to all but her chosen target, and shouting the
first thing that came into her head; to strangers mostly. Yet
somehow you felt she knew them all. Her irreverent gaiety,
and energy, the animality—I thought she was glamorous. She
made me think of moonlight. This presence whom I, only
minutes before, had turned up my nose at. Why, she had
more dignity than I would ever own.

And that is true. As the woman sat with the big arms
planted across her stomach, her head reclining on the green
plush seat, her breathing slow and melodious, I pictured her
crooning to a newborn lamb. What else mattered if you had
love in you?

Passing through on his return from the rear coaches, the
conductor stopped at her seat, his head bent low in conversation. I still couldn't make anything out, but his tone, the look
of him seemed more formal. His effort was wasted; she paid
not the slightest attention, eyes shining as she surveyed leftover deposits from his ticket-punching, sticking like bits of
white confetti to his vest, his navy serge suit. She reached up

and began brushing them away. Downward! Brushing further down, where there weren't any. His voice rose in a provoked crescendo, cracked, like a boy's.

"Come on Percy. What's the matter?" she cackled, and moved his cap to the back of his head, turning the peak sideways with a yank. As the conductor observed himself in the plate-glass window, turning his head this way and that, I could see that his earlier, rueful expression had taken on a kind of puckish glint. And with a sweep of his arm, he took hold of the band and adjusted his C.P.R. who's-who, tilting the visor rakishly, laughing at himself with a mischievous though somewhat guarded pleasure.

Her wink, like his, urgent and secretive, languid as she nudged him again; this time in the abdomen.

And guess who else was watching, taking everything in: my mother, slowly a flush rising. Someone near by, behind, blew their nose, a sharp self-conscious sound, like the one I could feel enclosed in my mother's body, a split-second vibration grazing my own insides. Why was she staring at me? Uneasy—because of me? No, something more than that, I think. The embroidery hoop, like her hands, like all of her, ready to snap. The toe of her shoe opened fire against my ankle.

"Stop gawking," she said between her teeth, "it's none of your affair." (My father got it that night too; after I went to bed I heard Mamma say, "What did you expect of the girl, you sitting there with that silly smirk?")

*Stop gawking.* Round and round in my head, the words thrown back at me from a voice inside the train wheels. I slumped back, mad at myself. I wanted to tell Mamma she didn't understand, it wasn't as if I were being a rude person. But I didn't know how.

The train wheels swept along, across the aisle I could hear the woman's voice, and I realized I did not care. At that moment I no longer cherished Mamma's approval. I would defy her, and have myself another eyeful; quietly though, it would have to be subtle. I wouldn't look across just yet, I thought, but wait for an opportunity, later, when things had quieted down. Why not stand up on the seat, I told myself, either that or sit upright on my heels, that would show I was looking some place else; then, when the time was right, I could ease myself down without being noticed.

"I wonder what the two bushloggers are arguing over," I

said loudly. "I think they're mad at each other, they're shouting," I went on, proving I'd found a new interest.

"What?" My father. "Bushloggers? You mean lumberjacks." He raised his head, bracing his arm on the armrest to pull himself up to listen. "Search me," he said. "Why don't you go down and ask them?" And my mother: "Just sit still . . . stay where you are," and glancing over at my father, "Give her an inch and she'll take a mile."

"I know," he replied and looked briefly out the window, turning back as he said, as though thinking out loud: "But still . . . her hat . . ."

"Her own fault," Mamma said. I didn't want to go anyway.

"Here," my father said, "change places with me, you can hear some of what the men are saying. One wants to get off at the dam first, that's all. They're not mad. People who work out of doors always speak loudly, they're used to big open spaces."

The lumberjacks. Four seats away; two bodies occupying a double seat. Mackinaws and gumrubber boots. Mud on the pair that rest, one leg over the other, on the velour seat. I don't look across yet, too soon; I feel movement though . . . a sway that jerks my neck around . . . the glass water-cooler . . . I remember swells of water slapping sideways inside . . . mackinaws swing from a hook, back and forth the sleeves, is it time to look across? I wonder . . . train blowing for the level crossing.

"Close your mouth and stop squinting," my mother says. "And get your things together or you'll be left behind."

Since my hat is gone, gathering my things amounts to picking up my schoolbag, and I open my mouth to ask, Why, what hurry *is* there?

"Make it snappy," Mamma adds, and promptly hands me her sewing basket to hold while she takes out her mirror and begins fixing her hair. "Know what, Cecil?" she says to my father, who perhaps doesn't hear her, he's bending down talking to the dog. She does not continue; she wasn't going to say anything anyway. It's her way of letting us know she's lighthearted again, we're supposed to get the message she was just fooling, she really wasn't cross about my hat, and certainly not at the woman. Confusing, now that she waits until the last minute; I might have had a chance to go over and say something, I thought. I wanted to ask her what her name was, and tell her mine.

She had moved over to the window seat, and was busy dissecting a candy bar. She had unearthed from somewhere, most likely one of the trussed bundles, a moss-green cardigan, which now strained to its last seed-stitch around a shape it must surely have fitted handsomely once. On had gone her hat, a funeral-black straw sprouting the pale curled undersides of a cornflower.

I could feel the train slowing down, the trees of Sumach Point, the high, spring-swollen river hurrying by; in the distance the farm up the hill, the beige sprawl of the sandpit below. As we bundled out of our seats, laden down, jostled by the sway of the train and barely able to see ahead, more baggage than flesh, suitcases, shoulder duffel-bags, fruit baskets, the dog kennel, our cargo as if having taken command, leading the way, I turned back to speak, the last one in line. I lingered wordlessly, shifting from one foot to the other. And lost my nerve.

And the last I ever saw of the woman, balancing myself in the aisle, fingers working nervously at my schoolbag in that hauntingly silent and fragile moment, not understanding why it seemed so, was the reflection of her face in the windowpane. Biting into a wrinkled Sweet Marie wrapper, pleased again as she looked out at the silver and white bushland gliding by. And in the same glass, standing just back of her, I saw my own image: hatless, navy and white middy herringboned by sunlight, swaying lightly. The moss-green sweater and middy touching shoulders in a pane of rattling glass, then moving away. Away from a moment that would never return, the window bearing as a cipher the image of a time that could not, in quite the same way, ever be known again.

# XIII

On hot summer evenings when the breeze had died down and the river went by as if at a standstill, I liked to take the boat out by myself. There was a certain lemony smell to the air, and as night drew near a moist coolness seemed to settle just above the water.

That summer a scorching wind blew through the inferno of days, birds and leaves wilting in the trees, stunned insects and chipmunks zigging from shade to shade, and once in a while, a solitary cloud moving through the sky like a barge. All day I would be back in the fields helping with the haying.

It was my job to sit on top of the haywagon holding the reins as Mr. Carman forked the thistly sweet-smelling hay onto the wagon, flinging it from below with the quiet and resolute passion of a farmer working his land, one by one the forkfuls being gathered in by the dark-haired (handsome, I thought, even if he was cross-eyed) hired hand spreading and packing the hay down behind me. Watching his profile, I'd wait for my signal, his wise and weatherbeaten face rearing above: "Git on up ahead." I'd pull on the reins and steer the team to the next pile, rising higher and higher on my perch up front, the high wooden rack creaking under my wrists as we jogged through the rutted furrows.

I was now almost fifteen, sitting there smudge-faced and goggle-eyed, fancying my lot, my long hair shoved up under an old straw hat, a pair of overalls Mamma had made to keep the sun from burning my legs, one of my father's shirts protecting my arms. Almost the envy of myself, the team at last my responsibility: "Whoa now, Diamond and Daisy, git on up ahead."

And now that the near hayfields were done, rattling along to the outlying fields, the mahogany-coloured mare and her black stallion breaking into a trot, Mr. Carman and the hired man sitting at the back of the empty wagon, legs dangling over the side, patches of sweat growing darker under their braces. On across the loose planks of the bridge at the creek and then the sudden drop down a steep clay valley, the horses' manes flying like a runaway team bent on destruction; harness tightening over their hind-quarters, climbing up the other side short of breath, glistening with sweat, their necks and flanks almost perpendicular; standing comfortably now, drowsy eyes looking straight ahead as another load is piled high. And Mr. Carman, preferring to walk the distance back, trudging along behind: "Get the buckshot outa yer ass," meaning the hired hand and me and not just the mare and her mate; chickens and hens scattering, running for cover as team and wagon galloped across the barnyard heading for the ramp and the pulley under the hayloft. Then out again for the next load; the hired man, in his thirties, Luke (known in the village as Black Luke), playing his harmonica, sorrowful ballads about lonesome cowboys, jails, and graves, I loved the songs, I never knew there were so many people in despair.

Often, on the return journey, we'd stop to rest the horses. There was a clump of trees in the centre of a field where shade fell on all sides of a warm rock and where a small well of spring water, in spite of the heat and drought, remained icy-cold. Mr. Carman, already at the well, since he did not have to climb down as Luke and I did, would douse himself with a dipper of water and, not wishing to be entertained, would wander off, finding himself a cool spot on the far side of the rock where he'd lie down for a snooze, feet up on a log, a hat perforated with air-holes covering his face.

Meanwhile, the horses nosing into the bucket of water I held. And Luke, leaning against a tree as he cleaned and shook the spit from his harmonica, singing away, as if to himself. But quite aware I was lapping it up! his very soul an orgy of anguish, his voice rising softly, impassioned, breaking in just the right place, a Neapolitan tenor with an Ottawa Valley accent, all the while pretending not to notice me, the pain of the world beyond the comprehension of all but the few who knew life from a long way off—until he'd pause to wash down a handful of berries, the rim of the dipper resting on the bridge of his nose and his tragedian's eye (the good one) suspiciously turned on me: is she impressed? or secretly making fun? Little did he know how wide-eyed *and* impressed my innards were, wrung with every catastrophe.

"Why do they always have a railway ticket in their pocket," I asked one day, realizing this distinctly uncatastrophic condition had found its way into every song, "and then say they'll never be on that train again?" such devotion to a train ticket escaping me.

"Because," he sighed, glancing distantly, knowingly, at the western sky, "they can never go home, it's too late . . ." (punctuated with a sudden jet of water spurting from his lips, the motion of wiping his mouth drawn out, timed to honour the weight of man's burden). "They've wandered too far, so they have. Far astray from their true loves;" pausing, "the seeds of destruction has ate their souls." I was silent, thinking about it. My, he certainly knew a lot about the world. "The ticket is their good intentions, but they know they'll never make it home," he went on, his voice slowing dramatically, obliquely. "For they're weary and spent," ardent now, reflecting the darkness of this last dashed hope, "and their time has came fer to go on to another world . . . where everything's forgot at the pearly gates. Even the blackest of hearts can go through."

"Gosh," I said with awe, thinking Luke must have been just about everywhere. While the sun beat down, the long yawning strokes of hot wind blowing languidly across the parched fields; me too sipping from the dipper, waiting, listening, watching his Adam's apple. "I heard the whistle of the postman . . ." ohhh! a minor key? ". . . his bag was heavy on his back . . ." what a swell tune! ". . . and he said, 'Good morning to you, Jack'," looking at the sky again, eyes half-closed, not a moment spoiled:

> But he little knew the sorrow he had brought me
> As he handed me that letter edged in black.

Mouth organ out again, low plaintive notes as a tattooed arm reached to untether the horses, the spread of distant fields around me throbbing and radiant with desolation.

"Good God!" Mamma exclaimed at the supper table that first week. "You're obsessed with sweethearts and mothers waiting on station platforms! Next thing you know you'll be demanding a harmonica. I wouldn't put it past you, traipsing around with a mouth organ shoved into your face."

"I already have," I announced. "Didn't you hear me yet?"

"What? When?" She was passing my father the bowl of mashed potatoes, her arm seizing up, the vase of sweet-peas rocking on its base.

"She unearthed George's old one," said my father, relieving her of the potatoes and setting them down in the middle of the table. "Didn't you hear her last night, Mimi? when we were down at the icehouse digging worms? I must say she's done very well with it, picked it up fast. A real pro."

"George Wade and his Corn Huskers!" Mamma hailed, like a barker promoting a feature attraction on the midway. And my father, grinning.

"Ask her to play you 'Danny Boy'," he said.

"Why not 'Roses of Picardy'?" she groaned. "What in the name of heaven does a fifteen-year-old girl want with a harmonica? or for that matter, a girl of any age."

"What's being a girl got to do with it?" George asked of no one in particular, eyes still on his plate; there was no need for an answer.

"Oh, search me," I said, replying directly to my brother,

and then glancing at my father, and shrugging, as if she weren't there at all. All at once I felt mean.

"You know what, Mamma?" I exclaimed urgently. "You can't just *sing* those songs by themselves, you know. They need a harmonica, to put the *feeling* in. The whistle-stop stations, and the prairie . . . *you have to make the sound of a train whistle lonely,* and the postman . . . when he's bringing that letter edged in black, it's like you hear him crying when he's coming up the walk. And there's another song called 'The Baggage Coach Ahead'. You see there's a coffin in there, and the . . ."

"Good God!" she said.

The stirring lyrics of these songs, to say nothing of what was for me a peaceful, lullaby kind of music, would, at the end of the day, leave me with a melodious glow in my insides; face, shoulders, arms, neck tingling, the edge of my imagination telling of a world I had not known existed, suggesting that romance was not one and the same as *true love.*

There would be something you'd feel deep under your skin, you'd want to give your *whole* self to a person, body *and* mind, and not just be the recipient of a kiss behind the light of a bon fire, feeling someone's mouth on a collision course against your teeth, as I had that summer, the night of the Dominion Day picnic at Wakefield. I gave him a good slap for trying to yank my pants off.

"What's the matter with you?" he had said.

"What do you mean, what's the matter with me?" I shot back. "There's nobody going to try to get funny with me." I barely knew what he looked like—beyond having fair hair and sporting a big ugly Woolworth's signet ring that dug into my neck. But that was three weeks before, when I did not understand these things; there had been no feeling inside me that I could think of. The only sensation I felt, all five seconds of it, was the sudden cold, naked clash of teeth banging in the dark.

I was different now. The ways of true love, as, in Black Luke's songs, were coming to me first hand. Instead of some sappy sixteen-year-old expert experimenting with me, I was isolating in my mind the image of flesh, sinew and confidence, someone like Luke, dungareed, vital, with a romantic Adam's apple, someone who rode the range and heard the cry of coyotes at night, who might sometimes have to be far away, someone thinking of you night and day, with a train ticket in his pocket. I would wait for that day, I fancied. I

liked things that were far off, that way it was more exciting.
And what was the hurry anyway? when I wasn't through
chasing around yet, Luke teasing me about how fast I could
run and climb, all those things I could do with my long legs,
he'd say. I still wanted to run and jump like that, be carried
away on my own. But! this other primitive response, this
pleasant ache inside. From songs I'd heard in the fields? I did
not know. What I did recognize was the beat of a pulse I had
not known before.

And that's when I started slipping away by myself in the
boat, evenings, when everything was quiet, the colours soft as
mauve. There was something special about the end of the
day, every night-stir, every rustle like a physical caress.

I knew a place where the only sounds were made by water,
and every evening after supper I'd row upriver under the
overhang of cedars and pines, past the bend of high rock to
the woods where a mountain stream flowed into the river. I'd
tie the boat to an old stump, and lie down on my stomach
among the ferns, listening to the rush of shallow creek water
tumbling over the loose flat stones.

When the sun's rays began to slant behind the trees on the
mountain directly across, I'd untie the boat and shove off. Instead of staying close to the shoreline, the centre of the river
now: I'd put the oars up and drift downstream with the current. Soon the cottage, seen from a distance, twilight,
darkness a breath away, drifting still. Somewhere a farm
dog's cry, and minutes later, the screen door of the cottage
opening and closing . . . one of my parents? George? Did
they want the boat? I had no idea. I wanted to stay out there;
mid-river, and dew falling in the magic, where sound carried,
where I was dreaming—of what? Sometimes it was as though
my body were a festival of tiny lighted candles, my mind
possessed as I rowed up and down the river, or drifted, Rachmaninoff and "Natoma" sounding soft and sweet across the
water.

One night, a dark and oppressively hot night toward the
end of July, when the moon had come up and hung over the
far hill more red than waxen, I remember taking all my
clothes off, and lying down in the bottom of the boat, the old
tub finding its own direction through the warm dark. How
strange and exciting to be naked out there in the middle of
the river, better even than swimming in the nude, I was
thinking. The marks of my bathing suit, where the tan left
off, were faintly visible.

The verandah lights blazed across the water, but I was out of reach. Silence surrounding me as I let my arms hang over the sides of the boat, my fingers trailing the water and my head cushioned on my shorts and blouse bundled on the seat. Not a stir to the night, breathless almost. Half way down the river before I realized I was almost at Cascades. Still lying in the same position but with my feet well braced, I rowed back up again, the centre floorboard sandy and moist under my bottom, oars bumping unseen logs and suddenly making a terrible clatter, nevertheless forgetting the discomfort, for there was more than daring nudity exciting me. I felt as though I had just seen my breasts and thighs for the first time, *really* the first time. It was of course the whiteness of skin, the pale glow flesh takes on under moonlight. Free of inhibition (which had never been the case in front of a mirror), I imagined I was lying on a silk couch, quilted and ornate like in the movies, a pure white evening gown and satin slippers beside me on the floor. I would be a dancer, or a bareback circus-rider, I decided. Logs boom behind my head, I wiggle my toes and close my eyes, wonderful; another log hits the boat broadside. I stand up and bang it away with the oar, and then lie down again.

"What are you doing out there?" my mother wants to know, calling out from the verandah and going back in again without waiting for an answer.

Funny. Had I told my father about this adventure, he'd have said it was only natural; and if I'd confessed it to Mamma, she'd have asked me what did I feel I had to go around exposing myself for? I'd soon learned I could go to one and not the other. Not that Mamma was strait-laced. Anything but. She was herself a true woman, and I think what she was trying to do, by instinct, was to tell me to protect and hold onto my mystique—seeing me as an extension of herself.

But haying back in the fields? Not what she wanted of me at all, she said.

It used to be George and his friend Jimmie, Mr. Carman's son, up there on the wagon instead; they had started out being the helpers, one driving the team and the other giving Luke a hand with a pitchfork. But they had defected—over the boundary-fence to the adjacent farm, where the farmer, on a smaller, more primitive farmstead, lived alone with his sister; quite happy to have them, stay the night if they chose! An adventure; a wilderness where owls screeched, and where, when they stole out of bed to look out the window, the dense bush was dark and swampy, enigmatic with loons waiting for an answer. They were ecstatic with tales, Mud Lake to jump into, or pole around in on a raft, pitchers of lemonade and fresh-baked buns and pies to stuff themselves with.

That left just me, offering my services; "I could handle the team," I said. And Mr. Carman shook his head and said no, if he was going to have a filly up there she'd have to have muscle, I didn't have enough brawn in my bread-basket. What would happen if one of the horses got stung by a bee or suddenly lost a leg down a hole? "The goddamned Jesus-loving frig of a load could end up in the crik!" What really clinched it for me, though, was the day Luke abruptly dropped the pitch fork and jumped down from the load to go for a pee in the bushes. He still wasn't back when I heard Mr. Carman call out: "By the Christ of Mary, what's the matter up there? Get the Jesus-lead outer yer ass." Out of sight, I climbed up the far side, took hold of the reins and brought the load in by myself. Mr. Carman didn't know the difference, I was hunched down low behind the wooden rack.

A tired walk home at the end of the day, even so I'd sit out on the verandah wondering where the day had gone, hardly knowing what to answer when Mamma said, "Daft, that's what you are. Why don't you stay put and content yourself with a book? Find something to read and take it out under the trees, and not be vaulting on and off a haycart all day."

I wanted to talk to her, tell her I couldn't understand why I got restless some days; perhaps that time was the closest I ever came. I wanted to be pals, like when I was little, and again like the day she was jockeying the spools in her sewing basket. What I had in mind to say was that right now reading a book wouldn't do any good, it made me impatient—I didn't just want to *read* about things, I wanted to do them myself. But I didn't know how to explain.

"Would you like this one?" she asked now, turning from the bookshelf and holding up *The Rosary*. "It's such a beautiful story . . . a love story, you know."

She sat down on the couch and opened the book, hesitating over a page near the end, was that the part she wanted to try on me? changed her mind in favour of Chapter One, and began reading aloud, inflections just so, hoping, surely this would be more compelling than somersaulting from a horse's back with hay streaming out of my hair. How could I resist being tempted?

THE peaceful stillness of an English summer afternoon brooded over the park and gardens at Overdene. A hush of moving sunlight and lengthening shadows lay upon the lawn, and a promise of refreshing coolness made the shade of the great cedar tree a place to be desired.

She closed the book and looked up, holding it out with both hands.

"No thanks," I said, remembering the last beautiful love story she had offered me. By Galsworthy, completely beyond me, couldn't make head nor tail of a single page. Luke's songs had better stories; he brought everything to life, even death.

"What a kid," she sighed getting up, and still clutching her beloved *Rosary*. "You can't be a tomboy all your life, you know. I should never have made you that pair of overalls, it only encouraged you." Watching me closely. "Look at you, just go and take a good look at yourself in the mirror. A girl your age . . . you've got half the fields caked all over your face." And the cry of a coyote wild and clamant in my ears.

———————

Another sultry moon to thrill me that same summer. The haying was over, and the threshers had taken over the golden fields beyond. And for the first time in my life I was to take off for a week in the city, a house-guest at the home of my best friend, Marian. Not only had I never been away on my own before, the only time I'd spent in the city in summertime was when the four of us went in to the Exhibition for the day. There wasn't even time to miss the cottage; before we knew it we were back again.

For several summers I had always hedged, managing to decline Marian's invitation. Finally, Mamma announced, "You can't expect Marian to always be the one to do the visiting, you know." Right in front of her too. "Why do you keep saying no?" she insisted, Marian standing there blue-eyed and reticent, looking from one to the other. I was embarrassed, for I'd heard people say there wasn't a blessed thing to do in the city, you sat around nights the same as you did all day, and after a while you just went to bed. "Did you never stop to think Marian might enjoy showing you what she likes to do at home?" Mamma persisted. Then, "Well?" I was throwing out the supper dishwater at the time, dumping it over the verandah railing into the grass. I remember looking up the hill and thinking, Who the heck wants to put on a dress and stockings just to sit around the steps of someone's front porch? I'd rather go fishing and dangle my legs in the water instead, or row across the river and see the train come in, who got off, what they said, things like that. My mind cavorted; we'd be missing *everything*, Marian and me. Not to mention George's tent he let us sleep in nights, where we had secrets! *True Story Magazine*, to mention one.

"Why don't you give it a try?" my father suggested. "You could phone me at the office, let me know how you're getting along. Would that be all right?"

"Okay," I said, in spite of myself.

That very same night, though, I went through my bureau drawer; what did I have that would be nice to take to the city? there was only a week to get ready, I'd have to see what was still in the wash, not end up with things full of darns. And yet, half an hour later, sitting on the edge of my camp cot, apprehension prevailed again: I'd still have to sleep on the idea. Did I really want to go?

Overnight, self-doubt already gone and I am leaping out of bed, the flap of the tent hurled aside as I stand on the hill stretching my arms to the sky.

How could anyone be that inconsistent?

At the top of my voice I started to sing

> How're you gonna keep 'em
> Down on the farm . . .

"Hey! calm yourself, don't get so excited," Mamma called from the vegetable garden where she was weeding, early, because of the heat. Marian poked her head out of the tent: "What'd she say?"

"Oh, she was just telling me to pipe down, control myself," I said, and clasping my hands around my knees, promptly rolled down the hill in my pyjamas. This comes as no surprise; the ground was there, handy to emotions refusing to be kept in check, in fact heightened, I recall, by the shock of the warm earth.

And oh my, the plans! This was no ordinary event, to be merely *discussed*, but by its very nature something that must be gone into in elaborate detail. Marian was going home in two days, I needed to get everything set up, know ahead of time what we'd be doing—the opposite to the way I am now,

I don't squander surprises. That wouldn't leave much time. Well, nothing we could do about the morning, that was spoken for, Marian and I had already promised Mamma we'd pick blueberries for the pies she intended baking. Visitors from the city were expected for supper that evening.

"They'll down those pies like gluttons," Mamma had said, "so see that you skin the bushes clean." But how could we *concentrate on plans* while doing something else? No question the discussion would have to be left for the riverbank.

"People pick the darndest times to ask you to do things, even your parents," I say: my apology to Marian as we stop for breath, reeling from the spring along the top of the sandpit, nonstop down the gully and up the far escarpment, bodies flung against the trunk of a tree for support, like two drunks, lard pails banging hollowly, dinning above the valley lying below and reminding us the third mountain is a long way off yet.

"I know," Marian replies, pails dangling from a wrist as she wipes the perspiration from her brow. "It's always the same at my place too. But I'm glad your mother asked us. When you're staying with someone, you like to, you know, show your appreciation. We can talk after!" Shielding her eyes from the sun, she hops over a fallen log. "We can be thinking about the *nights*, eh?" she cries, seizing my hand.

"Nights? What about the afternoons?"

"I meant it's best when evening comes . . . say, do you know what I like to do?"

"No. What?"

"I know it doesn't sound like anything much, but . . ." hesitating, plodding along with her thoughts, leaping over another log and then turning around; is she saving what she had to say? or did it not amount to anything?

"I'll bet it's lots," I tell her as we resume walking, pails rattling confidently. Best friends since we were nine, used to moving through leafy glades and rain and pavement and the soft swirl of blizzards after school was let out, heads crammed full, thoughts humming; this sense of immortality, a sense defined more by flesh than mind, limited to the force of the present, the moments just ahead where our feet, or bicycles, are taking us.

And now, squatting over gaps of rock between the blueberry bushes, forcing ourselves to keep silent and wait, contemplating, visualizing what? moving on to the next patch, sly knowing looks exchanged from time to time, sunburned faces peering above the bushes, for some reason on the verge of mania, why the cunning? what was so funny?

It's late afternoon . . . Marian on the wooden dock, slender, fine-boned, a kind of Nordic beauty, lips parted, she's glancing down . . . the river shimmers, slimy weeds undulate, and seen through the trees, a southbound freight train inching along. It's all a montage, we're both talking at once: "Ping-pong photos" . . . "how does this pose look?" . . . "they give you a telephone, you can pretend to be talking" . . . "who are you going to give yours away to?" "I don't know, do you?" Sitting up, suddenly lying down on the dock again, closing our eyes. Premonitions? viewing ourselves as golden (tanned) goddesses? Marian up on one elbow: "Know what?" She goes into detail, she's telling me about the night baseball in Cartier square . . . "Crowds of people cheering," she says, "the place is always swarming . . . league games . . . a real silver cup!"

"Gosh," I said, "golly," as though speechless, thinking of the small groups at the local games roaring themselves hoarse. Why, in the city, it'd be wild.

Sunlight pours down on our cache of free samples, the cosmetics and pharmaceuticals we'd been sending away for—what connection, for what purpose had these been carried down to the shore?—and cross-legged we sit before this collection, Marian's in a cardboard shoebox, mine in one of Granny's old shortbread tins. Tubes, bottles, packets: Forhans For the Gums, Ponds Vanishing Cream, Bluejay Corn Plasters, Neet Depilatory Cream, Sal Hepatica, poultices and kidney pills. Tangee lipstick, Campana's "Eye"talian Balm. Surely stale after two years? and the lipstick jelly in the molten sun?

Marian's hand shoots out: "Let's shake on it," she says, "Sure," I exclaim, "let's." I don't know for certain what it is we're shaking on, a kind of bond, I think, and pump her hand. Triumph as we fling our arms out like flippers, and from a sitting position fall backwards into the water, fully clothed, as quickly running out again, Marian squeaking, jumping up and down in the sand, and me following suit. Did we still have our shoes on?

"Let's the first day walk uptown to Sparks Street," Marian says, water streaming out of her wheat-coloured hair. "Woolworth's sells all those things you know, at the perfume counter."

Fancy. The miracle of it. We hugged one another, for crying out loud, standing there as though departed from our senses, a kind of inane chatter, feeling silly, it didn't sound like much to do. We didn't understand it was part of us.

And now we sit down in the water, the river lapping our waists, delicious cold water on the fever of anticipation, clothes sticking, blouses? sleeveless dresses? transparent in the wet? half-child, half-woman. Go slowly, life.

"As soon as we get to Woolworth's I'm going to give myself a squirt of Evening In Paris perfume," I declared scornfully (it being the one company that had let us down, not so much as a drop out of them; snipping out coupons and buying postage stamps all that winter for nothing), and lunged headfirst into the river again, surfacing to further announce that when the salesclerk wasn't looking, I'd uncap a bottle and spill some down my front, and if I still had time, I'd put a little on the inside of my wrists, the way Mamma did. And Marian the accomplice, nodding. Five o'clock in the afternoon according to the sun, and we gaze down at the sand, thinking, thinking . . .

---

"And remember. You're not to smoke." My mother's voice, her parting words. She has saved them for the very last, a command that must be made from a distance, twenty feet? She stands on the dock, her eyes fixed on the rowboat drifting slowly downstream as I bail. I don't answer, but instead wait until it's time to fit the oars into the oarlocks. I stand up and tease her, I pretend to smoke, my arm sweeps the air. She lets that one go by, and after a sufficiently effective pause, reminds me for the tenth time: "And remember what I said about helping with the dishes." The last I heard, or could make out, as I rowed upstream on my way to the train; my good white linen dress; the cardboard suitcase stuffed to its floral lining with God knows what besides packets of lavender sachets; two dollars to spend, plus George's fifty cents for an Australian stamp he needed for his album.

My mother lingered at the shore, wading up to her ankles, shoes in hand, looking as though she had taken a queer turn. She was ticking off hours and nights: someone else's mother responsible for a head she vowed would be the death of her yet. "George will always land on his feet," she'd say; "as for this one, only God or the devil can answer that."

Twelve noon exactly, and the train pulls into Union Station; coaches emptying under the skylight, the engine snorting great belches of steam. Behind me, in front, the shuffle of feet through clouds of cinders and the smell of burnt coal. In the front row of a crowd waiting behind the iron gate, Marian and her mother, an arm slipped around one another's waist, beaming, people back of them waving, the thrust of an elbow twice knocking askew the hat Marian's mother wears. My steps quicken as I hurry to meet them.

I had stepped off the train grandly. Instead of a schoolbag full of sandwiches and homework I had a suitcase with presumably my best clothes, a new kimono, I remember that, and, in an old Moirs chocolate box, handsomely gift-wrapped in used tissue paper tied with a brown shoelace, two bibbed aprons for Marian's mother. One pink, the other bright yellow, both trimmed with white zig-zag braiding and appliquéd pears and cucumbers, which Mamma had run up on the sewing machine—the night before, the bastings taken out only that morning.

Greetings done, I dropped to my knees in the thick of the crowd and snapped open my suitcase, scrambling through the neatly packed layers, and then stood up holding out the scruffy-looking Moirs box. Anxious to see her reaction, I asked Marian's mother if she'd first like to go in the Ladies; she could open the present there. She said no, why didn't we wait until we were home, what about at lunch-time? didn't I think it would be nice if she opened her surprise at the table? So we waited.

Nice. But a mistake. The next-door neighbour, a pumpkin of a woman with bristly hairs sprouting from the frilly open-necked jabot of her blouse, had also sat down uninvited, to dine. She peered at the "gift" box open on the table, postponing her comment until all was quiet: "For pity's sake," she said, "more aprons? How many does that make?" then turning to me, "They'll only go to the Church Bazaar you know. She never wears aprons."

"I'm sure I shall now," Marian's mother said graciously; and I wished then she'd had Mamma's tongue. If not that, then one of her other methods of the pounce—she'd have snickered first, appearing to truly enjoy the remark, and after a few minutes she'd have quite innocently reached across the table, asking the woman did she know she had a hair on her pretty blouse. Then she'd have given it the tiniest yank.

So *I* did, instead. I couldn't miss out on that one. I was helping to clear away the dishes at the table, and she sat there so full of herself, right under my nose, that's what made it easy. She jumped, the wedge of boiled cabbage she was about to fork into her mouth dropping in her lap.

Dishes washed and put away. Suitcase unpacked. Not a moment wasted as I put my things, in one fell swoop, into the bureau drawer—emptied for my benefit, a fresh sheet of shelf paper lining the bottom—in a top-floor bedroom of the house on Lewis Street. And then we're out on the street, as if our very lives depend on getting to Woolworth's.

The afternoon sun blazed fiercely, and upon reaching Metcalfe Street we crossed over to the west side where the sidewalk was lightly shaded by three-storey dwellings and an overlay of elms. As though on a reviewing stand, women and old men sat on front porches regarding us from hammocks, kitchen chairs and rockers; farther from view, though no less immediate, faces peered around potted ferns from the upper balconies. Heads barely visible above the bottle-green verandah railings, they squatted like nesting hens, their city-pale faces vague and indifferent, as though expression itself were part of their rationed energy.

My first real sense of summer streets in a city, and I am wondering if Marian is aware of the waves of heat coming at us from the sidewalk, and the pungent smell of tar being spread over a sidestreet. I take a sideways glance, and can't tell. It does not matter. There is a promise of adventure, we have a certain age on our side, aren't we almost fifteen? overnight, girlhood done with; sophistication reigns, in the skin of innocence.

Woolworth's cosmetic counter did not have us all to itself. Women coming and going, women killing time as they stretched corseted bodies and bosoms over the open displays, never putting anything back in its right place, I noticed. At first intimidated, embarrassed, feeling like frauds we hung around the department's classy three-counter spread, fingering, uncapping, squeezing the magic array. And paid for that privilege with the purchase of Jo-Cur setting lotion; at fifteen cents its outsized jar provided the illusion of grandiose spending.

Blessed ten times over with the holy water of Evening In Paris, talcum spilling from the neckholes of our dresses onto our saddle shoes, we decided to move on, the next temptation the ricky-tick sound of gramophone records which seemed to be coming from the back of the store. "Which aisle?" . . . "This one's quicker." Approaching. As I do in my mind now. I feel the warped, unpolished floors under my feet, and hear each banjo-strumming note, every syncopated saxophone's blissful dilemma, and what turned out to be the ultimate, the crooners:

> All of me,
> Why not take all of me?

Wedged between a sudden onslaught of five o'clock office workers, we dove headlong and grabbed at haphazard piles of records—scattering bits and pieces of hardware as well since that department shared some of the counterspace—the day's-end conglomerate of records there for the sweet-scented fingers of Evening In Paris to thumbmark.

Semi-delirious, as though stunned out of our wits by the spinning platter, we swayed to and fro, our minds as if in alien bodies clutching this new distance, its hope of what we could scarcely imagine. The salesgirl, "Sadie", not much older than us, if at all, with real silk stockings and peroxide hair, a permanent wave to boot, had been through it all. Sadie, who thrived on confusion and noise, and was quick to oblige with the crooner's pleadings:

> All of me,
> Why not take all of me?

playing the record nonstop without anyone even seeming to notice. End of the record; the turning wishoo-wishoo calling on the magic hand; mechanically it reached out, moved the needle over, then went on fitting the accumulated 78s back into brown-paper jackets as if doing it in her sleep, all the while mercilessly chewing bubble gum and blowing out elaborate pink bladders. Pleased at having someone share her musical tastes, Sadie, with calculated, childlike authority, ignored any and all proffered discs as she turned "All of Me" to the other side. The same passionate promises:

> Little girl,
> You're the one girl for me

Jammed against a counter that crooned its guileless heart, and Marian and I still memorizing and singing. Aloud. When we groped for words, or wavered on nerve, Bubble Gum was right in there, the wad consigned to a molar while she sang lead.

Jesus. What a sight we must have been. Truth is, I'd do it again.

Hunger alone dragged us away from the music. Fifty cents

between us guaranteed a spread at the soda fountain—two hotdogs with bottled Coca-Cola, and after counting our money, one banana split between us. This latter a copycat inspiration. While awaiting the arrival of our hotdogs, we'd been watching two ivory-faced nuns on adjacent stools, digging first into the cherries, then scooping pell-mell at the ice cream, ice cream that by this time was melting rapidly beneath the whirling blades of a ceiling fan like the kind we'd seen in movies about spies in Singapore.

Nearing the end of her demurely gluttonous spooning, one of the nuns dribbled ice cream on her crucifix. She dipped it (it clanked) into a glass of water, and with her pale convent hands dried the cross on the hem of her habit.

A sensible and practical thing to do, yet for all its everydayness, it seemed unreal. Made me uneasy. Unable to bridge that bleak immunity marked by a nun's habit, I began to feel a terrible emptiness, the more so since this nun was young and pretty, with a child's way of laughing behind a tangle of dimpled fingers.

In the mirror facing our stools, I kept watching her, unable to take my eyes from her. Visions poured through my head: charm bracelets and movie magazines, and Evening In Paris, the silver-fox fur I would save up for, the rich man's house I dreamed of giving parties in. And that's what made me feel sad. But then, a preconceived notion had already been set up inside me and I thought, Who now would ever tell her, Why not take all of me?

Such matters of self-imposed deprivation were beyond my comprehension. A life: to be silly, or radiant, or womanly. But here, a life handed back.

I sat there on my fancy-free stool, an inexplicable emptiness eating my heart.

A single recollection was alone responsible. Its impact I still lug around; a winter's night—the winter just past—walking home from my piano lesson. A cold starry night when my fibres as never before seemed to be sailing over the soundless rooftops. And then, all of a sudden, the feeling swept out of me when my attention had become waylaid. I had stopped outside a convent.

I was already in a highly emotional state, giddy, talking to myself even, no one about, the fields and the unploughed streets running into each other, which added to the weird sense I had of trespassing in a frozen kingdom. It had been snowing without letup for two days, and in the afternoon a further inch of sleet had glazed the mounds of drifted snow that seemed to go on for miles, like a snow-prairie.

Having figured out a shortcut through one of the slopes in Rockcliffe Park, I laid my music case on the ice surface, and flat on my stomach slid down headfirst: a good two city blocks' worth. Plunging back up the hill, I had myself another joy-ride, my blood racing half out of my skin. Starting out for home again I began to run, forging my way through the foot-deep crust. Stars twinkled and the moon twinkled back. Not a sound out of the night except for the earth cracking in the cold. And I thought: Winter has put its arms around me. Winter! I felt joyful and wild, as though I were swinging from treetops in that blue-white wintriness. A pageant I had for so long scorned. But then! Emotions pitched the other way; overtaken by a melancholy I could not push away.

Just why I don't know, but I stopped in my tracks outside the huge iron gate of the convent yard, my mitts gripping the bars, the metal slippery with ice and shining like candelabra under the moon. Not a sound as I peered through the gate, transfixed by the huge gold statue of Jesus, seven or eight feet high at the very least, its magnificent arms outstretched like wings against the bright cold sky. Riveted to the rim of the gold halo, a thin icicle had attached itself to the idol's lips. I pressed against the gate and gazed up at the statue, searching my mind for the symbolism it must surely have, the face, the eyes so gentle. I remember being put off by the thin icicle, it looked terrible, like a bloodless umbilical cord, a breathing tube created by the melting sun in the midst of winter's death.

I looked beyond the statue to the prison-grey edifice it seemed to be blessing, and under a lone light bulb, in one of the convent's back rooms, I saw a nun. Back and forth she walked, back and forth in that tiny cell. Bible, rosary, lips moving, draped in all that mourning. I found myself wondering if they'd cut off her hair, was her head shaved? would she still be pretty? I wanted to say: "Come with me and we'll take turns on my music case." But the statue was between us.

So now, at Woolworth's snack counter, I could make no concession. Sitting over my banana split, its globs of ice cream and cherries the symbol of my own freedom, I had to tell myself something, claim these two nuns into my own life. These robed figures were merely costumed effigies, theatrical and not real. Like a cartoon, or one of Grimm's fairy tales. Who ever heard of a nun at a soda fountain? And belching!

———————

Punctually at six o'clock, iron locks on the front doors slid into bolts, like gunshots. Flags of unbleached cotton whirling and flapping down over the counters. And gently, firmly, Marian and I are shooed out the side door. An hour and a half to put in before the ball game.

Turning east, sauntering along Sparks Street now, taking everything in, at intervals tricks of sunlight reflecting, elongated and ragged, the leggy stride of our bodies in shop windows. Once again our images, mirrored while we stand on the concrete bridge over the Rideau Canal, wavering faces superimposed on the canal's locks below Parliament Hill; companions on either side, potbellied, slender, white-haired or smooth-skinned, in shirtsleeves, some dressed to the nines, rubbing elbows as they leaned upon the cement balustrade, gazing into the blue outline of the Gatineau Hills beyond, still others contenting themselves with things nearer at hand as they dropped gobs of spit down into the water. Above our heads, the Château Laurier Hotel, looking fabled with its green-coppered turrets. "Do you think . . . ?"

"Why not?"

Through the swing doors. The newsstand: that looked safe, neutral, lots of people came in off the street to buy a paper. For three cents (maybe it was two cents) we bought the late edition of the *Citizen*, took two steps, hesitated, turned back, thumbed through movie magazines on the rack, bought *Photoplay*; that was for when we went to bed.

How immense and grand the lobby seemed: a Friday evening; cadences of groups, the chatter of new arrivals making for the elevators. This was all new to me, an experience both powerful and disturbing . . . all the fashionable sophisticated people . . . the clatter and motion . . . the sensation rushing at me; a kind of spell that remains in memory undiminished, the way a child remembers an emotional discovery, like a seashell or a stone, or rapids, or a dead animal's skull; at the time there is something about the colour and shape, but sooner or later it is the essence, the *feel* that is exciting and warm. I hardly said a word.

Where had the scheming minds gone, the daring of the blueberry bushes? one with a brown-paper bag in her hand, the Jo-Cur setting lotion, and the other with newspaper and magazine folded under an arm, shocked into good behaviour? Straight-backed and polite, we walked around, mingled, picking up our feet in a manner befitting the mauve twilight cast by chandeliers, the champagne in silver buckets borne by white-gloved bellhops, and the strolling old-timers who knew them all.

Explorations leaving no avenues undiscovered, to be sure. Up the marble steps to the Mezzanine, back down again, finding ourselves at the entrance to the side lobby.

A wooden stand just inside, like the boards they used in vaudeville, but lettered in gold leaf, formally announced: Peacock Alley. Gingerly, Marian and I trod across the Persian carpet, and set primly on the velour and needlepoint chairs along with the other transients—not a few of whom were living high off the hog for the thirties, men in tuxedos, their ladies in plum or silver-lace evening dresses. They sat with neither newspaper nor book nor conversation, putting in time as they waited for the decent hour to dine—in the Main Dining Room, where, at seven sharp, a salon orchestra would attack the first chords of "Glow Worm", or Tosti's "Goodbye", or somebody's "Ave Maria". And Edward German's "Merrie England" before the night was through.

French windows, facing west, opened wide to the warm summer evening: the clock in the Peace Tower on Parliament Hill bonging track of our time. Did we read the funnies? or just gape?

One final tour around before we leave—now that we've found our tongues, can comment.

"That girl looks *fast*, bold," . . . "The teller's just told someone on the phone to shut up" . . . "Is it vomit they're cleaning up?" Tinkle of plates in the Main Dining Room. "The Glow Worm" dancing to wrong notes . . . "Did you hear that?" You could have heard the violin all over the hotel.

Out the revolving doors, past the Union Station and over the bridge, arm in arm as we start down the Driveway to Cartier Square; springy, lush-green, federal grass to walk upon; the clank and din of streetcars receding behind. Dead ahead, sun deflected on the long stretch of canal, motionless as a pool; a scatter of people passing, and I'm conscious of blazers and bright frilly dresses, butterfly skirts that swing, the rhythm of slender legs, of bare arms, of voices. I can't believe I'm one of them; an ache of joy.

"Gee," I said, "I never knew the city'd be like this in summer. It's sure different."

"How do you mean?" Marian stopping, drawing back slightly. Had something gone wrong?

"Well, you know, Sadie . . . aren't you? . . . and no one knows where we are even," I babbled. "And those crooners . . . gee whiz." I could not understand, I felt light in the air, I wanted to do a handstand, even my heart was beating fast. I didn't know what it meant, to be moved like this. But then, it's a big move to suddenly go from one self to another, the more so when you're not aware it's happening—till afterward, when the focus has narrowed down, what season, what moment's very second? That's why this day stands apart, sometimes I think I've never been able to capture quite that same feeling again. I remember wanting to sit down on the grass right there and then, and spend the night talking in the dark. But I didn't mention it.

Marian's reply, cutting through my "Gee-whizzes", like a fleeting song: "That's nothing! Wait till we get to the ball game."

Silence. Words in our heads as we make our way. Breeze off the canal. Arms linking tighter. Then Marian says: "Me neither. I never knew it was like this either."

Footsteps scarcely heard above the tufts of grass, down over a dip of ground, twenty-five seconds of dialogue on an evening in the thirties, a slope where today the shimmer of flowers and stone terraces and floodlights of the seventies characterizes that same rapture, the passing crowd seeing themselves as others, hearing again a song that has not faded away; here, in sunlight, in snow or pouring rain, how many dialogues? how many returning to the wings or back to their seats in the National Arts Centre?

Cartier Square, and the game has already started. We sidle past the baseball fans—an avid, formidable lot not anxious to let latecomers flop down in front—and stand shielding our eyes along the first-base line.

This, the real test. Never mind the five-and-ten or the Château Laurier; Marian and I are getting messages—what's going to happen now? Besides, what had I been so nervous about? Hadn't I been half-expecting this, anticipating the day this feeling would flow through me? I nudge Marian's arm, on the chance . . . no fear, she knows.

Boys.

Boys!

Did we live around here? . . . they didn't remember
seeing us.

In our lives so far, what has matched this? what single perfection? That's the way it was in that decade; it took so little
then. Our innocence perhaps an advantage, freeing us to discover and rediscover?

Dialogue of these boys, who stand beside us in their white
ducks and blue sweatshirts; mild-mannered, the smell of clean
sweat. What exactly did they say? The lanky one is nice. He
stares at me and I feel my face getting red, that's dippy,
*feeble,* but I can't control my skin can I? I wait for Marian to
speak first, and realize she's waiting for me to do it, she has
her problems too. We cannot even give them an answer, but
instead look down, or off in the distance to Elgin Street, pulling at blades of grass and letting the pieces slip through our
fingers.

When they moved on, ventured further, we did not mind.
The turning point had been passed. There has to be a first
time, the turn of a head (and I don't mean being startled out
of your wits by some bare-toothed joker in the dark behind
you, deciding to take a chance on a kiss and felling you with
a flying tackle), only that one wonderful first time, magical
because you had no idea you were being looked at, chosen.
And then you know, you never wonder again, never afraid a
boy won't come toward you. . . .

Someone has made room. "Would you girls like to sit
down?" Front row, close up; down on our knees; legs drawn
around sideways as we sit, starched cotton dresses limp,
soiled, perfume and mustard stains.

We lean against one another and turn our attention once
more to the game, to the teams . . . to an individual player,
to his eyes as he smiles at us. Is he, will he be the one? He,
and the dark one who has his eye on Marian, keep glancing
over; are our dresses pretty? hair shiny? brushed enough? The
smack of a ball in the catcher's mitt and the umpire yells,
"Out!" Cries, screams all around us, we are the only ones
who don't make a sound, or move. Because there's someone, a
stranger, who's handsome, and an athlete, and old—he must
be eighteen. "Strike one!" I see Marian grinning back at hers,
he's the shortstop. "Yours has nice teeth," I whisper. "So has
yours," she says; except I don't know how she can tell, he's
out in centre field. Still, the view from here's peachy, all
that's needed. And even though I know that nothing will
come of it—I'd *die* if mine spoke to me—I've got lots inside

to think about. It's easier to be romantic by yourself, at first anyway . . . the beginning, that's kind of . . . you have to imagine, ponder a while. I'd like to touch him though, take his arm maybe.

Instincts, feeding their revelations, measured, like light through a latticed fence.

———

When the game was over and the crowd began to shift among themselves, or wandered in groups across the park, Marian and I circled about, slowly retracing our steps as we waited until the coast was clear; once the diamond was empty, we felt a need to go over the ground—that would be almost the same.

Back and forth we trailed along the deserted base-lines, the quadrangle-tracings whose warm sand tells us of eye-caresses. We feel them, embossed in the sand.

Summer dusk, falling into night as we leave the park, and walk along the Driveway once more, another direction. Not four feet away, the Rideau Canal lying narrow and still, willow trees skirting the banks, the dew-wet grass with a different, sensuous feel. On go the streetlights, frosted globes that spill footprints of light upon the water, like little continents, wavering, beckoning.

A year ago, a week ago, the life in us learning from the wind and sky. And now the risen moon, making us a declaration: I hereby grant you my magic. A gentle way to take us home.

Not so much as a monosyllable out of either of us. That was the nice part. We were listening to ourselves, thoughts at once preposterous, fragile, not yet ready to be given form. On the slippery grass our steps make faint sounds, as though we are tip-toeing, each within her own separate being. A certain knowledge: we are older now.

And I was thinking of how I'd asked George if I might bring his mouth organ with me, I thought if I was lonesome and couldn't go to sleep I'd play it under the covers. With the door closed nobody would be able to hear me.

But now! with the day's pursuits, everything that had shone for me. I must have been dreaming, I thought, when I prayed the week would soon pass. And while there were six days to go yet, six nights with the harmonica under my pillow, I knew I'd have no need of it. "From this valley/they say you are going" all but forgotten, seeming just then, surrounded by the city-scented night, almost like a song I'd heard a long time ago, a refrain more emotion than melody in the back of my mind, remembered for its yesterday.

"Marian? What do you say we sit here in the dark?" I said after a while. I was thinking of a park bench, the apricot moon, remote stars to look at. It wouldn't even be necessary to talk.

"What time is it?" she gasped, clasping a hand over her mouth—was it late? what excuse could we give? what would we have been *doing* all this time?

"I'll take the blame," I said, "I'll tell her it's my fault. We didn't have watches, and there was no one to ask . . . we thought we shouldn't ask a stranger. . . ."

"We could tell her . . . we can say this is where we were! Momma can't say anything about us being only three blocks away."

"She might though. I know Mamma would. She'd say, 'What's the number of blocks got to do with it? What difference does it make whether it's one block or a hundred?' I can just hear her! 'The pair of you sitting alone in the dark. How would you know who else was hanging around a black canal?' It couldn't just be the Driveway or the Rideau Canal. It'd have to be *a black canal*. You know her."

"Mine's different. She wouldn't say anything in front of you. Momma will save it—till after you've gone. She wants you to be our guest, and she'd be afraid you'd leave. Ever since I got back from Sumach Point she's been saying, 'We must see you both have a good time.' I never had a friend stay over before, you know. Momma's always making excuses, she says it's because she doesn't know their mothers. Isn't that crazy?"

"Mine's the same. Only she puts it another way: *'What kind of a home do they come from?'* And I tell her, 'How do I know? Like ours, I guess.' There's one place I go sometimes: not to visit, just for supper or after skating, things like that. Do you know Janet? Maybe not, they used to live near the cemetery. Anyway, her father has a habit of putting his thumb on a chair just as I go to sit down, he points his thumb straight up; it's supposed to be a joke. But that's dizzy, if you ask me. And now I feel so embarrassed whenever I see him; I have to pretend to like him. I try to be on the lookout, but how can you remember every time you go to sit somewhere? It spoils things, so I don't go there much any more."

Marian was silent, grinning, stepping over the grass as though

it were a soft new rug she was testing in bare feet, absorbed
once again, each step sensuous, full of concentration, changing my own thoughts, returning them to hers. "The way
things happen," I said slowly, reflectively. "When I woke up
this morning, I didn't want to come. And I almost didn't.
George said exactly what Daddy had said, 'Why don't you
give it a try?' And now I'd like to stay and stay. Today's the
best day I ever had."

"Me too. And didn't I tell you right about the ball games?"
I feel her arm in a sudden movement, is she hugging her
sides? She looks so pretty shaking her head, eyes sparkling. "I
never had a boy look at me before," she says, pulling the tip
of a willow branch under her chin. "Have you?"

"No," I reply, and lay my hand on the backrest of a
wooden bench. "Maybe they were going to, and we didn't realize. I don't know . . . I always look away. I feel so foolish."

"On the diamond did you notice how . . . I mean when
they were waiting to come up to bat? both of them coming
over to stand right up close to us."

"I guess they wanted to see what we looked like, eh? because they didn't say anything."

"That's what I was trying to figure out a while ago, why
they didn't."

"Maybe that's what boys do—when they're *serious*."

"Serious?"

"You know, *interested*. Gee, the way they were staring, I
felt kind of funny, more scared than anything. If I'd of had
to stand up my knees would have turned to jelly. You'd have
thought I was going to have an operation or something."

"Me too. But I didn't want to say anything about it. I
thought it was just me."

"It's kind of crazy," I laugh, "us not knowing anything, not
much anyway. I'll bet Sadie does, though. She'd know a heck
of a lot."

"Do you feel the same as before," Marian asks thoughtfully, drawing out her words, "before tonight, like?"

"Yes. No. Not exactly. We never talked about guys before,
so how do we know if we're different? We went so many
places today, but I guess the last one was the best. I got so as
I couldn't even hear all that shouting around me. Remember
that record Sadie played? 'You brought a new kind of love to
me'. That's what I was hearing in my head." Marian's voice
low, she's singing, eyes straight ahead, triumphant: "If the

sandman brought/me dreams of you . . ." And all of a sud
den it's not how you look any more, what dress you're wear
ing, the shine of brushed hair, the band of velvet ribbon
adorning it. It's what's inside you, and you don't know what'
doing it, you can't even answer to yourself.

"Holy cow!" Marian exclaimed. "This is the best talk we've
ever had." And her eyes following a black roadster as i
dipped around a bend, the rumble seat with two couples, one
sitting on the folded-down top, the other a curve of shoulder
leaning back against the velour upholstery. What secrets die
they hold? The girls, had they once stood as we were now
quiet with ourselves once again, feeling beautiful, the move
ment of our hands slight, almost nil, conscious of a grace
within, standing, as if in half-lighted shadows, before a
opening of clouds. And I hear Marian say, "Momma's going
to shoot me, but let's stay," stooping to pick up a leaf
"whether Momma says yes or no about staying out tomor
row . . ." Turning her head. "It's tonight that counts, isn't it?"

A thin yellow-and-white striped dress, the other a pink
and-white cotton eyelet. On a low park-bench we sit close by
the water, arms linked, feet crossed one over the other, white
bobby-socks like silver brocade in the moonlight, hair scented
still with Evening In Paris, rustling lightly above our shoul
ders, our faces like cream-coloured masks reflected in the
canal. And the trailing willows around us in repose, illu
mined, abstract as sculptures; the summer night quiet, the
listening ear of a city when it's standing still. Against the
blue-black night, into the space of time, the world hums in
the telephone wires behind, and in our veins. What does i
mean? We stare into the dark shining water that says nothing
back.

# XIV

A winter evening—or the small hours of the morning, depending on how you look at it. Anyway, a frozen middle of the night when soon I must fall asleep, where it's warm in this bed and the pleasant exhaustion of my body, not cold any more, nestles against the pillows; shoulders, the nape of my neck even, every last cell feeling things the way they *used* to be—due, I fancy, not only to where I've just come from, but other things too complicated to explain.

In the half-light shining through the lamp above the kitchen sink, I can just barely make out my overnight bag where I dropped it on the chair. Has an hour gone by? The temptation is to turn on my side and be done with staring at the ceiling. What is there to explain? Strange things happen.

Hours ago, in a dazzle of silence 300 miles from here, I watched the setting sun, orange in the winter sky, shot through with wisps of black, smoky-looking clouds and the hang of bare trees distant in space. I was standing at the top of the hill behind the old cottage, leaning against the wooden gate midway between farm and cottage, knee-deep in snow, hands in my parka pockets as I inhaled the crisp air, watching the shadows lengthening across the hill, beyond the fence the scatter of sumachs elongated and violet-coloured, more shadow than limb. This was something I'd not done for fifteen years (perhaps more than that) in winter time, and I wondered why. Why always in late spring, or in autumn?

No one, not so much as a beat of life to see, not even rabbits or winter birds, the farm abandoned: farmhouse, the huge barn, chicken coop as if standing in the grip of an auto-wrecker's junk yard, no windows or doors left on the house, the same with the barn. Tarpaper on the farmhouse hanging like twisted charred metal; the machinery shed without a roof; the front half of the cutter lying on its side and coated with ice.

Yesterday, on a sudden impulse, I decided to take off. I had a delivery to make in Port Hope, three weeks' worth of lampshades, and since I'd arranged to settle my cat and dog with their other mother, the lady who lives upstairs, I took a back road out of Port Hope and cut over to Highway 7; no traffic, taking my time through the winding snowscape. I would by-pass Ottawa, I thought, and stay overnight on the Quebec side; there was a ski chalet I'd heard about at Mont Cascades, and that would give me a chance to see the new highway they've cut through the bush, across the Gatineau River at Chelsea. And early the next morning, after breakfast, I thought if I saw a pair of snowshoes hanging up—to rent or borrow—I'd find me a woods or a valley. Failing that, I'd just wander.

Fine. I snowshoed. Mont Cascades. Never still a minute, whoppety-whoppety-tharrump, falling all over the place. I'd forgotten how you spot twigs and rocks, instead of assuming they're clumps of snow. But the quietude! I was *free* of myself! eyes and face smarting in the wind where no tracks led to—or away from—places I'd been.

But, when it was time to leave for Sumach Point, I stood with my hand on the car door, my eyes drawn to the slope of virgin snow I'd thumped across, back and forth, the ragged flapping of cross-hatches up hill and down dale, and I thought what difference does it make where you are, when the tracks are made by the same soles, the pattern left bearing the same inner knowledge, the discord and harmony sprung from the original? and in the end, still resonating? For me anyway.

And so an hour and a half later, I stood on the hill behind the cottage, and held my breath. To think I was here in that snowbound perfection again; beforehand, the walk across the icebound river serene and deep and vast, the current gurgling contentedly under the weight of concrete-ice; reaching the farm gate at the top of the hill, I could still tremble with joy as I looked across the river at the village, up and down the sweep of white slopes, the dark woods of the mountain like blue-grey brush strokes, closer to heaven than I remembered. And no farther away than the Luke I remembered, his brown-eyed squint, the smell of his dusty boots and dungarees, the sweat of him drying in the shade of the cool barn, his tender devotion to the horses, the morbid devotion to his harmonica, what this ground meant to me then. Just as it did in winter, Mr. Carman and Jimmie with the horses and sleigh waiting at the station to meet George and me as we stepped off the train; buffalo rugs, bells jingling, Diamond and Daisy galloping us back across the river and up the hill to the farm for a weekend. I couldn't think of anything else just then, our home away from home. I thought of the whitewashed walls, wind whistling around the corners of the roof, chairs drawn up in the cosy kitchen, learning to play Euchre and Five Hundred, wondering what the animals were doing in the barn now that we had bade them goodnight. And always the fields to wake up to, looking at them: what if one day they were no longer there?

I plodded back down the hill and stopped briefly outside the cottage, staring as though seeking an answer from the boarded-up windows and doors, the secret within: will I finish my quest here? Is this where I'll discover myself, the end of the line? like railway tracks, footprints have to come to a stop somewhere, there's no more ground to cover; feeling my way as I mounted the piebald drifts of snow on the verandah steps, and telling myself, That's all there is, you've exhausted the trails, the woodpiles and pieces of buttered toast, the before and after and everything in between, what lies ahead belongs to the songs you've heard, from Rachmaninoff to ragtime to "Redwing". Strangely, it was not even Rachmaninoff I hummed as I sat on the verandah railing, not even "Natoma" I sang, but

> Beat the drum slowly
>
> And play the fife lowly
>
> For I'm a dying cowboy
>
> And I know I've done wrong.

And I don't know why. I lie here against these pillows, and I don't even know why.

A light snow was falling as dusk came down and I retraced my tracks back across the river to where I'd left my car. Allowing an hour or so for dinner (a French restaurant I knew of in Hull), and another half-hour to drive through Ottawa, I'd be home before eleven.

And would have been, had I not seen a bright red neon sign: DIXIELAND JAZZ, the jagged letters TONIGHT flashing on and off, beckoning. Why not? I thought. Hadn't the small print read: Continuous from seven? It wasn't as though there'd be a wait, like for a floor show, spending half the night and your wallet before the action begins. Yes, I shrugged, why not tap my feet or a swizzle stick to a few tunes, I go berserk when I hear real Dixieland, and when was the last time I'd done this?

There was a party going on inside: parents, grandparents, all the relatives and friends, sober and otherwise, of a twenty-one-year-old man who'd brought his banjo along; the kind of party where the other patrons join in, and turn out to be the best mixers (high-flying and earthy they were, what did they care if some tight-assed relative threw a wet fish?). Save for Grandpa and Grandma! with their tapping spoons and old-world observations, calculations pricking the air, getting slightly tipsy, the snap in them beating the rest of us by a country mile. Grandma wore a toque and smoked a pipe; and Grandpa, in a double-breasted suit with padded shoulders, and wide-legged trousers, rising from the feast to approach a girl he'd had his eye on (quite obviously the date of the taken-aback young man sitting next to her, a shy, dark-haired, sexy-looking girl, lovely enough to be Miss Canada, if not Miss Teen-Universe), and whirling off to the dance-floor with her.

And! for a man whose dancing days you'd have thought began and ended with the Schottische—Western style—such a spirited and graceful high-stepper the other couples soon vacated the floor and stood around applauding (how do you *dance* to New Orleans jazz?), the girl quite up to every mad seize and turn of his hand, giving him the odd boomps-a-daisy with her shapely little bottom.

This is swell! I thought, sitting between two uncles (one deaf), pink faces all around me, fat hands reaching for another helping of roast suckling pig, glazed apple in its mouth, just like the ones in the butcher's calendar we used to have on the kitchen wall at home; Baked Alaska for dessert, cognac, beer, and dandelion wine someone had brought in a thermos; the end of the table growing distant as room was made for more, tables being shoved together, a new linen tablecloth, Grandma's eyes and mouth gleefully snapping directions, the police coming in for a sip and departing, and Miss Teen-Universe, this time returning to our table, falling exhausted into Grandpa's lap: "Grandpère!" while Grandma cackled out to the waiter to bring another glass. Just swell, said I aloud, cackling to myself as I thought, Who knows what time I'll get back tonight, and who cares?—until I looked up and saw a man coming in the door, his tunic-over-coat and sealskin cap white with snow, standing there shaking the blizzard off like Nelson Eddy playing a Mountie in the Northwest Territories.

My God!! Snowing all this time! An avalanche coming down? the visibility driving . . . would the roads be impass-able? I bolted my *crème de menthe* and tore out of there, ex-pletives erupting as I grabbed my things at the check-room. There was an appointment in the morning I had to see to, a matter of life and death—like money. A contract that could easily go to someone else. Why hadn't I thought to check the weather forecast? Not that they're even close.

Zipping up my parka as I ran to my car. Bitterly cold, and the parking lot gleaming like marble. I'd have to chuck the idea of Highway 7 and take the 401 back, I decided, at least they keep it salted. And now, if I could just keep awake, make sure I stopped for coffee, drop in at Maxim's along the way; and, if I could stay in the westbound lanes, and if the cars in the eastbound ones stayed in theirs, I didn't see why I couldn't make it back before 3:00 a.m. Which I did, on two coffees, one doughnut, and one windshield wiper.

What I had not bargained for, though, was the condition of the rear service-lane where my garage is, and where for some inexplicable reason no snowplough has ventured these past three winters; a single lane of deep ice ruts that never thaw because the sun never reaches them. Almost impossible to manoeuvre around when a foot of snow has fallen; a foot and a half to spare on either side doesn't leave much, not when you're making like one of the Hell-Drivers trying to get traction on the ice. The urge is to stop, or slow down. Ten times to none, you get stuck.

Practised and all as I am (the Ontario Motor League and I having parted company one bright frosty morning: "Lady, where's there room for me to turn around? The Emergency Truck . . . do you want me to hang it from a tree?"), 2:45 a.m. and the blinding snowstorm still in a rage, and here she comes, Lucky Teeter herself, full of wine and roses and coffee, approaching, taking the ruts cautiously, increasing the speed gradually, a medium-compact car trying to make the do-or-die turn into the garage. And failing.

Stuck broadside in the foot-deep ruts; and fifteen minutes later, the bag of sand all used up, no sign of life anywhere; the snow shovel, plus a smaller one, lying against the elm,

useless. Three o'clock in the morning, and the garages that
serve two streets, mine and the one back of it, a gloomy reminder I couldn't just walk away and leave the car, or sit
endlessly with the engine running. I'd tried to keep warm that
way, whistling Dixieland as I tapped the plastic windshield-
scraper against the wheel, hoping for the miracle others before me had hoped for. No, I couldn't very well go to bed.
What if someone an hour from now had to get by? Would I
write a note and stick it under the windshield-wiper? What
good would that do? it'd be covered in no time.  —

I locked the car up, leaving the lights on. Maybe there'd be
someone abroad: people have to get home sometimes, they
can't always wait for the worst to let up. Would taxis be running? There'd be no point in phoning for one, that was certain.

I plunged over to Yonge Street, and stood in the lighted
doorway of the green-grocer's at the corner; a good intersec-
tion, an unobstructed view if a car loomed in that tunnel of
swirling snow—looking through what I could see of it anyway. I leaned against the door laughing, slap-happy: why
didn't I call the Humane Society? tell them I *had* to get to
the morgue: that always makes people jump, they'll do anything for you. And then along it came, a lone taxi, sliding
around the middle of Yonge Street. I ran out, fur hat in
hand, waving my arms.

No chat: he sat, blowing his nose into a handkerchief as I
explained through the half-open window, then opened the
door and asked me to get in. "Might as well drive there," he
said off-handedly, skidding a huge and perfect circle as he
turned the taxi around.

The operation? took a good half-hour.

What did we do? Dug, clattered shovels, heaved chunks of
ice, leaned against the post holding up the roof of the garage,
walked around the car, stomped our feet to keep the circulation going, carried shovels of more snow behind the elm and
dumped them on top of the winter's pile, rested, shook snow
out of our hair, flicked it out of our eyelashes . . . "God, but
it's cold." I said.

"Yeah, but it's bracing."

"What do you say we give it a try now?"

"Too soon yet, you may have snow tires but they're not
worth a pinch in this. . . ." Clink of shovels crashing head
on. A foot thrust for the next dig.

"Nice neighbourhood, this," he says. "All kinds. Not too

much money. I knew a guy who lived over there." His head turns and nods at the row of garages immediately behind and down a bit.

"Yes," I agree. "It's great in a way." How do you start up a conversation in the middle of the night? Well, you do. Maybe you're ready for one, maybe you haven't heard yourself say a word all day. "Everyone's on the move in this neighbourhood," I say, "there's a certain flavour, a temperament I guess. I like to walk around. . . ."

"On your own?"

"How do you mean?"

"By yourself?"

"Sure. Don't you ever go walking alone?" Shovels clanking, snow whipping down from the roof of the garage.

"Can't say as I have. Here, let me dig that out . . . Christ, is it a rock? You'll get a rupture, it's froze right into the ground. Been here long?" Husky-voiced, abstract expression. And I'm thinking, You start up a conversation because you're alive. Is there a better reason?

"Five years," I reply. The rock won't budge, but he keeps at it because it's under the front wheel.

"That long?" Looking up at me now, and offering me a cigarette. Difficulty in getting the two cigarettes lit, but we manage, cupped hands, the butane flame about ten feet high. "What do you do for the juice of life?" he asks, putting his lighter back inside his windbreaker pocket.

"Pardon?"

"I said what do you do for juice?"

"Oh that. Haven't heard that expression in a donkey's age. No problem. The liquor store's only a couple of blocks away you know."

"Wasn't what I was getting at." Blowing into his hands, eyeing me.

"Oh? No? What then?"

"I'd like to lay you."

Open-mouthed, I splutter, choking on the intake of snow-flakes caught in my windpipe: "What'd you say?"

"I want to lay you." He takes a step back, a light from somewhere blinding his vision, and the end of a board flies up, hits the back of his head.

"That's what I thought you said." A pause. He's thirty years old if he's a day, nice looking, good body, outgoing . . . And those eyelashes! *contented* eyelashes. So what's all this in aid of?

"What for?" I say.

"What for?" fitting the board back in place. And down the lane, twenty feet away, the swinging overhead light throws runnels of gold-coloured haze up and down a snow-bank piled against a wooden fence, the metal lamp squeaking wretchedly, or beautifully, in this crazy darkness. Do I say nothing? just pick up the shovel and dig some more snow, wait for this to blow over? The car is still in its tracks. We haven't even started to try to move it yet. And I think, *What for?* . . . How *do* you answer that? And so I say, "You make me feel silly, do you know that? This is no time . . ."

"I know." He glances up at the snow sifting down, and holds his bare hand out to catch the flakes. "What are you thinking?" he asks with an honest, guileless, and disappointed expression, leaning forward on his shovel; we are friends, and his pride is hurt.

"I was thinking you're crazy," I said, "and we should try getting the car to move. Otherwise we'll be here all night. And you're losing flares."

He chucks his shovel into the mound we've piled, scoops some snow off the fender and tosses it lightly at my shoulder. I return the compliment.

"Try taking the wheel," he says, "and I'll see if I can lift the rear end. Roll your window down so as you can hear me."

"Okay."

After the second attempt, he stuck his head in the window: "We've shifted a little. Next time we should make it." He took a few strides and then came back: "Not too much gas this time. And be careful you don't go through the wall and out the other side. I'd say this garage is about ready to fall down."

Made it. Safe and sound in the garage; lights and ignition shut off; deciding I would get right out, roll the window up after he was gone.

Standing with his back turned, half in and half out of the garage and lighting a cigarette as I stepped out of the car. Now what? I decided that whatever it was, I'd take off my mitts again and shake hands, that'd be friendly, and warm, show him I appreciated his company. And then I heard him say, "I don't suppose you've got a drink? I wouldn't mind if you offered me one."

"Oh, but I can't . . . inside, I mean. There's someone . . . you see . . . a person who might not understand. You know how it is, jealous and all." I didn't think he swallowed that one. Why in the name of God would I be staggering around out on the street, in the middle of the night—to say nothing of a blizzard—if I had some healthy lump asleep inside? "Tell you what I could do, though," I went on. "How would it be if I brought you one out? You'd have something to warm you," my mind running on, what was wrong with that? wouldn't that be all right, glancing over his shoulder, the taxi with its lights hazed over, engine still running, the round dome on the roof submerged in snow, glowing faintly like a tiny igloo.

"Who said I needed anything to warm me? Got that already."

Poker-faced, I pushed my hair back, ramming my fur hat down on top of my head nonchalantly as I replied: "Well then, something to knock back before you hit the road? Yes? Rum? A bottle of beer?" Grinning at me now, and asking: "What's your name?"

"Hannah."

"*Hannah?* That's an odd name, you don't hear very often . . ."

"Oh I go by several names just now . . . don't ask me to explain, it's too complicated."

"Really?"

"Yes really. These days I hear my name being called: ten times a day, in my head I mean, and never the same one twice . . . Now, about that shot of rum. Or is it beer?"

"Jeez. You sure *are* complicated. Wouldn't have thought so."

"What's so complicated about giving yourself a bunch of names?" handing me his cigarette—for a puff? No. He's lighting me one. Nice.

"Is he asleep?" he asks, putting the cigarette between my lips, like an old movie.

"Is who asleep? Oh, him. Yes, I expect so. He sleeps quite a bit. What's *your* name?"

"Roy."

"Be back in a minute, Roy. Say, you still haven't told me . . . you didn't say what you'd like to drink."

"Got a beer?" Then, politely, very politely: "Wouldn't object to a bottle of beer."

"Cans—I'm afraid that's all I've got."

"Canned's fine."

"Why don't you sit down? In my car. I'll only be a minute."

I couldn't find the beer at first, and this delayed me . . . I knew it was in the cellar some place. Then I remembered I'd moved it to get at the Christmas decorations. After that I had trouble getting out the back door with my hands full, trying to balance two cans and a tumbler, creeping out backwards like a thief.

I saw that Roy had shut the ignition off in his taxi, leaving the lights on in case a car turned down the lane, and was back in the garage now, leaning against the front fender of my Hornet.

"Well," I said, handing him a tin and setting the other, along with the glass, down on the hood, "that was sure nice of you tonight. You were very kind to do that. Thank you, Roy." He blew into his hands and rubbed his fingers together. "Oh, goodness, what's the matter with me? Your hands must be frozen. Would you like me to hold the tin while you pull open the tab?"

"Would you mind?" Leaning into one another while I wondered if I should get the flashlight from the glove compartment.

"It's sticking," I said. "What's the matter with it?"

"Son of a bitch, eh Hannah?" Grinning. Husky-voiced again. But not looking at me. Foot braced against mine, fingernails scraping against the metal, completely engrossed. After a few seconds, he muttered: "Bloody thing needs a pneumatic drill," changing position, shoulders hunched, God he's big, I thought, he'd make two of me, leaning into me on the other side this time, one foot on a wooden platform—which gives way, sending him flying, his elbow clipping an old glass chimney lamp on a shelf, which he attempts to seize, but obviously that globe's been waiting for a moment like this, and crash! the edge of the wheelbarrow? or into the keg of nails? standing on my foot now, a thumb wrestling with the tab, too mortified to glance at where the pieces fell, muttering under his breath: ". . . bloody goddamn can." He flicked his fingers abruptly, as if he'd just caught them in a doorjamb.

Lord. Was this going to take all night? When could I retrace my steps across the backyard and call it a night? Not a sound, except for the creaking trees, and clumps of snow plopping down from branches. What a position to be in; if I shift, or move away a little, he'll think there's something wrong with his person, the grease on his hands maybe. I move my left foot, get more traction, he turns his head and smiles; I laugh and say, "It's taking longer than it did to get the car out." And the bedroom-look he gives me tells me something of what he's going to reply, which is: "I believe in taking my time in everything." I look down at the beer can, bend my head over his struggling fingers, and suddenly the can explodes in our faces, spray fizzling like a water-hose. "Oh, I forgot!" I exclaim staggering back, "I dropped the tins on the way out the door. I should've told you."

Exit laughing: a funny way to go, finally. I turn back and say, "Never laughed so much in all my life. G'night, Roy."

Not that I was speeding away all virtuous and proper, knowing my place and that sort of thing. For I wouldn't have minded in the least, the night full of lovely snow and the sweeping white wind brushing our shoulders; and I thought, The shoulders of a man trying to communicate. A love he just wanted to put somewhere instead of letting it go wasted. That's what I was thinking as I crossed the yard, you don't always need words, no language but the moment itself, rippling along on a beam, an inner-unknown crossing circuits, destined . . . oh God, but not now, *please* not now! It was—would have been—something gentle to put into the universe. And God knows that too is my need, but I can't. Am I not claimed, owned by something deeper, still buried under the past, neither child nor woman?

I shook out my wet parka and hung it above the tub; put the kettle on; turned on the electric blanket, pulled the covers back a little, three pillows fluffed out for a half-hour's reading. "Roy," I heard myself muttering, "you and that silly goddamned friggin' beer can." I started the bathtub running, maybe that would help get some of the kinks out of my legs—too much snowshoeing and clog-dancing with Grandma. I opened the kitchen cupboard and got out the bottle of rum, and then a lemon. By Jove! and wouldn't that go down well! The newspaper. That's what I'd read. Padding through the vestibule in stocking feet, and back to the bedroom. Oops, forgot to pull the drapes at the window-seat. Snow deepening in the backyard. When's it going to let up? A light, a single headlight fuzzed over, what . . . ? The taxi? Roy's taxi? Is *he* stuck now? The least I can do . . .

Not my parka but my winter coat, scarf flung around my neck as I turn off the tub, and out I tramp. Two headlights, yes, Roy's taxi all right, the ceiling lamp is on and he's sitting there reading a pocketbook—one of those street-guides? He hears me (or else has eyes in the back of his head that work) and rolls the window down.

"Why are you still here?" I ask.

"What took you so long?" he replies, motioning me to get in. Classical music playing on the car radio, Debussy's "Engulfed Cathedral". Is he . . . what about the fares he's been losing? is the cab his own? Not a word as he switches on the ignition, puts the taxi in reverse and backs up slowly, wheels securely in the ruts, eyes surveying my landlord's space in the garage. "Do you think I can make it the first time?" he asks. And I glance down at the bright blue cover of the pocketbook lying between us, Conrad's *Heart of Darkness*.

"What do you mean, what took me so long?" I exclaim haughtily, right up on my high horse. "I had no intention . . . I hadn't thought about it at all."

"No, I was aware of that. But Hannah's intentions don't always lay down the law, do they?"

"What's that supposed to mean?"

"It means I had . . . something told me you would be back." And before I know it, he's landed the car in the garage, and he's helping me out. He holds the garage door open; together we ease down onto the icy step. I'm off balance and stagger, and my coat is caught in the door, which he frees, and then picks me up, starts carrying me through the snow across the backyard.

"Tell me," I ask, as if used to being carried through snowstorms, "what gave you the feeling . . . how did you know? I didn't even know myself. I just thought you might be stuck."

"Hands," he replies. "You can tell lots by the touch of a person's hands. Everything."

"What!?" *Everything?* "And you! telling me *I'm* complicated!" He doesn't answer, nor even look at me, one step at a time through the snowdrifts, explaining in that unassuming way of his, "I'm used to the touch of hands, opening car doors, dollar bills going back and forth, silver, loose change . . . old people, middle-aged, kids. And us folk." Us folk? "Either they slap it at you, pitch it, hand it, shake it or press it into your palm, and . . ." gosh, did I leave the door open? well, the screen door . . . "and of course there's always a hat someone's left behind, or an umbrella, a book . . . you know? And your hands, Hannah . . ."

"But in this freezing cold, how would you know what you were touching?"

He sets me down on the kitchen floor and I grip the corner of the stove, while he reaches to lay the empty glass on the kitchen counter, and stands beside the counter, half in the bedroom doorway, his back to the bed. It's not my knees that are wobbling, it's my thighs, at the moment they don't seem to be part of me, and I calmly announce: "I'm afraid my legs have had too much of a workout today," and realize it sounds off-putting, the male in him doesn't quite know how to take this, so I tell him it's just an odd feeling of having no power over them, that I'm not tired or anything, it's momentary, the excitement of the day and that. "In a few secs," I add, looking down at my thighs, as if to make sure they're still there, and he says (protectively), "Where were you coming from anyway? Kinda late to be out alone. . . ."

He lies beside me now, half on his side, deep in slumber, one arm under the pillow, the other across my breasts, fingers closed loosely over ends of my hair; the most contented eyelashes I ever saw. I cannot imagine what he is dreaming of.

# XV

"What do you mean you have to go upstairs and get busy with the tongs?" my brother exclaims, his eyes giving me that "this-is-no-time-to-be . . ." look, holding me back, his arm reaching around behind my father's back, tugging at the armhole of my middy. "We've barely got started. Don't you know we have to leave in half an hour? Besides, who's going to see your hair anyway?"

"I know," I intone, and from where I'm seated, I cross one foot over the other and swing my legs, hard-pressed by the decision what should I do? Mouthing words, it's all right for George, boys don't have to concern themselves with such things.

Everything's in motion, a minute's worth of ragged but pleasant ruckus, the piano keys for one thing, and chattering

mouths, squawking mouths, a sudden high-pitched dissonance
and the cat flicks her tail in irritation, the half-asleep dog
whines and covers his ears—is there no end to this? A play of
shadows on the wall when the mahogany bridge-lamp gets
bumped, a hand shoots out to grab the stand. And while par-
ticles of dust from the lampshade twinkle under the beam of
light, things settle down again. I hunch my shoulders and
finger my hair, there's still the question—should I sneak upstairs and plug in the curling iron? Yes? No? I go on swinging my legs, ten seconds, fifteen. . . .Clearing off the dishes
from the supper table, Mamma trips back and forth, dodging
around us, where George and I sit with our backs turned, one
on either side of the piano bench, our father in the middle,
his hands moving easily, chords rolling, now fast, now slow.
Intermittently, our mouths open wider in song, we pounce on
a phrase and bellow, determined, it seems, on drowning out
the piano. It is a situation that finds us memorizing songs
again.

And not for Mr. and Mrs. Nolan either. "The Lost Chord"
is almost a legend now, for George and I have outgrown
pocketing crisp new shinplasters; our parents' friends no longer feel compelled to buy back our warts. At fourteen and fifteen, we have other fortunes in store—beginning with this
very evening. Instead of wandering upstairs to our rooms,
dreaming up ideas as we hunted around for bits and pieces to
make things, like the hundredth peep-show, or do homework,
or *boring* jigsaw puzzles, or deciding to put on our skates and
see what's doing at the Lindenlea skating rink, we were stepping out, about to set forth for city lights!

A time we had often dreamed of, the special privilege, the
freedom, of one day vanishing into the night, no longer children. And it had hit us there on the piano bench, the house
surrounded by the outside sounds of mid-winter. I remember
the brittle creaking of treetops out in the yard, the wild and
windy draughts of east-wind rattling the storm-window in the
dining room. Yes, what freedom! as we envision lighted
cafés, doorways thick with blue smoke and rollicking with
applause and draft beer, pounding along again, no less a part
of the muted sounds of passers-by and who knows what?
Why, the trip up town by streetcar, that in itself. And not
just to an early movie (the "pictures", as Mamma called it),
but two orchestra seats for an operetta. Famous artists in person. It was all I could do to contain myself. Stars of stage
and screen, people who sang on the radio and made records,

maybe. At the Capitol Theatre, no less! the moviehouse with a big expensive stage, not a squirt of a thing like the one in our high school auditorium, or the one at the Rio near the museum, where the nuns gave a concert for the poor and had to sit half down in the audience, but a stage big enough to hold armchairs and a sofa and bed, we'd heard, there was even room for a stairway with a banister. . . .

"But look at this mane," I faltered, "just look at it," urgently holding up two long hanks of hair, at-odds in length, poker-straight and coarse as horsehair. "See?" I argued, my voice rising, then, sinking into inaudibility, muttering to myself, "Who wants to go up town at night looking like this, for crying out loud?" I sat down again on the piano bench.

"That's better," my father said, pushing up his shirtsleeves. "You ought to be familiar with some of the music beforehand. Just hearing me play the odd excerpt from time to time isn't the same. This way, you'll be able to understand what the story's about: what's happening with François Villon and his Lady Catherine, the guillotine . . . here, tilt the lamp over more this way, so you can follow the words better."

"I love this," George says, "that marching song. But I've forgotten again how it goes." My father smiles and says, "Where were we?" looking from one to the other, itching to get back at the music. "Well then, why not go over it from the beginning, once more, eh kids? We've got time." He glances down at the pedals, hands now in motion, feeling out the key he wants to try this time, and his shoulders give a curious shrug as off he goes, in his element. He crouches over the keyboard, swings back, forward again, soon all three of us are rocking, wild with random words; and now, for the first time, we're all in tune, lungs and piano bringing the roof down. George, or I, or both, leaning closer. "Hey wait! I lost my place." Shouting again, "And to Hell with Burgundy! . . ."

"All right, all right, muzzle it, the pair of you," Mamma sighs en route to the kitchen, carrying empty plates and the sugar bowl. "You're not auditioning, you know. Leave the histrionics to the tribe on stage." The phone rings at the opposite end of the room, and she turns back, sets the dishes down on the table. Crash! "Fool of a cat," she explodes, "always underfoot." Brrr-r-r-r-ring. Brrr-r-r-r-ing. She makes it to the mission table where the phone is, by a window in the corner, sits herself down on a chair, taking her time as she lifts the receiver. "There's nobody home," she announces with a straight face, stroking the cat who has jumped onto her lap.

"Besides, you've got the wrong number." Click. "Well, that's that," she says calmly. "Wonder who it was, Flinty?" she purrs to the cat's head. "Never mind. What's one more telephone call? Can't have anything interfere with the Metropolitan Opera."

---

Not half an hour ago, shortly after we had sat down to supper, our parents had asked, "How would you like to have our tickets for the show tonight?" Go in their place? Am I hearing right, I wondered? their precious tickets? Holy crow! Hadn't they written away for them long before Christmas? What's more, how many times had they taken them out of the envelope just to look at them?

"Oh well, we've seen it often enough," Mamma replied when I asked how come, wasn't *The Vagabond King* one of their favourites? my eyes dancing as I threw my knife up and caught it. "Your father and I decided it's about time the two of you saw something on the stage, the legitimate stage."

"What's that, legitimate?" George wanted to know, suspicious, his tone suggesting he was perhaps being roped into something, an evening that in all likelihood would fail him. "You don't even know what it is yet," he said, eyeing me. And my father, returning to the table after putting another piece of cannel coal on the grate fire, said, "Legitimate's another way of describing a professional outfit putting on an actual performance, son. And you're seeing one of the good ones tonight," he added, his face expectant, quickly reflective. "Ah," he exclaimed, tapping the handle of his fork up and down on the breadboard, one, two-three, four-five-six, self-conscious tenor voice taking over: "Sons of toil and danger . . ." The fork sails through the air, is left where it is on the floor as he tells us of the vagabond poet who wanted to be king for a day.

"Hey, Mister," Mamma remarked, this time it's her knife, reaching across to tap his plate, "your meal's getting cold."

Afterward, when it was time for Mamma to go to the kitchen to fetch the dessert, I gathered up my empty plate, following on her heels: "Is it all right if I use your curling tongs, Mamma? Can I curl my hair?"

"If you eat your bread pudding. And that doesn't mean picking out all the raisins. You're not taking one step until you've cleaned your dish."

Ten minutes later . . . plunk onto the floor goes my plate

and the dog laps my pudding. Who's to see? Mamma's out in the kitchen making another pot of tea, and Daddy and George are over at the piano, already engrossed. Foxy me. I have to hang around for a minute, here at the table. Still, I'm watching, and listening: "The Song of the Vagabonds," that's the one George likes best, he says that "Only a Rose" is a girl's song. But wow! Burgundy again. What a din! Will the piano be okay? Can it stand that? Softer now. "Huguette's Waltz". Quickly I pick my plate up off the floor, I realize it's empty; the dog's teeth were banging against it, giving me away. I remove the evidence, a wet dog hair, from the dish, and put it back where it was at my place at the table, spoon across just so, and proceed to the piano bench.

"Play 'Some Day'?" I ask my father, edging in. "That's my piece. The words are beautiful, they're absolutely *beee-eut-eeeful*."

And from the kitchen: "Some day/you will seek me and find me." Mamma's voice, she's singing, makes up words for the next line: "Oh my/ the Heinz pickles are finished," which means Daddy stops in the middle of "Huguette's Waltz". He likes when she joins in. Does he ever! I bet when George and I leave, I bet you anything in the world the second we're out the door, he'll play her bloomin' "Finlandia". And then Handel's "Largo". After that, a little of Dvorak's "New World Symphony". All her favourites. He'll play and play until I don't know when—until they've had enough, I guess.

In the downstairs hall, the feel of the oncoming night is relative: our parents on the one hand, watching us putting on our galoshes as we prepare to leave, caught in the momentum, knowing what it's like to be in our place. And not just that, not just thinking of the thousand times they had been, nor even the first time flashing through their minds—wouldn't there have been a moment of sudden reflection, all at once their children growing up around them; why, they've never done anything like this before, their own tickets . . . no, not like this. And on the other, George and I, intent, all thumbs, giddy inside, a silent flow of thought. Mamma switches on the porch light; this being a Friday there's no need for the usual curfew, it will burn steadily for hours. I'm ready, straggly hair brushed and combed, shining under a green tam, hands in pockets feeling for a hankie, discarding a stick of gum, do I have both mitts? I hear the hands of the electric clock whirring on the mantel as I observe George, not saying a word, the brown eyes delighted as he puts on Daddy's white silk muffler, taking his time, casually smoothing the folds, whistling now as he crosses left over right. He holds the over-lap down with his chin, twirling his coat behind his back and onto his shoulders. For Pete's sake, you'd think he was put-ting on a cloak or something. At last! Finally he's ready.

"A silk scarf looks silly with a hockey toque," I tell him, and then wish I hadn't. Because all the time he was fixing the scarf—so the monogram would show—he was whistling "Some Day". My piece! Gee, it was his way of telling me he liked it too. He glances in the hall mirror, takes off the toque, and on second thought puts it back on. The feeling he had, being pleased with himself, maybe it's still there. He likes that toque. He shoves the two pink theatre-tickets into his over-coat breast-pocket, making certain they show too, like the monogram. Mamma and Daddy move toward the door: "Have a good time kids. . . . Got your cartickets? And remember, don't be whispering while the performance is go-ing on."

Oh, the solitude of decoding the process of growing up. How clearly the night speaks to me again, a night that seemed—from the day I was born until that time—to stand above all others. Nothing of its freshness has since dimin-ished. Nor is likely to. Difficult to explain. The fulfilment of anticipation perhaps a lesser dimension. Because the other, more subtle stroke was the real mark left. Deep in the gut, as deep now as then. It was as if we were setting off to the moon. Turning a time into what I think of now as that glad night: engulfed for the first time by the outside world, discov-ering in a vague sort of way the direction of one's life, life stretching far, near, whatever it was, creating itself, ours to conquer; sharing that discovery as defined by our homeward journey, deliberating under a dissolving sky, four inches of pure white snow to leave fresh tracks in, five inches, six, and *feeling* what we cannot yet express, no words to give the night some shape, nothing but the sensations of knowing . . . something.

Setting off to the moon indeed. Mauve streetcar tickets, one apiece, held between lips while we pull on lumpy woollen mitts, slowly, done with great care, very carefully: they must look proper, elegant, refined, like kid gloves, we're not on our way to play hockey. It's just past seven-thirty; our parents, seeming subdued as they turn and walk slowly back to the living room, and the front door closes behind us, weather-stripping muffling the sound. Yellow porchlight falls across the verandah steps. It's not snowing yet, nor is there any hint of the fall to come. Down the icy steps, two abreast instead of one behind the other, what did we say to each other just then? white silk muffler, green tam, out into the frosty, still-starry night. A shortcut across the side lawn, where there's a well-beaten path through three feet of accumulated snow-drifts, passing our late-November snowman, frozen stiff, there for the winter, dusted off after fresh snowfalls, given new pieces of coal so the eyes won't look sunken in, his hat made out of black oilcloth, askew, off to one side, as though bidding us good-evening.

We see our breath in the air, funnels pouring forth into the soundproof night. Are our mouths that wide open?

The streetcar—is it going to park down there all night? It's cold standing here waiting. Maybe the conductor's gone into the bush to pee; they do that in winter, I've noticed. They can't do it when the spring comes though, because once the snow's gone, people start taking shortcuts through there, and sometimes go looking for trilliums at night. I've seen them poking around with flashlights; why do people pick flowers in the dark? When the conductor has to go . . . I wonder where they do it then? This April I should watch where he goes, that'd serve him right for locking us inside the streetcar.

The conductor is back now, he's opened up the rear door and is sitting on the step having a smoke. That means it's going to stink in there, that *awful* shag they smoke . . . you can't get rid of the smell. *"Défense de fumer"* the signs inside say. Even so, it'll *reek* all the way up town, the *fumée* stays in the clothing. I don't think they send their overcoats to the cleaners from one end of the winter to the next. What's more, I don't think they even *change* their uniforms, and every time they stop for a smoke it does nothing but stir up what's already there.

George smiles to himself—he knows what I'm thinking, and also attempting to do. Because at the window seat, I've scraped snow off the frosted pane, and cupped it in my hand so that I can hold it to my nose. That helps some.

"I don't mind shag," he says, "to smoke, I mean. I tried it once and it's not so bad."

"Just because you've tried it doesn't mean I'm supposed to suddenly like it." The snow has melted in my hand, so I drink it, renew my efforts at scraping for more. "I had a puff on a Sweet Cap once," I say, going one better on the brand. "I got dizzy though. Did shag make you dizzy?"

"No. I got sick."

"Oh."

Idle chatter. What confidences dispensed! Time passing, minutes, as we glanced around. A time of your life when everything is profound. It would be lonely, I think, if you couldn't think of things to say, weren't inspired. And that's what made the night so important. So far, everything's been more or less exterior, and now you're aware of your inner being, not questioning what it can be, except that it's a nice feeling inside; there's a change that's different and it's not measured by last year's dresses that are too short, the style kiddish, or a boy noticing the cuffs of last spring's new pair of trousers are up above his ankle bone. You don't realize the mind is growing even faster. First you couldn't eat your supper you were so excited, and slipped the dog chunks of stew and filled him up on bread pudding, and now you're merry, clanging along in a streetcar. Isn't it—wasn't it—also a kind of identification one with the other, in this sense of time and place?

George examines the monogram of his scarf, head tilted half upside-down. He likes that scarf, he turns to see his reflection in the glass and tells me it's sharp, "Neat, boy." And so I offer to make him one for Christmas, or for his birthday in November.

"In white silk? Gee, that'd be neat." And then I wonder, Where and when would he wear a white silk scarf? I guess he might have occasional use. Next January, he could go dressed as a man at the Lindenlea Ice Carnival, that'd be reason enough to make him one. "Would you do me two initials, I mean instead of just having the 'W'?" One end of the scarf is out now, the monogram lying open to view across his coat lapel. Eyes almost crossed as he examines the scroll. "Yes," he affirms, "there's room for a 'G'."

"That's be okay," I say. "Easy."

The Capitol Theatre on Bank Street. White lights ablaze on the marquee, rows of bulbs blinking on and off. Taxis pulling up and the doors flying open. Men in white kid gloves fumbling for change, ladies in long dresses touching down on the snow. Are those ear-rings real diamonds? I take off my mitts and shove them into my pockets; my bracelet, that shows; the charm won't be overlooked, it's genuine silver.

"There must be thousands here tonight," George says looking around, mitts still in place, toque bunched in his hand. The scarf is all.

Splendour on either side of the entrance: four-foot bill-boards, "On Stage Tonight: *The Vagabond King*, Music by Rudolf Friml". Out loud, we read off the list of names. "Never heard of any of them, have you?" . . . "That's because we can't pronounce them." . . . "Oh, do you think so?" . . . "I don't know" . . . "It's because they come from Italy, all the singers do, the good ones" . . . "Oh, is that it?" Painted drawings; photographs; swords and banners; and a king in a hooded purple velvet robe. George tells me to get a load of François Villon's pointed cap! "Sharp," he says, and I say, "Yeahhh, but look at Lady Catherine's gown! And the people in the tavern, they're in lovely rags. What costumes! eh George? But hey, what's the guillotine for? Who dies? Do we have to see it happen?" I go back to the first poster, re-examine, and find George has already gone inside.

"Wait for me!" I yell. "Hey, wait up." I trip on the carpet, "Hey, *George*!" Faces turn around, I am aware of tight mouths, women mostly, and a man who looks like one—it's his hands, don't you know? fussing with the black velvet collar of his coat; his mouth opens and shuts, telling me to "shush". I guess considering the occasion I should have kept my voice down, it'd have wakened the dead.

And so would the Overture. All those wrong notes. I heard Daddy say it's quite understandable though, the orchestra only gets together when something big comes to town, they all have jobs in the Civil Service or some place, he said, and working all day they never have time to practise, they're too tired to feel like it. Heck . . . you don't notice so much when they get all mixed up. It's very nice—watching songs tell a story, the Dauphin sneaking into the poor people's tavern, *disguised* so he can find out about François, and Huguette in sleek black tights, standing on a bench with her hands on her hips so François will notice her, and forget about writing his poems. But! Gee whiz, why does this lady beside me have to fall asleep? She doesn't even wake up when there's applause. She should have got a good night's sleep last night. Or else had forty winks this afternoon, taken her shoes off and put her feet up then, and not here on her husband's galosh when his legs are crossed. Oh well. Say! Why is Lady Catherine . . . oh, she's arriving disguised on purpose. . . .

"George! Know what?" I exclaim, forgetting where I am. I put my hand over my mouth, pawing at his shoulder as I lean into him: "Do you remember that silent movie in Edinburgh, remember that time Granny gave us money?"

"The one with John Barrymore?"

"Shhhh!" from the row in front, a sideways face, ear-ring
bobbing.

"Yeaahhh . . . give Granny a drink," a man's voice behind. And suddenly the scaffold lights up in dark blue; Lady
Catherine throws back her hood, black robe trailing as she
mounts the steps, her arms are outstretched . . . but
François's are tied behind his back. I'm trembling. "Some
day/you will seek me and find me . . ." The swing of the red
velvet curtain.

We're the last ones to leave, still craning our necks at what
is almost like an encore: the spangles on the curtain shimmering. The pit orchestra replaying the Overture, piping out
the slow-moving file of the audience. Not until the last violin-
ist has closed his violin case do we get up to go.

---

It was snowing when we came out, a brilliant haze of slanting snow that had brought milder air, dumping cushiony-soft
accumulations in what had seemed so short a time. The street
throbbed with an impetus of silence, canyons of whiteness in
place of sound: a car or two, inching along, slipping sideways; pedestrians, blinded by the steady fusillade sifting
down, making their way with things on their minds. And,
with shops and business-offices closed for the night, the tea-
lounge directly opposite, as bright and gay as an arcade, figures taking coats and hats off and looking for places to sit,
pink and amber table lamps burning cozily, turning the little
settlement into an incandescent enclave, like a mirage.

In this diffuse, almost startling quality of shimmer and
dazzle, we stood off to one side under the darkened marquee,
wordlessly pulling on our mitts, snow melting on our eyelids
as we glanced back at the interior of the half-lit foyer, turning around once more to observe what was going on in our
midst, the last of the top-hats and evening gowns still
watching for a taxi, pant legs being rolled up; a wilted corsage hanging from the back of a head, caught in a hairnet; a
man taking a flask from under his overcoat for a fast swig.
Did it give him cramps?

"What time is it?" George is saying. "Must be nearly midnight."

"Gee, I don't know, do you?"

"No, I don't, I couldn't tell you."

"I suppose it's pretty close to that." Pulling my tam down

over my ears, I squint at the lights across the street. "Maybe if we went in and asked at the tea parlour . . ."

"Yes, let's go over and ask them."

"What do you want to know the time for anyway?"

We are overheard, and are handily rewarded with a smile: that beneficent facial expression meted out to tots, embalmed-looking faces mentally giving us a pat on the head as though we were children, and not the teenagers we are, who stand in a new-found, quieter grace, accepting this lapse of judgement by beaming back. A patch of snow falls to the ground, landing close enough that we vacate our rooted spot to look up and see where it came from. "What do you want to know the time for?" I asked again, placidly gobbling at the flecks streaming onto my face. And George, likewise sampling the atmosphere; but for a briefer spell—his scarf and that, the monogram might run into the silk. He dusts it off, then replies: "I thought instead of taking the streetcar, why don't we walk home? I'd sure like that."

"What? All that way? Egad. I never walked home from town before. It'd take us two hours!"

"Well the streetcar takes almost that long, at this hour it would, don't you think? Don't forget they only run every half-hour, and if we just miss one . . . It'd be nice, we'd have all that time."

"Time?"

"So we could talk, I thought."

"All right, let's. I don't care what Mamma and Daddy say, do you? Besides, they'll probably just tell us not to do it again, that's all they ever say anyway."

The end of the evening, with two more hours to tag on to floodlit parapets and gallows and poppy-red cloaks in a seething square, and take up again where the drop of a spangled curtain left off.

The babble is gone now, almost. There are serious things to discuss, comparing notes as we draw one another out: "Huguette died for Villon, fancy! imagine her stepping in front of him." . . . "Was that a real knife?" . . . "A sword, I think." . . . "I didn't know that's what 'legitimate' meant." . . . "Me neither." Breaking into silence, a solemn smile to ourselves, one of the dreams you walk on the edge of, whistling, humming a bit. Sodden tam, sodden white scarf, stumbling along; patience itself, pleased with the state of blocked roads and drifts piling up. For the night is resplendent, snow sprinkling down from rooftops, veils of it blowing across our

vision as we walk in the centre of the road. Lights in dwellings over shops on Rideau Street being switched off, and I
am wondering if our parents have called it a night too?
Should we write them a note? slip it under their door in case
they get up in the night? Wouldn't they like to know our eyes
are still held by the stage, that the tunes in our head will
never never be silent? and that we say, Thank you? And en-
close the two cartickets, they'd be able to guess why we
wanted to walk home.

Rounding the corner of Charlotte Street, and on, over St.
Patrick's Street bridge now, the squat, wrought-iron light
standards like clusters of white balloons, sheathed, mystical.
We pause half-way across the bridge; no one to hear us as we
hang over the cement balustrade and sing to the snow-dumps
on the frozen Rideau River:

> Some day, when the winter is over,
>
> Some day, in the flush of the spring,
>
> My so-o-oul shall discover . . .

Because George stops in the middle, I glance up at him, surprised. "There's more," I tell him quickly: "Some day / of the
days that will be . . ." Did he hear me? I hang over further,
swivel my head so I can see up into his face. Are his eyes beginning to droop? Is he getting sleepy? No. I get the impression he's thinking about something, there's no telling what
it is though, I don't have any idea at all. He bends down and
scoops up a handful of snow, and tosses it straight up; a
shower of snowflakes falls, ten seconds of blurred patterns
going round and round.

"How does it go again?" he wants to know.

"Some day / of the days that will be . . . That one?"

"No. Sons of toil and danger. . . ." Another handful of
snow, showering up, scattering down, covering us as we open
our mouths and rhythmically stamp our feet, the vagabonds
marching:

> Sons of toil and danger,
>
> Will you serve a stranger
>
> And bow down to Burgundeee-y!?

"I feel silly shouting when I sing," I break in, but George
doesn't hear me. Holy Nelly. I've never heard him letting him-

self go like this before! And suddenly he doesn't seem so
reserved, not shy any more . . . I don't think he will ever be
shy again. An emotion floods me, I don't know what it is. I
want to cuff him one, right then and there, lightly, a good
hefty bunt on his arm . . . but then I'd have tears streaming
down my face; I don't know for what reason, but I would.
Why would I want to do that?

Hands in pockets, I am silent, my eyes following the icebound river as I listen to my brother sing. I rock back and
forth with every word, I swallow, for I see now that his head
is to one side. I'd forgotten that gesture, he's thinking through
the words—what comes next—and I am tugged at the roots,
not just by music and things like winter stars hiding behind
the swirling snow, not just the night itself, but by something
else I have never experienced before, an inner cry I do not
yet recognize: rejoicing in the bond of a blood-line, I rock
forward and backward.

This emotion is something separate, different from the
celebration of being part of a family—because home is what
you're used to; you gather round, you go to school, you come
home from school, and gather round once more: like tides
going out, coming back in again. And when the shrieking
night wind blows and doors and windows rattle, making
sounds you want to cover your ears against, there's always
someone there, the same as when the waking ears are turned
to the sanctuary of other interludes. The porridge burns;
someone wins a bike in a raffle, and another is chosen to sing
in a Dominion Day choir on Parliament Hill; Mamma's
galoot of a milkman trips over his big feet and breaks two
bottles of milk on the front steps, "Who's going to volunteer
to pick up the glass? And don't all speak at once!" You pick
May flowers, and ring doorbells in some other neighbourhood
trying to sell them, finally your parents cough up; a burglar
steals a sack of P.E.I. potatoes out of the cellar and misses a
crate of tinned lobster someone in Halifax sent for Christmas; a Sunday morning and the doctor is called, another
Sunday and we're all in bed asleep, there's been a picnic, or a
circus, or a concussion, or the cat has a litter of kittens and
the dog is jealous and bites the postman. Or some other delirium. Everything merging, but *defined*. And here in a snowstorm on a roadside bridge, you sway with the beat of a song,
you lift your face to the sky and wonder what it is you want
to say, there is no knowledge . . . and all at once I think of
what George said under the marquee: 'So we can talk.' Does

he sing—*was* he singing—did he burst into song, being so very near to what is revealed and not seen: that we are chums and have come into our own, with a long way to go?

"Don't forget you promised to make me a silk muffler," he says without looking up, his gaze concentrated on a row of ice-blocks below, studying them, eyes shining, as if his dream-scarf was there, preserved in ice. "With a fringe. The fringe'd be really neat."

"Okay, gotcha." Bending over the railing again, below us the white space snow-pitted, wind-heaped, rising like crystalline bluffs, contours of two shores sloping away, disappearing, the vast darkness beyond. The shift of a foot, and a sleeve brushed across a face. Hunching up our shoulders now as we climb to the cement ridge above, feet braced, hands gripping the stone openings, leaning down, down, the visible, the invisible. Silenced by it. Deep night: one day we will be going somewhere, moving on with time. . . .

*So we can talk.* And in these moments of silence, feeling the wonder of existence as never before, the shock of emotion that we've come face to face with ourselves as individuals, what speaks better than silence?

# XVI

———◆———

My knees were bent, jack-knifed in a crouch, like a runner ready to spring: an awkward position to maintain, but if I stood up straight I couldn't see my head in the mirror. I was in my bedroom, comb in one hand, hairbrush in the other, humming away, green-eyed and flushed, unmistakably fancying the lot of my seventeen years as I dolled myself up for a Saturday night. Immediately below and in front of me the heavy wooden-framed mirror propped against the side of the cottage windowsill—a less than perfect arrangement, due, in part, to the big tree at the corner of the verandah. To my parents' chagrin, the silver maple they'd planted ten years before had taken leave of its roots and run away with itself, a sprawl-limbed windbreak that made the room dark as a broom-closet. Nevertheless, I had discovered there was a certain hour when rays of the sun shot through gaps in the foliage, and if I hit it just right, the window-ledge caught the blaze dead on, I didn't need a flashlight.

Supper over with, I was alone in the quiet, a little after seven in the evening, mid-July, and the baked earth already cooling under a light condensation of dew. Intermittently, I could hear the faint splash of a fish jumping in the river, and now that the wind had dropped, the first choruses of keyed-up crickets and frogs leading off, urgent with life as the tumult of purple and pink and orange in the flowerbeds folded their petals, bedding down for the night. Over in the village someone was piling lumber, the sudden sharp crack of planks reverberating across the water, whaaack, a few seconds of silence, and then, whump . . . whaaack . . . whump; pleasant and impersonal, the kind of sound distance and water combine to make infinitely lovelier; here, a sound of solitude evoking the smell of fresh sawdust and timber, suggesting too the damp sheen of a man's sweat, the ease and rhythm of his bare arms heaving with the force of his body. The air thrummed with an intimate sense, all the things I could hear and not see. Every sound went rippling through my insides, and oh it was wonderful to float like this, the breathing of the outer world like an exalted voice saying, Hurry up and get a move on there, you too surrender to the freedom of this night. My cheeks burned with the joy, and tension, of emotion.

I shook my head vigorously and scooped my fingers through my hair; a loose hank flopped down over my nose and the part disappeared again. More hair than I bargained for, I thought, holding up the coarse layers, discovering more underneath, as if questioning what had always been there. "It looks awful," I moaned inwardly, for half an hour I had combed, brushed, flattened, frowned, squinted, pushed and poked at spaces, more than once ruining a super arrangement over my ears, outside sounds half-heard, forgotten, the bare floor creaking under me as I strove to ape the style of the day.

That summer it was all the rage to have a saucy wave hanging low over the brow; no barette, no cheating with a bobby-pin to anchor it in place, the fad decreeing that one's vision be plagued. I had not worn this style before and was trying to ambush the ends, catch the wave up in the mess of tangles I'd purposely worked on for effect—to look wind-blown, undisciplined—vowing that even if it took me all night, I wouldn't budge an inch until I had my hair exactly right. From the neck up, isn't that what counted most any-way? It wasn't as though I could change into something really peachy, like my new wide-legged beach pyjamas with the hal-ter top; I had to make sure I didn't look any different from when I got up that morning, and the excuse for doing my hair was that I got it wet diving. Taking no chances on giving myself away, I had also planned that when the four of us sat down to supper that evening, if either of my parents, or my brother, asked why I'd washed my hair for the third day in a row, I'd look up surprised and say, 'Washed what? Oh *that*! The soap happened to be on the dock, so why not? I wasn't doing anything else, I had *stacks* of time.'

Word for word, exactly what happened. What a hope to think Mamma would let it pass. The first still minute: "Don't tell me you washed your hair again." She reached over, jig-gling a curl on my forehead.

"There's salad dressing on your fingers," I said, "and it's rancid." And Daddy, back from his round robin of tennis, triumphant and sunburned, sing-songed: "Time on My Hands", attempting to divert the focus. Mamma winked at him, postponed further teasing until she had finished licking her fingers, and then said that I'd soon have no scalp left. "All that scrubbing and lathering," tittering as she slid her gold bracelet back in place. She had this look on her, the same as when I used to dress up in her clothes and she'd try to keep a straight face, eyes darting from the bunched hem-line I'd be holding up, to the high-heeled shoes flop-flopping as I crossed the room to stand before her, grave and impressed with myself. The difference now, though, was that I wasn't playing make-believe, a difference not to be trifled with at seventeen; what did she find so surprising, and yes, comical, about having nice, soap-shiny hair, I wondered? Of all times to call attention to it. My brother *hearing every word*. I knew she would, sitting there like a broody hen, as if her daughter had just achieved fame, or notoriety. Why couldn't mothers be content to sit quietly, share your secret and look around at the air? Why did they always have to give you away? I glanced across at George. At that moment he didn't seem to be paying any attention; for one thing he had raised himself up to see if the woodbox was empty. I couldn't tell for sure, though; a sudden preoccupation with the supply of firewood could have meant anything. And George was the one I was concerned for, getting wind of something at the wrong time, and when I sat down at the table I was on edge every minute for fear Mamma would tip her hand, or more precisely, mine. Well, the damage was done, and while its moment was short-lived, think of the ones in store! it was still only six o'clock, at some point in the coming night such moments were going to be legion. But I would have someone to help me.

That was the dialogue I was carrying on by myself after Mamma put her foot in it. I kept right on eating; I didn't have to answer, my mouth was full and my jaws were working overtime.

"No wonder I can never find the soap when I need it," Mamma laughed. Plunk! the other foot now. "And oh dear, will you stop cracking your jaws like that? You'd think you were eating coal. Did you bother to bring the soap back with you?" Cripes! My father, returning from the kitchen, where he had gone to fetch the teapot, chided her and said: "You were washing your hands with it half an hour ago, Mimi. It's in there on the washstand where you left it, sweetheart."

Vulnerable to this discussion, and exasperated, I'd worked the butter dish over to the edge of the table while they were talking, and I exclaimed suddenly, "Look out! The butter! It'll be in a million pieces!"

"How did it get there!?" Mamma asked, puzzled, the train of her thought at last stopped in its tracks; hadn't she just been buttering herself a piece of bread?

Though dying to get started at my hairdo, I decided I'd wait until the supper dishes were done and everyone had cleared out. And now, crouched in the glare of sunlight striking the mirror on the sill, I'd all but forgotten the embarrassing goings-on at the table, the odour of rancid salad dressing gone from the curl on my brow. What am I going to do, I was asking myself. *What am I going to say tonight?* If only the night were over, behind me. . . .

Strokes of the hairbrush rasping, each stroke slanting up and down through the mind's words, their soundlessness buried in the thump of the brush against my head. Momentarily laying the hairbrush down whenever I caught my stare, hands against my face now, trembling; eyes that should be merry, considering who was coming to call. I left the mirror for a minute and sat down on the bed. Was this the way it was supposed to be? To find this sweetness: was it made harder, did it follow that one was not to escape a sense of trespass? Was guilt part of the dream?

I wasn't going anywhere that night, not that I knew of anyway. But that's incidental. There was another direction, an interior one; I had to find out how to open the door. George and I passing through change again; lives of our own, ready and waiting, no, at hand, arrived. A force of nature had now laid claim, and this time we could not go together.

His name was Frederick; his attentions the past two weeks had suddenly sent me spinning. Prior to that—the month before, and the previous summer—I don't know what I was thinking, puzzled perhaps more than anything. Like any girl, I was of course flattered, and more than a little curious. But there were always others present to divert attention, for instance the corn roasts over at the roadside hotdog stand, and nights of dancing under the stars at a place called the Tip Top three miles down the highway at Cascades. The Tip Top Inn was to me a grand place, and I was so excited I scarcely noticed Frederick in the crowd. And the strange thing is, whenever I caught him watching me, I deliberately freed myself of his gaze, drawing back into groups seated at the rustic cedarwood tables under the overhang of trees, slinking into the shadows where I could be invisible. I didn't want to have to have this presence, whose name I did not know, coming over to me in the night's darkness, solemn and serious-looking as he introduced himself, or asked me a made-up question. Not right away. What could I find to say in the silence, while I glanced awkwardly around? Shake his hand? and say, 'Pleased to meet you, Frederick, I'm sure.' Did he sense, know? and was too gentle to press, make me uneasy? deferring to this silhouette who concealed herself, always moving away, the back turned?

Until one chilly and moonless night the following summer.

I had been to the post office in the village, and because my friend Anna and I had decided to race one another back along the road, I was now catching my breath, sitting by myself on a log at the river edge, out of immediate range of the flamelight and bundled-up shapes huddling over weiners and burnt rolls, most standing around with their hands in their pockets, a few clasped arm in arm, others drawing in closer, attracted by the fire, their faces orange and glowing like jack-o'-lanterns. And I heard this voice, Frederick's, whisper in my ear, "When you get a chance, would you mind?"

Whereupon he pulled from his pocket a tiny bleached wish-bone, and dropping to a semi-squat position, one knee on the log, held the wishbone between a thumb and forefinger, look-ing not at me but across the soundless water—moving darkly, itself a presence when all else failed.

*When you get a chance!* "Sure," I said turning sideways, and with visible uncertainty, hooked my little finger around one end. Snap. And the ice was broken, a spike of dry bone snapping like a twig underfoot, and our heads held down, rendered silent, as though time had stopped on our last breath.

At that instant a cherubic, ruddy-faced youth called Hooley appeared out of the long grass, carrying a hotdog. Be-fore handing it to me he took a small bite, wiped a dribble of mustard with a sleeve drawn across his chin, and suggested to Frederick he might like to get his own. And off trudged Hooley, back to the fire, a boy alone, the inward hurt of his acne and pink overweight body returning him to the sum-mer's sad loneliness, as represented by the élan and affec-tionate pushing and shoving gathered there. Extending both arms, Frederick grabbed hold of my hands and pulled me up. I was to accompany him? I didn't know what else to do: I just couldn't still be sitting there, not now after the wishbone, he'd have thought I was waiting for just him.

There was no need for conversation, for the world was suddenly mysterious again and had to be rediscovered; it would take a few minutes. Candy-bar wrappers and shredded, Coke-stained paper napkins blew around our feet; coloured lights strung across the stand blazed gaudily, burning red and blue and bright yellow holes into the blackness; all at once, blasts of heat rushing at us. Looking down at the flames, how swiftly the grace of a single gesture, culminating an hour later in three minutes of what you might call dancing—the grass was drenched with dew, dotted here and there with sharp little cut-down stumps of sumachs. A mantel radio, plugged into one of the light sockets and facing out from the front counter of this classy snack-bar, staticky from a loose wire and all but teetering under the force of its output, was playing "Stompin' at the Savoy". He didn't ask me would I like to dance, nor hold forth his arms in the mock gesture of preparing to; we just took off. And then, when Benny Good-man, or Gene Krupa, whoever it was coming to us from high atop The Great White Way, or a turnpike (what was a *turn-pike*?), announced: "That about wraps it up, folks," I handed back to Frederick the piece of wishbone I was still clutching in my left hand, and without giving any reason, I said, "Goodbye, but I don't need you to walk me to the boat, I like to go by myself. Do you know what I mean?" Since I didn't myself, I wonder if he did?

Yes. How swiftly the wash of sleep that night.

"I think Frederick's sweet on you," Mamma had said only the week before. And I thought, She doesn't know the half; he was sweet on me last summer too, but I didn't bother myself about him, I didn't think he was so hot. "Handsome too," she added, "lovely brown eyes. And nice manners to go with them. At least he knows enough to get up on his hind legs when your father and I appear." My father turned to me and said, "Are you fond of him? Do the two of you have fun? Seems to me Frederick's a bit old for you." Mamma had been hulling wild strawberries in her lap on the wicker chair and, balancing a white bowl in one hand and a saucepan in the other, had just left the verandah and gone inside.

"What if he is?" she called out, an afterthought from behind the screen door. I jumped down from my perch on the railing and sat beside my father on the couch.

"He's not, you know," I said. "He's only twenty. Maybe he looks older on account of the way he dresses." I was thinking how nice it was that Frederick didn't wear smelly baseball sweaters and rumpled pants, but spotless white shirts, open at the neck with the sleeves rolled a certain way above the elbows, and swell grey flannels, with a leather belt that had his monogram on the buckle. And when he came into a room he didn't slouch, or stand smoothing his hair as if he owned the place. And! You never heard Frederick boasting about how fast he'd taken that dangerous curve in the road at Cascades so he could beat the train to the level crossing. Not him forcing us to sit there taking a deep breath as he helped himself to a Coke in the refrigerator, having to marvel at how he took the cap off with his teeth, the lid of the icebox left wide open and a new block of ice melting while the bottle was glugged down in one manly breath. As for bragging, it seemed to me Frederick had lots more than hairpin-turns on a gravel road to boast about; he had his pilot's licence, didn't he?

Out of nowhere he'd wheel down from the sky. Early in the afternoon, or sometimes shortly before suppertime, I'd discover the single engine circling the hill, then off down the river again, back to Uplands Flying Field on the outskirts of

Ottawa. And not a word out of him afterward; no demanding
to know: "How's that for flying a kite?" And so I didn't say
anything; I wanted him to first. But Mamma was not quite
that content to wait—things tended to neutralize in her mind
if left for too many hours. And so after the second time
round, that very evening, Frederick was scarcely in the door
when she wanted to know what he was doing scaring the wits
out of her like that. "Heavens! I thought you were going to
blow the roof off the cottage, Frederick. I was out on the hill
and I could feel the wings practically on top of me." Frederick glanced at me and winked, sheepishly though, I thought.
Mamma went right on: "Could you see me? I was taking the
suckers off the strawberry vines. And when my hat flew off I
thought for sure I was a goner."

"He wasn't *that* close," I said, "the grass wasn't waving."
Frederick, by now a little more than embarrassed, sized her
up for a moment; she was reproaching him? being jovial?
Then he said, "I was doing a practice run. One of these days
I'm going to see if I can't fit the missing bricks back in the
chimney." And Mamma, understandably, rosy and glassy-
eyed, almost bubbling out of herself. *She believed him!* I had
thought a shriek might be forthcoming, some quick afterthought in the corner of her mind, exploding: "What? From
up there?" But not so much as a snort rippled the drink of
fruit juice she had half-raised to her lips. Nosiree. The
mechanics? Pure and simple: the nature of things, automatic,
like earthquakes, like a microwave, anything was possible.
She never questioned technicalities. And furthermore, if she
was fond of you and you said black was white, then fine, it
was.

For the briefest instant she stood swilling the juice around
in the bottom of the glass, eyes fixed on Frederick. "That'd
be some trick," she replied, grinning cunningly; "I wouldn't
put it past you either," and with that promptly set the tumbler down and went outside to the hill. I watched her tiptoe-
ing around the flowerbeds, shading her eyes, not quite
certain, wondering, glancing up again, a sort of furtive peeking as she inspected at range the chimney's caries.

My God. It's a wonder she didn't come back in for the
binoculars.

She'd have been close to forty then, her face and soft black
hair lovely as a lyric, slim and spritely as ever, still full of the
old hoopla, a kind of babbling radiance speeding her out the
kitchen door, hair tied back with a bright yellow ribbon,

scented from head to toe with Quelques Fleurs and wearing a
halter and long frilly skirt, bare feet dodging crusted rings of
fresh cowflaps. Yes, I'd forgotten. How marvellous! How
marvellous that she would do that. Lurching around in the
grass, eyes screwed up, not a sound out of her. Faith in everything. The fact does not startle me. It's a dimension of
the romantic, neither stupid nor blind to the absurd: on the
contrary, a self-credence endowing it with its own luminosity.
Doesn't believing come from that? Isn't that what trust is?

---

I reached for my father's cigarettes, knees bunched together while I opened the box and offered him one—a reflex
emphasizing that a serious discussion was under way.

"Why do you think Frederick's too old for me?" I asked,
watching him closely, puzzled. Too old? What did that mean?
didn't he like Frederick? Resistance massing inside me, doing
my best to conceal it as I braced my feet on the wicker chair.
I was counting on him, my father—they were both part of
my life now and I wanted them to be pals. And from the beginning. I didn't want there to be a wobbly start. "I wasn't
expecting you to say that at all," I went on uneasily. "So how
come? You must have had a reason."

"No. No reason. I was just thinking how very quiet he is,
much more reserved than the other boys you've been
seeing. . . ." He paused to light his cigarette, and leaned forward, intent, as if listening to the reverse of wind overtaking
the motionless Lombardy poplars lining the path to the river,
eyes following the quick shiver of leaves breaking against the
skyline as he added, guardedly, "You're still pretty young,
you know."

"How do you mean? The way I act?"

"Oh my—no. It's just that up to now you've preferred lads
your own age. And it seems to me Frederick has gone around
with a much older crowd, don't you think?"

"I know," I said, fitting his pack of cigarettes into his shirt
pocket, "but even so . . . I'm comfortable with him, I really
am. It's nice not to feel like a kiddish schoolgirl any more, or
some apple-cheeked tomboy. Gee, for a while I thought I'd
be ending up as a girl athlete or something. The other day
Marian asked me was I turning out for basketball practice
this September and I told her she made us sound like football
players. I said to heck with that, I'd rather join Gwendolyn
Bishop's Dance School. What kind of a boy wants to ask a

basketball player out on a date, for crying out loud? I know Frederick wouldn't."

"Oh, I think he might . . . an attractive girl, realizing she's . . . well, flying the colours of her high school. Why wouldn't he?"

"Maybe. Anyway, he won't be here in the winter. Besides, after I saw myself, that awful photo in the school magazine, I decided I wouldn't be there next year you bet, all those horsy bean-poles with their big kneecaps. I'd rather put on a satin blouse and black velvet shorts, like I did when Lisgar Collegiate sent me to Miss Bishop's to learn that slinky fandango."

*"The Gondoliers,"* my father said, shaking his head as he recalled the school's annual concert. "It was very nice, well staged. You and your red shoes certainly hoofed it up."

"To say nothing of those castanets she couldn't work properly," my mother called out from the living room. "What a racket!" A garble of words—was she stuffing herself with the last of the season's wild strawberries? Is that why she decided to finish the hulling inside?

"You're not supposed to be listening," I shouted teasingly, banging my heel against the door for emphasis, a shower of rust and dried chips of putty scattering down on my head.

"Say!" she went on, "whatever happened to that vest?" spitting out the words through clenched teeth—fingers removing a twig? ants? She was of course referring to the makeshift woollen cover-up I'd been instructed to wear under my costume. Along with three other girls, I'd been selected to perform the Spanish dance the school was presenting from Gilbert and Sullivan's *The Gondoliers*. At the dress rehearsal we slipped off our coats the moment our names were called backstage. And the girls' gym teacher—doubling as wardrobe mistress and stage-director—when she saw us dart past, spangled and jingling in the flamenco costumes our mothers had made, long, bright-scarlet ruffled skirts with short, skin-tight velveteen boleros, grabbed the nearest arm and swung the girl around. Twitching and shouting above the orchestra's spirited opening (sundering an exotic score), she let fly with a resounding smack, the back of her hand whacking the poor girl's bare midriff. "You should be ashamed of yourselves," she cried. "Have you no sense of shame?" and then released her. "Go on out, the four of you, and do what you have to do," the bloodless face hissed. "We'll see to this later." Didn't we look all right? Our costumes weren't *awful*, were they? Hadn't they been made from a McCall's pattern? exactly like

the one in the painting the dance teacher took us to see in the
Art Gallery? Brass and tambourines crashing, our hips . . .
What'd she have to hit Lois in the solar plexus for? She could
have winded her. What on earth? . . . Damn. Hips, thighs,
triumphant feet and legs whirling and stamping, castanets like
gun shots through the din of the orchestra, bodies gathering
momentum. Why did she lose her temper? We look *swell*.

"Tomorrow night!" the gym teacher trumpeted, blowing
exasperation all over us the instant we came panting offstage,
"see that you have that bare skin covered up! And that's final, do you hear?"

"What for?" looking down at our middles, four heads examining six inches of ordinary, racy? flesh, heaving ecstati-
cally above an extravaganza of lace-tiered frills. "Why?" we
groaned, a tongue sticking out the corner of a mouth, another
mouth working up a storm, and the gym teacher poking her
flint-tipped drill baton into the soft velvet of the nearest
breast. And lowering her voice so as not to further accom-
modate the boys lined up and waiting to do their trampoline
act, she narrowed her eyes and said, "The minute you get
home tonight, have your mothers look through your mended
underwear and tell her she's got to get a box of Tintex tomorrow and dip it . . . first thing in the morning so it'll be
dry in time."

"Dip it?" . . . "Underwear? We have to wear *underwear*
underneath?" . . . "A dirty old shirt?"

"Don't be smart! See that you have four flesh-coloured
vests here tomorrow night or you sit in the audience." I
seized the tip of her pointer, holding it away from me, and
said, "If my parents didn't feel there was anything wrong
with my costume, then I don't see why you should." She eyed
me coldly, her upper lip curling as she retorted, "I knew all
along I'd have trouble with you. It wasn't my idea having the
school spend money on dancing lessons for you. You were
chosen over my dead body."

As for my vest! Mamma ended up borrowing a package of
Tintex dye (Mulberry, the box said) from a neighbour, for
when she telephoned the drugstore, they informed her they
didn't keep every colour and all they had was black, brown
and navy-blue; she wasn't making a special trip up town, "to
please that silly crop-haired baritone of a woman!" She
thought if she added some pink food-colouring to the water,
that'd do the trick. And so my shirt came out a lollipop-red,

shrunken from being boiled, and blotched in deeper shades where it was darned.

"Let Miss-what's-her-name see you putting the blasted thing on," Mamma announced when I came in from school that afternoon, "and then when she's not looking, rip it off." She picked the shirt up from the ironing board where she had laid it alongside my costume. "I've cut the shoulders off and sewn dome-fasteners down the back. See? You'll be able to get out of it in a hurry. Lord, it's a wonder she didn't demand to have the slit up the front of the skirt stitched as well."

"She couldn't," I said, "we have to practically turn ourselves inside out when we dance, and slowly too, so the ruffles will fall around our legs. That's the most important part of the dance! We're supposed to be señoritas, the dance teacher told us, 'tempting the patrons in a cabaret'. Mamma! She *loved* our costumes! She's even asked us to appear in her dance recital this spring. She'll have a fit tonight when she sees us in . . . in this crazy underwear."

"Then don't wear it. Do as I said, pitch it away. And if she's got anything to say, tell her she can say it to me. Why don't you just keep your coats on, then wriggle out when her back's turned?" Which is what I did—what we all did.

———

"Hey! What did you do what that shirt?" Mamma called out again, clear-voiced, no munching twigs and berries. "I haven't laid eyes on it since."

"No?" I said, turning around to protest through the screen door. "You tied it around the floormop when you were doing your spring cleaning . . . the walls and ceiling, remember? And you didn't bother to take it off either, you've been mopping the floors with it ever since. And now, do you mind if I continue talking to Daddy—alone?" I turned back to my father.

"Who'd have thought then?" I said, twining my fingers. "That Friday and Saturday night, gosh—ringlets and flowers in my hair, and doing all those intricate steps on a stage! Who'd ever have imagined that . . . that Frederick would come along. Gee, eh?" And I thought just then, I must have grown up a lot that winter, suddenly realizing I'd no longer be content to stand mumbling to some gaunt-eyed boy under a streetlamp, discussing how we'd go about dropping Latin, talking about football, or plans for decorating (and fumigating) the gym before the Valentine dance. Pretty heady stuff—once. But I was *not*, as my father had said a few minutes before, "still pretty young", for I had been into the bubbly of a riper age. And I must . . . oh, I'd have to tell him exactly. I'd have to tell my father of this other world. But could I, I wondered? What would I say?

I hadn't planned this moment. I seemed to be walking around in my head. And yet, easing myself closer to my father, somehow content within my dull and helpless brain that this sudden contact, the eagerness with which it was charged, was its own communication, I found myself saying, "Only last summer you said the day would soon come when I'd be wanting to make myself pretty for someone, and . . . do you know . . .?"

"Of course," he replied. "Of course I know." How could I tell him about a silly piece of balled tin-foil I had crossed the river in search of, that I kept this discarded grimy memento in a box with porcupine quills and my necklace of moonstones, and that I took it out in the dark each night? 'Of course I know.' His words light in my head. And the breeze blowing full again. Splinters of shade twisting on the verandah. A giant spider running sideways across the floor. And my father, exhaling cigarette smoke: "I must say I like Frederick," he said after a moment. "There's an endearing quality . . . a modesty about him. He may not be the most talkative person in the world, still, he enjoys hearing what you have to say. I like that." And I knew why. During the winter there's been a couple of boys ("lumps", as Mamma had observed, muttered into a skein of wool she was winding, having singled them out as dead wood, to be given the bum's rush) who'd taken to dropping in at the house Friday and Saturday nights, Sunday afternoons if the spirit moved them, one or the other (or both) camped on the chesterfield in the front room, neither finding very much to say whenever my parents addressed them—unless "Huh?" and "Uh-huh" could be classified as conversation. Finally my father laughed and suggested next time he'd see that he escaped to his transmitter in the cellar. It wasn't a question of their apparent boredom, he didn't object to that, he said, it was to be expected of young people nowadays, but he just didn't like having a couple of cigar-store Indians lounging around. Whatever a cigar-store Indian was. With his sense of the immediate, the mutual air being breathed, he liked an occasional response, *anything*, ridiculous questions, even an expert on something—cars, or kite-flying, or leather-tooling, or the Oxford Group, or faith-healers—holding forth. He'd get right into it, interested, thinking through what they had to say, five minutes, an hour, he loved it. So that now, sitting on the verandah couch, I thought, How wonderful my father hasn't missed the quiet turn of feeling in Frederick, and that his quietness is not rooted in indifference. The alert that had sounded through me was gone. For wasn't it merely a casual observation my father had been making, as one is moved to comment on change, such as new neighbours moving in across the street, or someone's style of dress, or the way he parts his hair? Why did I jump to conclusions, when he had given no sign whatever of scuttling me? "And don't you think Frederick has, well, have you noticed his nice affectionate way, in little things?" I said.

"I certainly have. And what also impresses me is that he meets your eye."

"Boy! does he ever! I nearly got the kinks the first time he did that to me. I mean, I didn't know where to look." And that was true; it was the day after he'd pulled the wishbone on me; I had never seen him *that* close in daylight. A Saturday afternoon it was, and I'd been across the river at the village store and was now putting the groceries in the boat when Frederick, returning alone from a trip in to Ottawa, drove past on the river road. He braked and backed the car up. My heart gave a little leap, and my knees buckled, double-jointed sockets sounding like castanets as they clicked back in place. Not twenty-four hours had passed since we'd been stompin' at the Savoy-Gatineau, high atop the dazzle of foil from chewing-gum wrappers and potato chips. Damn, I thought, just when I was going to stay home the next few nights and let last evening's diffused pleasures linger in the mind, sift through them; that way they'd mean more.

By-passing the footpath down the embankment in favour of a shortcut through the waist-high burdock, he scrambled up onto the sloping flat rock and asked, with what seemed like a kind of closed-in shyness, could he help me untie the chain? I flushed, hesitated a moment, and told him the boat was already unhitched, so he said why didn't he tie the boat up, and then undo it again? I liked that, it meant he had a sense of humour.

"Better give this an extra knot," he said, crouching between the boulders, "so as the boat'll stay anchored." Straightening up; rubbing his hands together to get rid of the rust. Back down again, a second knot? third? in a double-length chain heavy enough to sink the *Bismarck*. "There," Frederick said, "that ought to do it." Standing up again: "So much for that." And then in the next breath: "Here, I'll unfasten the chain for you. Let me do that." Three knots to untie, while I cupped my hand over my face to keep from snorting and sniggering, absorbing every ludicrous second, until finally a sobered mutter, "Thank you very much."

This time he did not bother about rust marks on his hands, but instead stood holding the boat with his foot on the seat, the lanky six-foot frame giving the illusion of being twice my height, his large, sleepy brown eyes studying my face, the dark spill of lashes, tinged with the same chestnut-brown of his hair, almost finishing me.

It was here; not at the bonfire, where all thoughts were interior, standing side by side, eyes straight ahead, staring into flames cracking with white birch, turning around to watch the smoke-screens of dust released in the wake of cars as they passed, a sudden spurt as we danced across the grass; expression communicating itself reciprocally, awesomely, in some form of motion, characterized by the spell of small eruptions, pleasant abstractions. No, it wasn't there, but now, here at the landing. Not an explosion going off in my head, nor anything remotely resembling it; something more than that. He was smiling, and there was a powerful, masculine gentleness to his face, a tan shoe placed squarely on the seat, the bend of his knee, the flex of his thigh directed at keeping the rowboat still. It was then I started to like him; I didn't know what he was thinking. He was wearing a light-brown suede windbreaker with leather buttons, and as he helped me into the boat my face brushed against the suede. It smelled good, I don't know what of, just him I guess.

The sun, the moon, mornings, afternoons, with the softness of love I stood among minutes that sang, sensual currents not just a peripheral surprise, like a blush, but sweeping through the whole of me, my body consuming what was left of my mind. I wasn't used to this feeling. Did everyone turn away from food, I wondered? did they want to faint dead away? go off somewhere in the dark in search of a place to lie down by themselves in the grass?

---

"Where is Frederick from?" my father continued. "The States? Didn't you say he and his family had come here from Washington?"

"No. Pittsburgh. Why? Does that make him seem too old for me, being an American?"

"Heavens no. I was thinking maybe he's had too much city, that's all. Either that or growing up too fast. In the States kids are inclined to, they're more independent. Somehow I don't see Frederick as ever having been young once, like George and Jimmie, for instance." My father smiled and shook his head. He leaned back, shoulders resting against the clapboard wall as the cigarette smoke drew into the netting at the window. Was Frederick too sophisticated for me, is that what he meant? Just then I was remembering someone had said that in fact Frederick was not twenty but twenty-one past. Well, that was still only four years older than me.

"I love to watch those two," my father said softly, the set of his face absorbed, a breeze blowing up, and tracing imaginary circles on the coverlet while he went on: "Always up to something harmless. Infectious too. Have you ever noticed their expressions? Since the time they were . . . wee gaffers, they've had this, oh, I don't know . . . this capacity for joy in life, a feeling for nature that makes them contented. And you know, I wouldn't be at all surprised if it stayed intact, no matter where they go in the world." *Was* my father trying to tell me something? I didn't know. "What I'm doing of course is comparing," he added after a pause, "and I shouldn't. But here now, why am I getting on that tangent, when other things . . ."

"No, you shouldn't compare," I cut in, seeking to qualify my own reasoning. "Think of all the summers George and Jimmie have had to do everything, what with the barn and the creek and that, and their log cabin, and a team of horses they could hitch up any time they took the notion. What's more, who else has fathers like they've got, fathers that are their buddies?"

"Well, I get the impression Frederick wants to let loose, but *can't*. And that's the whole point. I thought you might feel disappointed after a while, expecting him to."

"No I wouldn't. I like the fact of him being quiet and serious. I guess that's the reason I picked him, I mean . . ."

"Isn't it the other way round? Seemed that way to me." Hearing the words. Confirmation. Beautiful delicate star-shaped words, like darts of joy, sweet pain catching me unawares. I whirled around and grabbed my father by the knee, wanting to shout and laugh and sing. And so I did just that, I

jumped up and flung my arms above my head, as if I had
just been saved at a Revival Meeting, and I started to sing.

> Maybe I'm right
>
> And maybe I'm wrong.

and my father, skipping a line while he waits for the beat

> Maybe I'll live
>
> A life of regret

at the top of our lungs we harmonize, unleashing

> And maybe I'll give
>
> Much more than I'll get,
>
> But nevertheless . . .

Mamma opened the screen door and stuck her head out.
"Count Screwloose of Tooloose and his daft daughter!" she
snorted. "They'll be coming for you any time now." And the
screen door clicks shut. But not without her mutterings trailing off, the tune's in her head; she's trying to get it but she
can't, she's got the words in the wrong place. She returns to
the door, the screen bulges, it's her face pressed in our direction, and now the wire netting is being scraped, she's thumbing her nose with both hands. "Think you're smart the two of
you, don't you," she exclaims, "think you're the Pope's glass
eye," disappears again, with a whack at a mosquito, you can
tell by the smack, they're the ones she hits hardest; another
swing, hands smacking the air? and another. She's mad,
feeling guilty, she hates it when a tune gets the better of her.
Silence.

It was always like that, one person or the other skewered,
turned into a cartoon-creature in the comics, or some irra-
tional, unworthy, miserable but lovable incongruity of fiction.
Always plunging headlong into some song of wisdom, whose
bristle of words and tempo fitted the conditions. Must have
been a crazy house. But isn't that the way everyone carried
on then, back in 1937? screwy, rather shy, compromising, a
spontaneous gleam in the eye, laughing at oneself and the rest
of us, with a gentle kind of willy-nilly affection? Things have
changed somewhat. Boy, have they ever! Take back a pair of
shoes they deliver, both the same foot, and they tell you to go
stuff it!

I sat down on the couch again, feeling the instant heat of the mattress, as if the sun had set fire to it. "Know what?" I resumed, pulling my legs up under me as my father said, "What a sky! Same blue as the river," and then, "No, I can't even guess. What?"

"Know what I like best about Frederick?" I said, stroking the coverlet urgently, eager and sibilant with the vastness of my insight. "He's not always acting silly, keeping up a steady line of nonsense, doing knee-bends or pretending to shoot a hockey puck when someone's talking. And he doesn't try to make jokes all the time, those awful corny sayings like things being all wool and a yard wide, going up to every tall person he meets and asking what the weather's like up there."

"See here, Miss Powerful Katrinka (the nickname my father had given me when I was fourteen; by accident, not looking where I was going, I had ploughed the rowboat onto a raft of logs in mid-river, and instead of backwatering and rowing around them, I kept on going until every last log had rumbled past underneath), we can't all be perfect you know. You should be a little more tolerant. What gives you the idea you're blessed with perfection?" Eyes fixed on me, displeased, as if I had let him down. "I take it you're referring to Jack Humphreys," he said bending down to pick up an old tennis ball, throwing it up in the air and catching it. "What does it matter what someone says when they're stuck for words, but still want to be heard? You can't go around thinking badly of them, acting superior. Jack's only a lad, he'll outgrow it."

"Not if he has to keep listening to his father. He's worse." My father leaned back, rubbing his thumb back and forth across the seam of the tennis ball. "Jack even refers to you as Pops," I said. " 'How's old Pops?' he'll say. So I politely inform him, 'Who's talking? *Your* father's the one that's old, that big stomach hanging half out of his pants, and those *veins* in his hands! they're like dewworms. What's more I don't see *him* playing in tennis tournaments with guys half his age. In fact there's not enough breath left in him to even pick up a tennis racquet.' That holds him. But then, next time he sees me, right back again: 'How's old Pops?' Jack thinks that's smart." With the flat of his hand he began rolling the ball along the side of his pantleg, involving himself, in an abstract way, with the back-and-forth motion of his palm as he—what? summed up the situation? or thought that last one over, not relishing the idea of being tagged "Old Pops"?

"Frederick's interested in all sorts of things," I said

brightly, "not a smart-alec at all. He even plays the trombone."

My father was about to say something, but paused, tipping
his head back as he searched the leaves of the silver maple,
his eyes still thoughtful, resting on the verandah railing as he
said, "Don't be falling for him too hard; make sure first.
You're barely seventeen," and then, looking pensive, much
less; in fact joyful, "just be yourself, lass." For the next
minute we sat quietly, the murmur of shivery poplar leaves
and sporadic faraway sounds a kind of verbal accord, an
avowal that Heaven existed. "Tell me," my father asked as he
got up to leave, "you didn't mention it, but when did you find
each other?"

"Find?"

"Become sweethearts." What a question!

"Last week, I guess." I told him about the wiener roast
then, wondering if I could explain what it was about the incident involving the wishbone that had touched me inside—
that was the part I *understood*, and I didn't even know why.
My father shook his head again, instinctively nodding with a
whimsical twinkle, as though he were witnessing it this very
minute.

"Who got the lion's share?" he asked.

"I don't remember. I think I did. Yes, I ended up with it."

"Did you make a wish?"

"No. I forgot to."

---

A week had now passed, and during that time I assume
my father and Frederick had wandered off somewhere by
themselves. The sequence of days is somewhat blurred,
overshadowed by the focus of another, quite different conversation. An unexpected element had found its way in, a
situation had developed, and I was to learn about it only that
Friday evening when my father, upon hearing the six-fifteen
train whistle, suggested, "Why don't we row across for the
mail?" There was no particular significance to this; he was on
holiday and it made a change, he was glad of the exercise, he
said, after sitting all afternoon beeping away at his ham radio
station. And while Mamma usually went with him for company, she was busy making jam; my father had asked me instead.

About a hundred yards out from shore, and even though
the topic had not changed, its complexion had. As we came

abreast of the island, my father, assuming an air of non-chalance, stopped rowing. He lifted the oars and sat with them held above the water, the boat drifting slowly upriver, the motion of the river subdued in the reverse of current. Only then did I suspect I wasn't there solely for the sake of company; something was on his mind. I remember quiet plinks of water dropping from the oar-tips, a sudden whirr of birds on the island darting through the foliage, and my father, his hazel eyes less definable against the sun, slipping me a sideways glance.

"I'm afraid your brother thinks it's him Frederick is coming to see all the time. Are you aware of that? Did you know?" Scrutinizing my face as he went on: "George thinks the visits are meant for him." His brows knitting. And I, with my mind stuck, unable to get past the first sentence, hearing it over and over, like a gramophone needle caught in a groove. "What makes the situation worse is that for George it's more than just a new friendship." Jagged discs of light spun around in my head as I sat with closed eyes, stunned, no longer thinking of Frederick, my mind seized, trying to shout back, No, wait a minute, your father's *wrong wrong wrong*. And my father's voice, composed, making it plain he's quite himself: "In the last few days haven't you noticed how George waits for him to arrive, just as you do?"

"Waits for him? *George* waits? I never saw any sign of it, he's never given me that impression. All those times . . . every night I went across the river, I went by myself. George wasn't there, he wasn't bothering, he was always off somewhere with Jimmie."

"Ah yes, but that was before Frederick got into the habit of suddenly arriving. And the indirect way he goes about it, cutting back the engine of the motor long before he's reached the dock, detouring around, up and down the bank of the river, putt-putting back and forth through the weeds . . . as if he were out for a jaunt and wondered if anyone was home, should he drop in."

"You're right! At first I never knew whether he was going to land or not land." My father was silent for a moment, and then said, "Such an informal arrival—quite understandable that George would assume it had something to do with him. After all, he's sixteen now, beginning to feel he's a young man. That's a sensitive area. And along comes another young man his own type, open and honest, and just enough years his senior, no more than a rung or two up the ladder and headed the same way he's headed. Someone who's sincere and has taken the trouble to show interest—because that's the kind of person Frederick is—and that's the devil of it."

"Oh Daddy, what makes you so sure?" Dead words, buried in my fingers as I bit into my knuckles, not sounding like a question but an affirmation of fact.

"It'll work out fine, you'll see. Just thought I'd make sure you knew. I have the feeling somehow that Frederick has already sensed; and if my guess is right he'll find a way, Frederick will know what to do. Here now, what's this? Better splash some water on your face, come on now, put that Irish light back into those eyes, can't have Frederick seeing you like . . ."

"He's not coming tonight, he's in town; it's tomorrow night. This evening he had to take his grandfather some place, put him on a train or something, I guess he's pretty old. . . . There, does that look better? the water's pretty cold. I wasn't crying, you know. Something in my head seemed to go away, for a minute I couldn't see your face and when your voice came back I was asking God something."

He looked at me, a thought passing fleetingly through his mind: would he ask what it was? or let it pass? He waited, bridging the seconds by checking to see that his white tennis ducks weren't dragging in the wet sand covering the floorboard. And then, perhaps feeling the weight of his recent discovery and needing someone with whom he could share one of its exact moments, he said, "Only this morning, George asked me what I thought of his new friend, didn't I think Frederick was a very nice person, the way he sat down and talked to everyone? 'He's not only friendly but kind too,' he said, 'and he doesn't mind staying around the cottage, he never feels we have to be going somewhere all the time. Look how he brings another chair out on the lawn and joins in with everybody, and doesn't care if we sit on the hill all night, so many things to talk about.' Your mother is innocent of what's been happening, of course. She thinks it's just a matter of the two boys hitting it off. Another summer in full swing."

"Swing is right! Last night, do you remember? were you outside when we were trying to fix the canvas on the deckchair? She came marching out with glasses of root-beer and shandygaffs, banging a knife against the tray and singing, Hail! Hail! The gang's all here. But what did you say to him? to George I mean."

"Oh, *I* can't say anything. It will be easier on George to find out for himself. One has to experience these things, I'm afraid. And that's why only you and Frederick, particularly Frederick, must deal with it in your own way. It'll work out okay." He was silent, and so was I. I was thinking of how only that morning the two of them had gone for a swim before breakfast; I'd seen them taking that huge log out again, standing on it and rolling it together, laughing to beat all heck. Why didn't Daddy tell George then, I asked myself? I drew my legs up and clasped my hands around my knees, wanting to lay my head on my lap; what *was* it inside me, this nameless clawing, making me recoil. What was it, in addition to loyalty? "Look at the boom the Gatineau Power's put around the sandbar," he remarked, "now what do you suppose that's all about?"

My father, resting on the oars again; green-striped water winding itself into eddies, and dark and cool in the shade of trees the near shore without sound, waiting to receive us. And the dip of the oars once more, curving upward, blue-painted tips flashing in the sunlight, and I hear my father say: "Haven't seen you like this before. You're taking this much too seriously, don't you think?"

"No . . . you don't understand."

I could not have put it into words, for I myself did not know at the time.

---

And now it is the next evening, and I hear once more the whump and whack of lumber, a man in the village; he is not alone in his island of thought and sweat. Crickets, rooted to the spot, making conversation, compulsive talkers. Fish jumping, a flopping sound, the river must be very still. Where is everybody anyway? have my parents taken the boat and gone up to Wakefield? Did my father . . . no, I think George went somewhere with Jimmie; he did, didn't he? What time is it now? Every last curl in place, bright red-orange lipstick I taste as I lick my lips, it's Tangee, in a black metal case; slanting sunlight and a crack in the mirror divide my face. There. All done. Whaaack . . . whaaack-whump. And then the sound is gone.

Except for the creaks, and the slow drip of water in a pan under the icebox, the cottage seemed deathly quiet. And I was all ears again, listening, while I debated: would I put some of my Evening In Paris perfume on, or just let it go at the way I had fussed up my hair? Any minute now I would be hearing Frederick's trombone.

From his summer place, high in the woods on the far side of the river, roughly 300 yards north, he would be signalling his departure—by means of the trombone. That week, at least I think that's when he started to do this, he would play a song through, always the same piece: from beginning to end, without pause, wrong notes notwithstanding, "I'm Getting Sentimental Over You"; which to me, in spite of Frederick's never having made any mention of this quaint exercise, had become a kind of musical love-letter, sounding across the water as rich and startling as black velvet, like a gentle command, like a thousand trillion original love-notes.

That recurrent serenade. Tommy Dorsey's theme song, whose words were as familiar to George and me as the alphabet. Wouldn't that have told George something, I wondered just at that moment? and in the next instant I'm colouring. No, why would George think anything of that, when I could be mistaken; for all I know, I could be dreaming Frederick's playing it to me. Gee, if you can hear it all the way down here, it must be hard on the neighbours, when they're sitting out and all. Does someone shout out, "Dry up and bust!"? I pick up the mirror and hang it on its nail, and start humming, "Time on My Hands" . . . oh, that rancid salad dressing . . . I'll just bet Mamma's fingers left some on my hair after all, the smell, I mean.

Heavens, another tack's fallen out of the backing on the mirror. . . . Time on my hands, dah-dah da dee . . .

> Nothing but love
> In view . . .

I feel good again, and if I do say so myself, I look kind of pretty, like Mamma when I first knew her, in my mind I mean, the first time I saw her as a girl, she and Daddy were dancing to "Just a Little Love, a Little Kiss". I'm glad I don't have black hair though. Girls with black hair strike me as, oh, they're always so *darned* proper, so white-skinned and virtuous, like that prissy Melba. She let the priest in the village talk her out of wearing shorts. I wouldn't. When he stopped me in the store I just told him I wasn't a Catholic and let it go at that. Mamma said I should have told him he shouldn't be looking. Next time I will. Where's George got to

I wonder? Better stop dilly-dallying, why don't I go and wait outside, look at things while I listen for the trombone. . . .

When I went outside, there was George sitting on the verandah steps. Spruced up, I noticed. He'd changed into a navy sweatshirt, the sleeves rolled up and tucked into tight bands high on his arms. As for his hair! The curls brushed back and slick with Brilliantine. Was that the way it was, I wondered, two nights ago when Hail Hail The Gang's All Here were "hitting it off"?

I didn't think he heard me open the screen door, or even knew I was standing there. He was sitting with his hands flat together between his knees, opening and closing them in a kind of easy rhythm as he listened for Frederick's motor, a low soft whistling going on between his teeth, with his head turned, looking upriver.

He was taller than I now, seeming even more so just then, the set of his shoulders assured, arms once gangling (when? this morning at breakfast? last week?) glimpsed now as the arms of a youth with force in his body, firm and muscular.

Without saying anything I settled myself down alongside him, feeling, in a strange way, innocently, and yet powerfully, the difference in his boy's world, the self-knowledge that was his alone. How do you talk, how can you ask someone about things like that? that from a resortful to choose from, he had been singled out as a special friend. And four years his senior at that. Not just another boyfriend you went catching frogs with when there was nothing else to do. This was Frederick, fellow-friend, colleague, confidant; his other self? Someone who changed into shiny brown shoes at night, and wore white flannels with a crease, and took out a comb and ran it through his hair the way men did. Yes, George was devoted. How well I knew that tender reserve that ruled him, having to make certain first, I was thinking (one, maybe two more visits from Frederick), then he would tell me his feelings, assuming a casual air on the chance its importance to him might sound ridiculous.

Perhaps only a matter of seconds had passed, but I felt then as though I were drawing inside myself, locked in with words stuck in my throat, my whole being two halves, torn between my own growing-stronger attraction towards Frederick, and my affection for George which, until this moment, I had not realized was a deeper thing. How was it you could care about a brother more than anything in the whole world? That's the question I kept asking myself . . . why he came

first. I did not know. At this time in my life there were too
many other questions, which seemed more pressing. A common bond is not something you're aware of until there's a
threat of its being damaged, or broken; in this case, a bond
I'd had no grasp of, just a feeling that always was there.

If as children we'd only had the odd set-to! Or sounded off
with a good kick once in a while, maybe taken a swing. . . .
But we wouldn't have known what it meant to slap one another.

In the inches separating us, George on one step and me on
the one below, I couldn't help but feel the joy inside him.
Smiling at me a couple of times, but that was all, intent on
the river again, an opening of sound in the air. Patiently
waiting, the same as I was. Boards creaked under my bottom
as I leaned forward with my elbows on my knees, cupping
my face in my hands, taking a brief glance, surreptitiously,
my hand pushing back a wave of hair, accounting for the
movement of my head. In his eyes I saw a kind of triumph.
There was a trust he had earned, I was thinking, which I
wanted to acknowledge, to share his new joy. I tried to think
of something to say, it had to be just right, but I didn't know
how. Because whatever emotions we had shared before had
always remained intact; we'd never had to divide them, rip
them down the middle.

Only two nights before I had gone to bed with everything
so full of promise. I sighed inwardly, remembering how I had
twice gotten up to lean on the windowsill, wondering if Frederick were back from trying out that seaplane at Blue Sea
Lake, the quiet-voiced poplars and silver maple moving in the
slumbrous wind, their own emotion breaking through the
middle of the air. While the tom-tom beat of my heart broke
through me. Frederick, who liked me. I was his girl.

Now I felt miserable, half-sick. I thought of the dreamy
look I'd been practising in the mirror all that week, putting
Vaseline on my lashes to make them grow thick and lustrous.
Why, I was a silly Dumb-Dora, that's what I was. Good for
nothing but saving boys' baseball sweaters and samples of
perfume. If I hadn't been so concerned with making myself
into something I wasn't, I'd have seen what was coming.

———————

It was now around eight o'clock, and the quiet of summer
murmurs had settled across the valley. After the height of
day, with its runs of sound and brilliance, you felt the hush

more acutely; sometimes a kind of quiver went through my
flesh as I felt the night coming on, soon the moon and stars
and the thick darkness, and lights suddenly glimmering across
the water, and somewhere beyond, the sound of a car horn
distant in the hills opposite, its far headlights moving slowly
down the winding mountain road into the village. It was as if
you belonged to the night and the night belonged to you,
once you were seventeen. In my mind the night had taken on
mystery, something heavenly, exciting. I would lie awake
wondering what it's like, what happens when you fall in love.

And any minute now Frederick would be arriving, and the
thought of it made me ache. With my eyes on the river, far
up where he would make the same diagonal cut across the
water as if he were following a path, I saw in my mind the
tracings his boat had been making for more than a week
now, the dart-shaped line that followed him as he headed
downriver. To the eye and ear the boat in the river was
something that caught your attention, like an airplane. At
that time, Frederick's was the only motorboat around. Sometimes, when I wasn't expecting him, its nearing sound sent a
surge through me. Was the boat going down the far side of
the river? was he merely on his way to the village store? or
taking his grandfather fishing? I would never look. Trees par-
tially blocking my view, I'd stay right where I was, on the
verandah, or in my room, out on the hill, wherever, assessing
the direction of the sound . . . listening. If the boat seemed
headed elsewhere, I didn't want to see it, that way it was the
same as if I hadn't heard his boat at all. Then once I was certain, almost certain—did the blades just thump a log? it
sounded close, our side of the shore?—after minutes of fend-
ing off disappointment, an inexpressible joy, legs under me
weakening, my equilibrium . . . where? Why me? Is it true?
My mind repeating questions and answers I kept to myself; I
never let on to anyone. Was this all different from what I had
imagined?

Merciful heavens! Hot patooty! Right now, for the first
time, now, this very minute, I am that girl again! And I must
go slowly, carefully.

What I felt for Frederick *was* something else, I sensed that
much; my feelings were much more real. As soon as I was by
his side, the moment I was with him I forgot about being
dreamy. I wanted to be myself, the same as he was, at home
with himself, free of the ructions and crazy antics of all of
us. He gave you the feeling you could be quiet when you

wanted. And it was me he had chosen to serenade across the water, for the whole of the countryside to hear! I'd go into my room, I remember, not wanting to seem over-anxious, indulging my independence and thus making the joy all the more acute. Timing it to the last second, I would saunter down the path to the dock, picking my way slowly, feeling awkward, almost wanting to run back up the hill. Until I heard myself speaking; conversation, first between Frederick and George and then the three of us, and everything became the same as the day before. I was real again.

And now, feeling desolate, yet anticipating the best of all moments; George with his soft whistling as he watched the river, keeping to himself the shift of his inner being. Suddenly I didn't want to see Frederick at all, not then, not ever. As if the ache in me was his fault.

I uncrossed my legs and stretched them out full, heels plopping on the third step down, and George, as if directed by a reflex, like following someone's yawn, immediately did likewise, his feet dangling over the edge of the step below, the pair of us in running shoes, newly whitened, the laces tied into neat perfection as a final touch; itself an emotion. Between us, an exchange of grins, a thought. "What time is it?" . . . "Boy, did I get a sunburn today!" . . . "A fish just jumped, did you see it? What a splash. I bet it was a black bass."

Idly we banged our toes together, out of rhythm, into it again, the rubber thuds of our sneakers seeming to speak for us, saying more than we could.

It was nice: the river pale golden from the sun at that hour, an outdoor pavilion living a life of its own, the homeward veerings of swallows, and the drone of a blue monoplane heading north. Our eyes followed it indifferently, then turned back again to the moving river out front, our senses responding, fed by the lean of the two pines down at the river bank, the grown-wild tiger-lilies Mamma had planted between them catching the low slant of sunlight, long stemmed and tilted westward, like paper lanterns strung along the shoreline; above the dock, the boom-line my father had wired together when we were learning to swim, the boom we helped him replace when the logs rotted or had been loosened by the spring breakup of ice. And further out, sunlight striking the weeds floating on top of the water, green hair, shiny, slippery like the wet boom. Nothing was missing. All the things that had grown with us, that we had grown used to. So many years of play, the cowbells of Bessie and Myrtle, the station platform where we waited for the train to take us to school, the sandbar, leaves changing colour. . . . But inch by inch the playground was getting bigger; a field of competition, the human heart the competitor.

Now that we were older we had often sat like this, mornings, evenings, often before going to bed, our minds strolling the reaches of the day just passed, the night to come, the week about to begin.

I remember George getting up suddenly, and I thought he had heard Frederick's motor, but no, he was only going down to the bottom step to secure a block of wood that had slipped, a makeshift until the new hardwood plank arrived. When he came back up the steps I winced inwardly at his concentration, the effort to contain himself; I remember too, the grin he attempted to hold in check as he eased the knees of his pants, first one then the other, as though they had creases, as if only minutes before he had just pressed them.

"You're all dressed up," he said. I was in a baseball sweater and shorts. I didn't call that being all dressed up. Still, the shorts were brand new—white with red braids down the sides. "You'll see yourself coming a mile off," Mamma had said when I'd first shown them to her in Simpson's catalogue.

"You're dressed up too," I said.

"Nah. All I did was change my sweatshirt. The other got mud all over it back at the creek."

"So you did go, you and Jimmie went to fix the bridge after all?"

"Yep. Before milking. And I went back again after supper, but I had to tell Jim I'd forgotten Fred was coming, I'd have to be back early." Jim? Fred? Now it's Jim and Fred.

"Lucky you changed your shirt," I said. "It'd have smelled of more than mud!" The bridge George and Jimmie were shoring up was at the creek bed where the cows spent the night slopping around in the cooling pool-water. And that week they'd had their TB injections, you could even taste it in the milk.

"That terrible stink of disinfectant," I said, "boy, no one would get me back there this week. Could you still smell it?"

"A little. Not so much." It was good to talk. I didn't want to hear the trombone, the motor, in fact I didn't want to have a boyfriend at all.

"I never used to mind the smell of manure before," I said.

"On clothes I mean." George lifted the waistband of his sweatshirt and sniffed at the fleece. "Is it niffy?" I asked.

"Nope, but maybe the smell's come off on my skin," he laughed.

"Tell me," I said, "what do you think we'll do after Frederick gets here tonight?" *We*. I winced inside again, the sound of my words slapping me with guilt.

"Maybe go into town," George replied. "Fred said he'd drive me in one of these nights, and Saturday'd be a good night to go."

"Drive into town? What for? What's there to do in town?"

"Oh, hang around. You know. . . ." No, I didn't know. It was news to me. And suddenly I felt better, asking myself was it possible that long before now, maybe right from the beginning, Frederick had sensed, had an inkling from something George might have said, a funny gesture or secret exchange like men do when they're by themselves? Wasn't Frederick the one who took time to notice things? I told myself he'd know what to say, I wouldn't have to say a single word, and whichever way things went, coming from Frederick, George wouldn't mind so much.

"When did Frederick mention going into town?" I asked, my head down, intent on my feet. I didn't know whether to laugh or cry; either way, the feeling was the same. Frederick liked him, George wasn't just some girlfriend's brother.

"When? Last week," Geroge said, a low tone, triumphant, impressed. "And he mentioned it again yesterday when I saw him in the post office. You can come too if you like."

"If he invites me I will. And if not, then I won't."

"Why not? Don't you like Fred?" Fred again. I wanted to tell George I hated that name. I didn't though. I decided I would wait for a week, or the week after, depending.

"Sure I like him," I said. "I just thought if he asked you to go . . . well, that doesn't say he wants me along as well." I reached down and picked at a piece of rotted wood. I didn't want to go, and yet I did. I kept contradicting myself, turning the question over in my mind. Did I appear to be disconsolate? Did I seem put out?

"I'll ask him for you, if you like. We won't be doing much you know. He said he sometimes goes in and parks outside the Standish so he can hear the trombonist in the orchestra. He's supposed to be better than Tommy Dorsey even. Fred knows the manager there, and he lets him park in back . . . near where the orchestra plays."

I'd never been to the Standish, not yet. I'd only seen the place driving past on the way through Hull. And I thought now of the big black and white sign: STANDISH HALL HOTEL. Beer and Wine. DANCING NIGHTLY till 2 a.m. I'd have to change into a dress, I was thinking, I couldn't park outside the Standish in shorts. I decided the coast was clear, now I could put on my new beach pyjamas.

"Would they let us in?" I asked. "To dance, I mean?"

"You and Fred maybe. But that's okay, I wouldn't mind. I'd wait in the car. That'd be okay." His reasoning so practical. She doesn't have a boyfriend right now; it's up to him to see she has fun too. That's what I sensed going on in his mind.

Across the water the first sounds of the trombone, feeling its way, notes rising and falling, seeming close at hand, then distant, a pause after a wrong note, and a run at a new phrase, from the beginning once more, clear and strong now, confident. "Never thought I'd fall . . ." Those minutes were the worst of all. Sitting there, self-conscious, the music throbbing in me, trying to keep the tremble in my breathing— dread, joy—from making any sound. How could I tell George? How do you explain, give an answer when there's been no question asked?

"You wouldn't mind?" I asked. "I mean . . . if Frederick asks me to go inside and dance? Even if you did, I wouldn't care. I think he likes me."

"Nah. Why would I mind? I'll smoke a cigarette, and maybe take a walk over to the Chaudière Bridge. I've always wanted to stand on top of those rapids."

"Hey! I didn't know you smoked *cigarettes*. When did you start? After that time with the shag, or what?"

"Last summer. Jimmie and I get the makings over in the village and then roll them back at the creek."

"For Pete's sake. No kidding." I said, and punched his shoulder, and his arms flew out like a wing, a shove against my ribs, which I promptly returned in the solar plexus. I remember how we laughed, absurdly; hysterics come at odd times. Instead of poking him in the windpipe, I wanted to put my arms around him and hang on tight, I wanted to say, 'Please don't be hurt, I can't stand it if you are.' Instead, a jab of my elbow.

The interior of Standish Hall rises before my eyes; not the "Entertainment Nightly" room but a reasonable facsimile, I am thinking, a substitute much closer to Heaven. Scarcely twenty feet from the orchestra, outside in the red-carpeted hallway, Frederick and I silently, wordlessly, dance across the rug; a ceiling fan whirs faintly above rose-coloured lights mounted on the walls. In Frederick's arms I do not cling loosely, nor chatter, nor sing to the music; we are not disguised, we are not dancing at one of the bonfires. I hang on tight, the top of my head resting under his chin, as if I were asleep, the lovely noise and scatter of people streaming past, who do not seem to care, or wonder why we choose to dance here instead of inside where there's a dance floor.

Through the din and clatter, the bump of bodies, cadences of music, loud and then soft, a crooner sings about the wind and rain in someone's hair. And now the orchestra grants a request, the trombonist repeats a tune he played not ten minute ago when Frederick and George and I were sitting in the Oldsmobile. Was that when Frederick got out of the car and announced: "I want to dance with your sister"?

Rose-coloured lights dimming again, that's the second time, is the power going to go off? A telephone ringing, and a waiter carrying a tray covered with a white linen napkin dekes around us, says something to Frederick over his shoulder, something about a piece, ". . . third time tonight for that piece." And now the trombonist, inspired by the recognition of yet another request, swings his swinging music:

> Never thought I'd fall,
> But now I hear love's call,
> I'm gettin' sentimental over you.

My throat, my heart is gasping, and I think, Oh Frederick, please . . . Do you *know*? do you not know after all? about George? I can't say the words, I can't tell you myself! My mind floats, melts sort of, down through my body, flowing down, down, and I feel the pull as Frederick steers me away from a potted plant, which someone has just spat in, a man with a wig, it's crooked. He stops to fix it, it got caught when he bent over the palm leaves. We dance around him, moving away because he's drunk, and smells of vomit.

We're dancing out in the hallway for a very good reason: there's no point in paying a cover charge for a couple of dances. Besides, we'll be gone soon, long before the floor show.

While George smokes his cigarette, and stands, or leans, over the cataracts of the Chaudière Falls, the gossamer of my brain, my body, claims me, these dim lights, the trombone, the thump of Frederick's heart, knocking hard as my own, and his arms, the biggest I ever felt, so tight around me, why, I can scarcely breathe. In a few minutes, when the music ends, we won't be embarrassed about not paying the cover charge. We will come back; just the two of us maybe, we can pay then.

The vocalist has stopped, and the piano does a trill, like a three-second finale. That means we must go now. We will leave, we will walk beneath the ceiling fan, past the potted ferns and palms, hand in hand out the side door as we return to the car. And we'll be sitting inside, with all the windows down and the moist night air beginning to cool, not saying much, which says more, still holding hands when George gets back. Which George does, in ten minutes? fifteen? He looks expectant, excited.

Our plans are to drive back home, and home this time is Frederick's place. He has said twice, first on the way down and again now, "Why don't we go to my place and put on some records? Maybe try out George's new dance step he's learning." His folks are away, Frederick says, we can play our own music.

But first George must tell us about the rapids. "You should try it sometime," he declares, and reminds us that being there is nowhere the same as driving past in a car. "You have to stand on the bridge," he says, "it's that *wild* you can see the whole thing with your eyes closed." His arms rest on the car door, head half in and half out the window. Before getting in, he must tell us more about the Falls: "They look silver under the light, silver and brown." More water than he's ever seen, he adds. "Honest! You should try it sometime." He doesn't seem to have noticed Frederick's arm around me, the way he's trying to rearrange the flop of my Jo-Cur curls; Frederick is looking at him, and not at my hair at all.

---

Frederick's folks are away all right. From the look of things, the way it feels here, they're never anything else but! . . . unless they come back to sleep. You can tell when someone's around a lot; things aren't this tidy. There should be some dust, at least on the end-tables there should be. People, even if they're sitting around doing nothing, can stir up dust overnight. Maybe they don't like having company. I get the feeling they don't have anyone in much. So we should be careful not to disturb anything.

Frederick returns to the room, two glasses of beer, the tall thin kind of glass that has a base. They don't make rings. George sets his down, is more interested in examining Frederick's trombone, wants to know where the mute is. "Where do you keep it, Fred?" he asks.

I wander off down the hall into the bedroom; I like to see what people have in the rooms where they sleep, if they have rugs or mats on the floor, and if they've got nice bedspreads. Some of my friends' parents use dark maroon blankets instead, they don't have to wash them. Boy! Get a load of the bedspreads in this room! exactly like our good white damask tablecloth in town, the only difference being they're gold-coloured, with tassels to match. And the lamps! Are they pure china? made in Japan? or Limoges? Pure silk shades too, is this his parents' room? Golly, they must be wealthy, I'll bet they're rich. Holy mackerel. On the dresser . . . is that a real diamond? I thought they only put diamonds in ladies' rings. I try the ring on my biggest finger; won't even stay on my thumb. I better put it back in the tray. Which way did they have it turned? Did I see the sparkle in the mirror first, or was the diamond facing me? Oh, what a lot of ties. Ye gods! Are those all his father's? They're puky-looking, only older men would wear navy, or maroon; as for dark green . . . they're certainly not what you'd call smart. And not a single spot on any of them that I can see. Maybe after he's worn them a few times he just throws them out.

I try one of the beds, and wonder why there are two. Why don't they have a bed big enough to hold the two of them? Maybe his mother sleeps in another room. She's got her perfume on the bureau though, and a pincushion with a pearl brooch in it. But I don't see anything else of hers. I should open the clothes cupboard. Locked. Now why do they leave a diamond ring in full view and then turn around and lock the closet? I shouldn't be snooping. I'll tell Frederick what I did though, otherwise it would be cheating. I'd certainly expect him to tell me if he went in my parents' room . . . that's what's called having scruples. Mamma says she doesn't mind when we do wrong if we've been taught a lesson, learned something from it. Own up, she always says, be above board about things; if you can't trust yourself, how do you expect other people to? I won't be able to tell Frederick just yet though; he'd be thinking I'm not sophisticated, that I act too young for my age. I just wanted to feel close to him, see what it's like where he lives when he comes home; this is a good way of doing it so it doesn't show.

There's one more thing I need to know before I leave. Do they have pee-pots under the beds? Nope. Nor fluff, nor a steamer trunk. I shouldn't be so nosy. But while I'm here it won't hurt to use this comb and fix my hair. Where will I put the hairs? the waste basket is empty, spick and span. Ah, my purse! When I go back to the living room I can stuff it inside when they're not looking.

"Where were you?" George wants to know. "Didn't you go to the bathroom before you left the Standish?"

My trips to the toilet, or George's, discussing them has never seemed out of order. I see no reason to change now. The time to be modest is when you're with strangers.

"Did I!" I announce emphatically. "I went in the wrong one! I saw W.C. and thought the W stood for Women. They should have the Hommes on top, and in bigger letters so you can read it in the dark. That's what I told a man in there. Say! I didn't know you had . . . things on the wall to go in. When the man turned around I said, 'Oh, I'm sorry,' and he laughed, 'No, no, why would you be sorry?' and I said, 'Yes, well, goodbye then.' Then I left."

"No kidding!" George exclaims, startled, his voice stretching in disbelief. "You really went in?"

"You said you felt like doing something different tonight," Frederick observes with a wry smile. "I should have taken you down the hall," he adds softly, "when they were having all that trouble with the lights."

"I don't need anyone to take me, Frederick. I mean you have to find your way in different places." George I see is nodding.

"And did you?" he asks. "Did you find it okay?"

"No . . . I held it. I thought why don't I wait till after? I could go here."

"Feel better?" Frederick asks affectionately, sipping his drink, bronze lamplight flashing on his ring.

"Fred thought you'd gone home," George says quietly, spilling out his concern for his friend Frederick's private thoughts. Is that what Frederick was afraid of? Did he think I might leave? Walk out on him? I don't know as I should be too quick to say I'd never do that. I don't believe I'll say one way or the other.

"Hey, listen!" I say to George, plunking myself grandly on the green and gold sofa, sinking, foundering in feather cushions that make a wonderful sound, like someone sighing in their sleep. Halted by this sudden plunge into the deep, I sit upright in my pit of down, temporarily putting aside the request I was about to make of George, and, squeezing the top of an adjacent cushion, I turn to Frederick: "Are they made out of real feathers, or cotton batting?" And with no change of expression—which means Frederick's tender though slightly amused grin remains faithful to the demands of this unlikely quizzing—he replies: "Yes, as far as I know they're feathers."

"I thought so," I say, pinching down the corner once more; that's expected of you, it's a way of confirming that if you didn't before, you now recognize something in keeping with people of good taste. Returning to the subject I was about to embark on, I hesitate briefly, waiting for George's attention—he has come over to feel the cushions too.

"Neat, eh?" he comments, goes back to his chair and sits down again.

"Hey, George?" I begin, transferring my purse down beside me on the sofa, so as to appear casual. "All night you've been calling Frederick 'Fred'. I wish you wouldn't call him that. It doesn't suit him. Fred sounds like a name for a horse."

I feel my colour rising; it's an admission, an open declaration of my feelings for Frederick, which I do not want him to have, not yet. Still, I could merely have been indicating my sensitive taste in names. Well, it's as good a way as any of letting George know he and I are not sharing Frederick in quite the same way. "I could never get used to calling him Fred," I said airily, picking up a dainty porcelain ash tray and turning it over to examine the back to see where it's made. "How come you started it in the first place, when no one else does?"

"Slipped out one day. I guess it caught on once I got to know him, you know?"

"Sure. And it's okay. Fred's your name for him. People often start calling someone a different name," I say absently, trying to decipher little marks of gold paint smeared on the back of the ash tray. "Besides, when you're just getting to know someone, it shows you think a lot of them," I add, still examining the bottom of the ash tray; doesn't seem to have been made anywhere, and that's no bargain. I better put it back with the others. I never heard of an arrangement of ash trays before.

"I don't know if I'll remember, though," George says, pausing. "I might forget sometimes."

"Remember? Remember what?" I ask looking up.

"Not to call him Fred all the time . . . I mean when you're there."

"You don't have to. Call him whatever you like. I'm sorry, George, I shouldn't be . . . just so long as you don't call him Freddy."

"All right," he laughs, shifting deeper into his chair and then crossing his legs, looking around as he settles back. "Pretty nice here, don't you think?" he asks earnestly, mindful of that small courtesy of discovery when you find yourself in a person's home for the first time, it makes them feel you're glad to be there. "I didn't expect it'd be this nice," he goes on, obviously pleased, indicated not so much by a cursory sweep of eyes, taking in walls, leaded-pane windows, the wide rugs and what fills the air space above them, as by the pleasure manifest in his eyes.

"It's very nice," I agree decorously, about to add, "It's swell," deciding against it. "Get a load of that stone fireplace! Did you notice how it's round, George? I never heard of one like that before. It goes in every room, I mean in the living room, and the dining room . . . it's got four round sides to it. It's a swell place."

Frederick I see is observing us, stumping out a cigarette in a spittoon-shaped ash tray that has S.S. *LeBlan*-something on it. From his chair, close to where I am, and directly opposite George, who has now chosen to try out the hassock draped with a black-and-white fur rug, he glances from one to the other, the brown eyes Mamma says are lovely and warm wander back and forth between us. He is thinking. Whatever it is I know it would be pretty to hear, in a way it's the same as though he was talking to us, saying something without having to. I guess that's an art. He also looks happy. Is that because George and I are doing all the talking? Is it our company? So this is where he lives. From the look of things, I guess he can afford anything he wants. It seems kind of quiet here, though, kind of lonely-feeling. But maybe he doesn't mind. After all, it's home.

He puts a cushion behind his head, and leans back, like a man who's used to sitting in this room. Is this where he plays his trombone? in that chair where he's sitting? They must be out those times. I wonder where they go? Maybe his father and mother stay in town a lot, or go off playing bridge at another rich cottage. I wonder who plants the garden? On the way in I saw flowerbeds ten times bigger than the ones outside the Civic Hospital. And fancy: the same as what's out in front of the Parliament Buildings; under the porchlights I saw coloured lilies and things. Who does the weeding and watering? It'd take more than one person, it'd be a lot of work looking after these grounds, to say nothing of the lawn. Do they hang washing on the line? Do they have a dog? or a cat? No. Rich people have a horse instead. Yes. I bet his mother and father keep a horse in town, out in the country somewhere. I should enquire.

"Where are your parents, Frederick? They must be in the city a lot, I never see them in the village, or out on the river. Come to think of it, I don't think I've ever seen them—unless they passed me on the highway in their car." Brown eyes, warm, like his smile. That's a good sign; he likes his parents.

"They went to the Seigniory Club for a week."

"The Seigniory Club?" George exclaims, surprised; it's because he's heard of it. "My father goes there too," he adds.

"For meetings, conventions," I announce proudly, fancying such a distinction as far grander, much more important than just *staying* there.

"Then why don't you come over to our place for meals?" George says eagerly. "Until your mother and father come back. I wish you would. You wouldn't need to bring anything. We've got lots."

"They're supposed to be home tomorrow," Frederick says. "But I think I might come along in any case. I might just do that." He is not answering, not replying to George. For the first time, in all the time we've been here, Frederick's eyes focus directly on mine. Penetrating. Sudden and fierce as an interruption. And the warm night sends a chill down my spine, which comes out through my middle, high on the left side. I think I might die. My pink cotton-eyelet dress . . . oh, I wish I'd worn my beach pyjamas instead, the holes in the eyelet show through . . . my slip is . . . it's my heart jumping under my breast. I seize upon my purse, there's maybe a bobby-pin or my lipstick I could fiddle with. I unfasten the dome, and find my loose hair back in my hand; I'd shoved it behind the torn lining.

"How about playing us your trombone?" George says out of the blue. "How about giving us a tune, show us how it's done, and after, I wouldn't mind having a turn myself . . . see what comes out."

"If you do," I say turning to Frederick, "then will you play something else? . . . if you know what I mean?" I study him, fully recovered now, I can look him in the eye again.

"I thought you liked your theme song," he replies. My theme song? Mine? Is it mine? His eyes . . . I can't tell whether he's joking or if he's serious.

"No. Yes," I say. "But you've already played it . . . earlier. Remember?" Why doesn't he answer? "*Before* you got in the boat," I hint. Does that do it, or was that the wrong thing to say? Oh, when he's got a perfect opportunity, why doesn't he tell George a little bit, explain, now that he's got the chance. Why doesn't he wink at George or something; well, he *could* start by saying, "Do you think your sister has caught on yet? Do you think she knows I'm trying to . . . woo her over?" No, that's not the way Frederick talks, it's what Mamma'd say . . . well, "trying to ask her to be my girl"; that's better. I—it's true he sensed something was up, isn't it? Daddy promised me Frederick had already sensed, from the beginning, he said so, and that he'd handle it. But what if—? He's so busy flicking the horn end of the trombone up and down I can't tell. I thought now that we've been together tonight and all . . . And suddenly I'm relieved; I didn't know my knees had started to shake. I take up where I left off. "Instead of playing your theme song, Frederick, why'd don't you do 'Song of India'? Or, 'Marie'? How about 'Marie'? I've heard you at both of them, I hear you practising sometimes."

He moves to the sofa and sits down beside me, takes hold of my left hand, and rhythmically bangs my wrist up and down on the upholstery, which has a rough feel—brocade upholstery.

"I've got a better idea," he says. "Why don't I bring the trombone down to your place tomorrow, we could go out in the boat some place and all have a turn?"

"That's a swell idea, Fred," George exclaims, and takes a sip of his beer, then promptly recrosses his legs on the hassock. In all this time, his first swig. I guess his very first of all time; he made a face. I wonder why he didn't take a sip right away, just to try it? I guess he's been too busy; it's exciting being here. More fun than I ever remember. Fun? Yes. Everything's like it was yesterday, that is, before Daddy and I went for the mail—last night.

Frederick has left the sofa and, on the other side of the
room, is standing with an armful of records, his back to us as
he flips through, flip, flap, flop, flip, there must be twenty
records in the crook of his arm, like a cardboard book he's
looking through. Not saying a word; he's choosing.

"Which ones you think he'll pick?" I whisper to George,
feeling like a guest now, Frederick having left my sofa, the
intent of his back a sudden distance, formality, formal host.

"I think we're supposed to be trying that new dance step,"
George replies in a low voice. "And I'm not even good at the
old ones yet!" He shakes his head and laughs at himself. "I
could learn though, I wouldn't mind."

On goes the record. Good night, I knew it! Darn him. I
might have known he'd put that one on. Striding over to me
now, his arms and his right hand pretending he's playing his
darned old trombone. He expects me to get up. Which I do;
he hasn't done anything wrong.

"You're mean, Frederick," I stammer. I stand there like a
dummy, a baby wanting to cry. It isn't fair. The music,
there's no vocal on this record but I hear every word: "But
now I hear love call," I hold my hands at my sides, with my
head down. I won't budge. "If you think you can make me
dance, you can't. I won't."

"Why the tears?" Frederick asks and lifts my face, one finger under my chin. One finger, that's enough; my neck, my
will—nothing to fall back on.

"Why are you crying?" I hear Frederick say again, from
lips whose warm breath burns through my hair, my ears,
whose arm brings me, protectively, into the arc of his frame.
Such a big frame, big enough to hide me.

"I don't know," I mutter, and with him move across the
floor, slowly, around a table, back, in every direction, the
soles of my feet without any feeling, turning, the other side
of the room, where Frederick frees one hand and playfully
clips George's crossed knee, which jumps, making him spill
the beer en route to his mouth. Over Frederick's shoulder I
see George wiping the floor off with his sleeve, and then he's
gone from my sight; Frederick and I are turning again, our
feet, our shoes, slip, slip, sliii-ii-iip. My body is loose, not now
do I hang on tight, there must be at least a foot between us,
twelve inches of life separate, divide us, they must. Because
it's too soon for George to see. I must first—no, I want to be
the one to tell him, and yet I don't. Maybe Frederick . . .
when, though? tomorrow? And then I can come back in

close, and I'll hold on tight, forever. The music . . . I'm glad
after all that Frederick put that piece on; it's ours. I want to
sing the words in his ear but I can't. Frederick mustn't hear
me *say* them, there's something I have to make certain of
first: he could be sweet on other girls too. I sing in my head,
'Never thought I'd fall. . . .'

The music has stopped, just stopped, and Frederick is holding me as if we were still dancing, we're doing nothing but
standing here. I really don't like to move, his hand is clasping
the curve at the back of my neck, a finger, I feel his fingers
moving under my hair. Sometimes when music stops, you
keep moving anyway, pretend you're dancing. But he's not,
and I don't know where to look. It's a question of letting my
body do what it wants, sway a little to the music I hear in my
head; so I do, I raise myself up on tiptoes, swaying left, swaying right, and I see that George has gone over to the record
player. But he's not changing the record. He moves the
pickup head back to the beginning and sits down on the floor
with the pile of records. "Gee," he says turning around,
"here's a picture of the way they do that dip." He holds up
what appears to be a page from the coloured section of the
weekend newspaper. "They stick the leg out further than I
thought. How about this record next, okay? My turn next,"
he concludes.

"Me to teach? Or your sister?" Frederick enquires over my
head, towering over me, I swear he's twenty feet if he's ten.
Ohhhh. . . .

"No, you to teach, Frederick," I say, "not me. Because I
don't know how to do that dip either. George is good at it,
he really is, Frederick," I add, looking up, twenty feet. "He
picks up dances faster than I do. My legs get all tangled up,
they're too long to be any good at dancing. I have to learn
how to work them first."

"Come on," George says, changing the record. "I'll show
you," he offers coming toward me. "Want me to?" Frederick
releases his hand from my waist and passes me over to my
brother, casually, gracefully, in a personal way, and I think,
If it'd been that Jack Humphreys, he'd have had to do a little
trick or something before hand, take a step back and wind
up, as if he were about to heave a sack of turnips.

"Say!" George says. "Who says . . . I thought you didn't
know how?" looking down from his height, which is no more
than fifteen feet.

"Oh, I can do some . . ." I try again, my renewed faith is

over-exaggerated and I miss the next dip. "I'll never get it, George," I wail. "I can't seem to get the beat back, it takes me so long . . . I mean, when I slant my leg out I can't get it back in time."

"Sure you will. It's easy. You're almost doing it now. Here, watch Fred and me."

"Who's going to lead?" Frederick wants to know. "Who's going to be the girl?"

"Not me," says George.

"Not me," says Frederick.

---

Yes, I say to myself, what a crazy nut of a girl I am. I should be ashamed of myself. How come one minute I'm crying, and then end up . . . what?· What am I doing? Laughing?

It is quiet again, we have returned to where we were sitting a while ago; George is on the hassock, I am on the sofa, and Frederick is back in his chair. Reposing. Pensive. No palaver, no bursts of soft nothings; we take this seriously, you don't lurch around nonstop for half an hour without calling a halt some time, thoughts have to idle for a moment, they can't very well when a person's reeling all over the place, trying to count notes and plunge and swoop attempting to keep on the beat. What confusion! The three of us certainly went at that swing music whole hog. You'd think we were in one of those dance marathons or something. Frederick must be used to this, he's not even perspiring. Of course there's all that huffing and puffing on his trombone every day, his wind gets exercised. Intently, he's been turning something over in his hands—his lighter? that solid gold egg-cup they have in here as an ornament? Whatever it was, he's decided to lay it down, he's finished with the doings of his mind. The cushion, the one he used before, is resting back of his head again. Suddenly he reaches behind, and taking a firm hold of one corner, tosses the cushion at George, who also has been thinking about something; his eyes are on the floor but that's not what he's taking stock of. What's been passing through his mind I wonder? I swallow. Has the hassock become another lookout post, the Chaudière Falls no longer thought of? He gets to his feet and picks up the cushion, laughing, same expression as earlier, the same as an hour ago . . . two hours ago, three, the brown eyes no different from yesterday.

"Right," he says in reply to Frederick's throw. He shoves

up the sleeves of his sweatshirt, and lobs the cushion back at
Frederick, smack onto the chest, as if he were throwing a forward pass, then readies himself, face to face, hands cupped
off to one side to receive the return.

A soft sofa-cushion, royal-blue velvet and oblong, a bagful
of feathers, passing through the air, back, bck, back and
forth, why do they hang on to it a few secs first? what is happening? another two times, three, four as their eyes meet, and
hold.

It's their way of letting one another know.

They are gentle people, and they are two men.

---

Records scattered over the floor, rugs bundled into a corner. Two beer glasses with mustaches of dried foam, and Frederick's empty rye glass; one, no two, dirty ash trays. Did we
make all this mess? Never seems to show in our place. Oh
well. It's time we were leaving anyway. Must be way after
midnight. What will Mamma and Daddy think? Will they
worry? We forgot to tell them we were going into Hull.
They'd have seen us leave together in the boat though, they
were back from wherever they went and digging worms with
a flashlight, from the icehouse they'd have spotted us through
the trees maybe, the lights from the verandah and all, they'd
have been able to count heads, if not, then hear three voices.
And being as it's Frederick, they won't care where we got to.
Even so, they'd be expecting . . . listening for the motor to
come *across* the water, to have started out from the landing
opposite. Won't they get a surprise when they hear us coming
down river instead? I must remember to tell Mamma something. I'll say, 'Guess what we did tonight! Frederick asked us
to put on our dancing shoes.' That's part of her language,
and one of her superlatives: the thought of getting up to
dance, in a field, even, makes her elated. Any excuse and
she'll turn around with that racy expression and squeal, 'Got
your dancing shoes on?' or, 'Did you bring your dancing
shoes?' Now I know why this reckoning is always present in
her mind; it's not just a friendly saying, it's something you
feel. And if someone acts surprised, or tells her they haven't
danced in years, gave it up long ago, she'll say, 'Go to
blazes.' Well, if she was anxious tonight, had a premonition
we were driving up and down country roads till this hour,
there's no mistaking she'll grin and allegro-vivace: 'So it was
Standish Hall, was it?' And when she looks at her watch and

asks, 'Did you close up the place?' I'll . . . I know what! I'll do something she'll love. I'll get a piece of wax paper and a comb, do a little tap dance to the tune of "The Doll Dance". Can't wait to see her face.

"We should go now, Frederick," I say. "Our parents will be wondering where we are. We've never stayed out this late before."

"Oh yes," George agrees, and immediately shows Frederick his gratitude. George is polite and thoughtful that way, I always forget, but he jumps to his feet and shakes Frederick's hand. Not a farewell, though; the night's not over yet, he knows Frederick will be putt-putting us home, slow-motored so we don't wake up all the cottagers. No, George wants to show his appreciation here, right on the spot; the floor under him represents what he's expressing his thanks for. He will thank Frederick formally later, like you do when you say goodnight, the moment we step onto our dock.

Together we unroll the rugs and put them back in place. "Whew, it's hot," we say, "it's a warm night." And I am thinking, Gee, I wish we had only just arrived.

And now, at the far end of the room, George is pumping Frederick's hand again, somberly, not jerking it up and down. There's meaning back of this gesture; a word or two being exchanged, I can't tell just what, expressions alike, absorbed. No, I don't have any idea. Frederick is slipping into his jacket, and George, with his extra sweater already across the back of his shoulders, is looping the sleeves in front. Side by side, hands in pockets, they're walking to the front door. I have no idea at all what they're saying.

There. I've picked up every last glass, and put them all back in the cupboard, rinsed and dried; ash trays, the one they pinched from a ship, S.S. *LeBlanc*, where does this S.S. *LeBlanc* go? a clumsy-looking thing, reminds me of the dog's dish. I could set it down by that tall vase, the marigolds would take away some of the attention, if not hide it completely. Why would they have chosen to make off with this monstrosity? I'd have had my eye on the silver, helped myself to a knife or a spoon. Let's see now, what else . . . better pick up the records. Oh, the boys must've done that when I was in the kitchen. Cushions. I should make sure the cushions are exactly where they were when we came in. The blue velvet oblong—before Frederick put it behind his head, which chair, or what sofa did he get it from?

In the metallic light I hold onto the cushion, I hug the soft velvet—I wouldn't mind having a dress of this material—and lay it down upright on an empty couch.

At the door, I stand and glance around the room. No one would know we had ever been there.

# XVII

Of things to come. The unforeseeable. Was it January? Or February? the sparrows still huddled, shivering somewhere, frozen like the night? That diagonal snow; and the wet smell of my fur muff where I had laid it on the bureau next to my bed. Sitting there, half-leaning on a pillow, and the deflected light from the lamp above my bed falling across my shoulders. My fists were locked tightly, I could hear leather squeaking . . . a suitcase; shirts, ties, and a sock the dog won't let go of, the telephone downstairs ringing, ringing, the *awful* quiet, and the warmth of the dog's body pressed beside me, he has come into my room and jumped up on the bed. The sock, with its label showing, lies where he dropped it on the rug. And in the seize of this quiet I hear the front door close. If it had been earlier, hours ago, the night before even, the sound wouldn't have meant anything . . . someone arriving, a neighbour perhaps, or the dog being let out, a delivery from the drugstore, all the other possibilities: anything, except the one it was.

The unforeseen—before the dog started dragging things out of that suitcase, when it was still after supper. The first moments happening again as my mind treads the empty night, a mind's eye that turns to look back where a house still stands, and travels out into that night, when there was suddenly no sense of tomorrow; it was gone, tomorrow was yesterday. The road, the sky, my bedroom walls as though collapsing, a kind of confusion making me want to run for safety. To where? I wondered. That comes close to the feeling: pretend, pretend, I told myself, cover your ears and pretend you haven't heard, break into a run against the snow-flakes, run blindly ahead. For I was now staring into a night when the earth started to show signs of giving way.

It is the winter of my twentieth year . . . but shadows have converged, the portrait in my mind is blurred, there are too many shadows. . . .

Down the middle of the road we walk, my father and I, and neither of us is saying anything. In the chalk-white silence the sound of our footsteps is like static. I blink hard, and imagine my ears as blind to what was said, earlier, a while ago. But there it is again, reality as I plod through the snow and think back on the short conversation, and suddenly my father's words are a volcano in my brain. I feel my blood drain away; at my core a touched point sharp as needles, like bits of steel snagging a rib. I try not to let him see, my hands have turned into fists, hidden, out of sight in my fur muff. My father's hands are invisible too, less rigid, a loose kind of helplessness deep in his pockets, navy-blue overcoat, camel-coloured muffler bunched around his neck, brown fedora. After a while he will remove a glove, and without breaking stride will flatten his scarf inside his coat collar. We have to keep walking, it is a way of thinking up afterthoughts.

Everything around us silent, there's no one on the streets—maybe a car passing through the neighbourhood. Houses lit up; everyone's inside. Voices of children on a backyard skating rink, muted; the dialogue is their rapture. Smell of chimney smoke. I see its white trail going straight up, wrapping itself into an arch of bare trees, and, dangling upside down, a torn kite with the cord caught in the branches.

"What are you thinking about?" my father says at last, and I tell him I don't know, which is not quite true. After a pause, he says, "It'll work out," his voice low; "it'll be fine." Will it? I can't see that far ahead, nor am I equal to this moment. I take my hand out of my muff and slip it into his pocket, my fingers close over his. Silent words. A few seconds? A vision passing before my eyes: I was remembering something, an incident; the years had divided to a long time ago, a time seeming so distant even then. And yet, immediate. I could hear the wash of the river, and the bilge water sluicing around in the bottom of the boat. In my mind I saw the woods, the mountain back of the cottage drawing away, the red and gold leaves in thin patches and the earth covered in yellow and rusty browns where the leaves had fallen. I knew that feeling: the summer ends, it is time to leave, we're on our way back to the city, duffel-bags, cartons, suitcases, the dog kennel . . .

Flakes of snow fell that day in October, sprinkling our shoulders as my father rowed us through openings in logs, past the island and around, straight up under the overhang of pines. Mamma sitting at one end, George and I sharing a seat up front, the burdened boat low in the water and skimming upstream in the sudden turn of an eddy, out into the current again, my father glancing up at the overcast as he heads for a landing place near the station. It's seven o'clock in the morning. And distantly, not too many miles away—ahead of time—the train blowing. Panic in our eyes: which level crossing was that? Rockhurst? how many more minutes? will we get all this stuff out of the boat and onto the station platform in time?

Mamma had two cigarettes in her mouth, was on the verge of lighting them. Matchbox in one hand, match in the other, poised in mid-air. "Say we miss the bloomin' train," she said, the cigarettes bouncing up and down between her lips. And in the same breath, wanting our votes, "What do you say, kids?" With a sudden slash across the box she struck the match. My father let go of the oars and cupped his hands over the flare. Too late. The match went out. She would try again, she said, laughing, and tossed the burnt matchstick over her shoulder.

I couldn't remember, just then, whether we missed that train and caught the eleven-thirty milk train, or if we returned to the cottage for one more night; of that time I could think only of the moments that followed, a mid-river image whose vague impact had been locked away until its meaning could now be measured, revealed when the mind in reflection, seeking, wanting to be anaesthetized, went back over. . . . I closed my eyes, swallowing, the focus of an instant deep in the unconscious, borrowed from time. It was the way my mother lit my father's cigarette and put it in his mouth. There, in the slant of east wind and snowflakes, small grey waves lapping the boat and her fingertips briefly brushing his lips, was it five seconds? ten? Oars idling under my father's hands as he leaned toward her, the boat steering itself sideways, a corner of my mother's pleated skirt dragging in dirty water under the floorboard as she ruffled my father's hair, the rusty tin can their feet rested upon, it alone hearing their exchange. And George and me staying put as logs thump the side of the boat, as the train blows again, as the branch of a silver poplar sails by, while our parents turn into an expression, an imperceptible something. It is a portrait, still life.

Still life. How could we as children, as young adults, have guessed, have ever known . . . ? It happened so fast—or did it? Was it possible there were changes I didn't notice; did my eyes see one thing and my heart another? Didn't I remind them? Did I forget to say, 'Daddy is your sweetheart, isn't he?'

Walking beside my father I was trying to capture that image, the way they looked that day, but the spell was broken; it was a memory now.

We passed under another streetlamp, the white glare like a searchlight betraying the remnants of our thoughts; when meaning's gone—something that's real—that's what you're left with, remnants. He is my father, and the love in me cannot speak; he has asked me what I am thinking, but the cry in my throat cuts me off. And so we walk, it's somewhere to go. He won't wonder he knows I am like him, I tremble sometimes, and can't always release my mind. He's going, for some reason my father is leaving home . . . he'll never be walking in the door any more. What he's been trying to tell me has finally sunk in, numbed me, I can't even ask if George knows yet. Has he written to him? It'll take so long to reach him . . . the forestry station, they only bring the mail in twice a week. Maybe I'll write him; yes, that's what I'll do, I'll tell George everything's okay. I should go though, see him, my next pay cheque, on Friday I could take the train as far as Three Rivers and he could come down, his day off, meet me there. . . .

In the dining room, when we were by ourselves, that's when my father told me "There's something . . . could we have a talk?" He must have been waiting for me to get off the phone, for the minute I put the receiver down he was there at the desk, words on his lips, searching my eyes, and then adjusting a calendar on the wall. From the look of him I knew something was up; I think I turned cold then, that minute, without knowing why. They seemed just the same at supper, I thought, talking about library books that were overdue; Mamma mentioned the dogcatcher had been around again and picked up that poor Airedale, and Daddy had asked her what she had done all day, did she go uptown as planned, and she said no, her headache had come back, things like that. I had announced I would stay home tonight and practise my typing—did they know then, that I was to be told that evening?

It was around eight o'clock. Mamma had already gone up to their bedroom. I guess she just didn't want to be around when my father told me. I remember that after the dishes were finished and she had folded her apron and put it back in the drawer, instead of going in to sit by the fire she went directly upstairs. I assumed she had gone to lie down because of her headache.

I think my father had planned in advance what he would say, break into it gently, but with the coming of the moment, in cramped whispers he went straight to the point, he couldn't do it any other way. And it was clear he was using, quoting, direct words, words they'd perhaps have stumbled upon as they sought to articulate the cause, verbs like "smother", and "possess". They no longer wanted to possess one another, my father said. I was still sitting by the phone, my father in a chair he had drawn alongside.

I didn't know what he meant, possess; I was looking for blacks and whites. I was bewildered, my head was spinning. I wanted to wring my hands, I wanted to pray, Why? I asked, because I still believed then, why? Make things right again, don't do this God, do You hear me?; the impact leaving me stunned from head to foot.

It wasn't just a broken link; life was coming to an end, that's what I was feeling.

Other people weren't like they were, I said, close and loving; weren't things the same now as they had always been, the same as when I was born? Did it mean they wouldn't be together any more?

My father looked away, as if he'd heard something outside the window. Lamplight, beside the telephone desk, no longer the warm glow of the orange-silk bridge-lamp, but instead burning above us like a scar in mid-air, defining the fatigue in my father's face. Only then did I suddenly realize the weight of his thoughts, his face turning back slowly from the window. "It's snowing," he said, "why don't we go for a walk?"

Hadn't we always had our best talks when we walked in the snow, ever since when? nothing but soft white snow, you didn't even have to talk.

As soon as we stepped off the verandah my teeth began to

chatter. I could hear them; I put my tongue between and
lowered my head behind my coat collar.

"When did it happen?" I said, the air soundless and heavy
with aching.

"I don't . . . really know," hesitant, as though exploring
his mind, as if still questioning the fact himself. "I can't answer that any more than your mother could." Chunks of
snow falling out of the bends in trees, dropping in front of us
like broken white wings felled from the sky. "Possibly I expected too much from her." What? That was over my head.
"And perhaps . . . maybe I loved her too much. From the
day we first met. Maybe that was the mistake." And so was
that over my head; how could anyone love someone too
much? I remember he stopped briefly, and traced his toe over
a piece of ice; he needed to pause, do something else besides
looking straight ahead. He worried the lump of ice, saying after a moment of reflection, "I suppose after a while love becomes a burden. Either way, it makes demands, and you go
on, you carry on with that much less, assuming nothing's
been lost."

I did not understand, not one word of it. Love a *burden*?
How could love cease, how could love like theirs just stop?
My parents!

My father's hands were deep in his overcoat pockets, and
that's when I took my hand out of my muff and reached into
his pocket, gripping his fingers as though I were hanging on
to him for dear life, like a person that's drowning or has
slipped down a precipice, his life depending on that one last
fingerhold, an imprint left that cries *help me!*—which is exactly what I was doing to him, when it was too late: making
things worse.

In trying not to let my voice betray me, I had counted on
the communication of flesh; what else but the reach of his
own flesh and blood could give him what he needed?

And if not that, then at least a less painful sequence to look
back on.

Instead, my fingernails like crocodile teeth—both hands.
That must have been terrible for him. You don't think of
those things at the time. And that's what bothers me now,
how he would always feel that sense of me clinging so des-
perately, him the lifeline, powerless. A small death of his
own; in effect, he had to witness himself having to let me go.

My home. There's no other word for it. At that stage in
your life, that's all you've got. If the roof fell in, or a wall

collapsed, you know the rooms will soon fill up again, that sooner or later all the signs of life will be there as before. It's not the same as a light that's gone out for good.

The piano light; and the one over the panel of the ham station. In the dark of winter, the outside verandah light turned on at 5:30; and then their greeting. Hat and coat hung up on the rack, another greeting. "How's my girl? And where are the kids?" . . . "A letter?" . . . "Tired after a long day?" . . . "Want the fire on?" Next routine, their voices in the kitchen: "Not bad!" . . . "Hey, not here." Flashes coming at me in a rush. The mind races when it's lost.

He would be leaving that night, my father said, it was all arranged. He shrugged, nervous reflex; no one knew yet, he added, their friends would all know in good time, and for the first while would I try to take his place, Mamma would need me. I couldn't stand it, I wanted to run and run, bang my head against the trees. Every few steps I thought I was going to vomit. "See that Mamma takes care of herself," he said, his voice barely audible, patiently explaining how much she needed love, even if she sometimes turned away, went into her room and closed the door, he said, speaking slowly, searching for words as he reminded me she hadn't always been quick-tempered, her headaches had made her so, and maybe now they'd lessen, she'd be able to sleep better, he thought.

"Her headaches were exaggerated," I put in—suddenly aware? defensive? partisan? "She never did like being by herself," I declared, "and when you started working nights, the headaches . . . you remember, how bad they got after you began helping to build CKCO. I don't seem to remember her having them *before* that." I reminded him how they got worse, more frequent, after the long trips the Government assigned him to.

"I know," he sighed. "But it's my job, the way things have worked out. I can't turn down promotions. We'd still be in Canso if I had."

"After you left for Cairo," I pursued, "she kept saying over and over, 'What am I going to do for six months?' I have the feeling she was mad at you for being away, she was used to having you home."

"Maybe so, but there's nothing to keep me there now, your mother has said so many times. And what's the point of waiting until things are intolerable, letting hurtful words accumulate, saying things you don't mean?" Again, his voice dropping to a whisper, as if he didn't want to hear. But this was something he had to go over.

His shoulders arched briefly, brows knitting together; he was concentrating. "The first signs were a long time ago," he reflected. "Even then, I still thought love was enough. But it isn't." We had begun retracing our steps, on our way back now, the white coil of chimney smoke, and the torn kite, coming into sight again. "Love changes when people themselves change," I heard him say, "and before you know it, it just isn't there any more." No fancy words, no dictum, like It's all in the game; or, Life isn't a set of happy rules; Living can be rough; Some day you may have to accept whatever happens. I would have to learn all that on my own.

"See that Mamma looks after herself," he said again. "George and you, between you . . . once it's time to go to the cottage, there's a chance she'll take an interest in things again." But what about him? Didn't that matter too? He would be fine, he said, he'd find a furnished room uptown; near the office, he thought, so he could walk to work.

So he could walk to work! Making it sound like a fair exchange, tramping along beside me, surely exiled within, but still the same old self, refusing to let anything show through, nothing forced for my benefit, from time to time removing his hat and shaking off the wet snowflakes, as if it mattered.

Snow piling up, turning the snowbanks into tiny-humped valleys, the contours in heaped folds, as though crouched, like my senses. I saw myself in that form, surrendered to the white falling night, a lump with no interior. Except I had a choice; did I not have a mind that could be slapped out of its corner? Was I not the elder child, qualified to understand?

I slipped my arm through his, as though idly, pleasurably, at that moment feeling proud of him, sensing at last, if only fleetingly, that yes, of course there had been a change. I remembered a night—was I nine years old? ten?—wakening to the rise of their voices downstairs in the living room. I got out of bed and crept part way down the stairs. Through the banisters I saw my father, he was on his knees. I thought he was crying. I heard him say, "Don't do this, Mimi."

I went back to bed, and blocked the whole thing out.

As we walked, I remembered other times, there was something strange—the habit my mother had fallen into, pretending to turn away from my father's embrace when he arrived home from work, faithful to his way of seeking her out to kiss her hello. Openly she'd turn her other side, saying noth-

ing. She seemed to want to hear him say, "What's wrong?"
She *enjoyed* that!

Why wouldn't I have blocked that out? I'd tell myself it
was because she happened to have the frying pan in her
hand, or had to adjust the oven thermometer, or suddenly
remembered the dog should be let in, or out. And me, con-
vincing myself, never for a moment allowing myself to acknowledge these were things that could wait, worse, they
were distractions she'd look for, think up. She *knew*!

I guess you keep waiting for the knowledge to go away;
you could be mistaken, soon believing it's all your imagination.

It wasn't as though I could suddenly point this out to my
father. I couldn't very well say, "Why did she do this?" I
didn't want him to know I'd noticed.

"I can understand, a little, why you're leaving," I said
slowly, looking for the right words, and not finding them.
"I've always been closer to you, somehow you've always
made sense for me, and you've never changed." I could feel
his arm move, drawing me closer to his side, as if the sense in
him were breathing easier. "You know," I went on, "when
George and I were older, once we were in high school, I noticed a difference in Mamma then." I spoke hesitantly, still
puzzling things out. "As if she wasn't enjoying herself like she
used to." And that was true. But I'd paid so little attention; I
was having a better time, I liked when it was after school,
things to do on my own. "Do you think Mamma was happier
when George and I were little, when she could do everything
we did? like jumping in the sandpit . . . and tearing up and
down the hills?" Just then, I was on the point of mentioning
her love of parades, and the days a circus was in town, how
she liked to stand marking time, singing out loud with the
band, toes tapping, then a wild scamper further down the
block as it moved on, so she could get a better view; often a
balloon in her hand, as if she were ten years old. But I didn't
add this long-gone rainbow world; it would only have reminded him.

"Do you think her happiness . . ." I stopped, for I was
thinking, If only I could know the right words! I knew what I
felt, but at that time I don't believe I'd ever heard the word
motherhood used before. "Do you think the best part was
being a mother, the times when we could all act crazy and
have fun? Do you suppose that might've had something to do
with it, wanting to stay . . . like a girl?" I let it go at that.

People were always able to say things better than I could, but
I thought that sounded nice, something I could say that
would tell him I was proud of her, having grasped only moments before (as he looked at his hands, then off in the distance, repeating 'there's nothing to keep me there now'), an
awareness that every step he took seemed somehow trans-
fused with his love for her: it was locked inside, as if nothing
had happened. It was also something to say that would let
him know I thought she was wonderful, 'wanting to stay like
a girl', for she was a girl to me, I always saw her in that
light. But how come, I wondered, it was he who told me, why
was it my father? my mother keeping to her room; going into
George's room when my father was putting things in his
suitcase.

Was my father trying to spare me (as well as himself)
from hearing the bitter time-worn words, 'There is always
one who loves and one who is loved'? Was that what he was
trying to say, that it had come to that? Whatever their differences, the angry hurtful words he spoke of that night, I knew
only that this deader-than-dead distance that had come between them had neither distorted nor lessened his feeling
toward her. And that was what made it hardest of all. I felt it
in every inch of him, and I cursed my mother—but only to
myself. I'd have to be prepared, nothing must betray me, give
me away: words, flesh, nerve cells, I would never let her
down, any more than I would ever let my father down.

A new address . . . streetlights somewhere else, that's what
I was thinking as on we tramped. It had to be a mistake,
where had the telltale signs been? Like lips tightening. Was it
one of the times Mamma didn't speak to Daddy for a week?
There were two or three occasions; one was after a party,
there'd been a Government dance or something, and another
time, after an evening-dress party at someone's home, when
she came home early by herself. And sat downstairs all night,
sitting with her fur coat on. I saw her through the banisters,
twice I crept out of bed, and my father, to my surprise, calling me by the name in a story he used to read me, said,
"Please go back to bed, little Hannah, there's a good girl."
Things would be different in the morning, I'd tell myself. And
now next morning had passed, and the next and the next.
What did it mean? the way Mamma wouldn't answer, or
even speak. My father was talking, "Mimi?" . . . "Would you
like the fire on?" . . . "have you seen the kids' report cards?
Not bad, considering they were home with the mumps and

whooping cough." He was just the same, still bringing her little presents when he'd come home after work, like a new magazine, or packets of seed-pearls to make a necklace, skeins of Shetland wool to make herself a sweater, or a new pair of slippers. Did she look at them after we went to bed? It was so long ago, and all I could remember was the four of us sitting at the supper table and Mamma would say to George or me, "Ask your father if he paid Jolicoeur's grocery bill," or "Tell your father the roast has extra skewers in it." Panic gripped me, I shut it out, I didn't hear it. I didn't go out to play, I stayed in every day until I saw them holding hands again.

Were they talking things over then? had they flared up, fought out of hearing? my mother no longer radiant, her eyes dark with unhappiness, and in time withdrawn, a stranger to herself, as her friends had later said? I don't know. After all these years I still don't know. But then, no one ever does. A person could ask a thousand questions . . . and if I wasn't to have any answers when my own marriage broke up, how could I possibly know why theirs did? Well, they had their thing of beauty, and I mine. And I guess it's like everything else that's meaningful . . . its time comes. Leaving you to stare into a street, not understanding. Yet I can never bury a thing of beauty, even if it is dead.

———

My father and I plodded on, one block following another, silent with each other now, both my hands shoved through his arm, the heartbreak in us lost to the sudden leap of a cat from behind a snowbank, the icy screech of windshield wipers scraping back and forth on a car idling in someone's driveway; on and on we walked, past Ashbury College, along the side of the campus, turning onto Springfield Road, the wind whipping at drifted snow lying across the darkened grounds of the convent. And then came home. The blizzard streaming at an angle, heavier now, and we stopped on the porch steps to brush off our coats.

"That's some snow," he said, watching it sifting down under the streetlight.

"Is it ever," I said. "You'd think it was only just starting. I wonder where it all comes from?"

# XVIII

———◆———

Emerging slowly, apprehensively, I step out of the taxi, laugh and say something, nervous chatter. The music made me jump. I'd forgotten; odd that I would pause outside to listen.

The last minutes of "To a Wild Rose", the chords gaining in volume. And it's a haunting, full-of-life sound, where silk ribbons and cuff links and the colour of ice-blue dominate a Saturday afternoon. Briefly, there's a canopy of trees, and swallows on the sidewalk, the sunlit air motionless as the notes rise and fall through shade patches, through the ravel of ivy hanging loose above the entrance of a stone church. The oval door is open wide, and it is from the dungeon-dark inside that this music comes, this song by Edward MacDowell, being played by the organist of St. Bartholomew's Church, in Ottawa. I said I'd like to have that tune, was that all right? did he mind? "Why not?" he said.

It's August, August the sixteenth, 1941. Flowers? Flowers out here? A basket they forgot to bring inside? Did the delivery man set it down at the entrance because his hands were full and then forgot? Just as well. Ugh. They shouldn't let the groom's family choose the flowers for the altar, not the groom's mother anyway. Jeepers. I thought gladiolas were for funerals. Oh well, I daresay the guests in the church are wondering what the organist can be up to, playing MacDowell when he should now be into Mendelssohn.

Was it at three o'clock in the afternoon? 3:30? What time did we leave the house? The phone was ringing . . . I needed a few more seconds, and George called upstairs, "Take your time." Just the two us in the house; each knows what the other is feeling. There are peak moments of darting about, an occasional belly-laugh. Even so, there's a kind of subdued quiet underscoring the tempo. It is a day that can never be again, and it is enough: the power of a tenderness stands

244

alone, outlasts. In a few minutes we will look at one another
as we walk out the front door, and again, in the back seat of
the taxi. For on this journey it is not only the circumstances
of change we are riding towards, it is an end to something.

I stand in the downstairs hall, and look at the dust on the
windowsill; over my shoulder the piano, the fireplace. George
says, "Ready?"

Gusts of hot summer wind, the wave of green boughs re-
treating, a car passes, children with a skipping rope, symme-
try of wrought-iron fencing around Rideau Hall, taxi turning
right, slowing down, the curb, who's that standing there?

I'm in my bridal dress, pale ice-blue, fingertip veil to
match, hemline and tulle short length—because the war's
started, everyone's cutting down, those who know anything
aren't making a splash. At least so I was told: "A floor-length
gown wouldn't look right, not being done. Knee-length. Short
dress more fitting."

"Why?" I asked, at last getting my hackles up, "they can't
make parachutes out of rayon." Mamma should have been
there, she really should have. She was supposed to be, the
three of us were going, it was all planned. We would set out
on an afternoon, there was nothing to do but walk into the
store ... my future mother-in-law had already looked around,
she said, and knew just the right place, in fact there was a
shop where she'd had two or three outfits put aside.

"*Outfits?*" I heard Mama exclaim on the phone; she was
making arrangements which afternoon we'd go. "A jacket? A
wedding dress with a jacket?" Her tone not suggesting deli-
cacy.

"What?" I called out from my bedroom, and started down
the stairs. I certainly wasn't going to wear any two-piece.
Even if the woman had gone to great pains, who asked her
to? Why, I'd never be caught dead in a dress with a jacket,
not if you gave me ten of them. I'd as soon put on a curtain.

"I don't *need* to see them first," Mamma pressed. "No
doubt, but I fear we'll just have to look at what else they
have. Pardon?" She closed her eyes. "That's too bad." She
was sitting at the desk, and got up from the chair, shoving it
back in place with her knee, finger on the telephone cord,
eyes scanning the wall. She was thinking of wrenching the
cord out? would the plaster make a mess? "It occurs to me
we should leave it up to her, don't you think? The girl
knows exactly what she wants," she said firmly, patiently. No
answer?

"Long, and lacy-white," I whispered, affirming it to the suddenly complicated atmosphere, sticky air that was beginning to make my hands perspire.

"Yes, she has her heart set on it," Mamma concluded. "I thought we had been over that. Her father wants her to have . . ." Pause. "Of course, come along. Plans? Any day is fine . . . see you then." She put the phone down. "Upon my word," she said, "what a strange woman."

On the appointed afternoon, Mamma wasn't feeling well. In addition to a headache, she'd been up all night with cramps, was still running to the toilet. And when I saw her forcing herself to get ready, I pointed out that she was overtired, there'd been so much to see to, and perhaps the heat was getting to her. She wasn't used to being in the city in August; I said moving in from the cottage for the month hadn't been such a good idea after all.

"Just lie back on the bed and stay put," I said again. "There's no need to go. Why don't I just meet Brian's mother myself? It's not as though I need two mothers along, or even one."

She was waiting in the small dress salon when I arrived, seated in a straight-backed chair at the rear. Upon catching sight of me, she seized the first of two dresses, a lavender-mauve, from the lone saleswoman's hands, advancing to meet me. "Isn't it lovely?" she said, "Such a beautiful frock. They've agreed to make you a turban to match."

"Spit!" I moaned under my breath, wondering how I might stand my ground.

"Oh, my figure's too short," I said airily, "a two-piece cuts me off in the middle." Face stiffened but composed, determined as she ran her fingers over the fabric, and said, "Aren't the pleats pretty? Try it on." Pleats!

"No. I don't like it." I glanced about. Wasn't this shop supposed to specialize in wedding gowns? What did I want with a frock? And a turban! I wasn't Rosie the Riveter.

"Why?"

"Jackets are dowdy," I said. "They're for older ladies." I turned, and nodded towards the front of the store. "There's a nice one in the window,"—perhaps she hadn't noticed?—"with lace points over the hand." Before coming inside I'd paused in the entrance, leaning into the glass, all full of a vision of myself in such a gown. I would carry a basket of flowers, I thought, roses, pink Sweetheart roses. "At least it looks like a *wedding* dress," I added pointedly, my face flushing. I was uncomfortable. Had she forgotten that's what I had come to buy? "I think it's adorable," I said, "romantic, exactly what I had in mind." No attention. Organizing, arranging the second choice over her other arm, this one a deeper shade, varicose-purple, draping the folds, demonstrating. Flowers on the peplum! On Ma Kettle, maybe—no, Marie Dressler, she'd fill it better.

"I'd say it's between these two, wouldn't you?" Pleased, trembling with pleasure, her eyes travelling from one to the other, the mauve, back to the violet, Mrs. Regina originals. Material coarse enough for a tent, or a ship's rigging. "Which one do you think?"

"Neither. I'd rather choose for myself."

"Ohhhh," she said agonizingly, stricken, staggering back as if I'd hit her, her sad lips trembling, a helpless look about her. In the long silence I could feel my blood rising, anger an inch away from snapping. I held my tongue. We'd been friends; I thought she was kind, a very kind person, and she was Brian's mother (she did not wish to be called Mother after we were married, I got that message: she said, You already have a mother, I'm *Brian's* mother. There is no need to start that. I wanted to say, Well, it would have been an honour for you had I called you by that name). If I flounced out of the shop I would never forgive myself. My eyes burning, I returned her look, conscious of the two dresses suddenly displayed to fuller disadvantage, the pale mauve on one arm, the dowager-violet in the crook of the other, now hanging limp and pitiful. Wanting to clout the dresses and send them both flying, I eyed her for a few seconds more. I was not used to being made to feel guilty.

Some tableau. I remember the mannequin in the window, the dress falling into my line of vision, no more than a leap away, its insistence sobering just then, the reflection hazed in the glass, a virginal-looking alabaster dummy with an arm missing. How long had they had that one around? Surely dressed and undressed ever since the day D'Arcy McGee was shot; the black painted-on boots—or were they supposed to be oxfords?—sticking out beneath the lace-filigree hem, mock hair like plaster scrolls, the nose chipped. But the essential—the illusion of opaque snow-white lace on a figure my size—mounted on a varnished round wooden stand, and looming above me, lifelike, sideface expression, cupid's bow mouth, brown painted lashes lowered as if waiting, as if about to say, Well, what are you waiting for? Flesh more real than mine.

An hour later and I was back home again, my dress carefully wrapped in wads of tissue, under my arm the cardboard box pressing into my hipbone as I went directly upstairs to Mamma's room, the dress now a part of me, the feeling of what it stood for a kind of enveloping softness. Feet taking the stairs two at a time as I thought of the hushed church, the light dim over the rows of pews, someone I'd perhaps forgotten about turning around to look, my skin, the whole quick of me a tune of itself.

I could scarcely wait to get the dress out of the box, never doubting, never so much as the tiniest thought that Mamma was not prepared, how could she have been?

She clucked a sound sharp as a toy cricket, a second sped by. "You can take the whole works back," she said as I laid the pleated outfit across the bed.

"No," I said flatly without looking up. "It'd only be creating a fuss." I began to explain, from beginning to end . . . She swooped in, a rush of words diving headfirst as her eyes and fingers assessed: "Stiff as a board!" she exclaimed. "What's the material made of, for God's sake. Canvas?" Over her voice the sound of a crow as I rushed ahead, oblivious, my tone doggedly on its track. "I didn't want to start causing trouble this soon, I thought I best do it in easy stages."

She held the dress and jacket up, scowling. "What are you? A nun or something?" Stabbing at the pleats, they were to blame? "Is the woman deaf or something? I've a good mind to march over there this minute and ask her did she not hear what I said?"

"No," I said again, colouring, a sickly smile spreading above my teeth. "What could I say to Brian?"

"Ass of a woman, with her talk of wartime. There's more material in the skirt alone . . . there's enough here to make *two* long dresses. If you ask me, it's got nothing to do with what's fitting and what isn't fitting in wartime. Nothing whatever."

"How can you tell?" She hesitated, looked out the window, said she really didn't know, she hadn't thought about it before.

She settled back, as though dropping anchor. "You're the very limit, you know," she mused, "giving it like that." A ripple, settling across the slowed-down wash of her thinking. "You shouldn't have let yourself be talked out of . . ." Fingering her locket. Was she thinking of her own wedding dress? It was wartime then too, she wouldn't have had time when they got married, what with my father's shore-leave and all, she'd have had to wear something she had, one of the dresses in her cupboard, or perhaps out of one of the trunks at their boarding-house in Halifax. "What do you think your father gave you the fifty dollars for?" A corner of tissue-wrapping touched by a breeze, the movement is a sound. "On principle alone you should have put your foot down. If you don't do it . . ."

I stopped her. I wanted to say it would be more to the point if I put both feet down right now, in this room, on a more important issue. A matter having to do with my father. And for a minute I almost did, nothing else had pressed on my mind with such insistence, the consciousness of it a dinning sound in my head, like rain. And she knew, was every bit as aware; for when did this shadow, this blind idea of hers, ever stop hovering over us? But now was not the time; she might cry, I didn't want that. Looking at her as she sat on the bed, she seemed so tiny and fragile, for all her fireworks and outward vitality, so vulnerable, I thought. And so I didn't say anything. Later I would. tomorrow maybe, why spoil the fun we were having, that's the way things were going, she had liked the story of the busty saleslady in décolletage, tottering away in her platform soles and ankle straps in search of something pink on the racks, emerging quiver-bosomed and triumphant, hobbling forward with a gown of shell-pink see-through lace and silk. then cringing, euphoria gone, driven back by a petrified. granite stare to the dark passage from which she'd come: The funny side of it had reached her. But my ideas on the matter of principle would have to reach her too.

I put the lid back on the empty box and shoved it under the bed. "On principle. Mamma?" I said. "Gad, it's a matter of principle in another way. Brian's mother wanted her way, I wanted mine. And one of us was going to . . . well, come out of it spoiled. Let her be the one."

Sunshine streaking through the casement windows. Mamma lighting a cigarette now that she's hung up my dress—on the outside of the cupboard door, we still must have it in view. Whistle of the popcorn man coming along the street as I walk over and finger the hem, the buttonholes, my hand moves higher, fingers slipping under the lapel of the jacket.

"It's a beautiful shade of blue," Mamma says, and takes

the dress off the hanger, holds it against me, under my chin. "Try it on, lassie."

"Know what?" I say as I wriggle through the neckhole, "I think I'll wear my hair upsweep for the wedding."

"It suits you that way."

"Could you make me a headband, do you think a velvet? and sew the veil around? That'd be a dream, a velvet band." I pull the dress down, button myself in.

"The colour suits you too," Mamma says.

Wasn't it the same thing? Weren't dresses all alike? their real definition the feeling inside them? Otherwise I wouldn't have heard the popcorn man outside, smelled the peanuts, the sun, the lanes of the wind . . .

---

Out of the taxi and up the cement walk to the oval door, which is wide open, like the throttle of the organ; chords like a single harp meditating, it is the love of a wild rose. "Just a sec," I say. Are my seams straight? veil not caught again on the rose thorns?

I enter the church on George's arm. He, and not my father, is giving me away. To Brian. Today I am marrying Brian. He's waiting for me . . . only a few more minutes . . . And farewell, kind of. I've never had to say that before.

---

My parents were still together when I met Brian; whatever had ended in silence for them would not part them for more than two years. So there was that to be thankful for.

Maybe other girls were different. I knew some who were; being part of a family was a bother once romantic interests took over, parents only got in the way, "always expecting you to report everything." they'd say, and home was the last place they wanted to be. My love interests took precedence too, blissfully sallying forth with this new sense of inner freedom, its elusive element sneaking up on me: that the self was now capable of a different kind of love, the transition from girl to woman at last complete. Even so, that part of my life would have felt incomplete, and the freedom of less account, were I not able to report my sweet-nothings. And, not only did I want to, there was a need to. My brother likewise, I noticed, the more so after he had met Louise. So it wasn't just me.

"Pretty as a picture, and so affectionate," George had exclaimed triumphantly at breakfast one Sunday morning, home for the weekend from Rimouski and bursting to what Louise was like, head to toe, dark-haired like himself. "Only petite," swelling with pride, "tiny hands and feet . . . big brown eyes. Just my type." Pausing: had he mentioned her naturally curly hair? and oh yes, did he tell us about the dress she wore the night he met her at the formal? "Black velvet with straps. Made it herself! Copied it from a picture she saw in a frame." And a snapshot taken out of his wallet, "This doesn't tell you half! You have to *see* Louise—the way she laughs, and when she asks you a question . . ." Our heads in a huddle above the dining room table, the photo being turned to catch the light at the dining room window, a snapshot he'd taken himself, of a solemn-eyed girl with a gentle smile, dressed in a winter coat and standing in a doorway beside a young priest, with a white cat in her arms.

"Well, bully for you, George!" I cried. "She's gorgeous! But who's the priest?"

"That's Lucien, one of her brothers."

"She's a sweet-looking little thing." Daddy said.

"Ain't Nature grand!" purred Mamma, waiting her turn for a closer scrutiny. And George, raising himself from his chair to have a look himself, said, "Nice eyes, eh? You can't tell much from a snap, though," adding that soon we'd be able to judge for ourselves when he brought her home for Christmas, deciding maybe he wouldn't wait that long. Christmas was more than two months away, perhaps November might be possible. he'd see if one of the boys at the transmitter would cover for him, they often traded shifts. "Say!" he exclaimed. "If I phoned her tonight we could all talk to her."

"Sure thing," my father said, "then we could invite her for both times, next month as well as New Year's, if you can't make it for Christmas."

"Sure thing is right," Mamma repeated, photo now in hand, giving it the once-over, ecstatic, head to one side, longing to meet her, her mind planning. "I'll fix up the den . . . we must be sure to get the mistletoe up."

And again, that same afternoon, George expressing his thoughts in a one-to-one pow-wow with me, after we'd decided to hitch a ride and see what was doing at Sumach Point. He'd been in northern Quebec since August, and wanted to pay them a surprise visit at the farm before the winter freeze-up. "Once November comes," he said, "you can never count on the ice in the middle of the river being sound enough until after Christmas."

Picnic hamper in tow, we shoved the boat off into the up-river current and beached it at the island first. There was a pile of rocks where we'd often built a fire. "Why not toast the buns and wieners there?" George asked. "It'd save time hunting around for wood." As for kindling, "Wouldn't the smell of pine needles really be something in the October air?" we said.

Waiting for the flames to die down, chipmunks rattling around in dead branches and birch-bark, we sat with our backs against a slab of rock facing west, the water almost Mediterranean blue and the earth and shale warm in the bright sun. Tide-pools half in light and half-shadowed by pines, ribboned, changing colour, topaz, grey, black, marbled, and my hands cupping my chin, my head reflected in the dun-coloured ebb and flow in the crevices. How many times had I done this, I wondered. Making wishes, reading messages into my life.

I turned back to George. He had removed his heavy sweater and tossed it onto a stump, and was silently poking at smouldering twigs, suddenly diving at sparks that shot past into dry leaves. Without looking up, he said, "You'd think I'd never been knocked out by a girl before," laughing to himself as he raked in another spark, "but Louise is sure terrific. I wasn't going to say anything to Mamma and Daddy, not just yet. I was going to tell you, though." He eased the press of his trouser legs and settled back, arms resting lightly on his knees, fingers clasped. "Did you see Mamma beaming when I told her how Louise and I play records half the night? And she didn't go into a long rigmarole either, asking me what kind of a girl she is that would stay up late like that. She just said was it a good party I met her at, and did I bring her home that night?"

"She beamed even more when you said 'Louise wears black stockings a lot,'" I laughed, "and what was it Daddy said? 'Not bad.' Something like that."

"French girls do, did you know? Black silk stockings. Anyway, as I was saying, you never have to worry about what they'll say—about dates, I mean. Mamma and Daddy don't brush it aside, or start making fun, or catch you up on a question, like when you say someone's your type. That's important, don't you think?"

"Me too, that's what I think too," I replied. "That's the same feeling I get. And you know what? I'm like you, I always have to tell them too, about things. I even show them

Frederick's letters." I reached for George's pullover and put it around my shoulders, glancing upriver at the hollow space of bare trees, the ridge where Frederick's summer place now stood empty, the curve of road, the hill, the sprawl of mountain behind silent and still. "My but it's good to have you home," I said. "Last month, when everyone was gone, first you and then Frederick, I was sure feeling sorry for myself. I was really blue. No more running around. Going out dancing, though, that's what I miss most. Still, there's my job, there's lots going on there. And even if I am the youngest in the department, that doesn't mean I'm the dumbest."

"What about the ski group? Aren't you and Marian joining that Normal School crowd you wrote me about?"

"I will if they'll accept me. I'm such a punk skier. Lost the technique, and my confidence too, I guess. Don't want to break my head. Do you remember the winter before last when I hit that ice patch and ended up in the tree? Well, ever since then. There's a guy at work, Brian, and he says I should think of all the trees I missed, and not be worrying over one that got in the way. He says isn't it so, that sooner or later a person breaks a leg or a head some place, so why not come up covered with snow as well as blood? 'What's the difference?' he said. Not *their* head, but *a* head. At any rate, this Brian offered to get me going again. He says all I need is to get used to it. And you know what? I'm not sure yet, but I have a feeling I'll be bringing him home one of these days. Maybe not though."

"Why not? Frederick wouldn't mind." Coils of smoke spiralling up, trackless. What would Frederick be doing now, I wondered? Writing me a letter?

"No, I know," I said, "I guess he wouldn't mind. I don't know what Brian and I would do, though. He's not the kind who'd be content to go to the movies. And he hates dancing."

"He does? Why?"

"He says people look ridiculous pushing around a dance floor. He prefers to sit and talk. Trouble is I don't always know what he's saying; other people seem to, but not me, don't get the significance half the time. Plus the fact I'm never certain how to take him, can't tell when he's serious and when he's fooling. The other day he was standing in the reception lounge talking to a reporter from the *Citizen,* they were near my desk and I overheard Brian say, 'The way I see it, everyone's guilty until proven innocent.' Now what can a person make of that? He was laughing. But even so, I asked him later why he said it, and do you know what his answer was? 'It's practical; it's an objective way of thinking.' *Practical*? And then he just smiled. So I said, 'Don't you have faith in people? Don't you have any trust? What do you believe in, then?'

" 'Nothing,' he said. It beats me. Except I don't think he's fooling as much as he lets on. Daddy would like him, though; they'd get on fine. Brian's deep like him, you know? Maybe I could go out with him one night and just sit listening. Or talk. Like we're doing now, you and I. He's sure a conundrum. But at least he's not a smart-alec, or loud like the other guys at work, I will say that. Doesn't try to impress you with how sophisticated he is, or bored; according to some of the fellows, that's supposed to *send* you. Not me. What's so special about being *bored,* for crying out loud?" I scooped up a handful of pine needles and flung them into the air above the fire, watching them showering down, catching fire. "The funny thing is," I said, gnawing pine-gum on the heel of my hand, "I think Brian's kind of shy. What about Louise? Is she?"

"Shy?" George asked, leaning forward to tamp down a flame with the toe of an old leather shoe washed up on the rock. "No. I don't think so," he said. "Quiet maybe, but I wouldn't say she's shy. How old a guy is Brian anyway? Is he older or younger than Frederick?"

"Older. He's twenty-four. Maybe I could try going out with him one night. Yes, for sure I will, next week if he asks me, and I'll write you about it—if there's anything to tell."

———————

Nope, not a care in the world for George and me that year. Our home was still intact when these meetings took place, Brian and Louise the next turning points in our lives, the ones that counted.

It wasn't just a matter of caring what our parents thought. To be a parent, to have to think so far ahead, to plan, be responsible for us—it was a feeling of wanting them to experience our happiness. Didn't it belong to them too? a part of themselves? Hadn't they given us their values? taught us to love? Besides, being a parent didn't end once you started out on your own. They stood behind us, I thought, never asking anything of us.

The first night Brian called for me at the house, my father answered the door. I could hear their exchange of greetings, each other's names, presumably shaking hands; Brian as much a stranger to me, really, as to my father. And when I came downstairs he was already in the front room, about to present Mamma with a flower, a long-stemmed rose he'd had done up in a bright green sheaf of tissue tied with pink ribbon.

I was proud as could be, holding my hand beneath the paper in case the moss packed around the stem fell off, grinning from ear to ear, in fact blushing as a thick-leafed American Beauty, wet through to the paper, was gradually removed from its wrapping. No one ever did this before! they'd produce a pack of cigarettes and offer your parents one, or perhaps shove a stick of gum at them, maybe drag out a bag of humbugs instead. But to arrive at a strange house, having thought ahead of time to bring your mother a surprise. Wasn't this a mark of quality, Brian choosing a nice fresh rosebud for Mamma before he'd even met her? not something common and silly, like the lavender bath-salts that smirk of a Jack Humphreys gave her for Christmas one year, which she flushed down the toilet. "Must be twenty years old," she said. "Why, the smell alone would *contaminate* the garbage."

"Didn't I tell you Brian was different!" I exclaimed. Having spent the afternoon—that same Saturday—helping him choose a birthday present for his mother, I was now an authority. Mamma flicking her hand, wincing at her thumb where a thorn had ripped the flesh. "Bet you weren't prepared for . . . someone who reads books on philosophy," I chattered, babbling on in front of him. "Didn't I tell you you'd be surprised?" not knowing enough to save it until next day, nor content to wait that long for their marvelling: the look in their eyes might be gone by tomorrow, by then it'd just be a grin and some nice-sounding words, and what satisfaction would there be in that? the rose resting in a vase somewhere, upstairs on their bureau, for all I knew.

"Careful now," Brian said pointedly, cutting through my rhapsodizing. "You're putting your father and mother on the spot. After all, there might've been motive in the deed."

"What? What did you say?" Mamma asked, catching her breath, not certain what to make of it, fingers pinched together on a leaf, and then, recovered, ready to speak her mind. "Well, I'll be blowed! In the house not five minutes, and 'motive', he says."

"Don't believe a word of it," Daddy said, setting the tissue and ribbon-tie down on an end table.

"Oh?" replied Brian, poker-faced, "I'm not so sure," turning his head slowly, a faint, and what I see now as a wry, self-mocking smile at the corners of his mouth as he looked at Mamma, her disapproving eyes now expressing nothing, lost, bewilderment making her seem more out of it than anything else. "They say," he went on, "you can never trust someone bearing rose thorns," and retrieving the ribbon, laid it across the crown of her hair, arranging it through a curl. What? I stood there baffled. It was like a game of checkers, or chess: whose move was it now? What I could not know then—as my father did, had sensed—was what lay below the surface: I guess you would call it the human frailty. Everyone has his own way of presenting himself.

"Well, I don't, frankly," Mamma said, disoriented, in command enough to be aware of, and completely ignore, this beribboning of her hair. "I don't trust them at all."

"I certainly wouldn't either," Brian replied, winking at her, inviting her to join him on common ground as he lifted one of the strands of ribbon that had slipped onto her temple, and her staring at him, peeking around the side of his arm while he moved it to the back of her head, punctuating his words as he looped the end through again. "Not when they've got ideas on their mind. A mother can't be too careful when it comes to . . ."

"To what?" she snapped, jerking her head up.

"Brian!" I croaked, wondering if I could connect on his ankle without being seen.

"Well?" asked Mamma.

"When it comes to her firstborn," replied Brian, and turning to my father. "Wouldn't you agree, sir?"

"All right, then, smartie," Mamma retorted, cackling, pleased with herself, a piece of the ribbon dangling over one ear. "I can see I'll be having a few rounds with you before the year's out." And my father, now that he had seen she was at ease again, put in: "Well, for a fellow who can't be trusted . . ." hunching up his shoulders, twinkling.

"Or trust himself," Brian added, self-consciously pecking at the ribbon, putting it back in place. "You don't know the trouble I went to," he said lightly, "getting your daughter to go out with me. I had to think up ruses," reaching his arm out to slip it around my waist, and deciding not to. "And by God, I made it!" A house of loonies all right, I told myself, and now another to add to it.

I'd been more or less prepared for a meat-and-potatoes

conversation, realizing there'd have to be some kind of chat, even if it only amounted to whether or not you'd had your tonsils and appendix out, or if you hated or loved cottage cheese, or polar bears, the way people do sometimes when an occasion elicits a sudden burst of conviviality, submitting themselves, determined to cram a lifetime of tastes, sentiments, minor surgeries and predicaments into the space of five or ten minutes. So that now, on this finest of Saturday nights, with the instant foursome grouped, facing one another in the living room—where were the polar bears and cottage cheese?

I remembered how delighted my father looked taking in the byplay. For he had spotted the lurking, subversive humour in Brian, appreciating the fact Brian had not capitulated, had not thrown away the moment's questionable levity with a limp apology. And while I could do nothing but stand wordlessly, waiting for these weird formalities to run their course, my coat lying at the ready where I'd laid it over the chair in the hall, asking myself what's going on? what on earth? my insight into Brian limited—this new way of being a person—my father had instantly realized that Brian's vulnerability was at the core of the matter, feeling a responsibility to this virginal nineteen-year-old whose parents now stood before him; chatter, chatter. Both parents. And each one perceiving a different side of Brian: my mother drawn up short, going from high dudgeon to eyes sparkling with amusement, taking Brian at his word until she could safely turn it into a game; my father aware of Brian's sensitivity, feeling compelled to tell the parents he knew what was (or might be) on their minds, but having to do it his way, a deep-rooted honesty the only way he knew, meanwhile my father glimpsing the irony of it: a sincerity coming out as cynical, when Brian's true feelings were the exact opposite. Was it two minutes it went on? Five? And throughout, the dog whining to be let in. Why didn't the telephone ring, or something? I wondered, or someone come knocking at the front door? Or the furnace blow up. Anything!

"Well now," Daddy said. "Must be after nine o'clock. Don't you think the two of you should get going?"

"Will you be late?" Mamma asked, glancing at Brian, deciding to return his compliment by pulling the ribbon from her hair and draping it over the knot in his tie. "Never mind. You can sleep in tomorrow." Giving the ribbon a final pat.

"There. A present for you." A shuffle of feet, and a glove being picked up from the floor, car keys rattling.

"I'll leave the porch light on," my father said as Brian advanced toward me with my coat. Flushed and bewildered myself, puzzled more than ever as I wriggled an arm into the twisted lining of a sleeve. Meanwhile wondering what reaction my parents were digesting, in lieu of cottage cheese. I couldn't get out the door fast enough.

"Damn you," I protested weakly, trying to find words as Brian climbed in behind the steering wheel of his car. "Is that the way you always make someone's acquaintance? For introductions, that one sure takes the cake."

"I thought so too." Reaching for the ignition, muttering, "I've got couth coming out of my ears." Lights switched on, and the car vibrating. "Comfy?" Rolling down his window, brake released, looking over his shoulder and then into the rear-view mirror, "I like the dress you're wearing tonight," the car being put into gear. I was silent, concentrating on what the headlights turned up in the dark as we pulled away from the curb. But out of the corner of my eye I could see he was taking sideways glances at me—without asking what I was thinking.

"If we'd stayed any longer," I muttered, "there's no telling . . ."

"Don't you have any faith in me?" he asked gently.

"While you were at it," I went on, "why didn't you really clinch it and . . . it's a wonder you didn't say, 'What luck! your daughter's a virgin,' or something to that effect."

"Yes. Now why didn't I think of that? And are you?"

"Are I what?"

"A virgin."

"I could shoot you, do you know that?" I said, ignoring this next challenge. "Gosh, Brian, you do a nice thing like that, bringing Mamma a flower, and then you turn around and try to pass it off as a—"

"Oh?" he replied, saying nothing more, and instead, wagging a finger—but why at the windshield? My, but he's attractive to look at. And fun to be with. I like him! Eyebrows uplifted now: "I wasn't passing it off at all. There's method in my madness."

"There you go again!" I said. "Method . . . madness. Did someone say that in the *Mansions of Philosophy*?"

"Guess again."

"Noel Coward?"

"Could be. Sounds like something he'd say."

"Tell me, not that I'm dense or anything, but did you feel embarrassed when Mamma was thanking you for the flower? Is that why you joked?"

"No. Not at all. It's not complicated. The rose was a token to the future. Does that explain? . . . It was simply a way of expressing what I was celebrating."

I hesitated. Nothing could have sounded more complicated. "Celebrating?" I asked. "You talk in riddles. What do you mean, Brian, the rose was what you were celebrating?"

"I was saluting the occasion, that's all. Because some day I'm going to marry you, Miss Watson."

I snuggled my face into the fur collar of my coat, pulling the corners up and holding them against my cheeks. "Well," I said. "Fancy that. Except I don't see how you can. I'm marrying someone else. I told you. I told you about Frederick this aft. When he's finished college he's moving to Ottawa and . . . I promised him two years ago."

"You'll see," Brian replied. "And by the way, in Canada we call it 'university', not 'college'." I glanced up, a flap of fur half over my mouth, all set to reply. "You'll see," he said again, "a year from now, two years." And I thought to myself, *What is this anyway?* If it's just a case of him being sure of himself . . . but no, it's something he instinctively feels, a statement of fact he doesn't find necessary to follow up. No idle or racy pursuit of romantic movie-talk, no glib tongue telling me I'm gorgeous and beautiful, that I do things to him, and in all his experience he's never laid eyes on a girl to equal me, eyes, teeth, hair, chassis by Fisher. I am to discover this for myself? a matter of time until my interest is won over, trapped, absence from him unbearable? This would have been a good time to say some of it at least, surround me with words, where had I been all these years that he'd only come across me now? But no. Tapping the dashboard instead, the dial indicating the gas tank. No ploy—in itself a ploy.

"Would you like a cigarette, Miss Watson?"

"Not only is there Frederick," I said, bending over the flame of an initialled, tarnished-silver Ronson, "there's also another reason. I'd never marry a man with blond hair. I only like them dark. I've never bothered my head about a fair-haired man. Blond men are conceited."

"Oh? Not if there's nothing to be conceited about. But we'll just have to see."

On our way to the Gatineau night club, we had turned off

Island Park Drive onto the Champlain Bridge. And mid-way across we ran out of gas. Setting out in search of a filling station, the car off to one side, half on the sidewalk and half on the pavement, we stopped on the bridge, the late October wind blowing a soft rain in our faces as we stood leaning over the cement rail. Couples strolling in the park under the bridge, looking around for an empty bench, or heading farther back under the bridge for the hotdog pavilion ablaze with coloured lights; cars passing behind us, headlights picking up the slick black flow of water on the near shore.

I remember Brian singing to himself, almost as if I wasn't there, the misting spray carrying away his words, ". . . with the wind and the rain in her hair", and minutes later, another song current at the time ". . . that's why the lady is a tramp". (There was a connection?) And I thought, *Some day I'm going to marry you, Miss Watson.* I wanted to say, My but you're sure of yourself, aren't you? The girls in the office calling you dreamboat has gone to your head.

But I didn't. I just stood looking at the water, hearing sounds I'd not remembered hearing when I'd stood there before, the current gurgling over rocks where the riverbank bent sharply. What was I doing standing here like this with someone called Brian? chilled by the rain and happy to be so. Not ecstatic, just content. The lights of Britannia off in the distance; darkness out front and above, Brian's arm lightly touching mine.

He was wearing a light grey gabardine trench coat, unbelted, with the collar turned up, and a pair of brown suede gloves lined with sheepskin, fingers clasped, wrists resting on the cement ledge. And quite unexpectedly, catching me off guard, taking my hand out of my muff, he removed the black kid glove I wore and slipped my palm in with his, the two hands together inside the fleecy lining, not a word being said. All we did was lean into one another, and it turned into a beautiful and wordless dialogue. I don't know why, but it did.

I did not know then that this quiet, rather shy, contemplative, amiable, imaginative, sometimes grouchy, droll and tender person was to be the man I would choose to spend the rest of my life with. As if from out of that swift and immediate darkness, the unconscious and conscious dream I'd grown with for nineteen years had become the reality that now stood beside me. Not knowing that he was to be the most vital, the most caring person I would ever know.

It was only then, standing on the bridge. I wanted to stay

there forever, just the way we were, making no sound, the
night ahead a glitter of mystery, abandon, strange and hypnotic in a way, and I did not know why it felt so.

In my head I was going over the days leading up to this
night. I'd paid so little attention at first, an enthusiasm in
those early weeks that was as polite as it was indifferent. But
not deliberate. It was just that Frederick was on my mind,
and while he was far away, back at the Academy again until
the summer, I wasn't too interested in dates; the letters going
back and forth were a thousand times better, more rewarding
than going somewhere I didn't want to be, with someone I
didn't want to be with. Not Brian particularly, for he could
have been Buddy Rogers himself, or even Rudolph Valentino
reincarnated. At least that's what I told the girls at work
when they got all aflutter: "Cast your peepers on the dreamboat," they'd say. "Get a load of that guy Brian."

Because I remained oblivious, aloof almost, what else
would Brian have done? what greater challenge than to shake
me out of it? there was a long winter ahead, and what girl in
her right mind—if you ask often enough. What man isn't certain, believes there's none but he?

We'd both started work in the National Research Council
the same day, a handful of us taken on, Brian in one of the
labs upstairs, and me in another part of the building—sup-
posedly in the stenographers' pool but more often alternating
on the switchboard and reception desk. I saw everyone who
came and went, it was part of my job to recognize voices,
faces, to know the time of day when asked, the spelling of a
word. And to respond with grace when a trick was played on
me.

Like the Monday morning I came in and found my bowl
of goldfish! God! filled to the brim with black water. A bottle
of ink—no, two bottles, maybe even more—had been
dumped in. Turned sick, I did. Were they *dead*? my pencil
probing the swill, which one would I turn up first? Mitzi? Os-
car? Empty. My fist rammed in, fingers feeling around. No
goldfish. Where were they? And who . . . ? Who was it said
yesterday . . . Brian? Brian!?

I ran up the stairs two at a time, heels like gunshots, running lickety-split down the hall and bursting open the steel
door to the lab, bottles on the counter almost shattering.

"My fish! What did you do to my goldfish" trembling,
more tears than rage.

He'd put them in a crock, a huge stone crock, the kind

they soak beans in, and there they were, swimming around as if in the Caribbean, the four of them darting between sprigs of white coral, fins brushing over pearls and sparkling stones. "They can't *see*!" I stormed, bumping my head on a metal spigot above the counter, "they can't see where they're going! Don't you know glass is what they swim through, the same as water? That's how they tell how *far* they've gone!" Out I marched with the crock, staggering under the weight, water spilling down my front. Men in white coats passing me on the stairway, was I going to make them home-baked beans for lunch?

I stared at my desk, I could hear the automatic elevator out in the hall, doors opening, closing, staff leaving for lunch, coming back, and all I could think was, He took good care of them, he even bought them a new tin of fish food. . . .

Two weeks later, and I'm out of my office drab, the appropriate navy, or black, with white collar and cuffs, and into a pale blue crepe, a long string of pearls resting, sliding back and forth, over a wow of a pintucked bodice. At a table for two, I sat opposite him that night at the Gatineau, music blaring, five hundred people crammed in there? a thousand? One floor-show; two hours later another; at 3:00 a.m. still another. Fingering my pearls, and thinking to myself, The last time I was here it was with Frederick. But I had not remembered other moments like this, . . . turning my head to answer whatever it was Brian said, feeling the touch of his hand on my back as we danced, when the breath in me rose, as if wanting to cry, My own. He is mine. But is he teasing me? He has not *asked* me to marry him, he has *told* me I'm *going* to, once in the car, and now here at this table. Knotting and unknotting my pearls, sucking the end of their rope, green spotlights sweeping the barn-like cave, people swishing past white tablecloths, silverware blinding my eyes; kettle drums, saxophones, trombones taking the roof off the place, suddenly segueing into long slow notes while the band leader leans down over two sailors requesting a number: "How deep is the ocean?", waiters bumping into tables, a girl in a red satin evening dress sauntering past, ". . . how high is the sky?" "Would you like to dance, Miss Watson?" feeling our way in the dark to the dance floor, oh I must write George, I must do that first thing in the morning.

And now, watching the others dance. My pearls, my pearls and I in this island, green, gold, red, blue, greenish dark lighting up, eerie, the whole place seems at a distance; shutting my eyes, and I shiver, it's like being in the supernatural, for a moment I can't seem to think. I sit forward on the edge of my chair, observing a waiter's hands shifting things around on the table. I've just returned from the Ladies', and realize the waiter's concerned with where to put my handbag, there's no room left on the table. If I moved my elbows, and took my pearls out of my teeth, he could work around me. A streak of blue light flashes across my silence, where was I? and Brian leans across the table and says, "Boo!" A table that's squashed in with ten million others, no wonder the waiter couldn't find room to move his behind; a table I've been gazing down upon, where Brian has ordered oysters and sauterne. And while I try to gag down these puky oysters, making faces, choking on Tobasco sauce, he calmly tells me, "Eat them. They're a good aphrodisiac." And so I eat them, I don't know what aphrodisiac means, but not for all the tea in China will I ask. I'd never be caught dead asking, maybe it means they're good for your eyes, like spinach and carrots, or maybe your hair, or teeth, or skin? legs?

---

I feel George's arm tremble, that means two sets of knees knocking. The organ drowns out the feeling, calms us now that we've stepped further inside the church, where the air's cooler. "Okay?" George whispers. The carpet underfoot feels like a caress; there's nothing to be afraid of. The poor organist: he's the one, having to keep pace. "To a Wild Rose" is not meant for a slow processional.

I wonder if George is thinking the same thing as me? For an instant has his mind travelled to the St. Lawrence and back? We've turned left, the short aisle now behind us, all at once the sight of the long one ahead—merciful heavens, almost stopping me dead in my tracks, and the urge is to exchange an aside, whisper and point to some half-visible dangle of ribbon decorating a pew. I sway a little, and look up at stained-glass windows the sunlight catches at a peculiar angle, orange fireworks exploding above palm groves, a white city of mosques. From the rear, the organ, skillfully dragging; I guess he's trying to hold back, we're not exactly barrelling through. Eyes fixed on a point straight ahead, high up, and now down, hard light, momentarily blinding, the chancel is like a Vatican stage, it's the sun doing things to the brass. But Brian! Where's Brian? Ah, there! off to one side, he has to leave room for us. He's wearing a navy blazer and cream flannels . . . arms folded, looking up at the stained glass, and moving slightly: rocking back and forth on his heels—because of the music? or because he gets impatient standing, all this hushed silence, people, pews filled to the walls, he likes to be anonymous. Beloved Brian, who'd as soon toss a pebble up at the stained glass as have to stand facing it. Likely he's said as much to John, the best man. Well, it's all I can do to aim at what's under me, the carpet, make sure my feet behave, not have me tipping over, staggering into a pew. If Brian's impatient, he should try this walk. Gladiolas. I was right. Never mind. I'll find something else . . . Brian, image sharper, stronger, facing straight ahead, still swaying, what's he thinking? Again I see tiny flames in motion, this time flickering above the bronzed wingspread of an eagle holding the Bible; and of course, dear Matt, Matt in his red and white vestments, tapestry work on a cream-coloured flannel robe I've not seen him wear before. He has that benevolent look, hands folded as he waits. A good feeling to see him there. Why be nervous when it's a friend performing the ceremony, someone who's known us since the day we moved here from Canso?

If only Matt knew how I'm counting on him; as of this morning he's been elected to propose the toast to the bride. What if he's held up? Who'll we get? Mr. Mahoney was supposed to, but the poor man got sick or something, I didn't read the telegram this morning. I called downstairs to George, would he open it for me? I was busy practising how I'd get dressed. Something borrowed and all that. Where in Heaven's name was the blue satin garter Aunt Isa had made me? George was still reading aloud when he reached the top of the stairs, and came into my room visibly concerned, his fingers running lightly through his hair. He sat down on the bed beside me. "Don't worry," he said reassuringly, putting an arm around my waist as he laid the telegram on the edge of the bureau. "I'll take care of it. Wait a minute—why don't I telephone Matt and ask him?"

"Sure," I said. "That'd be great." I dove under the bed. Now where in the dickens could that garter have got to; did the envelope fall down behind somewhere? What's the toast to the bride supposed to do anyway? Does it come before you cut the cake, or after? And do I say "Cheers", or what?

In a few minutes George was back. "Matt says he'd be glad to, but could we hold things up a little? I'd forgotten that he has another wedding to do, back at his own church. After that he'll jump in his car and come right away."

Holy catfish! Does that mean Matt will arrive at the reception in these robes? or will he dump them in the vestry on the way out? Oh well, he could come dressed as the Pope and I'd welcome him. I wonder if he's appalled at my taste in a wedding tune? Did I prepare him? Well, nothing surprises him, and he knows I'm pigheaded. Under my breath I thank the organist for carrying through on my song. In the airlessness he's creating a sense of petals moving above moist earth, above rock; the man's an expert, he *feels* that wild rose. And any second now I think I'm going to cry.

But I don't; it passes as George and I lean into one another, advancing slowly. Diagonal pattern rushing up from the carpet. There's no need to stagger . . . look up and not down. The altar is farther away than I thought. I bite my lip, and take a firmer grip on George's arm, which is trembling. And that touches me.

Yes. That touched me; a split-second drop of time that's been posterity-deep, the quiet feeling in him, held back, locked up inside, the tremble a burst of rejoicing he could not contain. I remember the sad-sweet wash of emotion that passed over me, intuition communicating something of our inner selves. Swiftly, in an indefinable way, there had come the realization that whatever might happen, change, the arrangements of life, this day for one as I prepared to go my separate way, our beginnings had sewn us into one another's destinies. I did not know how I knew this, the flash of recognition dominated by the clamp that seemed to close around my heart. Each other's being. The safe secret place we had back of us, the only thing we were certain of, I was thinking. While we live we must make sure never to die, as our parents will one day. I remember closing my eyes, blinking rapidly to send the thought away; I was merely over-excited, not enough sleep the night before. And the organ . . .

Is the organ catching me off guard? I wouldn't have thought . . . surely . . . maybe I shouldn't have asked for that piece, the organ is producing a delayed reaction, I can't handle it. I must get a hold on myself. Just because someone's absent . . . that's no reason to feel faint again. Matt's the one with composure, I see his benevolent hands haven't moved. Will everything go off all right? the same as we rehearsed it last night?

A sudden movement and I look up from my bouquet: the

grin, the golden shoulder-length hair, a flicker of blue eyes
glimpsed through transparent veiling the colour of pale sand,
belong to Marian, my bridesmaid. Lovely, stunning Marian,
in buttercup-yellow, tall, long-legged, graceful; she's passed
me in height now. Over her shoulder she has given us a backward glance. Are George and I in step? Now that we've
caught up are we following too close? She looks a little
flushed, it's all these eyes watching. Is this the way we saw
ourselves? That summer, when we were fourteen, and I asked
her would she, did we imagine this? I certainly didn't waste
any time lining up a bridesmaid! but it popped out the day of
the ball diamond in Cartier Square—isn't that what the night
was all about, when we walked by the canal and talked of
orange blossoms and the dreams we thought of then?

In the front pew I can see Mamma's head, her lovely hat,
wide-brimmed, dipping here and there, dove-coloured, like her
crepe dress, all one shade. She should have her head up
though; what's she doing, praying?

She's all by herself.

---

"If your father sets one foot in the church I'll make a
scene." From the very beginning, "I'll make a scene."

This was the shadow, that blind idea of hers which kept
passing between us all those weeks, her determination to bar
my father from the wedding, holding fast to her threat that
she'd stand up in the church and say something. I remember
the ravage of her words, the stare in her eyes, dilated, too
bright: "Your father walked out, deserted us."

The first time she said it I shrank back in horror. In the
name of God what raving tongue was this let loose in our
midst, was this my mother speaking? I looked at her, incredu-
lous, my eyes blurring as I shot back the truth! Wasn't she
the one insisted he leave in the first place? And afterwards
hadn't she put the phone down every time he called? doing so
for more than a year now? "What do you call that?" I demanded, stalking her out to the kitchen, where I sputtered on,
inarticulate almost. "Don't say mean things!" I seized her by
the shoulders and shook her. "Don't ever say Daddy deserted
us, do you hear? He never would." When she did not reply I
turned away. I sat down on the kitchen chair, my feet on the
rung and my hands twisting about in my lap. "I love my father and I want him at my wedding," I said to her back; she

was wiping spilled gravy where it had dried on the stove. "Please, it's terrible . . . he has as much right as you have."

"I don't want to hear another word about it. The matter is closed."

"You don't realize what you're doing. If only you did. One day you'll regret . . ."

"I said I do not want to discuss it, not another word." A kind of choking in her voice, implying not provocation, nor even exasperation, but that she was wrought up. She sagged into the stove, I could see her small breastbone heaving, as if fighting for breath just then, the pulse in her throat making little throbs, like a trapped bird. I was trapped too. The defenceless, pitiable expression in her eyes got to me.

I got up and left the kitchen, and staggered upstairs. How did I know this was going to happen? My brain pounded. But what of my father, what about him?

I was torn between the two. My father with no anger in him, no sign of ill-will, as if the change in their lives had not taken place at all. 'What's new, lass?' he'd say, his slender hands fumbling for something in his pockets, or busy with some minor object near by. Didn't I know the silent breath in him cried too? And the day I told him, when I had to go and say what Mamma had said . . . about him coming to the wedding.

Never once did he mention it again. When one of our evenings came to a close, he'd hunt around for his keys and say, "I'll drive you home." He was now living downtown, and we drove through the late hour passing lighted shops and crowds strolling the August night, on into the sounds of one neighbourhood, and then another, voices possessed of their own individual trials and triumphs, vibrating and musical as they floated out of open doors. And in the dark I sat leaning back against the seat wondering what I might say to her. The awfulness of the subject. I would wait, I decided, maybe tomorrow, or the day after, or the day after that. Mamma would feel sorry, admit she was not being fair. Would there not be a moment, a longing in her, some swift memory that would prompt her to say, He is a good man?

But the days passed, and not a word out of her. She's trying to punish him, I thought. She's using the wedding, and he won't let her. I put off further discussion with Mamma for another reason: I wanted her to change her mind, herself, write my father a letter or telephone him. That would show she meant what she was saying, there would be no ructions in the church, and then I wouldn't feel the space between them, no cloud over me waiting for something to happen. . . .

"Gee. That's tough," Marian had said; "I mean about your father not being there. I don't know what to say."

"George stood up to her," I said, the pendulum swinging the other way now that the time was so close.

Ever since their separation, right from the first day, I was always aware of my mother's deep sense of loss, a quiet thing in her that made me want to protect her; without taking her side. So I saw that she was made to feel loved and needed, telling myself she just wasn't herself. But with the wedding so near, scarcely two weeks away, I found myself inwardly becoming angry at her, once or twice on the verge of letting her know so, until I realized I too would have burst into tears. I hadn't intended to say anything about it to George until he came home. He was in Halifax now, taking a two-month course in radio-wireless, training for the merchant marine. And when I realized he'd have to put in for that weekend off—in order to be certain that he and no one else would give me away—I had to write him. I tried to make it breezy, would he come to my aid? I'd need someone to wake me up that morning, and to see to it that I didn't forget my flowers, I'd be so busy pinching myself making sure I was alive, I might leave my bouquet behind. George surprised me by being firm with Mamma. The first time in a letter, and the second was when he arrived home on the Friday morning.

"What's this I hear?" he asked her gently, but firmly. "You're not being fair, you know, just thinking of yourself. Daddy has as much right."

I guess I knew all along I'd never have the . . . what? to speak up. I hadn't learned there's a difference in vulnerabilities. The one you can see, the vulnerability that shows, is really the lesser; it's strong enough to make demands.

"When you're older you'll understand," my mother says. Understand? I didn't realize it would be like this, doesn't make any sense. In one breath she'll say she doesn't want my father near the house, mad at him for taking her at her word, and then she'll turn around and say, "Why did your father have to go?" Loony, if you ask me. I'm so busy trying to puzzle things out, I keep forgetting who sent what present, and get the cards all mixed up. Not as though there's someone I can go to and ask, or explain. Who has parents that have separated? who's ever heard of it even?

Boy, I could sure tell them. Who can go to sleep nights

when you have to listen to your mother crying in the next room? Well, at least she stops after a while, and reads; I hear her turning pages. Often I go in, she likes when I plump her pillows, or play with the dog on the foot of the bed, smoke a cigarette with her, anything! The fact of me *being* there. What good does that do? Because soon I won't be? Each night I look at her, expecting she's changed her mind, that she'll say, 'I think your father deserves to be at your wedding.' But she never does, and I try to think of a way, there must be something. I could get mad too, or look helpless, like she does. What if I said, 'Now listen here . . .' My throat always swells, I shrink, a simple question and I can't find the words any more: 'What harm would it do? just give me one good reason.' I retreat to my bedroom, dialogue in my head, 'He's coming because I say so.' My words follow me, follow me wherever I go.

The night of the wedding rehearsal, the Friday night, I'd arranged to meet my father beforehand. That was something I wanted to do, just the two of us. After work he would call for me at the hairdresser's and we'd go out to dinner, we'd have until 8:30 p.m. I told myself it would be almost the same, what did the ceremony matter?

Not that simple. As soon as we met, the minute we left the beauty salon and stepped out into the warm evening air, the thrum of traffic, the rustling and laughter around, all at once settling down over me, its resonance as though far-off, sound-less. And loud in my mind, a single thought: tomorrow, to-morrow at three o'clock he will look at his watch. . . .

Friends of the Nolans had invited him for the weekend, he said suddenly, as if breaking in on what was on my mind; their summer place near Brockville, he added, they had a boat, and thought he might enjoy a run on the St. Lawrence. Looking straight ahead now as he guided me across the inter-section, and in the next instant: "Now wasn't that kind of them? You remember the Ryans?" Streetcar clanging over his words. "They came to the cottage once, do you remember? a long time ago. . . ."

Two people sitting in a restaurant, and the world going by. They walk past, sit, talk eagerly, or in whispers. For a hun-dredth time or a first. Whoever knows what's being said, what's in a person's gut? And there he is and here I am. It is not one of those times you can say, "What's new?" "Good to see you." "How's your mother?" It is not one of those times the river looks back at us and says "Hi!", no lash of the cur-

rent round my ankles as he ties on my water-wings and tells
me, 'Come back here, I want to teach you how to float.' History ties us with another cord. He has prepared me for, led
me to this turning point in my life. And suddenly it's not his
any more, he has to look at his damn watch tomorrow instead.

After a while he became silent. He had cleared a spot on
the table, his arms were crossed, resting on the white dinner
cloth. Brows working, perhaps a faint smile behind his eyes, I
don't know. I tried to read his thoughts, they were private;
for all its promise, I did not think he was visualizing a boat
on the St. Lawrence.

Our coffee cups had been refilled, and as I scooped at some
spilled sugar, I found myself suddenly blurting out: "Why
don't you come anyway? just say nothing and be outside the
church when George and I arrive, then George could skip on
inside. Mamma wouldn't carry on." I licked the spoon, staring at a coffee urn, it was somewhere to put my eyes. "She
was only just saying that. Half the time she never means
what she says, you know that." I stirred my coffee endlessly,
eyes fixed on the silver spoon going round and round. There
was so much more I wanted to say. But wouldn't that only
make things worse? sear him? if I lost out on my argument?
What was the reason he hadn't declared himself? what force
prevented it—himself? my mother? A gnawing inside. The
little lamp on the table communicating its orange glimmer
over my clammy hands, the silent waiter, brushing crumbs
away, onto the floor. Tomorrow so near.

What is my father thinking right now? When I look at him
I want to cry out angrily, "Patch up your differences, both of
you, forget them for a day, it has nothing to do with me.
Can't you see the real issue? Don't you know it matters, that
*your* feelings come first?" . . . No, don't leave him with that
. . . but say something! A surge through me. By saying nothing . . . supposing he thinks I suggested dinner because I
wanted to put pressure on, that I'm imploring he give me
away tomorrow for appearances' sake? It'd look as though I'd
suddenly decided he was letting me down. What a muddle in
my head. You have to be careful of regrets: sometimes, a
time like this, the more love bursting out of a word the more
of a backlash when you're left by yourself. I did not want
him to have to say what was deep inside him, no shadows lingering in his mind, for as long as he lived no strained words
to have heard himself say. And so I hurled myself into some-

thing he already knew: "At bed-time tonight, when Mamma and I are having a cigarette, I'll say if you're not there, everyone'll know she's to blame, it's her fault, and how would she like to have that said about her?" The lead-and-silver saltcellar turning in my hands. Someone in a raincoat being seated at the next table. "She'll probably want to box my ears, but even so, once she thought things over, don't you feel that in front of all those people she'd decide to sit there and keep still?" A man's arm pulling itself out of the sleeve of the raincoat.

My father paused, drank from his glass of water. "Can't take that chance," he said, and glanced away, drawing on his cigarette as he gazed around, the sense of him more wise than wistful. "Your mother . . ." he hesitated; he was reflecting, and now looked troubled. "Wouldn't be the first time, and with people present. I've thought for weeks, Just supposing I did suddenly appear? No."

Can't take that chance? That isn't it at all. He doesn't *want* to come. Because he *can't*? Both of them? are both of them unable to *see* one another? it's too hard?

The tone in them the same, but taking a different key. Deep down I knew my father was right, his final decision spoke for them both: whatever it was that divided my parents was too raw in their flesh. But all the knowing in the world doesn't change what you're feeling.

I did not think of my parents as ordinary people, I had created images, they were beyond human failings. And so I thought they should have done this for me, pretended, if only for a few hours. This was a day with a focus; I wanted to be able to frame it in my mind, I didn't want there to be anything to mar it. How could I have known then that hypocrisy—faking things—and not my father's absence, would have been the true wrong, robbing me forever of what had been real in their lives?

---

"Who giveth this woman?" Imperceptible movement. And the candles flicker. Brian's face, despite the dimness that's all I see. The face of a man with quiet authority. And eyes suddenly grown serious, he seems to be trying to tell me something—that I look pale? or beautiful? He reaches out a hand, withdraws it, and I hear George say, "I give her." The moment has come. Slowly George releases my arm, his nervous tremors gone, and with both hands takes my clammy one, presents me to Brian, who murmurs, "How do you do, Miss Watson?" Funny man. I could weep, but I won't. It's just that I'm not used to being this happy, not this way. That's why I'm shaking like this. Rustlings. The gathering at the altar shifting, moving closer together. I shiver, even my bouquet trembles, and Brian, who senses my every pore, leans down and whispers, "What did you have for lunch?" Matt smiles. I guess he's used to nervous jitters, *and* guests arriving late. That shuffling I hear behind me—is that someone just arriving? or changing pews? Brian regarding me intently, waiting for me to reply to his question.

"I don't know," I falter. "Pears. I had two pears."

"The ring?" Matt asks of John.

Fingers clasp, and a hush closes in. Lips parting, a solemn reply, another . . . A plain gold ring. "Let no man put asunder."

# XIX

———————◆———————

Looking back, that Saturday was the shortest day of my life. Well, in a way it was. I saw it as a beautiful thing, not just my future but all of my life was beginning, like the beginning of time. That's what I was thinking when the ceremony started. A sense of timelessness all mixed up, stained-glass windows vivid with the living and dying, the dazzle of brass crosses and urns, the *Book of Common Prayer* and words of old drifting down from Matt's carpeted elevation. Every emotion I'd ever experienced, the good with the bad, seemed massed inside me, turned upside down in a kind of helpless churning. For one brief instant, the sense of one's fate being folded into this moment, this overwhelming ritual—is it truth? is it fantasy?

Yes. The shortest day of my life. But I sure wasn't thinking that at the time, not a couple of hours later, I wasn't.

Thought I was going berserk. All set to shout, Will this mind-lessness never end?

I remember waking early that morning, sitting back on my legs in the middle of the bed as I looked out the window. It had rained heavily in the night and the streets were marbled with slicks of wet and dry patches. And while the skies were still heavy with overcast, the birds were now singing—though not quite so vociferously as when Brian and I emerged from the church. What a chorus. As if in our honour they were trying to drown out the noise the churchbells were making. That's a good omen, I thought: first the sparrows and chip-munks this morning, now even the swallows sing out.

Scarcely two hours later, at the reception, I was trying des-perately to retreat into their song. For there I stood, as if nailed to the floor, my sweaty hands clutching at the pink ta-blecloth, no longer feeling rosy and silken in my "nun's" wedding dress, but like a statue someone had stuck a wedding veil on, a statue wanting to become invisible, meanwhile asking itself: 'Will this never end?'

Well, how did it end? Squeeze into that waiting car, girl, Brian beside you, the day is only half begun.

———

Confetti on my lap as I ride to the west end of the city, to the house where the reception is to be. Chatter. John up front at the wheel, Marian beside him. Horns tooting. Happiness. I'm bursting, light-headed, a kind of fog of delirium as a breeze ripples my pleats, and Brian says, "Can't call you Miss Watson any more," and takes hold of my hand. "I love you Miss Watson." Fingers moving back and forth over my knuckles, resting on the seat between us, warm against our thighs.

What *did* we say? Tears come by my eyes. What do the words matter when they are witness to a greater depth, and rise up like silver castanets, a sound riding across a Saturday afternoon?

A long ride from the church. From St. Bartholomew's, half an hour to get here? My . . . all these people! Awkward for the hosts?—friends of my parents—did they know what they were letting themselves in for? They've gone to great lengths. I wouldn't have had gladiolas though; it's like I said, they're for funerals, and they're as ugly as the dahlias they've got in the front room. Still, this lace tablecloth is nice, looks like an heirloom. So are the pink linen napkins. Did they borrow the maid?

Mutterings. Brian's mother in a confab with the host and hostess, plus another man. She's buttonholing him for something—now what? and the house is suddenly still. Yes, of course, the speeches. About to begin? Why is everyone standing? Are they starting? But Matt . . . Why is everyone crowding in so? Where's Matt? Don't they know we have to wait a few secs? Too late. They've got someone else? I hope not. I focus on pickled walnuts, celery, pink serviettes. What? A woman's hands turn me around, it's Brian's mother, telling me I should be facing front.

"And so I've been asked to toast the bride. . . ." Who *is* that man? I give him the once-over; on sight I don't like his pursed lips, and you can't trust short men with slitty eyes. Who chose him to speak for me? rounded up at the last minute, like a minister summoned to give a eulogy to a stranger, all he needs is the name. He doesn't know me, and apart from shaking his hand a while ago, I don't know him at all. And since he's not smart enough to dream something up about me, why doesn't he play it safe and tell a funny story and not keep lecturing me, reminding me of my good judgement? For according to him, I'm a very lucky girl. Wow! Seems I've married a rather exceptional young man.

Two minutes gone? The coarse metallic voice drones a buzzing sound as he obliges, and lapses into something he's reminded of: "At the time, I was in the insurance racket. . . ." Racket? I'll bet! I guess Frederick will read about the wedding in the newspapers. Maybe not though. There'll be no way for him to see today's paper, by this time he probably isn't anywhere near Ottawa. Didn't he get married himself last Saturday? I could be wrong, but isn't that what someone said at the rehearsal party last night? I should have had a wedding like that, I hear they eloped. "Zzzzzzzz." Mr. Whatever-his-name-is. Who tells us he's out of practice. Does that mean he's just warming up? He straightens his tie, a marathon he's preparing for? and I think, Matt—get in here quick! "Gargantuan . . . the Tooth Fairy . . . no more perfect tooth than . . ." You'd think he was Brian's godmother or something. That one sure fell flat! What a hick.

I flinch, and wish Brian wouldn't keep squeezing my hand, people will think he's feeling sorry for me. Thank the Lord he can't say anything, I don't want him sticking up for me, I don't want him ever to do that. Five minutes? Candles burning, summoning me, I flow into the flame. "And so this fine young man . . ." Say, this is getting comical. Too bad Mamma's on the other side of Marian, I'd love to kick her under the table; she'd be good for a laugh. Well, since she's having herself a little sip, why don't I do likewise?

Tasted good. Tastes like another one. What? Oh, that was Marian's glass, she must've put hers down for a minute. "Zzzzz. As a rule I don't take this long . . ." Lord, who's Mamma whispering to? "Mercy, I should think not. Who'd have the constitution?" Did the poor simp overhear that?

Whew. Gosh it's hot! Must be ninety in the shade. Sticky too. The men in white flannels must be suffering, they make winter coats out of that material. I pinch Brian's flannels, are they sticking?

Ahead of time, before What's-his-name started to speak, did someone announce he was only pinch-hitting? I'd like to sock him right now, bust him one in those yellow teeth. Why, I wonder, at the very moment when I need to, why is it that I can never express my anger properly, the way other people can? Why does mine always have to come out in tears? The nerve of that man! To get a point across, he seizes Brian's right arm and holds it up as if he's declaring a champion prizefighter. I've got the prize. Brian's got nothing?

---

Dearly beloved, we are gathered here . . . better you should be some place else, but since you're not, take off your shoes, have a drink and let us get on with the scenario. That child over there, the small boy in the blazer and short pants, will you please stop pouring coffee down behind the chester-field? Someone, will someone please give him a glass of punch? And the mother of the bride, would you mind tilting the brim of your hat back just a little? We're losing a bit on expression. And you better stay in your shoes, you need the height. The rest of you, as you were.

---

That's right. Don't change a thing. Crazy, but I stare into this reach of an afternoon, and find in it a hidden serenity. What is happiness but a form of chaos? the mind skittering through dreams, coming to rest on what it has found? Were I there now, I would clap my hands and cry, 'This is mine!'

But that is today. What of then? my young friends grouped around, and I, awkward, blindly exhilarated, half in their

world and half in my own. And what of the poor guests?
Were the ladies and gents not slowly going out of their
minds? pleading for mercy? I can't for the life of me remember a single anecdote, nor even a thread of the discourse,
whose meaning *nobody* can have understood, apart from
Brian and his parents (and I doubt if Brian himself knew
what the man was talking about), interrupting himself,
jumping from one subject to another. For someone who
played such a prominent role that day, in retrospect it seems
strange I never laid eyes on him again. But then he came, as
they say, from enemy territory, and took his leave, leaving us
classified as the walking wounded, parched, hungry, teetering
on the brink of stupor.

For-better-for-worse. The scene at the table is not over, my
own offering is yet to come. Holy wedlock. Holy mackerel.
Fifteen minutes, that's how long he's been at it. I've been
counting on my watch. I treat myself to a small sip, a man in
gabardine frowning in the shadows, the butterfly panes of or-
ganza over by a window. There aren't any uniforms, no one
here is in the army—only the ones making their living that
way in the first place. Which is just as well. Now that there's
a war, the ones in the permanent force, those I've met, anyway, resent anyone who hasn't joined up. And things are bad
enough without some flag-waver provoking a head-on. It's all
I can do to stand here trying to smile inanely through this experience, swaying uncertainly, my eyes taking in walls, the
ceiling, and the lassitude of a straggle of arms raised, ready
and waiting through an August bluejay's cry, the noise of
traffic going past. I wait with glass in hand, I'm certainly
ready, haven't I been testing the distance, calculating how
long, rim to mouth? Mustn't bungle things. . . .

My bouquet, I should lay that down. Confetti drifts down
upon the rug, it has a wayward feel. I do too, feeling inade-
quate. I shouldn't take any notice, but—in the speech I wish
he'd mention me once, isn't he supposed to?

"Ladies and gentlemen, I ask you to . . ." Where's my
glass, what did I do with my glass, oh, there . . . "join me in
a toast to the bride." In one fell swoop I drain my punch.

"Ohhhh *no*!" A woman's voice, one I am well acquainted
with. Galvanized air. The rim of my glass presses into my
temples. My head swims, what have I done? And before I
can glance around, try to see what I've done wrong, Brian's
mother scythes on: "You don't drink to yourself!" What?
"Never! never drink to yourself." Is everyone looking at me?

She reaches over, tries to put my glass down, and Brian, fingers like pincers, nips her in the back of the hand, which makes her jump.

"You don't? And who says so?" Great! *Great!* It's Mamma—who else. "Who says you can't?"

"Lovely!" exclaims Marian's mother from the end of the table, her face beaming, expectant: what comes next? Mamma does, she's not finished yet.

"Drink to whoever you please, lassie, yourself most of all." Daddy should have been here, he'd have been proud of her.

"Bloody goddamn right!" That's the Colonel, Colonel Lewis having his say to anyone listening. Mamma winding up again, speaking her mind was not enough, she has that reproachful, dismissing look. "The girl was happy . . ." she says leaning forward, and, oh dear, glaring at her opposite number, who replies: "Didn't you think to tell her?"

"God's teeth," Brian says to his mother quietly, impatient, "what difference does it make?" an inexpressible anxiety in his voice, and now, turning to me, lips swiftly brushing my ear, "It worked! You pulled a fast one and it worked!" A fast one? But I . . . "And I'll tell you something else," he adds, facing front again, refilling my glass from his: "We keep our cards neat, Miss Green," the words enunciated quietly, clearly, like a pronouncement. And I think, What now? *We keep our cards neat, Miss Green.* What and who is Miss Green? I don't remember meeting her here, or any place for this matter. Can we talk here? Can I ask him to expl . . . "Oh," he says, anticipating my open mouth, "that has become quite a famous saying amongst we obsessive-compulsives," his head turning slightly to the right, "hasn't it, *Mutterschön?*" Oh God. *Mutterschön* stiffening, drawn up regally, staring haughtily ahead, visions of Emily Post dancing through her head.

"Oh Brian," I hear myself say, lips barely breathing the words, "I'm uncomfortable . . . your mother, it's bad enough . . . who is Miss Green?"

"Tell you later," he replies, placid eyes looking at me steadily, smiling. "A tale of martyrdom and righteousness beyond belief—remind me." I began to hiccup, pleased now, all at once ecstatic, What if I have made a blunder? Brian, Brian's all I care about. I want to say the words aloud as he stands with his arm around my waist, he never did that before, not in public, never.

Well. What wedding doesn't have its brutal moment? What
better entertainment than something of the precarious, if not
the bizarre? the bride's long-in-the-tooth sister, say, or maybe
a maiden aunt who has decided to sing a solo, and is poised
on the staircase in her maribou boa, a contralto, off key and
plastered? or else some camphor- or eucalyptus-smelling
grandmother, her quiet-eyed and delighted self also a little
the worse for wear, out cold in an upstairs room? or the
groom's father as he pauses to look down during a toast, realizing his fly is open and managing to catch it in a bridesmaid's veil?

Except that I'd never experienced such worldly goings-on.
Things like that only happened to Charlie Chaplin, and
Laurel and Hardy.

Congestion at the far end of the table? Yes. From all
directions, individuals converging on the punch bowl, the
whir, the sudden speed is like a frontal attack, immediately
diverting the focus from my faux-pas. I realize Brian's arm is
still around my waist, his free hand arranging my veil. I
know that gesture, he's done it with my hair, it's a way of
saying what you're thinking when a feeling of love wells up,
too realized, too strongly felt to be trusted to mere words. I'm
learning to do that too. Except I can't here, on account of
Brian's mother, she makes a fuss when I touch him . . . she
doesn't seem to understand . . . why? I wonder. His warm
body presses against me, my flesh is hot, moist, clothes sticking to me. Good thing I didn't wear any pants, they say it's
unlucky if you do . . . a man doesn't have to think about
these things. Funny, they like you to wear a garter though,
and a bra, when no one's looking they can undo it through
your dress. I feel beautiful, the spell is back.

"How are you doing?" Brian says bending low at my ear.
He straightens up, does not wait for my answer, there's no
need. I feel his quiet authority, unconcerned, the blond head
tall above me, sensuous mouth, lips that are alive, his face is
a message. No! None of this has happened at all, only the
fact I am his! I belong to Brian. Pink serviettes and cutlery,
the perfume of yellow roses, and cream-coloured ribbons
twined around an empty glass. The seconds start moving
again, I'm having a grand time! Now George has come over,
carrying his wineglass, and is standing behind us; a man has
interrupted his mission and he's trying to say something in re-

ply. At the same time he embraces our shoulders, first Brian's and then mine, head lowered as he draws us both in, a gathering of the clans. We smile at one another, the circumstances, the moments before this visit, are tempered, George's voice an intervening murmur, the brown eyes intent as he turns to me. "Pretty Bird?" he asks—that's what he's taken to calling me, ever since I told him, "I think I love Brian. Oh George, what am I going to tell Frederick?"

"Hey! Pretty Bird?" he says again. "I wonder if I shouldn't follow up Mr. Whoosit, and say I believe Matt has a few words he would like to add about my sister?" Brian hesitates briefly, then gently lays his hand on George's forearm.

"No," he replies in a low voice, "better I should, don't you think? I'll catch Matt's eye." I peer up from under the huddle, and glance around. "You won't need to," I whisper. "Look! Our host has his hand up, he's waiting for the conversation to die down." Matt, suppressing a smile. He has to cool his heels until the introduction is made.

A lone voice, and it's Matt's; he's begun. "Of course in Sunday School the Biblical bookmarks we gave the children were of the Virgin Mary and Jesus." What? Bookmarks? That's new. Matt, shifting his pipe to the other side of his mouth and grinning at me, and now at Brian. A good feeling. I turn to Brian, his eyes caress, and my heart races, the flames of the candles are like my insides. "And she informed me she knew exactly what the Holy Ghost looked like, that was easy, she said." Holy cow. Where's the punch, I could hold out my glass? ". . . table in the dining room at their house, and I said, 'Supposing you show me, take your crayons.'" Matt!! ". . . and I said, no, I was asking her, I wanted to know what *she* thought God might look like." Damn him. "I remember that she tore up the first one." I had to start over, I ran out of space, no room left for the feet. "I pulled up a chair . . . the hand over the drawing deliberately, didn't want me watching . . . Definitions . . . in a dressing-gown . . . wrist-watch. I'd seen a few versions, cloaks, Rip Van Winkles, a beggar in rags with a halo; one boy saw Him as Ben Hur driving a chariot across red-coloured clouds. Children sometimes talk aloud as they draw, but she talked to herself. . . ." Brian, not moving; he *likes* this? ". . . finished, the hand reached up, 'Like this?' . . . at first eluded me. And then I knew. For her, God existed in all men, in our time, as then, as He did in Christ's time. At a glance the face was . . . hands in the pockets . . . and she had put a knot . . ."

I gave Him the mumps, and a warm scarf tied around His head, and corns on His feet. I thought He was the same as my father.

———————

Five o'clock now? Five thirty? and my bouquet tossed from a landing on the stairway, the whole debacle behind me, the evening ahead—the dusk that would soon fall across cities and towns, dew on the fields and the darkening shrouds of trees tucked away as Brian and I drove to a log cabin in the wilds of Haliburton. But first, I was in an upstairs bedroom getting changed. My mother and Marian between them busily hither and thither while they went around the room ceremoniously sorting out my going-away dress (shocking cerise—the sheerest I could find). Where were the shoes put? the pin for the corsage? did I need any help with my stockings? and Mamma: "My God, did you not have any pants on? What a girl," turning back to her chore of folding up my wedding dress. Still riled at attention having been called to my faux-pas, she smacked at the tissue paper as she flattened it lengthwise along the pleats. "Achhhh," she said; now more than ever, the dress taking on a paler hue. Marian was singing, "I'll Be With You in Apple Blossom Time", I could hear the phone ringing, and chatter in a room down the hall, someone else was taking a shower with the bathroom door open. While the hubbub downstairs drifted up in faint cadences. From time to time, Brian's voice, and George's, within earshot—were they waiting near the foot of the stairs? a chance to be alone and talk by themselves? brothers now.

Someone knocked on our door. There was a long-distance call for my mother; the maid asked would she like to take it in the study across the hall?

The call was from my father, he had telephoned to wish Brian and me well, but he had asked to speak to Mamma first. That he would think of that—what more could be wished for?

"Long distance for you, Mrs. Watson, from Brockville."

"Me?" she asked, looking up at me from a scatter of tulle and tissue, "asking for me? I thought maybe you . . ." Her eyes told the tale, like they used to when she would run to meet my father.

"You see!" I exclaimed, standing in my slip, my face accusing as I took hold of her arm, pulling at her. "He could have come after all. I knew it!"

"Knew what?"

Amazing. She had no idea, something like a pent-up joy glazing her eyes. While I knew what had suddenly hit her, I don't believe she herself realized what it was, not then anyway: she had a need to share this moment, there was only the one person with whom she could have.

She grabbed the brim of her flouncy hat, and I watched it sail through the air and down onto the bed. The dove-grey dress rippled out the door, the swirl of crepe like a destiny, past and present, as it rilled above her legs.

"Can you beat that?" I said to Marian.

I can now. It's real life.

I picked up her hat and for a moment sat with it on my knee. I would miss her, I thought.

I was no longer angry with her, and never would be again. For although I did not understand, nor even know why, I realized then my father would never be back.

The door to the study was open, and I could hear Mamma's voice, animated, louder now. She was back on home ground: "The cheek of the man! As if your daughter was something the cat dragged in. If it hadn't been for . . . if the reception had been at the house I'd have punched him in the mouth." Silence. She's listening. "No. By telegram, I believe he's been sick. And Matt got here late . . . Oh, some local pip-squeak, a fart-in-a-mitt with too much to say." Marian and I in our stocking feet, standing in the bedroom doorway, Marian snickering. "Probably wanted Brian for his own daughter. She's a drip too." Yipes! Can anyone hear? ". . . her veil, and drank to herself. What, Cecil? . . . Oh you know *her* . . . of course . . . by promptly holding out her glass for a refill, defiant." Is that how it looked? I was only trying to cover up the evidence. "Yes, Brian did . . . yes, sharing something personal with her, and then! an aside to his mother. Lord knows what he said. I couldn't hear, but whatever it was, it left a few mouths hanging open . . . of course . . . No, but I had to laugh though, a while ago; when the man was taking his leave, she shook hands and apologized, said she was sorry Matt had upstaged him, she hoped he didn't mind, and was that why he was leaving? . . . Yes, it was fine . . . Did you? No, George has to get back tomorrow." Her voice low again, I can't hear. Is it her throat?

"She's in the next room changing, I'll call her . . ."

"I hear you got your Irish up," my father says. "What happened?"

"Everything but the monsoons! But it was OK. Now that it's over, you begin to see the funny side. Mamma was the one got her hackles up, and I thought I'd bust. She hasn't done that for a long time, she really hasn't. And hey! You know what? Did Mamma tell you about old Colonel Lewis putting in his two cents?"

"No."

"He piped up after Mamma gave it to Brian's mother. Before that even. Because all the time the silly twit of a man was talking, Colonel Lewis kept putting his head to one side and banging his ear as if he had water in it. What? You bet! Then, when everything was quiet, after Mamma was finished saying her piece about me drinking to myself, he suddenly bellowed—and you know that loud army voice of his, you could have heard him over in Hull. 'Bloody right!' he boomed. 'The bride had to do *something* to give us all a charge.' "

My father laughed, and said, "The Colonel was back on the square! his old drill-sergeant days. Tell Colonel Lewis I said that was quick thinking, will you?"

I asked him then was he having a good time, and he said, yes, he was, there were guests there as well, and in a few minutes they were all going out for a sail, he thought he'd take his camera along this time, he'd forgotten it in the morning.

"What time do you think you and Brian will reach Minden tonight?" he asked finally. "Those gravel roads . . . will you phone me tomorrow?"

"Sure." He gave me the number to call, and hung up.

I sat in the den for a minute, wanting to phone him back. There were so many things I had wanted to say, I could use the excuse I thought George was planning to surprise him with a visit in the morning, before he caught the Pullman out of Montreal for Halifax. But what else would I say? Blurt out that it was the quality of his presence that was missing, and not just his role as a father, and that I never knew him to seem so far away, even though he wasn't? I would be telephoning him later, I thought, by the time Brian and I reached Minden I'd have thought for a nice message to give him then. I bounded back to Mamma and Marian, back in action again with their glasses magically replenished, stocking feet going around in circles; where's this, where's that?

Finally, on the cement steps leading down from the front walk, I turned for a glance back, Mamma and George the

only ones I saw as I left; in all the excitement, above the
scented gardens and spill of guests clustered about the lawn,
their faces, their faces alone not dissolving among the crowd
as I slipped happily into Brian's ribboned, tin-canned, soap-
lettered Plymouth.

I couldn't think of anything to say as we drove off. Instead,
fingering the pendant Brian had given me the night before;
the fragrance of my corsage of gardenias, and the moist
warm intimacy of the two people in our shoes, enveloping
me, making me lightheaded. Holding hands. Weaving in and
out of traffic. We would find a side street, Brian said, shuddering at the pink and yellow streamers rippling across the
car hood.

"Oh yes," I said, the question of Miss Green floating in
and out of my mind. "I'll help you get all this stuff off the
car. It's attracting attention."

"Wonder what dull Babbitt did the lettering? Pretty risqué
stuff, 'Bachelor's Brothel'." I wondered too.

---

"And now, would you mind telling me about the tale of
Miss Green?" I began all of a sudden, the clatter cut loose,
soap-letterings eradicated, the city behind us at last, trees,
fields and silver silos flying by and the late afternoon sun deflecting across the windshield, just enough breeze to make the
air like velour. "You sure were in form!" I bubbled, hooking
my arm through his, easing over as close as I could. "I
thought I was used to you talking in riddles. Now I'm not so
sure. I thought for a sec you were joking at the table, making
something up. And then when I saw your mother, her face
like a mask, I knew that little saying about Miss Green must
be some kind of confidence between you. And it's not something you laugh about either, is it?"

"Well yes," he replied. "Yes, once in a while she's laughed
about it."

"But she wasn't laughing this time. Nor was your father. I
heard him clearing his throat, and it wasn't his catarrh I'll
bet. There was nothing in his throat. Before you start telling
me, do you want to know what else I think? It sounded to me
like you were getting something across to her."

"I was. Indeed I was."

"I don't blame you for pinching the back of her hand like
that, the way she reached across to put my glass down. But
then after . . . I saw her grip the table when you called her

*Mutterschön*. She knew what was coming because she closed her eyes. You'd turned to look at me just then, you couldn't see her, but I did. And when you whispered 'martyrdom', and what was that other word? . . ."

"Oh that's my mother, I'm afraid. She believes in things—people and situations—being very neat and orderly, that is according to her lights, which are always on high beam. She can't stand disorder, it's a compulsive thing with her."

"Boy, I've sure noticed that. Sometimes it makes me perspire. I get soaking wet. Once I thought I was going to faint—that time she said she wanted to go with me to see about ordering the wedding invitations. She didn't want me to include my father's name in the wording. So what! if he wasn't going to give me away? Whether he was or he wasn't, the announcement still had to say Mr. and Mrs. Cecil Watson were announcing the marriage of their daughter, not just my mother! And what a thing going on! I had to keep asking the clerk in Birk's if he could get me a glass of water, and my stomach got so full of water I barely made the washroom and threw up. I wasn't going to tell you. I thought I'd wait and see if you ever asked me anything . . . want to hear a confession? When she walks in the room, or phones me, I get prickly all over, she makes me feel so unworthy."

"Ah, but that's the idea. After all, you *are* unworthy of her beautiful son. Didn't you know that?"

"I'm unworthy? What do you mean?"

"In her eyes you are. But let's drop that part. It's the story of Miss Green . . . and it's an all too common one. Goes back to when Jesus was born."

"Jesus? What's . . . oh, you mean Christmas?"

"No. *Me*, for Christ's sake. The virgin birth and all that. And there was a certain nurse in the stable that night. Miss Green, alias Florence Nightingale—she was the nurse on duty. Did you never hear stories about when you popped into the world?"

"Sure. Only mine wasn't a stable, it was a pink cloud above the sea."

"The stable was only a figure of speech. Weren't you provided with all the gory details?"

"Heck no. Did you have some?"

"Did I!? Momsy walked through the shadow of death. And so poor Miss Green became witness to, and therefore part of the glorious sacrifice for a most worthy and filial son, her one and only offspring. A few years go by, I learn to walk, I go to school, and I'm a clever little chap the teachers say was born old. Ergo, they chuck me out—but that comes later. Meanwhile Miss Green retires from her nursing profession and is compelled to live in some rotten boarding house, Florence Nightingale activities gone from her life. And *Mutterschön*, possessing the martydom of a female Brébeuf . . ."

"Say! Are you drunk?"

"No. Why? Do I have to be drunk to be . . . by the way, Matt certainly made up for things, didn't he? I thought he was charming. I must write him. I feel I really got to know him today. I saw Dad shaking his hand afterward, you know the way he does when he's been won over, using both hands, rejoicing in the handshake? Anyway, do let me tell you of this great lady, Miss Green, who came to dinner to our house. Where was I?"

"*Mutterschön* possessing the martydom of somebody or other."

"Ah yes. A female Brébeuf; couldn't have put it better myself. Who takes it upon herself to resentfully ask Miss Green to dinner, approximately once a month. A kind of gastronomic period. Miss Green is quite infirm at this stage and . . ."

"How old were you then?"

"Ageless, Miss Watson. Ageless and wise beyond my rocking horse, and privy to the flutterings of this poor love-starved creature, who was trying so desperately to please. As she had done once. She wasn't just someone with know-how who had taken over in a hospital room, but the one person whose hallowed right it was to spend her day off paying homage, saluting every gleaming diaper and toy in Jesus' nursery . . . Miss Green, her gentle existence was still a perfection and not a weakness, until at last this angel of mercy, this goddess, fell from grace."

"How could you tell she had? And I don't mean for you to tell me more! I was just wondering how you caught on, to the martyrdom, I mean. I never would have."

"From conversation, I suppose. Likely at the dinner table. At least the first time was. She let something fall, her handbag, unfortunately, which apparently was lying open on her lap. Given to picking at her food, I imagine she'd just been told to eat hearty, but the thing was Miss Green had a surprise for me, and either it was inside her purse or else under her table napkin, ready to hand to me the moment I returned from washing my hands for the 'dinner party'. And when she turned to kiss me, she forgot what she had balanced on her knee . . . it was too late to make a grab for it. Without a word, *Mutterschön* went running for the carpet sweeper, there were pieces of aspirin and sugar cubes and tiny bits of crystal, loose beads from a broken necklace Mother mistook for a broken mirror. Down on her hands and knees wincing at zircons! about as sharp and harmful as rice. And the social outcast, sitting apologetically, trying to hold her feet out of the way of the furious carpet sweeper, the claw-like fingers clutching Golden Boy's surprise. The gift she had thought nothing of dipping into her hard-earned savings for—so that she could buy me a watch for my birthday the year my voice changed. . . . Anyway, as I said, Miss Green is quite infirm at this stage, her most notable features now being a set of green teeth in a bristly face, with two large warts to grow them in."

"My, I'm certainly glad you didn't have to toast anyone today. You're in fine form."

"Do you think so? . . . But to proceed. Miss Green is embarrassingly grateful for these outings, which are like a light in her bleak life, but by the same token the light can be rather terrifying, particularly if there are two bright eyes watching her every move from behind it. No, I grant you Miss Green's outings can't have been too hot, but since she was wallowing so in her gratitude . . ."

"You're awful, you are just *terrible!*"

". . . at being accepted at dinner and cards afterwards, she never questioned her own feelings. Nor did Momsy ever question *her* feelings either. Queenie was doing good work, the widow's mite she owed to life. But she hated Miss Green. She hated her for her green teeth, her hirsute face. . . ."

"What's hirsute?"

"Hairy. My shaving brush is hirsute. *Mutterschön* hated her bristles, her warts, her liver spots, but most of all she hated her vulnerability—her need. The poor old dame. The dinners and cards were a subconscious exercise for her masochism."

"How do you know all this? I never heard of such things. Never! What were you doing? Sitting there taking notes?"

"From the age zero. When you don't have company, like you having George, for instance, when people come in you don't talk so much as listen and watch, and then it's a game. You start catching on to the way the wind is blowing, a web that grows out of this cache of your own little secrets. And in this case, the more so when it's the nurse—I used to think of her as the first person who had picked me up—the routine becomes more suspect. I'd be doing my homework, or else reading a book on the chesterfield."

"Pretending to, you mean. What was your father doing?"

"Playing cards too. He made up the threesome, smoking, having his rye and water, now and again drumming on his watch chain as he decided which card he wanted to play, nothing out of order in his life, his Madonna, or his angel as he called her, always centring her life on others." Brian paused, frowning, silent words in his head. "Incredible," he said anxiously, as if to himself, "beyond reason . . . Anyway, Miss Green had reached a stage in life where she was perhaps not too adept at getting food impaled on a fork past the green barrier reef of teeth. Sometimes bits of food would lodge in a corner of her lips, or else fly out of her mouth when her upper plate fell onto her tongue, and you know who never missed it. That's right! It was fuel for her fun with Miss Green, and at the same time it assuaged her wonderful sense of goodness."

"That's the cruellest thing I ever heard. No wonder I didn't seem to be getting to know your mother very well. Why would she want to purposely hurt someone, someone who once took care of her, a kind nurse . . . You've said awful things about your mother, even though I know you're fond of her. I guess when it comes to our parents, we're loyal. But she . . ."

"I know. You can never understand things like that about a person. Don't misunderstand, though. I love her very much, believe it or not; she has a great sense of humour. The trouble is all humour is based on people's shortcomings, their mistakes, faults; listen to mine some time. And card-time after din-dins . . ."

"Don't tell me. I don't want to hear any more." Landscape going by. A dry creekbed. White chickens strutting around a barnyard, and children swinging from tires hanging from a tree.

". . . was a joy for Miss Green. She was being accepted into a home, fed and even played with as an equal—a competitor with these nice people in a lovely game of cards. Yet somewhere, somewhere a way back in Miss Green's mind there was a little pinworm of fear: was she holding the cards right, was she putting down the right ones? Card-time became a bit of a hell to Miss Green, although she would never admit it."

"You and that damn rocking horse! A fiend watching! Or was it *The Mansions of Philosophy* by then?"

"And through the passage of time, Miss Green's trained-nurse's fingers had become unsure: *was* she holding her cards right? *was* she putting down the right run of spades? *was* that wonderful wife and mother, that most beneficent of beings, that comforter of her in her loneliness (once a month)—*was* she smiling superciliously? No, the thought was blasphemous. Yet the worm of doubt had now wormed its way to the forefront . . ."

"While you flipped pages, looking up where it talked about such things . . ."

"She began to put down the wrong cards and then try desperately to retrieve, her already unsteady hands became even shakier, and she'd suddenly clench the ill-fitting green teeth together lest they sound like moss-muffled castanets."

"I'd have shut my eyes. Oh, it's making me sick. Your mother's a skunk. I'd have caught her eye, yes I'd have picked up a fork or something, she'd have known by the way I held it what I had in mind. Those watchful eyes . . ."

"Plus the monthly directive: 'We keep our cards neat, Miss Green!' and the hand pounced on her miserably arranged cards on the table, tapped for emphasis and arranged in perfect fashion. Mother had done another good deed, she had made another kill, she had set another soul straight, goodness and light prevailed—except inside of Miss Green the worm had invaded the addled brain and had now taken over completely. Miss Green never came to dinner again. Miss Green never played cards again. Miss Green called Momsy an angel. Miss Green died soon after. Momsy cried at her funeral. Who killed Miss Green?"

"I know why you're telling me all this," I said after a minute, having let the seconds tick by, the car taking a bend in the road, coming out into sunlight, butterflies, merciful butterflies a more beautiful picture, and the woods of green cedar, my hand in Brian's lap, caressing his thigh deep down, and him remaining silent for those first seconds. I didn't know what he was thinking. "But you don't have to, you don't have to keep my mind occupied," I went on. "I wasn't . . ."

"No. I know. And while we're on the subject, let me tell you how proud I was of you today. I felt your father's absence every bit as much as you did, and I was, well, just full of admiration, believe me. You didn't once look sad, not even coming down the aisle."

"I promised myself I wouldn't. Anyway, it's George who deserves the credit, not me. I could have been moping around, I know when I got up this morning I was close to tears. George must have sensed it right off. He saw to it there wasn't time for me to feel blue. Whatever room I'd go into, and no matter what I did, he was always there. You know how quiet he is, and that tender way of talking to you, coming downstairs with a new stamp he'd been trying to get for more than a year, and we had a swell laugh over the manual the merchant marine gave him. All the things the ships have to do! the crew, I mean; when night comes and there's a blackout, they have to run around stuffing every crevice, all the holes, they practise on dried seaweed, long strings of it like netting. Plus how to swing themselves into their sleeping-hammocks when the ship's rolling. He was showing me, and we were killing ourselves laughing. He knotted two sheets together and tied the ends to the door handle and bed post. I was determined to try it too. Guess I'll never make it as a sailor! And first thing this morning we went round to the Lindenlea tennis courts and had two sets. Did I tell you that? I was up before six, couldn't sleep. Maybe I had a premonition that Mr. Mahoney wouldn't be able to make it . . . Say, remind me . . ."

"Don't forget you promised to call your dad tonight. Why don't we stay the night in Minden, and then go on to the cabin tomorrow? There's a place on the other side of the town, a small summer-hotel on Lake Kashigawigamog. It'd be more private than phoning from a drugstore."

"Okay."

The phone was down in the tuck shop, and Brian placed the call for me, ping-pong balls being batted back and forth across tables, a jukebox at the far end of the room, couples dancing, others reading notices on a green felt bulletin board, someone taking a splinter out of his foot with a pen-nib. And I heard Brian say, "You bet we are! . . . No. We stopped in Kingston for dinner first . . . You betcha. And by this time tomorrow she'll have learned how to paddle a canoe, that's what she wants to do first. . . . Not far, a half-hour drive . . . no, she's right at my elbow . . . I can't fend her off. . . ."

Did my father and I talk for a few seconds? three or four

minutes? me describing whatever tumbled into my mind, Colonel Lewis, Matt, the terrace in the garden out back, where we were taking pictures when the neighbour's bulldog bit one of the guests on the ankle; asking him again what he thought of me trying my hand at a canoe and wasn't that a departure from the old flatbottomed scow, Powerful Katrinka would have to learn the trick of how not to tip over and land in the drink.

Our conversation skirting on the near side of things: the real words omitted. It never occurred to me to ask him if he knew I had been thinking of him, not just when I walked down the church aisle, but all day, in the morning when I wakened, and through the silence of the noisy house, doorbell, phone, feet running up and down stairs. I did not think to tell him that as I left the house, it was as though he were there with me; not just to make him feel so, but so that he could tell all his friends what I had said. But I was very young, there were no words to find; only my eyes said: 'Now that it's taken place, a father feels deeply on his daughter's wedding day, the breath that's in her is the breath of him.' I could have given him this release, but I did not know how.

———

And it has haunted me. Still, maybe it was better that way; perhaps it maintained a distance for him, the gone of what had been. That day, there was nothing where he was but blue water to reflect upon, the tulle of clouds passing beyond, his face in the mirror as he combed his hair for dinner that evening, and moths zinging in the night around a porch light as darkness fell. That's what he'd have to remember. Wasn't that preferable? Isn't it so? Tell me!!

It's as though I'm talking to him now: 'Wasn't it better to be taking those pictures you showed me? the group on the boat? not posed, like the ones you'd have taken of our entourage; and the flowers, blooming in that field by the cliff, the enormous bees you described, surprising you?

'Be thankful, will you? And be thankful too that Mamma was herself again. For a few hours. It took the wedding, but then I guess you knew that all along. You did, didn't you?

'And while I think of it, wasn't the faux-pas I made at the table a good one on me? drinking to myself, and then saying, "Thank you." You can't imagine . . . Yes. You can. Didn't you once say nightmares are the funniest jokes of all? like that time you filled up my water-wings in the middle of the night and drew cat's faces on them? one was called Felix and the other Alice. "Meet Mr. and Mrs. Nightmare," you said. I never forgot.

'Say, did I ever tell you . . . no, I don't think I did. The waterwings are still in the cottage! and will be till the day the place collapses, or someone sets fire to it. I made sure, you bet—isn't that where they belong? The week the place was sold, Mamma and I began sorting through things, and you should have seen all the junk—after what? thirty-five years?—and did I ever get a surprise! To think Felix and Alice were there all that time. Oh, doesn't it give you a good feeling? They were down in the ice-house, at the bottom of an old Shredded Wheat carton. The two faces staring at me, and I said, "Hi!" I almost missed them, the straps were tangled around a dead cedar branch. I shook off all the sawdust and cobwebs. Good as new, I thought. Except for the buckle—it was kind of rusty, and Felix had mould on one cheek. I took them up the hill and got the ladder from under the verandah and climbed up on the roof. And you know that hole where the chimney bricks didn't fit? Well, right there's where they are. I wrapped them first in some straw, told Their Highnesses to behave themselves and tucked them back to back between the attic slats, then I nailed two pieces of board over. It was such a lovely day, a real September one, you know that blue in the air? I think there must have been a brush-fire somewhere, you could smell that far-off smoke. That's why I stayed up there for a while, hadn't even noticed it earlier because the pickles had boiled over and all you could smell was curry and brown sugar sizzling in juice all over the woodstove. So I lay back on the shingles sniffing the air with my eyes closed. Next thing I knew the train was screaming around the bend down at Cascades. Yes, you guessed it! A mad engineer. Wild as all the others once he got his hands on the whistle. Even so, there's nothing to beat a train hammering through silence, seeing the reflection in the river, past the wooden bridge, the pond in the village, thinning pines. I watched it long after it was out of sight. . . . Oh yes, I almost forgot to mention the tar. Next day, before getting on with the packing, I climbed up on the roof again with a can of tar, then went up to the farm and snitched some cement mix. Guess I was making sure everything was watertight. Felix and Alice were the squires of the manor now, weren't they? Those spring rains might have carried them away. . . .'

Strange, the unexpected symbolism of a pair of water-wings that had been out of sight, and mind, for so long a time. I wouldn't have thanked you for anything else in the place, not then. Cottage, contents—as far as I was concerned it could all go. But Felix and Alice were not for sale. When I'd discovered them in the icehouse, and had cleaned all the crud off, I tried fitting them on, and suddenly there was this faint whiff of banana oil, spilled glue from one of George's model airplane kits, I thought, or else that sticky smell ants leave when you squash a bunch together. What, I wondered, was I going to do with the pair of them, the faces looking at me? I couldn't just dump them in the gully with the rest of the rubbish, or worse, heave them into the river to sink to the bottom in some fusty old carton of odds and ends. It would have been like drowning them.

My father, tell me you understand. "Do you see?" I cry out. "Nothing is lost! The seasons come and go. But what is silenced, what can be denied of faces and forms when echoes go jingling by, all the specks of the human sound?" I must tell him what I think is true, that long after the flesh is no more, eyes, hands, bones, faceless as dust, the earth sends back—something, I think. Don't the boughs and waters sigh with the peace of their exalted dead, who wander in space? Sometimes, in a winter twilight, or in the teeth of a sleet-storm, or when at sunrise you stand in a valley sparkling with dew, what curve of sound rides the stillness, like a caress from the core of eternity laid upon the brow of a human being, who instinctively turns around, mysteriously willing to accept the invisible? Yes, I must tell him, finish what I started to say. I don't know though; except the reach I am being pulled toward at this moment, there's a sense of contact—imagined? real? Oh, can I? that far? I never know . . . sitting alone here, where am I, in this room that's drawing away from me? Beyond the rug I see a vacant lot, or is it a field? with thin clouds moving behind trees, and rain sprinkling out of the sun over a path I'm stumbling along. . . .

I've switched off the lamp, and in the north and south darkness, the clock ticking in deep silence, I am conscious of my lips moving. "So many Septembers have come and gone. My father, what are ashes?" Voice! Don't betray me, I'm clear-headed, so let me? "A thousand seasons of ice and sav-age sun, coming and going like ground-shadows, like the whiskered chalk-white water-wings, like wood-fires and bro-ken toys and a harvest moon, like the fantastic thump of a

toboggan flying through frozen wastes on a city hillside; like
the legend of a wedding, when you stared into space and saw
me. As I see you now, this minute. Stand nearer while I
speak of the passage of time: of sea smells and shipwrecks,
of grasses growing under the travelling stars, 'brittle' stars,
you said that night in July, 'like tears the moon has shed'.
And you, guardian of my wings, explaining each new rise of
ground, chiding me as I reckoned the one beyond, and the
one beyond that, until higher and higher and higher . . . until the Tea Gardens Restaurant the night before my wedding.
Do you remember how we stood outside for a minute, words
escaping us? happiness my tail-wind as you eyed me, smiling
at me, grinning, and in a squall of rain you sent me on my
way."

# XX

I slept with a man who turned me to gold.

The warmest of sleeps. No one day ever like the other. But
it went, and nothing could bring it back. There was everything, and yet nothing, to bind us. In the end, anyway.

It is warm now, late May and the Toronto sunshine decep-
tively like summer, the outside world gathering momentum
behind its screen of faint leaves, buds changing to foliage
overnight, birds and houseflies flitting about, even the
ants. . . . The air is a billion exits, the ground lies waiting for
what you intend to do: run, skip, tramp, disappear. I should
do that, skip, just skip town and get lost. But I can't, I
can't. And it's making me restless. I don't know why, but I
feel so imprisoned within myself lately. Tracking a distance
that suddenly winds itself into a coil in my insides. Lately it's
become more difficult, this past week it has. Brain and
memory growing silent. I did an about turn and started to cut

myself off from the past, asking myself what more does it want of me? Haven't I paid my dues?

It's temporary I guess. What do I expect when I've been so many places in my mind these past months? Tramp, tramp, living in this house and that, rising from other beds, other tables. And under how many changing skies and winds? Strange to be this restive, though, unquiet as I never have been before. It comes as a shock. I'll hear a clack of heels on the sidewalk out front, the sprint in someone's step hurrying by, click-clack, click-clack. People I imagine as in love, or about to be. Springtime belongs to them. That's what I'm thinking as I watch them pass. Pastels, grey flannels, shirt-sleeves, miniskirts and maxis, blazers, recycled jeans. Clickety-clack, clickety-clack. Gatsby hairdos under cloche hats. Jazzy shirts and ties, long denim skirts. Male, female, swinging along. On their way to meet someone for a drink? a lover maybe; where there are flowers, and perfume, a bottle of wine, and music coming from somewhere. Why not? Click-ety-click-clack. People with phone numbers in their pockets, an address, a subway token, or maybe only a dream. Or trav-ellers' cheques and a passport? Off to Martinique or Tibet? Grenadier Pond? Bahrain or Ontario Place?

And me, where's madame off to? Where is me-myself-and-I going? I know there's a place. . . .

Sultry May night, where nothing stirs, no clickety-clack, the evening sleeps. Out back I see lighted windows, dim con-tours of houses, shutter of a window hanging on its side, a shadowed door. And, in a white satin slip, a red-and-white fringed poncho over my shoulders, I sit like a statue in my back garden, shoes off, bare feet on the grass; above me, high as the night itself, the big elm I wanted to climb a few months back that night the wind was so fierce. Where's the moon? No moon? Well, all else is perfect. While the pores of my body shiver. Dah-dah, dah-dee-dum, and my toes feather-ing the turf, what was that song? "Over the highway and un-der the sea . . ." Who knows I'm here but me? I'm mirrored in the night, and I see the face of a girl . . . where snow cov-ers the ground. . . .

Cold dumb flesh of mine, crying out at shocks running through its nerves. I bend down and pick up the cat, velvet fur, green eyes blinking contentedly. Soon now, while she sleeps in my lap, what will she be dreaming of when at last I reach that field, a field far from the sepia sandbar, more dis-tant than the hills?

# XXI

—◆—

Gales whip across open space, sweeping the white distance before me. Silent noise, a plaintive whistle in the wind that trails eastward to the heavens, out of hearing. Gone. What is happening?

Nineteen months later now, a year and a half after my wedding. Life, not just Brian's and mine but everybody else's, the whole world's it seems, is being *done* instead of lived. For the time being the future is postponed. People, faces, voices; they carry on as before, and speak of going home again. Everyone is somewhere else. The roofs they look out on are unfamiliar, dreary, and fill them with longing, 'Where will I be tomorrow?' they ask. Something will turn up: a buddy, maybe . . . someone to talk to, get drunk with if they like.

The war. Uniforms, civilians, always on the move, possessions forever at hand. Strangers brought together, joined by a common task. Days that seem out of order. But evening comes; in the cities, around the depots and bases there's always something they can find to do. They take a girl out dancing, big ballrooms and supper clubs, a canteen, small orchestras, pick-up groups who play Tommy Dorsey, Benny Goodman, Glenn Miller: "I've Got a Girl in Kalamazoo", "Sleepy Lagoon", "The Jersey Bounce", "Don't Take Your Love From Me". They raise glasses, a pensive, emotional toast to the future, two people alone together, or in company, wondering where they will be this time tomorrow. They laugh, and love, until the uniforms are on the move again, packing a kit and wishing that just for once they could wake up in their own bed.

The war. And the tail-end of a winter. Brian's in the army, stationed for the present at Three Rivers. And home is now the furnished house in Dorval that George has rented for Mamma and me. Yet though things have fundamentally

295

changed, so much seems almost the same as before: the
lovely autumn just passed, and the long winter passing too,
life going along; at intervals, Brian and George coming home
on leave; and twenty miles away, the bright lights of Montreal for a night out on the town. The Samovar night club,
the Normandie roof; dinner and an evening with my father,
seeing him off at the station on the train back to Ottawa. A
momentum entirely different—yet retaining a certain softness,
in spite of the anxieties of a nation at war. Being alive . . .
we're here, like everyone else. Each finding his own sleepy lagoon. Change? Somehow, the same as we've known. Except
for my father's absence from our home.

---

But what *is* happening? Leaden skies above the white space
that lies before me. My feet are cold and my nose is running.
It's taken me more than half an hour to get here on foot. Bitter winds twist across the snowy fields, fields that are bleak
and empty, punctured by the broken lines of fence-wires and
posts sticking out of the drifts. I see this landscape clearly;
why, in the last year I've come here day after day. Yes. I did
that. When it was *then*, before—when it was still a white
splendour. Or a green one. Mornings. A midday. Or an afternoon. They hold me, those times. Days I don't forget. Dorval. My lips part. Am I ready to tell myself the next? My
mind balks, as though turning away from what it's visualizing. Will I always do this?

A plane warms up, engines that speak to me, in a tongue
I'll always . . . on the frozen ground I lie on my belly, chin
on my hands, listening, waiting. I open an eye. A half-mile
beyond, a famous river, almost obscured by the rise and dip
of dreaming fields.

Vibrations run through the ground under my body, a
rumble, as if the earth were cracking. Over my head the slow
rise of a plane; painted circles on the fuselage, bull's-eyes that
are red and black over mud-grey. Camouflage. My insides
tighten, a split-second uneasiness inhaling the cry of wind at
its tail. Next breath, and the next, a kind of excitement—the
surge of noise, throbbing engines, the plane's lift into the sky.
Seconds later, another plane, and another. Suddenly I almost
weep; a moment of wonder: the long crossing over the North
Atlantic, travelling in darkness. Why, they're still pioneering—flying by the seat of their pants, as the pilots put it.

Sometimes I become overwhelmed thinking about the part being played, the ties. I can't help it. Some people grouse about the war, they get cynical and say it's England's war and not ours. But I never agree.

I lie with my cheeks flushed, wishing I could shout an emotion: apprehension, exultation, any sound of sense. Instead I lick my upper lip; my nose is still running. Look at this four-engined whopper roaring down the runway.

I watch the undercarriage lift higher, the nose pushing slowly, steadily against the sky. A downdraft ripples across the pelt of my electric-seal coat. Like shudders encasing my body. I rest my chin on my hands again, green woollen mitts one on top of the other, and study the slow climb into the clouds, which are bulbous and low, March grey. Into the greyness the plane heads east. It leaves. It leaves behind the snowy fields and leaden skies, the warm frozen ground under my body, and the rented house by the St. Lawrence.

Above me, the sound diminishing; a warplane, a Liberator bomber. Out of Dorval Airport and into the winds of 1943.

One plane, two, three . . . four more . . . One right after the other. Lancasters, Flying Fortresses, Hudsons, Mosquitoes. Bound, ultimately, by one or another checkerboard route, for Prestwick.

What I'm watching is the Ferry Command in operation. Air crews recruited from the R.A.F. in England, along with Canadian and American civilian personnel—bush pilots, and flight engineers, navigators and radio men who have qualified as air crew. Delivering heavy bombers, long-range and medium-range bombers; combat aircraft, manufactured as far away as California, now taking off on the first leg of their journey to Britain.

Is George in the plane that's just left? Or the Liberator waiting to take off? the one warming up? That brown aircraft with the propellers whirling—is it a Boston? Maybe he's in that one. They must get kind of jumpy, waiting, waiting . . . Gee. If you're not acquainted with someone in the Ferry Command, a person wouldn't believe the places, the distances these guys have to travel sometimes in order to make one single delivery. Holy crow. Checkerboard route is right! The planes going out today, for instance. Who knows where they'll end up ten hours from now, or even twenty? The weather briefings and flight plans given to them during briefing this morning aren't necessarily the final word, not at this time of year you bet. The elements can be tricky, and change in a matter of hours. Who knows? Maybe the planes I'm now watching *are* heading directly across from here, re- fuelling first at Goose Bay in Labrador, and again at Gander in Newfoundland. But after Gander, it's anybody's guess: Iceland next? and then on to Prestwick? Or by the time they've reached Gander will their flight plans have been changed? meteorological services now advise weather condi- tions over the North Atlantic too risky? It's happened a lot this winter. It's the head winds. Plus wind-force storms. How can those *crates*—oh, excuse me. I shouldn't be talking that way. It slips out when I'm nervous—I mean how can these bombers buck head winds for 3,000 miles? plus the hazards of the wings icing up? That's when they set course and head for the South Atlantic. Lord. All the way down to Brazil, and then across to Africa.

One thing about this trip, though. George knew last night where his first stop is to be. Bermuda. To pick up a flying boat, a Catalina. Bermuda to Greenwich direct, that means twenty-two hours' flying time, minimum. No wonder they refer to the plane as one of those "lumbering cats".

---

On days I'm not working—for the elderly doctor up the street who sort of retired—when I'm not over there, then for something to do I come here. George's departure days for sure.

Bombers taking off. I wait hours for minutes of this view. And I lie there feeling proud, excited, swallowing snow whipped by the wind, so full of awe I could bust! History being made. *It is* pioneering.

Difficult walking over today. Here it is, almost the end of March, yet nothing thaws. Snowdrifts keep filling the hollows in the fields, and if it weren't for the ice-crust, I'd have sunk to my knees. Days like this, when there's a wind chill, in or- der to keep my circulation moving I walk around, up and down mostly, or else I run back and forth until a plane stops warming up, which means it's time to plop down, flatten my- self again.

Not that I'm in the way; I'm not that close. Near enough though. There's this sensation I get when the plane lifts over me, it's as though I were being scooped up by the undercar- riage, as if I were going with them! It lasts so short a time— seconds? Then, once they're up, they're frozen into my vision.

Chin propped on mitts, legs crossed, one galosh over the other. My eyes follow them. Even when I lose sight of the plane, I follow them. I never wave. I have to put my hands in my pockets to keep myself from waving at bare sky.

Soon now, a few minutes? an hour? when all is silent and the familiar figures of the ground crews finally disappear in back of the hangars, I will retrace my steps, running home across the fields, up over the slope, along the creek of shell-ice, through the bush, and on down Pine Beach Road to St. Joseph's Boulevard. . . . Wonder what Brian's doing right now? In a way I'm glad I'm not there, near the camp, I mean. I'd hate to see him trying to be a bloke in the army, as he puts it. What a life. Just as well they don't encourage wives to live near the barracks. I thought about it; that was last April, after he'd joined up and was posted to Cornwall. But I'd rather wait and see him on his furloughs, have that to look forward to. "I'd rather go and stay with George and Mamma in Dorval," I said. "That's one of the reasons George took that furnished house in the first place, so we could all be together. And with you only a hundred miles or so away . . ."

"I won't always be, the way they move us cattle around. Sounds like a good idea, though. No point in skulking around a boarding house when you can have all the comforts of home."

What a darb of a house it is too! When I arrived and saw it from the outside, I said to George: "My God! It's a mansion. What rich millionaire built this for himself?" George could hardly drag me inside; he followed me around the grounds with my overstuffed suitcase banging his legs, patiently changing it from one hand to the other as I peered up at the stained-glass windows. "Is that a turret room up there?" I asked, goggle-eyed, standing on tiptoe, "Is that one of the bedrooms?"

"Why don't you come inside and see?"

Brian gasped when I first took him to my room. I ran up the stairs ahead to show him. He looked around and said, "Holy old dyin' Dora! Christ! You should see the fucking sleeping quarters I wake up in . . . not that I ever remember going to bed." And he sits on the bed to test it, stretching back on the pillows, hands clasped behind his head. A June night, and the open hearth crackling downstairs. Mamma putting another log on the fire she had set to welcome him home. George still away, not due back for a week or two yet. And in two days Brian is gone.

To stretch my legs I run back and forth across the snow; suddenly I trip, go sprawling, pick myself up, and sing to the grey skies:

> It may be that death's bright angel
> Will speak in that chord again,
> It may be that only in Heaven . . .

Tomorrow George and I were supposed to go skiing. But last night he got this bloomin' call from a pilot in Bermuda, would he get down right away? they needed him to help take a Catalina over. Twice now he's had to cancel a four-day leave. He must be one of their best radio officers! I wanted to say, 'You need some rest'; I was thinking of his last three flights, all the way down to Brazil first before they could make it over. But I checked myself.

When he came back from the phone he was laughing, chomping on peanuts, throwing them up in the air and catching them in his mouth. He never shows disappointment. He told me, "Bermuda tomorrow. Got to take a Cat over." Then he turned and went back to the kitchen to telephone Daddy in Ottawa. George never leaves without calling him.

Maybe that's why he woke me up this morning—something he's never done before—he thought I was disappointed about not going skiing. But no, I think there was something else on his mind. That last trip over from Natal . . . maybe *that's* why he came into my room! Never occurred to me. I don't like thinking about that Dakar business: an unarmed plane being chased halfway round the Mediterranean. Those fighters—I've seen them on the newsreels, I know how fast they are. The Ferry Command planes don't have much of a chance; a transatlantic crossing means they're almost out of fuel, and worse, unarmed! What was the matter with the ground crew at Dakar that they didn't alert them?

George doesn't know I heard about it. But word gets around. Even when he's away the boys still like to drop over for a meal, after a flight they like to go somewhere instead of putting in time in a room. And I hear them talking when I'm in the kitchen. That's when I get my info. The boys have to talk about the rough trips some time, I guess, get it out of their system, make out that it's nothing, joke about it. The Mosquitoes, for instance, being made of plywood, and the heat from the exhaust being too close to the wings. Who was it, the pilot? or the flight engineer? who just got the plane's fire out in time or they'd have dropped into the Atlantic. But they're uneasy, I can tell. They've no idea I'm watching them from the kitchen or listening in the hallway. First I bang pots a little, use the eggbeater, then the details start to come. Like the Mosquito that was on fire. I move across the hall into the pantry, and see them shift around in their chairs; then they get nervous and silent, cross their legs and lose themselves in the firelight. I come in the room and sit down and do the same, cross and uncross my legs whenever they do, which passes unnoticed. It's like a reflex, the same as a yawn. Are they thinking what I'm thinking?

---

Propellers. The next one to leave: I know that final thrust, the last whine of the engine. I turn around before I lie down, have a look to see "the job". Yep. It's a Boston all right. That means a smaller crew. Do I know any of them? Is Tommy with him this trip? George says Tommy's the best navigator the R.A.F.'s got, and his best friend now. He'd planned to bring him for Christmas dinner, but they were away then, in South America.

Up it goes, painted circle, khaki camouflage; faster this time, a slant up, and out over the St. Lawrence. This time I keep my hands pinned under my chin, and tell myself it's the ones heading over the Channel need luck: they're going into combat. The Boston, a dot now, has only the sky to worry about.

My breathing makes ice-webs on my mitts, and I'm thinking, no registers here to dry them on. Registers. Where the old furnace at home—home?—blew hot air up through the grating. My mind wanders . . . no, there are no warmed sleepers to curl up in. No "Charleston" and "Black Bottom" to take refuge in. I am here now, in the year of my dancing "Boogie Woogie" galoshes and my "In the Mood" sweater and skirt. With an extra pair of mitts stuffed into my coat pockets. For when I walk or run home to the house by Louis Bay on St. Joseph Boulevard. It's the wind makes me run, I feel I have to keep up. I'm in its pocket, that's the feeling I get, being carried over this white space; and singing a new song that's out, well, not so very new, 1940? two or three years old anyway. "Don't Take your Love From Me."

Would you take the wings from butterflies
So they can't fly?
Would you take away the ocean's roar
And leave it just a sigh?

For the life of me I can't remember, I don't even know
where I was the first time I heard that song but I think I
must have been somewhere special, maybe at the Standish, or
at the Gatineau Club with a gang. Wherever I was, I wrote
the words on a scrap of paper, which I brought to Dorval. I
took it out the other day, and put the thing back safe in my
snapshot album. Must have written it in the dark, the words
run all over the place. That's why I hang onto it: some day
I'll know what I was thinking of then. Was I at the Gatineau
Club with Frederick and his friends? Was that the night I ex-
cused myself to everyone and said I was going to the Ladies'
and instead went straight out the front door into a taxi and
all the way home from the Aylmer Road to Elmdale Avenue?
If so, if that *was* the night, then that's the reason I can't read
my writing: I was feeling guilty, there was someone else . . .
I had fallen in love with Brian, I couldn't sit at that table another minute. It was Brian who made me go in the first place.
That was a surprise. Brian said: "You owe it to the guy to at
least see him, don't you think?"

I couldn't tell Frederick. Couldn't face him. He was too
gentle, too nice a person to do that to. I must still have cared
about him too much to have seen his pain. I guess not
enough though; he had a right to have something more than
an empty chair left behind.

The wind, in fact the gale, will run me all the way home.
And I'll still sing that song, the one about butterflies and the
ocean's roar. I always do in a gale. I'll run every step of the
way back. And I'll put the fire on, maybe play the record
player. Yes. "To a Water Lily," that's what I'll pick out first,
and the "Indian Love Lyrics" next. A change of music that's
quiet. I'll stack the records on the spindle and let them spin
away. Then once the fire gets going, as soon as the kindling
stops shooting sparks onto the rug, I'll pour Mamma and me
a nice rum, Myers Plantation. George smuggled it back two
months ago from Puerto Rico.

Yes. I'll break open the Myers, and Mamma and I will
take our rum-and-coke to the living room where we'll sit in
front of the fire. I know exactly what she'll say! "Well lassie,

did you help them get off the ground?" She and I are having
fun now. It wasn't like that at first, not those days last spring
and summer . . . we were still trying to get used to living together again. I was a gloomy sad-sack, wanting my own place
with Brian again.

"You bet," I'll say. "And you know what, Mamma? Another Boston left today!" They're her favourite. (On George's
departure days she never goes to the airfield. She says it
might bring bad luck, so she watches instead from the back
porch.) And the next thing Mamma will say: "Did you draw
them something in the snow again?" I did that once. I traced
a message with the toe of my galosh, big block letters that
said: K I S S E S. But I never did again. When I stood up
and looked down at the letters, I thought it looked silly.

"Well lassie," my mother will murmur again, without adding anything in particular. And both of us will giggle, at the
fire, at the rum, which we have yet to sip. Then one of us
will say, "For what we are about to receive . . ." And the
first swig a long one, the gullet burning deep down, deep
down, further. While we sit with our thoughts: are the planes
still on an eastward course? over the frozen wastes of
northern Quebec yet? and George, Radio Officer R. L. G.
Watson, civilian, in his navy-blue uniform with its blue
flashes, busy at his panels?

George says the civilian crews have to be in uniform in
case they're captured—there's always the chance they'll fall
into enemy hands, and the uniform guarantees them
prisoner-of-war status. The Ferry Command gave them officers' rank, and came up with a swell-looking uniform, I
must say. Dark navy gabardine, silver buttons that have the
R.A.F. crest on them, and a cap with the traditional Latin-in-
scribed badge.

Poor Brian. While I have the pleasures of a grate-fire, a
comfy chair, and nice kitchen premises to prepare a few
rums, he's slugging it out in an army camp. Right now he's at
Three Rivers, taking advanced infantry training. He joined
the infantry because he was afraid they'd try to make a clerk
out of him, put him in an office filing blotters, he said; anything was better than that.

"Even that hole in Cornwall," he announced, home on
leave. Two months of the army under his belt and not sitting
too well. "A tin shaving mug to eat out of, for Christ's sake.
Or else a chipped granite plate some lout's urinated in." And
then, a more resigned tone setting in: "Oh, well," he sighed,

having no illusions, "there was bound to be another war. Our so-called heroes in the permanent force were getting restless, time for the desk clerks to play toy soldiers again. Can't have them gathering dust, now can we? How long's it been? Twenty years?"

Boy, do I remember that day. It was the best time I ever remember. Six months ago, seven almost. Labour Day weekend. A Saturday afternoon when Brian and George were both home, the first time since we'd moved to Dorval that they'd had leave together. On the Friday, to the surprise of us all, old Doctor Marais had said why didn't we borrow his car, wouldn't the four of us like to spend the holiday weekend at the cottage?

We piled into the maroon Studebaker that afternoon. Brian driving, and George and me beside him; Mamma in back with her feet up on the velour seat, chattering away to the dog Jimmy (named for Jimmie Carman at the farm), pulling him (under protest) onto her lap and showing him the landmarks, for God's sake! Beside herself at the thought of seeing Sumach Point again.

Next morning, Saturday, George and Brian and I had driven to Ottawa to have lunch with my father. And now we were back at the cottage, sitting out under the trees having a beer, the two boys glad to be in civvies again, old pants and striped cotton shirts they'd dug out of a carton in the attic; musty-smelling, I remember, yet still redolent of country air, the mingled odours of pine, sweat, and puffball-pulp.

"Toy soldiers my foot!" Mamma exclaimed, appearing through the sumachs on her way back from the privy. "Whatever makes you think *they* could start a war, Brian? It's the munitions makers who are behind it. With their fat bellies! Same as the last war; we were saying it then too. Munitions makers and international bankers. They're the ones! The whole lot greedy and power-mad with their fat bellies!" She sat down on the grass, ready to proceed, her hands clasped around her knees.

"Hitler doesn't have a big stomach," I said. "Who's *they*?"

In her entire lifetime, my mother's one and only soapbox; a diatribe that began the winter we spent with Granny (perhaps before that, even), those long Sunday afternoons when she and her brother and sister would be having their wee tots, arguing between themselves, or with friends who'd dropped in (like their second cousin from Glasgow who had lost an arm in the War, the empty sleeve folded and rolled up flat, pinned to his jacket where the shoulder socket would have been; and another man, a worse casualty: a hole with puckered skin grown over where his eye had been). All of them, going on about the plight of the boys home from the trenches. "Your Uncle Tom was a stretcher bearer," Mamma would say for the umpteenth time, turning to George and me with despair, or anger. Or both. At that point Uncle Tom looking quite pleased with himself. "And him a boy of seventeen!" she'd say again, beseeching him. "You could have been one of these shell-shocked wrecks wandering the streets. Or come back with your face blown away. Well, they'll get no son of mine!" *They!*

"Don't worry, Mamma," I had said the first time. "Don't be mad. Everything's all right, isn't it?"

"Ach, Mary," said Aunt Isa, sighing, shaking her head. "They're too wee, Mary. Mercy, they're only bairns. They weren't even borrr . . ."

"Their father—two and a half years on a minesweeper!" my mother went on, walking up and down. "Out there in the Atlantic, up to Greenland and God knows where else. I never knew from one day to the next if I'd ever see him again. And that's the point I'm making, Isa," she said, stopping in her tracks, her face softening as she beckoned George and me to her. "I want them to understand *now*, impress it on them when they're young!" Pulling us in, one on either side, the three of us like a triumvirate, standing on guard. "It's the children growing up, today's generation who'll be in charge of the world. They'll see to it that there will be no more wars. . . . Run along now, kids, find something to do," she said, less intent, almost over the wild and oblique moment that had consumed her. Almost, but not quite. "Heroism is a thing of the past, anyway. What glory is there in war?" Muttering away: "Krupp making his millions . . ."

And so here we were, the children of this new world she had spoken of. Still a world of ideals, our thinking scarcely a generation removed from that of her own. What was idealism? Wasn't that what we had always known? It wasn't a big word that had suddenly come from somewhere, but an inherent condition—like one of our vital organs. What difference was there between idealism and breathing? We had grown up in a quiet, merry, hopeful, at times precarious, but for the most part blissful culture that had not yet had time to go through transition, the Depression banding us all together. Yes. The world still seeming a very small place indeed. For

its known dimensions were one's backyard, perhaps a town
you took a train to for a visit with friends, or a city where a
parent went on business. Why, the telephone and the radio
still seemed a miracle. No one needing to do "his own thing".
And human beings everywhere were not far-flung, but close,
millions of people you thought of as like yourself: on the
face of this earth, the other guy somehow a part of your own
spirit, no one felt alone. As for the war, it was simply a matter of an isolated race that had suddenly risen up and was
threatening your existence. You had to defend yourself the
same as you would against someone coming to burn your
house down.

That was the external and internal climate of my time and
the generation from which we had sprung, chattering away
on a 1942 Gatineau hillside, discussing the war. Something
we did rarely when we were all together like that; the same
when we were with my father. We talked of music, the Metropolitan Opera, baseball, hockey, the revival of an operetta
and when did anyone think a touring company might bring
*Bittersweet* or *The Vagabond King* to Ottawa, or Montreal?
We spoke of ration coupons getting low, and what friend
could we invite to visit? someone who ate like a bird and
obligingly divested theirself of a fistful of unused coupons.
We would compare notes on a funny new book; agree that
Amos 'n' Andy must be well-to-do by now; wonder what it
would be like to live on Sable Island. And while the earth
turned on its axis of hard cold reality, we were asking one
another: *"Did you see that pure white moon the other
night?"*

Dialogues and interrogations like that, spiked by my
mother's occasional outbursts about armaments and the youth
of the world, waiting her opportunity to shout at the helpless
skies, the ground, the walls. As pointless as that. And now,
hadn't I just tried to switch her from "fat bellies" to her even
more visual, if less ranting, views on Adolf?

"No," she said, getting up from the grass to straddle a
bench, "the squint-eyed little runt's avoirdupois is all in his
lungs. He's bow-legged, have you ever noticed? As for that
fat pig Mussolini . . ." She wrenched a tattered strip of dry
cedar bark from a corner of the rustic table, and, intently
coiling the shreds around her thumb, turned to Brian and
George. "Gun fodder, that's what you are, nothing but gun
fodder. Wee Willie King may be a sap, but the man was on
the right track when he said no conscription. If all the na-

tions of the world got together, if every country forgot about the blasted League of Nations . . . what were they but a bunch of dreamers? with their disarmament conferences! If the countries of the world decided to call on the little man, just let them sit down and talk . . ."

"You shouldn't be taken over by all that propaganda, Mamma," George said quietly, getting up from his chair to retrieve a birdnest hanging from a twig, an empty nest that had been there for years, surviving how many winters? "There's more to it than international bankers, you know," he added thoughtfully, looking for a more secure place higher up. "You get one man who goes berserk," he continued, reaching around the tree-trunk to shove the nest into a higher fork where the tree was split, "and before you know it he has the whole country behind him, trying to take over the world. First it was the Kaiser who had to be stopped, now it's Hitler. Sometimes I can't help but feel this is only a continuation of the First War. Do you remember me telling you about that flight I went over on the week before Easter?" coming back to sit down again, "when Tommy my navigator invited me to spend the weekend with his parents in Yorkshire?"

"Tommy?" Mamma asked. "Yes, I remember, George. What about Tommy?" Still twisting the cedar, up, down, over, under, listening, wanting to understand, but knowing there would be no answer for her. How could a mother, my mother anyway, accept theorizing in any form when it meant accepting the possible maiming, or even death, of her son?

"I thought I would tell you," George continued, "about the time I came to this conclusion. It was the night we drove over to an R.A.F. base outside Tommy's home town. He had wanted to see if some of his old buddies from before were still at the station. When we got there, most of the guys were out on a raid, so we relaxed in the officers' mess waiting for them to get back. And that's when I learned something." He stretched his legs briefly, then crossed one knee over the other.

"There were only a few of the older guys there at the time," he said. "In their late forties, I'd say, and what interested me was the fact some of them had been in the Flying Corps—I could tell by their ribbons. We were all just chatting away, they were telling us about the raid on Liverpool the night before, or the night before that, some of them wanting to know about the Ferry Command, which aircraft was the toughest to fly, and was it rough going when we en-

countered gales over the Atlantic, things like that. After a
while, they started swapping tales about what it was like in
the First World War, and how this one was no easier, the
destruction and frustration. Listening to them, I got to thinking about it, I mean about *both* wars. And it seemed to me
all we're doing is trying to finish what had begun then, in
1914. And on the drive back I said to Tommy, 'It's not just a
matter of King and Country, is it, patriotism and that sort of
thing?' I meant it was something deeper than that, something
else besides duty. I tried to say it. I remember he was looking
straight ahead while I was talking . . . he's kind of a quiet
person, you know, and I wasn't sure what he was thinking.
But do you know what his answer was? He said, 'It was
scribbled down in a single line of poetry one of your Canadian soldiers wrote in the trenches in 1915. Colonel John
McCrae.' "

"No kidding, George?" I exclaimed, pleased as I thought
about it, silent for a time, as we all were. There wasn't any
need for George to tell us which line or phrase of the poem,
for what Canadian, then anyway, was not familiar with "In
Flanders Fields"? "To you from falling hands . . ." "That's
it!" I said to myself. I didn't know which line Brian and my
mother had thought of. Nor did they say.

"That's the only time Tommy and I ever talked about it,"
George said after a moment, "that way, anyway. But it felt
kind of good to have someone . . . well, you don't like to
force your sentiments on anyone, start making a spiel, especially when you don't know them very well." He stretched
his legs forward, and leaned his head back on the rim of his
chair. "It's the way Tommy and I both feel, Mamma," he
said, not so much soberly or firmly as idly, looking up at the
leaves, his eyes with an expression I had not seen before, as if
some half-forgotten sensation of the mind had regained its
original significance: ". . . that the war is a kind of faith,"
he said in a low tone. "You know what I mean, don't you?"

"George is right, Mamma," I said. "He's damn well right
and you know it."

"Do I?" she replied, eyes downcast, the cedar holding her
thoughts. I remember she was still in her bathing suit, with a
multi-coloured cardigan pulled around her shoulders, the fes-
tive-looking orange velvet ribbon tied around her hair still
damp.

"Try to see it that way," George said gently, reaching
across and taking her hand, shreds of cedar bark suddenly

uncoiling under his fingers as she released one end. "What does it really matter *who's* behind the war?" he urged, pressing down on her wrist. "*It's happened.* What's everyone supposed to do? Go and live in the Arctic? let them take over Canada as well as Britain? And! what about all the innocents? The innocents on both sides?" he added, slowly sitting back again. "We all just have to say 'damn it' and get it over with. Can you understand that?"

"Innocents on both sides?" she asked, stunned. "*Both* sides? I don't care a hoot in hell . . . What are you saying, laddie?" Hot sun drilled through a parting in the branches, my mind seizing up for an instant, drifting away by itself in thought, wondering what my father would have said had he been there. While I did appreciate how my mother felt, though not because I agreed—how could I form a picture in my mind, let alone believe that there were villains, villainous politicians seated around the table planning destruction?—it was her anxiety I sympathized with. I was now only beginning to grasp that these highly charged emotional responses were simply a crucial, honest attempt to make the whole *world* face reality (as she saw it); she didn't want to be doing it by herself.

As for my father, the politics of war did not lie as heavily on him as did its injustices, the loneliness and anxieties brought about by displacement. These were things I was feeling myself and could sense in him, parents raising a son to manhood and hoping the day would never come he'd have to drop what he was doing and deliver himself, happily or unhappily, to the ultimate test, be it beaches, skies, seas or the mud of battlefields. And in that instant I thought, These are the things my father would be conscious of right now, when George has spoken of his talk with Tommy, and the innocents on both sides. For the sight of a uniform was familiar to him; crossing streets, or as he looked out a window, just working away in his office even, he'd be remembering when he too had been part of an ideal.

Not until several months had passed (had war just broken out?) had I begun to see the quieter, more resigned approach my father had. For example, my mother would refer once more to the young German soldier, Paul, in *All Quiet on the Western Front*, whose final act (in the movie version) was to reach for a butterfly he had seen. A story that haunted not just my mother but my father as well. And during one of those times, an evening when the movie was being discussed,

I heard my father say, "Don't you think the butterfly represented an ideal, Mimi? . . . Wasn't Paul's reaching up an affirmation, that he had attained that ideal before he died?"

"The butterfly represented his life," she retorted, "and he reached out because he wanted it back! Cecil! How could a butterfly . . . how could you possibly see it as standing for an ideal, when it appeared above a rat-infested trench? Some ideal! The cause of him being shot by a sniper."

"He wouldn't have known what hit him," my father replied, "it was over so fast."

"If only he hadn't stuck his head up . . . Armistice was hours away . . ." Gravely abandoning herself to thoughts of how she had wanted the story to end.

"The lad was transfixed," my father said. "In spite of all his training, he was so taken at seeing a butterfly, the beauty of it, something alive . . . the death around him all those years and now there was new life, *there was something living after all*. So he raised himself up to touch it. And in his mind, he *had*—before it was over for him. A transcendence . . . that's what I meant. It suggests that the end doesn't . . . that it's not always one of agony, even in a trench."

"I never thought of it that way," she said. A "transcendence"? I asked myself. What did that mean?

Now, of course, it was another war, and the time was 1942; two years since my father had been present to *understand*, to assuage and divert Mamma's reasoning—in short, to lift screaming Mimi down from her soapbox, telling her she was talking through her hat, that people would take her for a crazy old woman and if she didn't watch out a famous international banker in Switzerland would be suing her for libel. Three years had passed since we had heard Neville Chamberlain's broadcast: "This country is now at war with Germany."

And, had my father been with us at the cottage that day, the conversation veering off in a direction it had never taken before, with the children of my mother's world trying to find a middle road in the face of the words she knew by heart, my father seeing her argument growing silent, thoughts behind the mask of her face sinking deeper and deeper into the curl of cedar, I wondered if my father would have said, "Whether we rail outwardly or inwardly, there's no one escapes asking himself about the whys of war. But, in the his-

tory of man, who has ever found an answer?" As he had
done the day war was declared?

I had no idea. His face appeared briefly in the vision of
my mind as I glanced at my brother, seeming so like his father just then, the thoughtful deliberation which had now returned, searching not for a logic but some remote and
nameless point to it all, wanting to find something worth-
while, to see something beautiful no matter what the laws of
fate. And somehow finding it, I thought. I sensed then how
far my brother had come within himself.

Even though I could not have defined it at the time—any
more than George could have himself—he had gained the insight, as I had yet to, that one's responsibility did not begin
and end with one's own person and the lives it touched.

How much of this would he have known consciously then?
Aware of this intangible new allegiance, perhaps wondering
what it had been born of, or even why. Knowing only that
his life belonged to the universe as well as to those he loved.

No. I could never have expressed it at the time. I just knew
that deep inside, something meaningful had been added to his
life. A radiant yet dark and silent truth. Gone was the
longed-for thrill of flying, dipping down over lakes and
mountain streams, climbing again into patches of blue, or
into a blizzard. Was it only my imagination, I wondered? or
intuitive truth? *Had* there been too many flights over convoys
at sea? that'd be bound to give you a sinking feeling, you'd
be looking down at the future instead of ahead, or up; and
too many take-offs and landings at bases in the Azores, Africa, Gilbraltar, at Dakar where men were hunched over the
anti-aircraft batteries I'd heard pilots discussing in a Montreal
hotel lobby. Montages through my mind as I thought of
newsreel footage, with the played-down score of music behind a narrator's voice, entire cities in England being levelled
. . . that in itself!

But then, I thought, total belief in what you were doing
softened the edges, didn't it? Or did it? Wasn't that what
Brian was thinking too? What were his *real* thoughts? Well, I
said to myself, of the four of us, only Brian in his own way,
that sense of irony, half in earnest and half in jest, never taking himself seriously, could swing a world without brightness
(and it was, that's the way we all felt, those times we allowed
ourselves to think of it) to one of gleeful and wretched
amusement. In a war where innocence and idealism fought
yet another, inner conflict—would this mindless boredom,

this loneliness and discomfort ever end? when could we all go home and get on with our lives again?—so far, Brian had maintained his equilibrium by having no expectations beyond what the next day might bring. "Swill, and a hot bath if I'm lucky, or a forty-eight-hour pass," he'd said that afternoon. "Isn't eternity now made up of that?" Adding something about the large intestine being poverty-stricken, and, "Maybe I should try eating the soap, at least it's clean. A sensitive chap like me is particular . . . What's so funny?" And so it went. With the flow of his words, I was left thinking, Isn't it crazy? It's not so terrible for them . . . not if a man can inwardly keep his distance, remove his thoughts from the dust and grime, the exhaustion. "Once more over the barbed wire," he said. "The obstacle course, the shooting range . . . it beats living any time!" Yes. So it went.

For Brian had taught me that a man in the services went to bed at night, wondering, Why am I here? What am I doing? My life's going by . . . I've only got my youth once. Either you lay awake cursing your lot, he said, or else you stopped asking yourself questions, and instead looked back on a certain day, the one just passed, for instance, spotting incidents you would caricature in your mind to keep you from dying of frustration. Self-knowledge of a different kind. In Brian's case, the paradox of caring, and yet not allowing yourself to care. And yet caring anyway.

"Sure, I can understand it, George," Brian said. He was replying to George's declaration that the war was a kind of trust, refilling my brother's glass from a chilled bottle he'd taken out of the paper bag at his feet, an auxiliary supply of Old Vienna lager we'd stopped for in Hull on our way back to the cottage. "But that doesn't mean I'm in love with the idea. Why should I get my head blown off? My head and then some! But you're perfectly right," he added, the words coming less quickly, but emphatically. "While I'm not promoting the goddamn army, or for that matter anything to do with this hellish way of living, I know what you're trying to say, what you're feeling." Plunging a rubber stopper into the neck of the bottle: "I know exactly, believe me. Deep down it's what we all feel, whether we like to admit it or not. Eh Myrt?" (The name he had taken to calling my mother the previous summer; when I asked him why? he said, "It suits her, don't you think?") "Speaking of faith," he continued, not waiting for "Myrt's" reply (knowing full well she would resist, at that point anyway, not allow herself to take off her

mental blindfold), "there's no race in the world comes close
to the British. God, think of the poor bastards right now,
incendiary bombs raining down around their heads, spending
night after night in bomb shelters. How do they ever get any
sleep? While our lousy, and I do mean lousy, camp squats in
tents. Scratching their wretched bodies to sleep, a chorus of
basso-profundos singing 'Oh Nelly put your belly close to
mine'."

"What blasphemy!" Mamma cut in. "The nerve of them!
*tinkering* with . . . Brian, do you know that's 'The Road to
the Isles'? How does the rest of it go?" He glanced at her
quickly, cheeks reddening as he made up words, and lost the
tune: "Wi' a skurrr-lll o' the pipe, and toot o' me bonnie lips
. . ." and without a pause, continued his fetching account of
army life where he had left off: "Or like me, when I lie on
my cot, retching up the shit—oh, excuse me, Myrt—the crap
and dung they feed us. The cook has no pride, not an ounce
of dedication in his smelly bones. The Canadian Government
goes to the expense of paying him a dollar thirty a day, pro-
vides him with truckloads of turnips and salt pork and vintage potatoes, plus his choice of the best rotting carcasses in
the land: a golden opportunity to show what a chap can do
in a soup-kitchen—and the son of a bitch turns out swill.
Imagine! You'd think he'd never heard the world cuisine. The
prick should be made to eat what he dishes out, eh Myrt? instead of high-tailing it off to the Chinese Dragonfly, or whatever they call that joint in Cornwall. It's as filthy as the
latrines, and about as appetizing." George was killing himself.
He just about spilled his glass all over his pants, caught it just
in time. I don't think he even heard what came after the
smelly bones—about the army cook having his choice of rotting carcasses, I mean. He was laughing so hard he choked,
spluttering beer all over the place, a mouthful went flying out
of his mouth. And Brian! aghast, flicking regurgitated beer
(if there was any) out of his eyes as he went on about the
army cook.

"Pretty Bird?" George asks, drying the front of his shirt
with Brian's shirt-tail. "How do you stand him? Does he always talk like this?"

"Like what?" Brian wants to know, asking George why
doesn't he use his own shirt-tail? telling him it looks as if it
could do with a rinse, or a lighted match. And there's silence
for a while, we're still laughing to ourselves, and there comes

a quietness of a different kind as we watch the logs going by on the river. And I am pondering: maybe when Brian gets his commission he won't have to eat that swill, or live on milkshakes and Sweet Maries any more. Not only that, he won't have to keep digging into his savings. When will that be, though? Any day now the money he got for his Plymouth is going to be all gone, and he'll end up cashing that War Bond he put away.

George says the pay in Ferry Command is good, more than he ever dreamed of; by next June he'll have enough saved to buy the cottage outright. Now that he's talked the owners into letting it go, now that they've agreed to sell the "dump", it's all George has thought about since he got back two days ago. Buying the cottage is his goal, he says, he wants it more than anything else in the world. I can understand that. Who else should it belong to? It's always been ours. . . .

Brian said those cheats should give it to us, free. "A present for living in their goddamned chicken-coop all these years," he laughed. Chicken-coop my hat, I chuckled inwardly. I noticed His Lordship had no trouble making himself at home right from the start. Bad as the rest of us, I told him the summer before we were married. Even planting his own trees, lugging them from a bush two miles away and then roping them off as if they were forbidden ground, like at a royal garden party. And! Two days later he's ordering us to take our feet off a section of verandah railing he'd painted. Bile green, if you please. "You *love* the place."

"Who's talking?" I said, giving him a peck on the cheek. "You *love* the place."

"Just shows you can get used to anything," he replied, sniffing.

One of the barn cats, half wild and half tame, had wandered down the hill from the farm and was perched on top of the woodpile at the kitchen door, cleaning its face and ears. I decided to go inside and pour it a saucer of milk, a chance for it to lap to its heart's content without fear of a cow's hoof sending it spinning into the troughs. When I came outside, the conversation had shifted from salt pork and soup-kitchens to life itself, emotional concerns. I could hear Brian saying something about love making the difference.

"Are you still going with Louise, George?" he asked.

"Yes. Though it's mostly by letter. I mean, the family has

moved to the Gaspé, so we've not seen one another for months. Her grandfather died and left her dad the business, a small hotel she helps her parents run because there's no one else in town wants the job. We sort of became engaged a month ago, if you can call making up our minds by letter being engaged!"

"Really?" Brian exclaimed. "Let's drink to it! When's the wedding?"

"Give him a chance!" Mamma hooted, clapping her hands at crows circling the pine at the river. "He's not even twenty-two yet."

"You mean," scoffed Brian, "he's not an old curmudgeon of twenty-seven like me." I leaned my head against the verandah post, thinking of my own wedding, conscious of my body now in summer clothes, shorts and a halter, barefoot, loving the way I felt, the greedy cat purring as it splattered milk over my hand.

"I wasn't twenty-two yet either when I got married," I called out. Mamma was now sitting with her legs straddling the bench beside the rustic table, and she turned suddenly. "Why didn't you tell me?" she laughed, a look of amazement, hair blowing wildly in the breeze. "I had no idea . . ."

"The wedding's in the future," George said. "I'd like to take a course in forestry at U.N.B. first. Got the bug for it when I was in the tower up north of Rimouski. We used to go out on portages a lot, after we got to know the wilderness a bit better. And the quiet! nothing between us and civilization but wildlife, and the lakes and forests. We'd hack our way through. . . ."

I left the verandah to get the cat more milk. What a lovely day, I was thinking. Why couldn't it always be like this? Even when the boys weren't home. Why couldn't Mamma and I seem to find things to do, and make jokes the way we'd been doing the past few days; why didn't we gabble and talk more when we were by ourselves in Dorval? Brian and George can always get a rise out of her, they seem to bring her to life in a way I never can. I should try harder; it's not her fault, it's *mine*.

What did she have in her life that was as interesting as mine? Even if I was alone, or felt myself to be, an army wife still had, in body and mind, the fierce, tingling sensation left by the flow of her husband's semen . . . to last her weeks and months if need be; and, one day, it'd be for the rest of her life! What did Mamma have, when the two of us sat by ourselves? and me counting the days. . . .

I stood watching them through the screen netting, the low hum of voices like music, like life never standing still. It's a wonder Mamma doesn't start singing 'Hail! Hail! The gang's all here,' I thought. But she wouldn't, I realized. She never did that again after my father left.

The cat was gone, nowhere to be seen, and so I went back inside to change from my shorts, doing up the buttons of my beach pyjamas as I ambled around in search of a box of matches, and returned to the kitchen, thoughts skittering here, there and everywhere, trying to pin down that indeterminate feeling of a while ago, that soaring sensation I'd felt in George when, all at once, and fleetingly, his thoughts of Louise had seemed to lift him sky-high. One of those trinkets of discovery, the happiness that surprises the maturing adult mind. Like what my parents would have experienced when they were young, I was thinking; as Brian and I had discovered; now George too. My brother has found the magic on the other side of the hill, that's how I described it to myself. For in spite of the fatiguing and faraway order of his life, which the war had so suddenly caught him up in, an emotional conviction, heightened by a still-present sense of adventure, charged his being.

I struck a match against the stone fireplace, watching the glow until it went out. And I thought: George has passed me now. He has touched hours I have yet to reach. The ground under his feet feels something of this . . . this *what*? And then I was puzzling: what word was I looking for? This *gain*? No. That's too materialistic. A triumph of spirit, then? I read that somewhere. I couldn't expect it to be a plateau or peak I would know one day myself—not in the same way, I mean, being a girl and all. Well, what on earth was I trying to figure all this out for anyway, when George himself wasn't—or was he? Come to think of it, though, the way he wakes up and bounds out of bed. Like I don't know what. Most times, anyway. Some days, after he's been up a while, he gets deep in his mind, there's *something else*. It's a *thing* he wants to put behind him, I guess. . . .

This was the mixed-up conversation I was having with myself on my way back to the kitchen. I wanted to shout, 'What more could a sister ask for?' I was so glad for my brother.

Just then the screen door opened.

"What treats are you making for supper, lass?" Mamma asked, hands behind her back, sniffing at empty pots on the woodstove and making a slrr-p-slrrr-p sound with her tongue, as if I'd already started proceedings. A hint that I would be in charge of the kitchen for the next hour.

"I think what I'll do," I shrugged, "is boil a lot of mashed potatoes," doing a full knee-bend to get at the basket of provisions under the table, "and throw in a can of tomatoes and some mushroom soup . . . did we pack an onion? and with the cold chicken we've got, and three or four cakes of Shredded Wheat, I could take the potato-masher and mush it all up. How does that sound, Myrt? I know what! I'll put in a whopping big tablespoon of curry, and when Brian asks what the hell it is—and he will, just you watch! . . ."

"The rascal. I'd fix him."

"Well, I'll tell him it's the latest thing in Indian goulash. Ha! Then he'll *want* to eat it."

I took a set of bowls out of the cupboard, put them on the kitchen table and went to stand beside her at the door.

"My but it's good to see them get on like that," I said. "Really, they're like two brothers."

"Well, that's what they are, isn't it?"

"You don't expect brothers-in-law to have much in common, though. Or even *like* each other. . . ."

"Oh," she broke in, "George would get on with the man in the moon."

"And Brian wouldn't? Is that what you're saying?" I went back to the table. Now where in the world was the curry?

I heard Mamma's reply: "No. That's not what I'm saying at all. George and Brian are different, that's what I meant. Not their basic natures; but Brian's more wary, he's got to size a person up first. And even then, he sure takes some getting to know. He's the very dickens at times. You have to know how to *take* Brian, how to handle him." She paused, thinking about it as she moved up and down on her toes, the rubber soles of her tennis shoes bending softly and soundlessly, up, down, up, down, on the inside of the wooden doorstep. "Ach," she said glancing back at me, "his bark's worse than his bite. Brian's a softie at heart, the same gentle soul as your brother, and your fath . . ." She stopped, and looked away.

"As my father. Why didn't you say it? He doesn't have any trouble saying nice things about you. C'mon now, let's not go

pretending you're going to start sniffling. And don't be flying
into a rage at me. You're having a good time! You've talked
more these past two days than you have in a month of Sundays. But cripes! You and your munitions makers. You remind me of a suffragette!"

"Get on with your curry-making, woman, and don't be telling your mother where to get off at!" She strode across the
kitchen floor, a sweep of her tiny arm scooping the air: "One
to grow on," she said and spanked my bottom. With that she
started for the screen door, and stopped, running her finger
around the rim of the bowl I'd handed her. Round and
round, slowly. "What's up?" I said.

"George hasn't changed, has he?" she asked, putting the
bowl back in the cupboard. "Why did you say, 'How could
he help but come back changed'? He's just the same, isn't
he?"

"What? What are you talking about? When did I . . . ?" I
paused, looking at her, puzzled.

"When we were brushing our teeth at the river this morning. I only got half of what you were burbling."

"Oh, that," I nodded guardedly. "I'd been thinking back to
the early days when George was on the cargo runs to Goose
Bay and Gander, then all of a sudden he was flying off to
war zones. I was also saying don't forget he's been over there
and been touched by the war in ways we haven't, and that'd
make him seem older. That's all I said. Anyway, I think he's
having the time of his life. And Brian thinks so too. Don't
you?"

"No. I don't think so at all. Far from it." There was a
sharp clicking sound as her finger let go the spring of an old
mousetrap she'd been toying with. She reached to lay it on an
upper shelf. "Whoops!" she laughed suddenly. "I'd better
shed this bathing suit before it sheds me! Time to get into my
finery. Are we still going to the square-dance at Wakefield
tonight?"

I nodded yes, my arms in motion now, hands extending
left over right, grabbing at imaginary partners as I waltzed
about the kitchen, chanting, "Oh-a-do-si-do, and an elbow
swing with the dear old thing," wondering if we'd be seeing
any uniforms at the clubhouse, friends home on leave, most
of the boys were gone now. "Promenade till you meet your
girl . . ."

"And circle left with the pretty little thing," she sang, turning a pirouette with her arm raised above her head, "And do it once more for the good of the hall. Now run away home and swing your own!" and with that was off to her bedroom, whistling a reel, beautifully off-key, as bureau drawers and wire coat hangers rasped and banged behind the beaverboard wall.

I sat down to peel the potatoes. What I had felt earlier, the shock of awareness that shone under the trees, was gone from me. And listening to Mamma in the next room squirting Eau de Cologne from the carnival-glass atomizer she'd won playing bingo—the rubber bulb sounding like a Fly-Tox gun, as if she were going after a nest of hornets, or a bat—I kept peeling away, dipping the potatoes in and out of a small basin of water, an anxiety beginning to prod me, a touch of it anyway. *Was* there an underlying restlessness in George? The day that first entered my mind he was leaving on a flight, and I was on my way over to sit at the end of the tarmac. It was raining, and I sat under a tree. Well, I said to myself, it's not as though he's set in one place, one country. Why wouldn't he get restless at times? Look at where he goes! Flying half around the world in those cramped bombers. Ice-fields one day, tropics the next. Jungles of South America. And how many bases do they sit by the hour in, for days, standing by for weather and whatever else keeps them waiting.

At that moment Mamma returned to the kitchen.

"Where in the name of God did you get that frowsy dress?" I asked, half appalled, half delighted. "Did you pull it out of the rag-bag? With everything that's been stuffed in, since the day I was born . . . couldn't you find something near the top? a dress that's no more than ten years old, say? Or did you have to root down to the roaring twenties?" She thumbed her nose, standing at the screen door, emerald-green and faded pink roses falling in folds, rust stains shimmering at mid-calf as she attempted the Charleston—in bare feet. "No wonder you doused yourself with cologne," I said. "The thing's probably high with mice pee." And the swirl of chiffon subsiding, her thoughts returned to the rustic chairs occupied on the hill, the murmur, at times tumultuous, of Brian's and George's exchanges; the wood in the stove catching fire and crackling; drops of water under the kettle I had just filled starting to hiss. Potato-peelings on an old newspaper pushed to one side, wetting the green cardboard covers of those 78 records of Tschaikovsky's "Fifth Symphony" we had been playing the night before; George had plugged the turntable into a light-socket on the verandah, so that we could hear it out on the hill, cigarettes glowing in the dark, a bottle of rum, cokes and a lighted candle on the rustic table attracting night moths.

"Tell me," my mother said, suddenly, abruptly, "that evening last week, when we were pasting the snapshots in the album at Dorval, what was preying on your mind when you mentioned Dakar?"

"I've no idea. What do you mean?"

"Were you hiding something?"

"About what? Don't know what you're getting at."

"The Mediterranean . . . and the fast take-offs."

"Search me. Oh, *that*! No, I wasn't hiding anything." Steady, keep my voice steady. "I was just saying the trip to West Africa must be the trying one. Now that I've heard the other side—from some of the boys, they'd been talking in the pantry. It wasn't that I was keeping anything to myself."

I went over to the stove and lifted one of the lids with the poker, holding it in mid-air as I talked into the burning wood, moving it about, adding another log. "Don't you remember, that lady up the street came in? and you went next door with her? You've forgotten, that's all. I was starting to say I don't think the Ferry Command air crews can ever move very far from their quarters, in case word comes to take off fast—the next hop is clear for them." I lowered my voice; I didn't want George to overhear, and read into this conversation the sense of uneasiness it might be conveying. I put the lid back on the stove, opened the oven door, my head half in as I began banging pots around.

"Anyway," I continued, "the boys were saying how the crews all have to sit around waiting for weather, and that it's tiring and boring." I backed out of the oven. "Hey," I said, "would you like another beer?"

"Boring? When did they mention this?" she asked, going to the icebox in the living room. I waited for her to return. Then headfirst into the oven again: "I dunno when they mentioned it. A month ago?" I reached up to put a pie plate on top of the stove, bones in my elbow cracking at the awkward arm movement. "I was in the kitchen. I think I was looking for a light bulb or something, or maybe I'd gone upstairs; I forget. Two of them were getting some ice in the pantry, Ray was one, can't remember who the other was, and they were

asking one another was he still bringing his Arctic and anti-
malarial kits along on the flights? or did he say to heck with
it too? Things like that."

"What else did they have to say?" she pressed. I'm down
under the table now, shunting baskets and milk bottles about
as she bends to hand me an opened bottle of beer: "What *are*
you doing, child?" squatting on all fours, eyeing me.

"What?"

"First your head's in the stove, then in the oven, now here.
Did you lose something? Lord, where did all these cobwebs
come from?" she mutters, and with that pulls herself up, returning to stand at the screen door while she sips from a glass
stein, little finger crooked, as if it were a cup of tea.

"Not much, really. They did say they get jittery sometimes,
and that it's the waiting around, particularly if you're with a
crew that's not your type. Some old story, I guess. There's
nowhere to go to get away from each other. And isn't that
exactly what Brian said too?"

"Yes," she agreed, "poor wretch. Poor wretches, all." I
turned around suddenly, bumping my head on one of the
supports under the table trying to shush her, oilcloth covering
the upper half of my face: "If Brian heard you call him that
he'd skin you alive! But to finish, just so you won't think I
was keeping something from you, they do manage to find a
buddy once in a while, and try to be posted on the same
flights after that. Like Tommy." I surfaced, went back to the
giant mixing bowl, contents more like vomit than anything
else. "Damn," I said, licking my fingers. "I think I've put too
much curry in. Wasn't watching what I was doing."

"No wonder! All this talk about war zones."

"What? I didn't mention the word! Who said anything
about war zones?"

"Well, somebody did. Didn't they? Or did I dream it?
Seems to me . . ." her voice stopping half-way through.

I had purposely avoided telling her the main reason for the
fast take-offs. When they're waiting to leave Dakar, or one of
the other bases in Gambia, for the second-last leg of the journey—the all-night flight to Gibraltar. Grabbing their things together—because more than the weather is clear! Allied
Intelligence, plus radio ground crews, have notified them that
the German fighter planes have been chased back across the
Mediterranean, they've returned to their bases in Italy, or
France, or wherever they came from. Either that or the Ger-
mans are busy elsewhere; anyway, the coast is clear.

Sour milk going into the mush, have to kill that curry somehow, can't count on potatoes alone to do it. Or the soy sauce. What's making this curdle? That never happened before.

Plum jam . . . a little more, one for the pot, as they say . . . "Oh Nelly, put your belly" . . . and the rest of the cut-up chicken. There's more skin than meat, I'm thinking. And I hear Mamma asking me something. Golly. She's been at the screen door all this time! I thought she'd gone back outside to sit on the hill. But no. Emerald-green folds still as a breath, a finger picking at a loose piece of wire on the door-spring. Words forming on lips; it's hard to tell. And I thought then how much I loved her, all the things she stood for as a mother, giving us countenance not so much in words but in the inner strength of her rich and tranquil woodland imagination, her sense of right-and-wrong and the world be damned. What if anything happened to her? Thumb and forefinger picking away at the bent wire on the spring.

"Why do you think they get jittery?" she asked, having the sense to lower her voice.

"*I* didn't say they get jittery." I said. "I think what the boys meant was they get fidgety, at Dakar anyway. The town's off limits at night, you know. Besides, you'd get that way too if you had to keep yourself awake playing bridge—in case they get word."

"Yes, I guess I would. But is that the only reason? Do you think . . . ?"

"Oh well," I replied, shrugging, brushing this next query aside, "at least George enjoys all the places he sees. What's more, he's happy doing what he's doing. His letters prove that. And I guess that's all that counts. You know what, Mamma? It's a funny thing, but when I see the planes take off, I mean when I'm lying in that field and I know George is in one of them, I completely forget the long hauls ahead of him . . . that maybe he's finding it an ordeal. Because I remember how he looked the night before, or that morning. Always excited, laughing, even playing with the dog and remembering to say goodbye to him too. I lie on the ground thinking, What's the matter with me anyway? Just because he's in a hurry to get back home . . . he's just as happy when he's getting ready to leave."

"George would be happy no matter what he did," she replied, standing in the light of the doorway, her eyes bright and sad at the same time. "Looks like he's explaining something to Brian. They've got bits of wood spread across the table, and two pieces of blue paper they've made into . . . pontoons or something."

"Likely he's showing Brian the undercarriage of a flying boat, how it's equipped."

"So they can let the wheels down?" she asked. "Would that be it, do you think?"

Her eyes were sad, and I didn't want to think about it. She had asked a question, her voice rising faintly, *So they can let the wheels down?* half dreamlike, more thoughts than words, a small voice into the netting, rising like the lift of a heron. Her eyes were sad, yes. Was it because of my father, that he wasn't there too? I didn't want to know.

———————

Sometimes I get the feeling none of this ever really happened. I mean the afternoon on the hill, for instance. As though I had dreamt it. I'll press my fingers against my eyes and say to myself, You only dreamed it. Like the rest of that year. Oh, the fact that our wedding gifts and furniture were in storage, the displacement of our lives, the hours of being together like moments snatched from time—that was real; the bombers roaring over my head, too; and the quiet of my turret room, facing out over flat green fields, and snowy ones; glittering Baie Louis when the sun came out after that terrible ice-storm, the time the huge trees in the front yard were felled. The same winter the war news was getting worse instead of better, and was the invasion never going to come?

But no! No pressing of fingers against my eyelids, no denying any of this, telling myself this too is what I dreamed, that it never happened. And then I am silent. For I know it did.

But that late afternoon, that Saturday in 1942 sitting under the trees, and the supper hour that followed—in fact the whole Labour Day weekend—how strange to feel as if it never happened, that it is only what I dreamed. When I can recite every word? when every rib, vein, artery, every fiery cell cries out: 'Tell me again!' Eugene O'Neill once said, "You can't kill the dream without killing the man." So whether it's fantasy, or the pull of an impossible conflict, or just a once-happened reality, an illumination of something I'm trying to recapture but never can, it's the trust, not just the hope but the *conviction* of its existence that forever beck-

ons. And claims me, the sweet and the bitter, until I am
dead?

---

The mush I was making. Into the oven at last. Two cas-
seroles filled to brimming. It'd take a good hour, maybe longer; slow baking was the secret. That would brown the top a
little, give it a nice crust, too. How would Brian know what
the turmoil of guck was, bubbling underneath?

Gathering up scattered sections of the Saturday newspaper
we had brought from the city, Mamma had announced it was
time for her to "Have a wee read. Stretch out on the living
room couch so my gams will be all set to promenade at the
Wakefield clubhouse tonight!"

"Gangway for the Highland fling at the hoedown!" Brian
teased, getting up to hand her the sports page he'd been doo-
dling on—putting whiskers on a lady tennis player, an apron
round the waist of a pro golfer.

It was still only a little after five in the afternoon, and
Brian and George and I decided we'd walk up the hill to the
farm. Mr. and Mrs. Carman were alone now. Jimmie had
joined the army the previous summer, and after six months
of basic training exercises in Nova Scotia had been sent over-
seas to complete his advanced training in England.

"Hello there, Johnny!" Mr. Carman called to George from
the porch. "What are you up to, Johnny?"

"How's yourself, Papa Carman?" George asked, mounting
the steps and embracing Mrs. Carman, turning to shake
hands with Jimmie's father. Brian and I did the same.

And then it was into the front parlour, a crock of
homemade chokecherry wine brought from the cellar, four
rose-coloured goblets taken from a shelf above the sideboard.
Easing back into our chairs, we fell into talk of other days,
"the good old days", we agreed, holding the wine glasses up
to the light of a window. Mr. Carman asked, "Do you mind
the time . . . ?" Yes, we sure did. "Ambrosia. That friggin'
Ambrosia," he went on. Then it was the afternoon the boys
got the rooster drunk on applejack, and then the morning I
was driving the haywagon when Diamond broke loose on the
dip down the gully, upsetting the wagon and sending us head
over heels into the "crik". "And he's still going!" Mr. Carman
added, slapping his thigh. "By the Christ, the bugger's been
dead these past three years but that'd never stop him! Hell

no." And turning to Brian: "Got yourself a filly just like him, lad. Do you fix her wagon fer her? . . . And are they treating you right in Cornwall?"

Lighting his pipe, preoccupied now, amusement gone from him, striking a match on his rump, and asking George: "Any chance of you and Jim meeting up? Ever get to the south of England? Christ Jesus, though, don't even know where those sons of bitches have him billeted." Straightaway, a letter coming out of Mrs. Carman's apron pocket. She shook her head, puzzling, looking first at the postmark and then turning the envelope over. "I'm sure I don't know where it is. Can you tell, George?" she asked.

My brother leaned forward, trying to read what appeared to be a series of numbers. "Seems to me I've seen that address before," George said, "and I think it's some place in Sussex." He opened the drawer of the sideboard, searched for a pencil, and copied down the address on the back of a card he'd taken from his wallet.

"Did Jimmie switch to the tank corps?" I asked, having noticed a large framed photograph on the sideboard, the kind they used to do in photographic studios, so perfect then, head and shoulders, the neatness of the uniform standing out, nothing in shadow, the poised calm so lifelike.

"That's the Artillery, isn't it?" Brian asked, going over for a closer inspection. "The badge on his beret . . ."

"He's a gunner," Mrs. Carman replied in her soft voice, rocking back and forth in the pine rocker. "Mercy me. Why do they take you lads and turn your light hearts into killing?" her voice becoming silent for a moment, and then, "Sure, weren't the two of you more at home in the barn with the lambs?" She reached across for Jimmie's photo, and sat with it in her lap, arms clasping the glass side against her bosom.

And Jimmie's father, his blue eyes filling as he glanced out the window, at the fields, the far mountain to the south, and back again, back to the green-coloured velour curtains separating the parlour from the hallway, the folds parted slightly and a thin darkness showing where the stairs led up to the second floor. No more words for him to say, except: "The lad's room is there for him when he comes back, so it is." And wasn't this exactly like my own father, I was thinking, that same expression? when George and I visited with him, one more flight behind George, and my father, cheerful, laughing quietly, asking my brother did he have everything he

needed? and was his Leica camera (the one Daddy had
brought him from Europe in the thirties) still travelling by
his side? and then gradually a silent thought overtaking my
father, his concern hidden, vanishing into a restaurant wall's
tapestry, into the coming and going of train passengers hurrying along the platform beside us: "Well, son. Back in two
weeks, do you think? Maybe we can get in a couple sets of
tennis."

A short while later, and we make our farewells at the
farm. "Our supper's about ready," we say, and tell them we'll
come back tomorrow when we can stay longer. For how can
we sit prolonging the conversation? After months of not having seen us, our sudden arrival has evoked a rush of words as
if times haven't changed, mirrors of the past unsmudged—re-
living a long-gone rooster's dilemma, the fire in the barn
when lightning struck the rod installed to prevent its happening. But how long had it taken till memories led us straight
into the present? feeling Mr. and Mrs. Carman's quiet fear
developing, perhaps even panic trapped in their innards as
they rock silently, the growing sense that there is something
they want to ask, but never will: is Jimmie preparing, is he
marked (now that the raid on Dieppe has failed) for a full-
scale Allied invasion of France?

It was George who got up from the sofa, looking eager as
he set his wine goblet down. "Papa Carman?" he asked.
"How would it be if I brought my camera up tomorrow? Will
you be somewhere around at noon? I thought I'd like to take
a couple of snaps of you and Mrs. Carman out by the barn.
And how about that new colt you were telling us about, get
him in the picture too. Okay? I expect to be in Prestwick
next week, and I could mail the photos to Jim from there."

"We wouldn't want to put you to any trouble, George,"
Mrs. Carman said, beaming.

"Get out your best bonnet, Ma," said Mr. Carman, "and
don't be after putting my good pair of overalls into the wash
in the morning."

Setting out for the cottage, and chickens pecking about the
barnyard, the distant moo of a cow as we opened the rusty
gate. Closing it behind us, and realizing how much in need of
repair the hinges and hasp were, and the fencing too. On
through the cropped hayfield, the same field where the cows
used to lie in the shade of the elm: the hoof-marked patch of
ground where Bessie and Myrtle and Yvonne had lain, I was

thinking. Times had changed; I had changed; but not this field, not this dozing terrain leading us to the top of the hill behind the cottage, its rutted stubble scorched and arid, shining in the September light. Who had ploughed the fields, I wondered? who mowed the hay, stacked it, brought it in, milked the two dozen cows, put the milk through the separator and took the cream cans to the station next day? Who fed the livestock? when all the hired hands were off working in factories, or in the services? And I heard Brian say, "Those two, people like Mr. and Mrs. Carman, they're the real heroes of the war. And no one cares." Glancing over his shoulder, the stillness of a machinery shed with its equipment lying about, as if all activity had come to a standstill, and you knew it hadn't: a farmer on his own now, with only his wife to do what she could helping out, both of them well on in years. "No one gives a good goddamn," Brian added. "Christ."

My brother was walking slowly, hands in his pockets, head down as his eyes followed the trodden path to the gate at the top of the hill. Without looking up, he said: "Maybe there's a chance I could get down to see Jimmie, give him all the news. Perhaps if I asked one of the R.A.F. guys at Prestwick . . . see if he has a way of finding out the exact location of Jim's unit, then if I caught an overnight train from Glasgow, I could bring the snaps—you know?" He stopped, and bent down to break off a dried stalk of goldenrod growing through a hole in the fence. "I'll bring him this," he chuckled. "Boy, we'd sure have a good laugh. Hey, Brian? did you know we used to smoke this once? Jimmie and I. We'd dry it on a log in the sun, and then crumble the pulp and roll it in a sumach leaf."

I remember that day for many reasons. Isn't the sight of two men examining a crown of goldenrod itself a kind of dream?

Supper. The last of the daylight fading, evening breezes gusting through open windows. In the living room, above the dining table, the parchment shade swinging to and fro, its octagonal wire frame banging against the light bulb. And the goulash, with all its last-minute additions—Corn Flakes, cut-up chunks of tinned Spam, the remains of the previous night's rhubarb preserve. Devoured in the end, every plate wiped clean with crusts of bread, nothing left but the pattern on the plate, fanning curry-hot palates as we fought over the pitcher of well-water, drinking from the spout and passing the amber-coloured glass jug to a waiting hand, talk idling back and forth, muttering whose turn was it to go back to the woods for more? or would we take a chance and boil the river water?

And just as I got up to carry the empty plates to the kitchen, George reached behind one of the sofa cushions for the surprise he had been saving: a bottle of liqueur he'd brought back from Port of Spain.

"This'll help put the fire out," he announced, removing the cap. "Can't wait for you to try it. It's my favourite."

"Put it out!?" Mamma said, burping. "You mean start another one," she observed, eyeing the bottle, turning it around so she could read the label. "Is it over-proof?"

"Banana liqueur!" Brian exclaimed, taking the bottle from her hands and tipping the neck for a quick whiff. "But what the hell are we going to drink it out of? Jelly glasses?" Then apologetically, "Do we have anything . . . ?"

"Egg cups?" I suggested, setting the plates down on the table again, not wasting a minute while I hurried to the kitchen cupboard. Were there enough to go round? Three. Three rooster-decorated egg cups, and a medicine glass.

Between sips, shuddering at the initial shock of the fumes, warm-flowing, catching my breath.

"Good, eh?" I said.

"Like it?" George asked.

"Like it!? I *love* it. Never heard of banana . . ."

"Who needs well-water?" Brian asked. And, suddenly rising to his feet, he raised his egg cup. "Here's to Myrt," he said, taking her by surprise, her medicine glass poised, held at a distance from her lips as she waited for him to finish. "She's the one who keeps the home fires burning."

"I'll drink to that," George said.

"Myrt's the gal we depend on, eh?" Brian smiled. "Never mind us with our pithy concerns, Myrt. Me anyway. Me and hellhole Cornwall," he added before downing the last few drops of his liqueur. "Where would we be without the chatelaine of Burdock Villa? Thanks to you . . ." Hesitating, then pouring himself a refill. "Whoa . . . spilled some! By golly, should've used the jelly glasses. And now, here's to dear Miss Watson, who thinks she's going to get me up on that hick dance floor tonight."

"Go soak your head!" I retorted, removing one of my

moccasins and throwing it at him. "Bet I will, though," I laughed, for Brian had been won over the previous summer; at first merely relenting, then with a kind of fascination, the ham in him taking over—determined to follow the dialect of the caller's chant: "Wink at the next girl on the sly and alle-mande left, circle-on-down-and circle-on-down." "Bet you a dollar you're up for the first square," I taunted.

"And finally," said Brian, bending down to retrieve my moccasin, ignoring my rejoinder as he handed it back to me on a plate, "last but not least, a toast to the one who—in my outstandingly patriotic absence—has given Miss Watson a roof over her head. Listen. I know a lot of people in my life that I hope I never see again, and they're not all down in Cornwall. And I'm going to meet a lot more people I'll see for the first and last time on the same occasion—at least if I can help it. But there are two or three people who are so dear to me that I . . . that when I try to say it out loud I . . . To good old George."

Looking embarrassed, but glowing, a smile breaking across his face, George paused for a moment, standing, shoving his chair back against the wall before replying.

"To my sister and brother," he said.

I felt the warmth between them, their individual selves so different in many ways, and yet, in spite of it, the tenderness of their masculinity a silent and vital brilliance: for me it was the one permanence that filled the room. I remember thinking, in a strange and inexplicable way, I remember thinking that each one, in the gentleness of his person alone, seemed to represent the space, the accumulation of my life, the whole of me. And I heard Mamma say: "To the chicken-coop and all us soaks!" egg cups and medicine glass clacking above the table, a splay of arms saluting the breeze that wafted through the open transom above our heads, and a cry of "Sip up, ye sinners! But slowly. Slowly down the hatch."

"Long viva Burdock Villa!" said Brian.

Two and a half days later, early in the morning, and the boat loaded down with suitcases, Brian's duffel-bag, turntable, records, a football, the electric toaster. And we're crossing the river; it's back to Dorval now. Mamma seated beside me at the end of the boat, back turned, legs over the side, her feet trailing the wash behind. Brian, irritably uncomfortable in his corporal's khaki serge, in the seat in front of us; George be-hind him, rowing, in the white cable-stitch pullover I'd

knitted him, the Ferry Command crest on the left side a
lesser reminder of the part and parcel of their lives. One
voice at a time, or all four, humming snatches of Tschaikovsky's "Fifth", or the "1812 Overture". Brian keeping time
with his prized and awful-looking runty shillelagh, beating the
air or the side of the boat. And Mamma splashing a foot in
and out of the water, looking back at the hill and saying,
"Well, that's that. Won't be long now till the snow starts flying."

"Brrr," we said.

———————

And now it was March, at the tarmac. I thought of the
rustic table and chairs, the pots and bowls and potato-masher,
and the slept-in beds left last September as they'd been lain in
(not made up, I remember, in our hurry to get Dr. Marais's
car back in time for his Tuesday afternoon rounds), every
last chair and water bucket locked inside the cottage. Cottage
and contents as silent and sheltered as the deep snow I now
imagined as heavy on the warped roof, snow I thought would
still be up to the windowsills, perhaps higher than that at the
back where it drifted. And up beyond, near the farm, slanted
fence-posts sticking up through the snow, the same as here in
this overcast; likely a train whistle had echoed across the valley, also the same as here, the train that went by a while ago,
heading east, a passenger train trundling across the flat plain,
filled with how many longing servicemen? a thousand years
since they've been home, looking out the window at the unan-
swerable snow, at the flight of a winter bird whose life could
outlast theirs.

March. That same March day of leaden skies. And the low
bulbous clouds reshaping, the whistle in the wind still trailing
eastward, a plane on its way, pushing against the sombre yet
peaceful cloud-hang, a plane gone into the silence, the wind a
reach of sound folded somewhere in behind as I lie on the
frozen ground. Green woollen mitts under my chin, one fist
on top of the other. Why *did* George come into my room this
morning? Was there something he really wanted to ask me? I
was so sleepy . . . but I sat up, and that's when I heard him
say, "See you."

Starting to blizzard a little now, a thin scattering snow, and
through the haze I see the last aircraft's a Liberator.
George's? Slow in the take-off, slow even for a Liberator.

Must be carrying extra cargo, ammunition, cabbages, eggs. I wonder what else? You'd think it was never going to gain altitude. But it will. And it's just possible my brother's in that one. Maybe it's loaded with cargo for one of the bases in Africa, and on the way they'll drop him off in Bermuda to pick up his Catalina for Greenock.

I open my mouth and yell, that emotion I always want to show, and never can. But now, am I trying to say something, am I trying to ask the *wind* why George came in? And up it goes, altitude at last, my eyes follow the plane . . . follow it . . . I yell into the tunnel of downdraft as it shudders across the pelt of my coat. I scream and scream, as if I'm being dismembered. . . .

———

I never saw George again.

He died.

One week later, on the seventh of April, he was shot . . . the Catalina, it ran into terrible storms over the Atlantic, the "April Equinox", they told us—twenty-five hours up there—the flight, and the instruments—the plane, it was driven over the coast of France—attacked by German fighters near Brest, and George . . . with bullets in his head and spine, he . . . tried to swim.

# XXII

It is not the past you mourn, but the expectations of the past. And that is the dream you follow.

———

Yes. A far dream, more distant than the hills. But the earth's atmosphere cannot burn up what a man stands for. The space of time he has lived leaves *something* . . . a force

that can be felt, like a communication you find yourself trying to decipher: an inner vibration? or a rattle out of the
earth's firmament? What voice cries through the ether? And
you look up into space. *A far dream.*

That time last winter, the day I snowshoed past snow-
buried fences down the side of a valley and back through the
dark white woods with their toppled trees, and then afterward, when I walked across the frozen river and stood by the
farm gate at the top of the hill, I had touched my own infinity. For once again I was living on the edge of that dream:
that once there was an identity I shared, born of the same
flesh and blood, two existences predestined to lie in the dark
of a womb, one by one, waiting. And then the everyday
miracle, open mouths announcing themselves to an unknown
world; in a sense, like two homecomings, as if tossed up by
the surf. There was no place else we belonged. While the wild
boomings of a Nova Scotia coast gave us our place in time.
Two beings created to master the world—their speck in it.
The hope of everyone. But not always his destiny.

---

And when you get a cable that simply says, "Missing", it
isn't final, and you cling to hope.

April passed. And then May. June. I did not pray. Not
now. I just kept saying, "Be lucky, George."

Mamma and I had moved back to the cottage now. It was
July. I roamed the hills and fields alone. Who was there to
pray to? What was blind faith but mere fantasy? I'd wander
through the bleached spaces of ripening grain, over the bridge
at the creek, down the far slope, telling myself, 'There was a
time when God believed in the fields, but He doesn't any
more. That hour is gone.'

For it was. The longest of days when you learn there will
be no homecoming. And my hand, crumpling a letter.

On a summer's day, after three months, July: the details in
a letter from Tommy. Written from a prisoner-of-war camp
in Germany. I stood gutted to the core.

---

As I am now, this moment. Toronto behind me, Canada,
and in a communal cemetery I stand beside this white stone
marker, a slab I sense as icy-cold, sunwarmed in an alien
land where the seas and winds of Brittany hurl sprays of

foam on this July afternoon, as they must surely have done that day of the April storms in 1943, thirty-two years ago, beyond the cemetery wall. I've come! I'm here. And I think of Tommy's letter, fresh from its envelope, and my mother crushing it against her lips, rocking back and forth on the ground, the flowerbeds at the side of the cottage verandah darkening in the shade of early evening; rocking, as she would do again, the following afternoon when I returned from Ottawa where I had gone to be with my father—so that he would have me standing beside him as he read, instead of the emptiness of my voice at the other end of a long-distance call.

On the bus into town next morning, Tommy's letter in my purse lying across my lap, it's opening words burning through my brain cells: "You will perhaps have heard from the Ferry Command that George is now in a happier world, and it grieves me to be the bearer of news that confirms this." And the sidewalks stretching before me as I walked to my father's office. Uniforms, inanimate objects, stoplights changing, closing my eyes to the blur, walking like a blind person until I reached the Hunter Building.

"Dear George," was all my father said. Slowly he put the letter back in the envelope, whispering, as if to its handwriting, while he collected himself. "We will talk of him again one day. . . ."

But we never did.

The pain in my father was never to leave him. He carried it without anyone knowing the silence that was in his mind. But I knew. For it was the same with me.

And those drawn-out minutes—arriving back at the cottage later that afternoon, dazedly walking back up the hill from the dock, aware of the bleating of cattle coming from somewhere, rounding the corner of the verandah, past the rustic table and chairs, and the previous night's newspaper with its interminable war headlines lying on the table where I had left it. And now I was putting the letter back into Mamma's outstretched hand. I had left her with Mrs. Carman at the farm, where she had agreed to wait till I came back from the city. But here she was, sitting where she had sat the night before, close to the flowerbed, as if in a trance, staring blindly at the roses.

"You still have me," I said, groping for that one word that would make contact, reach her.

"It wouldn't matter if I had *ten* children," she cried. "It's the one that's gone who you . . ." One hand holding the letter, the other pulling up tufts of grass. And then the violent rocking back and forth all over again. Now tearing at the letter with her mouth. I was kneeling beside her, and she suddenly got to her feet, ran, like a frightened animal, into the kitchen.

Stumbling after her, and the dog biting at the hem of my skirt, his eyes as if pleading to understand what had happened, and I heard my mother's piercing wail as she dropped the tattered ends into the woodstove, setting fire to the ink-smudged page with lighted birchbark I could not now retrieve. It was Tommy, *Tommy's words* she was burning.

----

But now it is my own wail, thirty years delayed. A cry once soundless, soundless as a plunged chasm, that rends this aching air, the green plumes of foam like shards splintering above the seawall at Ploumaneau. And the cry in my throat more piercing than an exile's plea: "George! You brought me this far. Help me to go further!" No one is here, no one is watching or listening. The afternoon is polished and glittering, vital as life; above my head, the dance of flat slippery leaves brushing the wind. What sound, what other? . . . what reply?

My scalp contracts. And the armful of poppies I picked along the side of the village road, gathered from the sand and weeds bordering a farmer's field, tumble from my hands as my wail is suddenly stilled. What is different? *What is happening?* I cannot explain. You have to believe in something, even if it's only yourself as an instrument being played upon. But how can I tell anyone, a stranger even, what I suddenly hear?—the reach of a voice I do not mistake.

I sit down, and one by one gather in the poppies, wilted petals, the scraggle of fuzzy stems. I lay them in order across the small white stones, then bunch them, the largest flower at the base of the marble stone. George's voice: not the fact of it, but that it was so *urgent*! I bend low: "Why did you ask me that?" Cloud shadows moving swiftly across the ground, and I hear him once more. "Find Tommy. Find Tommy and go to him. Will you do that for me? *He needs you.*"

Needs me? Oh, but how can I? . . . it's more than thirty years. And Mamma burned his letter. I don't even know his last name. . . .

"Is it Tommy's need, George, or mine? Oh, don't go, George, don't leave, not yet, please don't go away. How can I find Tommy?"

"You will."

# ABOUT THE AUTHOR

Oonah McFee grew up in Ottawa where she worked for the CBC prior to moving to Toronto.

## Other Canadian Bestsellers from SIGNET

☐ **JOHN AND THE MISSUS by Gordon Pinsent.** A brilliant writer's roaring novel of an indomitable man and the woman who went with him all the way . . . "Extraordinary, marvelous, shattering!"—**Library Journal**
(#W6779—$1.50)

☐ **THE ROWDYMAN by Gordon Pinsent.** The raw, ribald, and riotous story of a man who can resist everything but temptation! The unblushing, best-selling smash hit novel by Canada's brightest new storytelling superstar . . . "A winner!"—**St. John's News** (#W6850—$1.50)

☐ **WILDERNESS MAN: The Strange Story of Grey Owl by Lovat Dickson.** The startling saga of the man of mystery who became the uncrowned king of the Canadian wilds . . . . "Beautiful, sensitive, honest!"—**Ottawa Citizen.** Illustrated with unforgettable photos. (#J6513—$1.95)

☐ **BOOZE by James H. Gray.** Here is the rollicking, roaring, entrancing saga of the wildest days of the Canadian west, when men were "wet," women were "dry," and whiskey was two-bits a shot. (#W6121—$1.50)

☐ **RED LIGHTS OF THE PRAIRIES by James H. Gray.** The bonanza years when the wide-open frontier was a hooker's happy hunting ground! (#W7828—$1.50)

☐ **TORSO: The Evelyn Dick Case by Marjorie Freeman Campbell.** Canada's most lurid, sensational, and suspenseful murder trial, with all its scandals, shocks, and still controversial findings, has been re-created—in a fascinating narrative no novelist would dare invent, and no fiction could surpass. "It all comes alive again!" —**Hamilton Spectator** (#W6971—$1.50)

## SIGNET Canadian Bestsellers You'll Enjoy

☐ **MORGENTALER: The Doctor Who Couldn't Turn Away by Eleanor Wright Pelrine.** The case that rocked Canada! The candid and intimate story of the remarkable doctor who dared to challenge the abortion law. With eight pages of photos. (#E7100—$1.75)

☐ **LOVERS AND OTHERS by Joan Sutton.** Forty-six delightful essays that capture all the facets and moods of love, re-creating moments and feelings that will be familiar to every reader. "Earthy, tender, amusing and, yes, loving with advice for everyone you know, maybe even for yourself."—Victoria Times (#W7013—$1.50)

☐ **SOMETHING I'VE BEEN MEANING TO TELL YOU: Thirteen Stories by Alice Munro.** From the author of **Lives of Girls and Women,** fiction that probes the inmost depths of the female heart. An irresistible triumph by "one of Canada's best writers . . . wonderful . . . a sheer pleasure!"—Seattle Post-Intelligencer (#Y6732—$1.25)

☐ **LETTERS TO MY SON by Eric Nicol.** From booze to bedrooms, from morals to manners, the Old Man offers some startling advice to his freewheeling teen-age son. (#Y6851—$1.25)

☐ **THE CANADIANA COOKBOOK: A Complete Heritage of Canadian Cooking by Mme. Jehane Benoit.** Add flavor to your life the "Provincial" way with this outstanding collection of recipes dating back to the frontier days of Canada. A taste of the good old days from Canada's favorite cook! (#E6736—$1.75)

**THE NEW AMERICAN LIBRARY OF CANADA, LTD.,**
**81 Mack Avenue, Scarborough, Ontario M1L 1M8**

Please send me the SIGNET BOOKS I have checked above. I am enclosing $_____(check or money order—no currency or C.O.D.'s). Please include the list price plus 35¢ per copy for postage and handling. Prices and numbers are subject to change without notice.

Name_____

Address_____

City_____Province_____Postal Code_____
Allow at least 4 weeks for delivery